# AFTER DANIEL

## REDEMPTION ROMANCE
### BOOK ONE

## IVY WINTERS

*For you, the reader.*
*Thank you for taking a chance on me.*
*If you hate the book?*

*Tell no one.*

# CONTENTS


| | |
|---|---|
| Prologue | 1 |
| Chapter 1 | 11 |
| Chapter 2 | 19 |
| Chapter 3 | 27 |
| Chapter 4 | 33 |
| Chapter 5 | 41 |
| Chapter 6 | 47 |
| Chapter 7 | 53 |
| Chapter 8 | 63 |
| Chapter 9 | 71 |
| Chapter 10 | 79 |
| Chapter 11 | 87 |
| Chapter 12 | 95 |
| Chapter 13 | 105 |
| Chapter 14 | 113 |
| Chapter 15 | 119 |
| Chapter 16 | 125 |
| Chapter 17 | 131 |
| Chapter 18 | 137 |
| Chapter 19 | 145 |
| Chapter 20 | 155 |
| Chapter 21 | 161 |
| Chapter 22 | 169 |
| Chapter 23 | 179 |
| Chapter 24 | 185 |
| Chapter 25 | 191 |
| Chapter 26 | 197 |
| Chapter 27 | 205 |
| Chapter 28 | 213 |
| Chapter 29 | 219 |
| Chapter 30 | 225 |
| Chapter 31 | 233 |
| Chapter 32 | 239 |
| Chapter 33 | 245 |
| Chapter 34 | 253 |

| | |
|---|---|
| Chapter 35 | 259 |
| Chapter 36 | 265 |
| Chapter 37 | 273 |
| Chapter 38 | 277 |
| Chapter 39 | 287 |
| Chapter 40 | 293 |
| Chapter 41 | 299 |
| Chapter 42 | 305 |
| Chapter 43 | 311 |
| Epilogue | 321 |

# PROLOGUE

DROPLETS OF PAIN spatter my wrist, and I recoil with a hiss that rivals the sizzling of peppers frying in the cast iron pan.

"You good?"

Three steps backward and I'm at the sink in the middle of our kitchen island. "I burned myself." I flick on the tap and shove my wrist under the cold stream of water. The burn ebbs away, and I let out a relieved sigh. "Too much oil in the pan."

Daniel pushes up from the kitchen table. His mother bought us the set when we got our first apartment in New Westminster. At the time, the walnut piece had been the nicest thing we owned. I used to polish it every other day before lighting a white gardenia Bath and Body Works candle and placing it right in the center next to some fresh-cut flowers. It drew the eye to the table and away from the peeling paint on the walls and the stained ceiling above.

Now, ten years later, the table fits in with the rest of our furniture and our lives. We've come a long way from that rundown one-bedroom apartment, that's for sure.

Daniel slides in behind me and puts his hands on my hips. His touch is warm through my leggings. He gently pulls me backward, my ass lined up with his fly. I know what he's up to before he brushes my hair from my neck and presses his lips to my skin. His stubble, nearly black and just past the point of prickly, gives me goosebumps, and I tuck my chin to my chest and giggle.

"I can take your mind off the pain," Daniel purrs.

"Then who would finish dinner?"

"Dinner can wait." His lips glide up my neck to my ear, and his voice drops an octave. He hardens against my ass. "I want to put a baby in you."

When my husband used this line on me two years ago, it made me soak my panties as I went weak in the knees and clawed his shirt off. He'd been wearing the white polo shirt with flamingos on it I bought him as a gag gift before he had to go golfing with my dad. He hated golfing, but he went every year on my dad's anniversary at the golf club. Like clockwork.

What else had Daniel stuck to like clockwork?

Tracking my cycle for the last twenty-four months more diligently than I had. We haven't missed a single ovulation cycle.

And we haven't gotten pregnant, either.

"Daniel," I breathe.

"Baby."

"Not tonight."

"What if tonight is *the* night?" He presses himself more firmly against me. My hips meet the counter as he reaches around me to turn off the cold water. The spots where the oil hit my skin feel hot, but they're not painful anymore. Daniel turns me around. I keep my eyes downcast on the white marble kitchen tiles. "Baby, I know it's hard, and I know you're tired, but–"

"Please don't."

"But all it takes is one time."

"Not for us."

"Until it does." He presses two fingers under my chin and gently guides my face up to look into his eyes.

They've always held galaxies of possibilities for me. He's a dreamer, that's for sure, but he also knows how to get things done. It is because of Daniel that we have this beautiful house with the long driveway and the front gate. It is because of him that I drive the white BMW with the custom red stitching in the leather seats. And it is because of him that we are still trying for a baby. Daniel thinks he has enough hope for us both.

But it still hasn't been enough.

"I'll tell you what," he says, galaxies of blue swirling as he smiles at me. "We go to the bedroom, I make you come, and then I'll run you a bath and finish cooking dinner while you soak the troubles of the day away. What do you say?"

*Why can't my body do what she's supposed to do?*

"A bath sounds nice," I say.

He smacks my ass. Hard. "I'll run it now. Rose or coconut bubble bath? Or both?" He winks, and the corner of his mouth twitches in that sexy smirk that made me drop my panties for him the first time.

"Both."

"You got it, baby. Meet you in the bedroom. Give me two minutes!"

Daniel disappears up the stairs, passing white-framed photos of us and our families on his way. Our mothers, fathers, siblings, aunts, uncles, cousins… everyone but children of our own.

I run a thumb absently over the phantom burn splatter on my wrist.

*You can do this, Charlie. What's one more try going to hurt?*

The image of a negative pregnancy test flashes in my mind, and it feels like my stomach is going to fall out of my butt. A girl can only take so much disappointment, and after the universe denies her the thing she wants most so many times, the weight of it all can become too much.

*I can't break my own heart again.*

The sound of the bathtub running leads me upstairs, and I find Daniel sitting on the edge of the deep soaker tub. The gold faucet pours out water as he squeezes two bottles of bubble bath in at once: one blush pink, one pearly white. He's lit candles around the ledge and placed the book I had on my nightstand within reach beside my face roller, a face cloth, and some of my favorite skincare products he knows I use daily.

My heart is already breaking.

The way he takes care of and loves me is a testament to how good of a father he would be.

In another life. Not this one.

He smiles over his shoulder at me. "Why are your clothes still on?"

"Daniel…"

My husband stops pouring the bottles of bubble bath and sets them on the edge of the tub near one of the many vanilla-scented candles. He turns the water off. The drain hums for a moment before the bathroom goes quiet and still.

"Not tonight then?" He rests his hands on his thighs and slides his hands down to his knees.

"Not tonight."

Daniel leans his elbows on his knees. He drags his hands down his face and exhales. I am reminded by his sigh that I'm not the only one who feels like she's carrying the weight of the world on her shoulders.

But he's lucky. He's not the one who's broken.

"Maybe not for a while," I say. "I…"

"Are you calling it?"

I shake my head. "No. I just need a break."

"How long?"

"I don't know."

He rubs his eyes and nods once. "Fine."

"I'm sorry."

"I get it."

"I'm still sorry."

"You have nothing to be sorry about."

I wish he'd yell at me. Maybe it would be easier. His endless patience and understanding only make me feel more guilty. My therapist tells me that's because I'm a people pleaser. Daniel tells me he loves me too much to ever be mad at me, which feels terrible because I'm mad at him all the time.

I'm mad that he never folds his laundry and always leaves his hamper at the end of the bed, which totally ruins the aesthetic of our dreamy bedroom. I'm mad that he takes the last of things and never says anything–eggs, milk, cookies, chocolate, leftovers. He has three brothers, so he grew up having to take what he wanted. I have one sister, and we fought over clothes, not food. I'm mad that he doesn't like wine and that we aren't one of those couples who can sit on their patio on a summer evening sipping a merlot. I'm mad that he's so kind and deserves so much better than me.

But most of all, I'm mad that he hasn't given me permission to stop this pregnancy journey altogether and try something new. I don't have the strength to tell him I'm done. I need him to do it. To set me free. But that's the thing about him being so hopeful.

He won't–can't–throw in the towel. It goes against everything that he is.

Daniel stands and walks to me. He's handsome in his dark jeans and black shirt. He always looks handsome.

He puts his hands on my upper arms, rubbing with his thumbs in reassurance. "Hop in the bath. Enjoy it. Might as well. I'll still make dinner."

I feel that oh, so familiar tightening in my throat. It's suddenly hard to swallow.

"Hey," he breathes, cupping my cheek. "It's all right. I've told you a thousand times, baby. You don't owe me this. And all good things come with time. We can take a break. Catch our breath. Focus on other things. Like your sister's wedding," he adds with a grin. "There's more to be excited about than our future child."

*Our future child.*

How can he be so sure that the idea of this child will come to fruition?

"You know what will lift your spirits?" he asks, pressing a quick kiss to my cheek. "Ice cream."

"You don't have to."

"I know, baby, but I want to. You hop in the tub before the water gets cold. You'll be done by the time I get back and finish up dinner.

Then we'll sit on the couch and watch whatever shitty reality show you've got in your 'to be watched' list."

He turns to leave, but I catch his wrist and pull him back, drawing myself up against him so I can catch his face in my hands and kiss him. His lips feel like velvet amidst his soon-to-be-beard. His kiss tastes like lime from the Corona he'd had earlier, and he smells like the sandalwood cologne I put in his stocking last Christmas. I breathe him in and drape an arm behind his neck, letting my fingers sink up into his blond locks. He needs a haircut soon. His mother will probably tell him as much when we go to her house for dinner this Sunday.

She'll probably ask us when we're going to give her grandbabies, too.

I push the thought aside as Daniel wraps his arms around me and holds me close. His arms have always made me feel invincible, untouchable, and feminine.

"Is it too late to change my mind?" I whisper.

He turns his face and presses kisses to the side of my neck. "Don't tease me."

Gripping the hem of his shirt, I pull it over his head. The fabric passes between our lips before we crash together for a kiss. He backs me up against the bathroom counter and takes hold of the waistband of my leggings so hard I hear stitches tearing.

"Watch it," I breathe. "These are new."

"I'll buy you another pair. I'll buy you as many as you want." He tugs again, and they tear in earnest. He lifts me up and sets me on the bathroom counter next to my silver tray of perfumes—almost all gifts from Daniel. He makes a fortune for us, and he likes to spoil me.

He deserves someone else. Someone better. Someone who can give him his truest desires.

"Stop thinking," he breathes in my ear. "Relax, baby. Let me take care of you. There's no pressure. We're not trying tonight. Just let me make you feel good."

He pulls my panties to the side. My legs are still trapped together by my leggings, so he rips them off and discards the tattered spandex on the tile floor. I reach for him so I can trace the ridges of his shoulders and the swell of his chest while he undoes his belt. Unzips his fly. Drops his jeans. His boxers.

He steps in close, his cock grazing my inner thigh before he finds my entrance. I'm already wet. There's no resistance, but he takes his time, giving me his length inch by inch until I'm panting and clawing at his back, dragging him into me, hooking my legs around his hips, pleading for more.

He slides his hand up my spine to seize a fistful of my hair and pull my head back. He kisses my throat and collarbone while his other hand moves down to grip my ass. I know for certain he's staring at my ass cheeks in the mirror.

"You feel so good, baby." His voice is thick with gravel and lust. He buries himself deeper inside me.

I whimper.

"Fuck." He pulls out and drives back in. Our rhythm quickens. "I can't get enough of you."

Our skin is tacky. Humidity has built from the tub of hot water. The room smells like vanilla and his sandalwood cologne. I feel like I'm floating as he lifts one of my legs so he can fuck me deeper. I gasp as he fills me up, and he silences me with a kiss that hurts my lips but sets my skin on fire. My pussy throbs and tightens around him, and he feels that I'm close.

"That's it, baby," he whispers, tightening his grip in my hair. "Let go."

His words push me over the edge. My toes curl so intensely that my feet cramp, but the pain has nothing on the wave of pleasure flooding my body. I cling to him, hot and breathless, and murmur his name against his shoulder. He loses control, bucking into my slippery core until he comes undone, filling me with his warmth. I love the feeling and hold on more tightly to him, a silent request for him to keep making love to me even though we're both spent.

He does. He's slow and gentle, and his cadence brings us both back into ourselves. Still inside me, he pulls back to kiss me softly, whispering sweet nothings against my lips.

"I love you, Charlie."

"I love you, too."

We close our eyes and press our foreheads together and stay like that until he moves back, leaving me empty, and tenderly finishes undressing me. He lifts my sweater then undoes my bra. He folds it all neatly on the counter, gathers me up in his arms, and lowers me into the rosy coconut bath water.

I run my fingers through the suds. "Join me."

"I promised my wife ice cream." He bends to pick up his shirt. I sink lower into the water as he cleans himself up and zips his fly. "And ice cream she'll get."

"Pralines and cream?"

"Obviously." He cracks a wry grin and leans over the tub to kiss the top of my head. "Enjoy. I'll be back soon. I'll lay your robe out for you on the bed."

He turns and walks away, but when I call his name, he pauses in the doorway.

"I…" I trail off. What can I say? I wish I could give you children. I wish things were different. I wish I could give you as much as you give me.

He raps his knuckles on the door. "Don't get in your head, baby. Read your book. Say some affirmations. I choose you. Always." He gives me a stern look. "I mean it. That voice in your head? Tell her to fuck off. I'm happy. I wouldn't trade this for the world. I promise."

Nodding, I hold back tears.

He returns for one more kiss, brushing his thumbs across my cheeks to wipe away my tears. He says nothing, and neither do I. Everything unspoken between us feels understood. He leaves, and I hear the front door lock behind him before his car starts in the driveway.

A few moments after the sound of the tires rolling down the driveway fades, I gather my book from its place on the edge of the tub, settle deeper into the grooved porcelain at my back, and open the pages.

I read three chapters before it occurs to me that Daniel isn't home yet. I close my book and strain my ears, listening for sounds of him cooking in the kitchen downstairs. Perhaps the chop of a knife, the hum of the pipes when he turns on the kitchen sink, the clanging of dishes as he loads the dishwasher. But there's nothing. Only silence.

"Daniel?" I call.

Nothing.

He's been gone a long time for just popping down the road to the local grocer for ice cream. Maybe they were sold out of my favorite flavor, and he had to go further. It's definitely something he'd do for me.

The water has cooled down, so I add a bit more heat and sink lower, right up to my chin. I'll get out when he gets home.

I wait.

And I wait some more.

How long has it been?

Half an hour? Forty-five minutes? Maybe more?

When the bath cools down again, I get out, leaving wet pools under my feet as I dry off. My robe is in the bedroom, so I throw on Daniel's, a waffle-textured navy blue with his last name stitched in white over the right side of the chest. It had been an appreciation gift from his marketing firm. I think I wear it significantly more often than he does.

I step into my slippers and go downstairs. Daniel isn't in the kitchen. The peppers and onions are in the pan where I left them when I burned myself. They have long since gone cold. Frowning, I go for my phone beside the oven, where I'd had dinner's recipe open. Just as I reach for it, my kitchen lights up with red and blue. I hesitate.

It takes a moment to register that the lights are coming from outside. They're shining through the large windows on either side of our front door and pouring through the large windows in the front sitting room. I move down the hall from the kitchen and stop in my tracks when I see two police officers walking up the long driveway. How they got through the gate, I'm not sure. And I don't care.

Something is wrong.

My hands suddenly go numb.

*Daniel.*

The police reach the door and knock, but I'm rooted to the spot on the white marble floors as their cruiser lights strobe from blue to red and back again. I draw my husband's robe tighter around myself and smell the lingering scent of sandalwood.

*Daniel.*

The police knock on the door again. "Mrs. Warren? We're with the Vancouver Police Department. Are you home?"

I sink to my knees on the marble and clutch at my chest.

*Daniel.*

# CHAPTER ONE

*Three Years Later...*

Women mill around in summer dresses, sipping alcohol-free bubbly on the wrap-around porch of my parents' home in North Vancouver. Among them, my sister rubs her very round belly and smiles radiantly. She has a 'mother to be' sash draped over her shoulder, and she's wearing a blush pink dress made of dreamy silk material. No pregnant woman on earth deserves to look as good as my sister, but leave it to her to get off looking like she's more youthful and joyful than her previously non-pregnant self.

"Are you sure you're up for this?" Mal asks, nudging me in the ribs with her elbow.

"For my sister's baby shower? I have to be."

"Considering the circumstances..."

"Daniel died three years ago." I lift my chin. "I can't pretend life isn't continuing to move forward. My sister is carrying my niece or nephew. I'm going to be part of their life. Might as well start now. Right?"

"That's very healthy of you. Is that what your therapist said?"

"Pretty much verbatim."

Mal laughs softly. "Nobody would blame you if this was too much,

Charlie, least of all Devin."

"I told her I'd be here, and I'm here. Come on." I start up the steps to the wrap-around porch of my family home. Mom insisted on hosting Devin's baby shower, and with the lush green gardens, plenty of outdoor seating, and gorgeous wisteria blooming over the lattice around the south side of the porch, my sister would have been an idiot to turn her down. I grab two flutes of faux champagne at the top of the stairs from a welcome table and press one into Mal's hands.

She throws it back like a tequila shot. "Do you think there's any *real* champagne for us non-preggos?"

"This is Devin we're talking about. If she can't have it, we can't have it."

"I should have brought my flask," Mal grunts.

"Charlie!"

I flinch as someone with a shrill voice calls my name. I turn toward the sound of high heels on the porch and manage to brace myself as a beautiful woman with long blonde hair in a yellow dress throws her arms around me.

"Stephanie," I say, patting my sister's best friend's back before she pulls away. "It's good to see you."

"You too, babe! I wasn't sure you'd make it."

"I RSVP'd a week after you sent the invites," I say.

"Yes, you did. I just wondered if it would feel a bit too heavy after what you went through, you know? Nobody would have blamed you." She turns her sweet, crisp-white smile to Mal. "And you are?"

"Mallory." Mal struggles to shift her grip and balance the gift on her hip and the glass in her hand while holding out her other hand. "Charlie's best friend." She holds up a beautifully wrapped square present with pink and blue ribbon. "Where do we put our gifts?"

Stephanie turns and points a perfectly manicured finger to a long table in front of my parents' living room window. There's a powder pink and blue balloon arch over the table and fluffy white clouds with raindrops dangling from the porch ceiling. It's beautiful–and everything I had dreamed of for myself when Daniel and I were trying. Metallic raindrops the size of my palm glitter from fishing line beneath the cotton candy clouds. I sigh, and Mal puts a reassuring hand on my back.

Mal and I drop our gifts off at the table, tucking them amongst the nearly fifty other parcels. We wander between bodies of beautifully dressed women, and I spy three pregnant bellies in the crowd.

I wonder how easy it was for them.

"Oh, shit." Mal takes my shoulder and turns me toward the porch steps. "Incoming overbearing mother alert. Flee. Flee!"

I regret wearing the strappy lavender sandals that slap against the soles of my feet as I hurry to escape being noticed by my mother. It's too late. As she sweeps down the porch, she spots me and hollers my name. Mal groans. I inhale deeply and brace myself for the storm.

When I turn, I have the most convincing smile plastered on my face that I can muster.

Mom is dressed for the occasion, and as usual, it looks like she thinks the baby shower is for her. I know she's excited. The baby in my sister's belly will be the first grandchild—the first-born grandchild, that is. Mom is wearing a shimmering silver dress that ends in the middle of her tanned shins. Her wrists jingle with bracelets, and a shawl covers her sun-freckled shoulders. Her hair, which started turning white a couple of years ago, has one streak of light pink and one light blue. I suspect she'll be sporting them until the baby is born.

"You look great," I tell her as we lean in for a hug.

She squeezes me tight. "Thank you, sweetheart. Oh, and you brought Mallory! My dear, it's so nice to see you." Mom pulls back and gives Mal a fierce hug as well.

My best friend makes wide eyes at me over Mom's shoulder. "Nice to see you too, Deidra."

Mom withdraws from their hug and reaches up to twirl her fingers in the streaks of blue and pink. "What do you think, Charlie? Devin says it's obnoxious, but your father likes it. He says it brings out my eyes. And it reminds me every time I look in the mirror that I'm going to be a grandmother in a month." She balls her hands under her chin and squeals. "Maybe even sooner if Baby decides to make an early appearance!"

Mal is watching me. I can feel her deadpan stare.

But I smile. "The streaks are fun. Devin is probably just bummed that she didn't think of it first."

"That's right." Mom plants her still-balled-up fists on her hips. "Enjoy yourselves, dears. I'm playing hostess today and going to check on my guests. I mean Devin's guests." She giggles at her mix up. "Let me know if either of you needs anything."

With that, Mom flutters away like a fairy in a garden, tending to nearly empty champagne flutes and removing empty serving trays from the food table on the porch. She makes small talk with other guests, pausing to put her hand on the belly of another very pregnant woman. I'm pretty sure she's one of Devin's colleagues, and she probably doesn't love the way my mother is feeling her up.

I get lost staring at the swell of her belly–the perfect ball of joy that makes her belly button stick out beneath the fabric of her dress. Her feet are swollen, but her cheeks are rosy, her complexion bright, and she's smiling even though Mom isn't giving her any personal space.

Mal notices that I'm spiraling. She loops her arm through mine and guides me through the chatting guests toward my sister, who is sitting on Mom's white wicker bench seat on the porch, propped up by floral pillows behind her. She lights up when she sees me, rises to her feet belly first, and sidesteps around the coffee table to hug me. Her hair smells good. Like roses.

"I'm so glad you're here," Devin whispers into my shoulder. "You don't have to stay the whole time. If at any point you need to duck out, just go. I get it."

I give her a squeeze. A silent thank you. "I'm good. Promise."

When she steps back, she regards me with that furrowed-brow look of concern of hers. She doesn't believe me. But she spares me any pushback and returns to her seat, complaining about her fat ankles and new stretch marks that have recently appeared.

Stephanie, who sits beside my sister nibbling on a plate of fresh fruit, leans toward Devin like she has a secret, but when she speaks, her voice is loud. "Coconut oil, babe. It's a miracle worker. I bought so much cream and oils marketed to pregnant women, and nothing worked. But coconut oil? It was the best thing by far. And I think I got lucky. I'm genetically gifted and not prone to stretch marks. I only have a few on my hips." She lifts her chin proudly and looks around at the other women, as if seeking approval. Nobody says a word.

Except Mal.

"Stretch marks are sexy," she says. "Take it from the lesbian."

Stephanie stops chewing her pineapple briefly.

Devin laughs, and so do some of the other women. "Mark keeps telling me he likes them, too. He says they will be my forever reminders of what my body did for our little one." She puts her hands high up on her belly and rubs them both in slow circles. She stares adoringly down at the swell.

I find myself wishing I'd gotten big enough to have forever reminders on my tummy.

The sunny Sunday afternoon crescendos into organized chaos—first a couple of shower games, then presents, then photos down in the garden with props, then another game, some prizes, and the slow inevitability of the party ending. Mom flits to and fro, packing up food and trying to give as much of it away as she can as guests leave. There are extra cupcakes and cookies, and Mom doesn't want them around the house. They'll go straight to her ass, she says, or to Dad's heart. Neither is good.

Mal and I find Devin to say goodbye. I'm ready to go home and plunge myself into distractions. A book. A show. A workout. Anything.

"Thank you for coming," Devin says, clasping my hands. "Seriously. It means the world."

I'm exhausted from putting on a happy face, but I manage one more smile. "I wouldn't have missed this for anything, Dev. I can't wait to meet your little bean and spoil them rotten."

"You'll be the best Auntie. Brett keeps saying so."

I smile. My sister got lucky with Brett, just like I'd gotten lucky with Daniel. Brett is a good man. Honest. Hardworking. A little OCD, but that seems to be more of an advantage than anything. He has to get things just right, so, needless to say, their baby has a downright magical nursery with nothing out of place. He'll be a doting father, and I know he'll take care of my sister postpartum. I'll be close by, too, but suspect my role will be more suited to helping her maintain boundaries with Mom and Dad. I offered to throw myself on the sword for her so that Brett didn't have to, and they could revel in newborn bliss.

Stephanie comes down the porch steps to meet us on the lawn and say goodbye. She runs her fingers through her long blonde hair and gives me a sympathetic smile that might be closer to pity. "Take care of yourself, Charlie," she says.

Mal throws an arm around my shoulders. "If she doesn't, I will." She turns me around, and we march down the paving stones and out the garden gate onto the sidewalk. Her car is parked on the curb a block and a half away, so we walk, our hips bumping into each other, our footsteps in unison.

"Stephanie is a bag," Mal announces.

I laugh. "She's... well. Yeah. Pretty much."

Mal brings her voice to a higher pitch and feigns a doe-eyed, feminine smile. "I'm genetically predisposed to *not* get stretch marks. My blowout cost three hundred dollars. Look at my tiny, dainty feet in my designer sandals. I'm *spectacular.*"

A snort escapes me as I throw my head back. "You sound just like her. Did she really tell people how much her blowout was?"

"She told your mom." We reach the car, and Mal opens my door for me. She gives a dramatic half-bow and invites me in with a wave of her arm. "My love."

"We'd make a good couple," I tell her. "You know, if I were gay."

"And ruin this good thing we have?" Mal shakes her head. "Never. Besides, I've tried having relationships with straight girls. Ends badly every time. I only date experienced lesbians now. A minimum of three prior relationships. And they have to be *out.*"

"Do you request their resumes on all those dating apps you use?"

Mal flicks me in the forehead. "Don't judge."

Giggling, I rub my forehead as she closes my door, walks around the front of her Ranger, and climbs in behind the wheel. She turns the ignition and pulls away from the curb. Billy Joel comes up next on her playlist, and she turns the volume down.

"Thanks for coming with me today," I say. "I know it wasn't your thing."

Mal puts her hand on my knee. "Having your back is my thing. I'm proud of you for going. You should be too." Half a mile passes under the tires before Mal speaks again. "I'm around tomorrow if you want help moving."

I shake my head. "I hired movers for a reason, but thanks. The last place I want to be is in the house while everything is being moved out. Daniel…" I trail off and gaze out the window as cherry blossom trees snow in the breeze. My dead husband's name has free range in my mind, but I hardly ever speak it aloud. I swallow. "He bought that house for us to spend the rest of our lives there. The last three years without him in it have made me painfully aware of how big it is. So many empty rooms…"

"It's good that you're getting your own place. A fresh start. No memories all over the place." Mal sounds matter-of-fact, and I wonder if she's trying to convince me or herself that my new condo in Port Moody is a good idea. It's out of the city–about a half hour drive from Vancouver and family. And Mal. She wishes I would stay closer, but every nook and cranny of Vancouver reminds me of Daniel. Our usual sushi dates. The Roxy, the club where we had our first kiss. Granville Street. Robson Street. Kitsilano Beach. The ocean in general.

I could have easily gone more than thirty minutes away, but Port Moody will do the trick. It is a much smaller suburb. Family friendly. Quiet, but thriving socially. The place is packed with outdoor activities, breweries, shopping, and new development everywhere you turn.

A new page.

"I'll have you over as soon as I'm settled in," I promise.

"We can find the best pizza joint near your new digs."

# CHAPTER TWO

THE MOVING company I'd hired was referred to me by the packing company I found online. After weeks of trying to pack the house myself, and half a dozen emotional breakdowns and multiple bottles of wine, I conceded. I couldn't do it on my own, and I didn't want someone I knew picking through all my memories. So, I shoved everything that reminded me of Daniel in what used to be his home office and told the packers to label everything with his name. I'll tell the movers to take it to the storage unit I rented out a few weeks ago.

Four hundred and sixty-three dollars a month to keep Daniel's things in a place that is secure, but where I can't see it.

Steep, but worth it.

The movers arrive at seven thirty in the morning. The sun is out, and so are the birds. I stand at the front door in biker shorts and an oversized tee–the ideal moving attire for the middle of July in Vancouver. Three men pile out of a moving truck with their company name slapped on the side in orange and blue paint, *Simon Says MOVE.* Apparently, they are the best in the area.

The oldest of the three strides toward me and extends a calloused, massive hand. He grins like he already knows me. "You must be Mrs. Warren."

I shake his hand. "Ms."

He doesn't realize his mistake and just nods. "I'm Simon. These are my top two guys, Dusty and Mack." He hooks a thumb over his shoulder at the two men at the back of the truck.

They throw the door up. It rattles and slams against the roof, a metal clap to wake up my neighbors. I wince. I wince again when Simon puts two fingers in his mouth and whistles. Dusty and Mack look up and begin making their way down the long driveway to greet me.

Dusty is tanned and frumpy. He has charming wrinkles at the corners of his eyes, stubble that connects to the frizzy chest hair showing at the neckline of his tattered white shirt (it's not all that white anymore) and dirty old Levis that are about two sizes too big. But he's friendly enough and shakes my hand. His grip is gentle and warm.

Mack, on the other hand, is less approachable, despite being better groomed. He has brown stubble trimmed short with clean edges. His eyes are dark, but that might be because they're in the shade cast by the visor of his ball cap. His skin is tanned as well–likely due to all his physical work outside–and his shoulders fill out his heather grey shirt well.

Very well.

Mack doesn't shake my hand. Instead, he nods past me at the front door. "Can we start?"

Simon rubs the back of his neck and chuckles lightly. "So long as the lady here says we can. Any special instructions, Mrs. Warren?"

"Ms.," I correct again, more sternly this time.

He hears me. "Sorry. *Ms.* Warren."

"Please be gentle with all the items in the office on the first floor. They're… sentimental. And I'd like those to go to the storage locker. Everything else can go to the condo."

Mack glances at Simon. "Storage locker? You didn't say anything about a storage locker. We only have one truck. We don't have time to take a load back to the lot and then go to Port Moody."

"I have to be out today," I say. "The new owners take possession tomorrow."

Mack doesn't even glance in my direction. He continues to stare at Simon with his lips pressed together in a firm line and his jaw muscles flexing. I thought that only happened in the movies. Apparently not. This Mack character wears his irritation like he isn't speaking directly to his employer. "What's the plan, Simon?"

Simon presses two fingers between his bushy graying eyebrows and rubs hard. "Damn. That detail slipped through the cracks." He makes a low sound in the back of his throat as his fingers move to his chin. He taps thoughtfully. "Would the items for your storage locker fit in the bed of a pickup truck, Miss Warren? It's just from your home office, you said?"

My cheeks are burning like I'm standing on the beach in the middle of August without sunscreen. I shake my head. "They won't."

Mack sighs.

Dusty scratches his lower back and looks unbothered.

"It's not all office goods," I say, feeling the need to explain. "It's… well…"

"Sentimental," Mack says. "Yeah, we got it. Looks like we're going to have to pack that room up last. We'll put those boxes at the end of the truck and hit the storage locker first." He points a finger at Simon. "Pay more attention to the moving forms. I'm sick of working past the clock. Dusty, too. He's got a kid to get home to."

Dusty looks like he's just woken up from a bong-hit-induced nap. "Huh?"

Mack pats him hard on the chest. "Look alive, Dusty. We've got a lot of work to do today. First floor office boxes go in the truck last. Got it? Oh, and they're fragile," he adds, shooting me a look.

I can't tell what Mack is thinking. Does he think I'm wasting their time? Does he think my sentimental items are boxes of old diaries and stuffed animals from my childhood? Would he see me differently if he knew each and every box was immaculately packed with Daniel's things? His clothes. His book collection. His nightstand and everything he kept in it, right down to the spare watch batteries and a small memo pad he used to scrawl dreams on in the middle of the night so he wouldn't forget them, and he'd have something ridiculous to tell me over breakfast the next morning.

I couldn't throw any of it away, and it has been three years.

Mack and Dusty shoulder their way inside, and a quick order of business is established. They both head upstairs and begin bringing boxes down and loading them into the truck. Simon tells me that I don't have to stay. He suggests I make myself scarce and do something with my day, which is exactly what I had intended to do, but I feel weird leaving the three of them with all of my worldly possessions.

All of Daniel's worldly possessions.

So, I linger near the front door as the sun creeps higher in the sky and the temperature rises. Mack and Dusty give Simon lip for not helping until he bends and starts hauling boxes into the truck. Restless, I try to make myself feel busy by doing another walk through of the house to make sure I haven't forgotten something. I find a roll of packing tape on the window sill in the kitchen from sealing one of the last boxes last night–the one with my French press, favorite coffee mug, and a couple of dishes and kitchen items I needed up until the last minute.

I continue walking through, pausing to trace my fingers over a dent in the door frame to our old bedroom. My old bedroom. I smile. Daniel and I put that dent there on move-in day. He was carrying one of our nightstands while I trailed behind him with a three-pound lamp. He was grumbling about how lazy I was and how I could have taken more than a lamp, and I told him the way the veins in his arms were bulging from carrying the solid pine furniture was making me too hot and bothered to be trusted to do any real lifting.

He'd laughed, twisted his head to grin over his shoulder at me, and walked smack into the corner of the door. The nightstand wedged into his stomach, winding him, and he wheezed out a string of curses as he struggled to put it down in the hallway and recover.

*"I can make it better,"* I'd whispered before slowly going to my knees, placing the lamp down, and reaching for his fly.

I withdraw my fingers from the dent in the door and step aside as Mack and Dusty come out of the primary bedroom with our nightstands.

"Can you put those in the storage locker, actually?"

Mack hesitates, the muscles and tendons straining in his arms, and his brow furrows.

"I bought new ones," I say, as if this explains my choice—not that I need to explain my choice to a moving guy *I'm* paying. He's supposed to do what I ask, isn't he? Why does that critical furrow of his brow and the hard set of his jaw make me feel so judged? I lift my chin and muster confidence. "Is that going to be a problem?"

Dusty grunts at the top of the stairs and uses his knee to balance the nightstand. "Not a problem, miss."

"Thank you." I cross my arms and hover at the banister, watching them descend and hook a left into Daniel's study, where they leave the nightstands to be packed at the back of the truck with the rest of his belongings.

I leave only to head down to the corner store to buy cold waters and Gatorades for my movers. I feel the need to do something or offer them something for their efforts, despite paying their wages. They're working hard and breaking a sweat in the summer heat. It's the least I can do.

When I return, Mack blatantly asks me what took so long before unscrewing the cap on the water bottle I hand him, tipping his head back and draining the entire thing in five gulps. He crushes it and shoves it into his back pocket.

"I can recycle that," I say, holding out a hand.

He gives the bottle back and lets me off the hook for having to answer his question. I didn't hit the closest corner store down the street. I haven't set foot in there since the night Daniel died. It was the last place he'd been that night, and when his body was removed from the driver's seat of our car, the pint of ice cream he'd gone out to buy for me was melted on the asphalt.

I always opt to drive an extra three kilometers to the next store.

I spend the next several hours watching from a distance and

making small talk with neighbors who come out to offer what they must think are words of support. They tell me how beautiful the house is. How they used to see the way I greeted Daniel at the front door when he came home from work. How well we took care of our grass. How much I loved the tulips in the spring. How they'll miss seeing me when they take the trash out on Tuesday evenings.

It's all so… bleh.

I don't know these people. Not really. And this is the most I've spoken to them since Daniel died.

Later, Simon informs me that there are only a few more boxes from the study left to load into the truck. I'm pleased by their efficiency. I'll be settling into my new condo in Port Moody earlier than I hoped, considering the mix up with the storage locker. While Simon and Dusty go to make sure they can make room in the back of the truck for the remaining boxes, Mack heads inside. I follow him into the study.

Only three boxes remain.

I lean against the doorframe and wrap my arms around myself as he lifts a box. Things rattle inside.

"Be careful," I hiss. It's a reflex. I hold myself tighter. "Please."

"Your ex sure did a number on you, lady."

"Pardon?"

He nods down at the box in his arms. "I've seen a lot of people hold onto things from previous relationships, but I've never seen someone with quite this much stuff. You know, there's power in letting go. Isn't there a book about that?" He offers what he probably thinks is a kind and supportive smile. "I bet you'd feel better if you purged some of this shit out of your life. And you'd save money on storage fees. How special could this guy have been?"

I stare at him.

*Who the hell does he think he is?*

"He's dead," I say.

"What?"

"All this stuff was his. My husband's. He died. So, forgive me for not being ready to 'purge his shit' and save money. I hired you to move boxes, not to give me advice."

Mack adjusts his grip on the box. I wait for an apology, but one never comes. He lumbers past me and heads out to the truck.

"Asshole," I mutter.

# CHAPTER THREE

DUSTY AND MACK lean against the kitchen island in my new condo.
The place is full of boxes. They've done what their ad promises:
placed each labelled moving box into its designated room for me to
unpack. Office supplies in the den. Primary bedroom items in the
bedroom. So on and so forth. While they drink water from a pack I'd
placed in the fridge the day I took possession, I stand in the middle of
the living room, my eyes flicking from box to box, acutely aware of
one unsettling fact.

*Nothing in here is Daniel's.*

Everything that was his—clothes that still smell like him, shoes I
begged him to throw away because they were hideous, his laptop, his
watch collection—sits in the dark in a lonely storage locker ten kilometers away.

Waiting to be forgotten.

"Are you all right, miss?" Dusty leans up against the kitchen island
while he strokes his beard. "You should sit down. It's a scorcher out
there. Here." He turns to the fridge, jerks it open, grabs me a water
bottle, and tosses it at me.

I miss the catch. The water bottle sails past me into the living room, hits the fireplace, and lands with a sloshing thud on the laminate flooring.

Mack grunts.

I crouch down, pick it up, unscrew the cap, and thank Dusty with a small murmur of gratitude before lifting it to my lips and drinking. It's cold and refreshing. I wipe my mouth with the back of my hand. "Thank you."

Dusty checks the time, glancing at the digital watch on his wrist. "Better get moving, Mack. Simon will start honking the horn if we don't move our asses. Need anything else from us, Miss Warren?"

I shake my head.

They move to the door, and I've already turned to stare at the mess of boxes I have to unpack when Mack clears his throat.

"We were gentle with them," he says. "The boxes in the storage locker. They're safe. Just thought you'd want to know."

I can't look at him. My vision blurs with tears. So, I nod vigorously and sniffle. "Thank you."

～

THE NEXT DAY, MAL COMES OVER WITH STARBUCKS AND A CHEERY attitude. She finds me in the ensuite off the primary bedroom, setting up my favorite products around the edge of my new soaker tub. They're all sealed and brand new. Untouched. Never used.

I haven't had a bath since Daniel died. As I set a cinnamon and citrus scented candle on the corner ledge, I wonder if I'll break that streak here. New home. New tub. New memories.

Mal leans up against the doorframe. "You never told me you'd be living like royalty in this place. It's *nice,* Charlie. Damn." She looks down at the floor. "Is this real marble?"

I nod.

"Get fucked."

Laughing, I push up from my knees and take the coffee she holds out. "It's the apartment of my wildest dreams, thanks to Daniel's life insurance."

I'd rather live in a shoebox and have my husband back, but hey, the universe deemed me unworthy of a happily ever after.

"Put me to work," Mal says. "What do you need unpacked most? Kitchen? You know my organizational skills are unparalleled."

"Says who?" I brush past her and move down the hall into the kitchen. Gold accents shine in the morning sun bursting through the floor-to-ceiling windows in the living room.

The apartment was built five years ago. My unit is on the top floor, and it's just shy of sixteen hundred square feet. Pretty big as far as apartments in the Lower Mainland go, especially considering it only has one bedroom and a den. Most of the space is designated to the social areas of the home: a top-of-the-line gourmet kitchen, sprawling living room with a towering black marble fireplace, and a dining room plucked straight out of an interior design magazine. The windows aren't only beautiful, but functional, and open like bifolds onto a sweeping balcony overlooking Burrard Inlet. If I get lucky, I might see a pod of orcas one day, swimming up the inlet to feed.

Mal starts familiarizing herself with my kitchen. She opens cupboard doors and slides open drawers, oohing and ahhing over the storage space, silent closures, sparkly white quartz countertops, and walk-in pantry.

"That's it," she announces. "I officially hate my house."

We spend the next few hours unpacking. By the time we finish the kitchen and living room, my back feels like a tightly wound spring. I fall into the corner of the sofa and kick my feet up on the coffee table.

Mal joins me with a huff. "So, all in all, the move went well? No broken dishes?"

I shook my head. "Everything was fine. Seeing Daniel's stuff get taken out wasn't easy, but... I know this is for the best. And I know where I can go if I need to, you know, see it again."

*Feel it. Smell it.*

Mal chews the inside of her cheek.

"I know," I say.

"What?"

"I sound crazy."

"I didn't say that."

"You might as well have. It's written all over your face." I shift on the sofa, tucking one leg under myself, where it will stay until it falls asleep and the pins and needles become unbearable. "Want to know what's *actually* crazy, though?"

"Tell me."

"One of the moving guys had the balls to assume all of Daniel's stuff belonged to my ex. He told me I'd be saving money and my sanity if I purged it all, and that the guy 'must have done a real number on me.'" I scoff and roll my eyes to the ceiling, where my sunken pot lights are set on a dimmer switch. Daniel always hated how I liked the lights dim. Ambiance over functional lighting. Always.

Mal's mouth drops open. "He said that to you?"

"Right to my face."

"What did you say?"

"I told him the truth."

Mal winces. "Really? That must have been awkward."

"You know, it might have been, had he said anything else, but after I told him Daniel was dead, he just continued about his business like he never said anything at all. No apology. Nothing." I feel heat at the base of my neck as anger grips my spine. "Such an arrogant jerk."

She rolls her eyes. "Men."

"Specifically, *that* man."

She smiles, and I know she's just humoring me. "So, not to change gears on you here, but I need you to come do the Coquitlam Crunch with me on Sunday."

I arch an eyebrow. "Uh, no?"

"Pretty please?"

"You want me to strap on some running shoes and spandex and climb a hill with you for *fun*? No thanks. I'll pass."

"You owe me."

I chew the inside of my cheek. "Fine. But can we make it early in the morning? It will give me an excuse to leave my sister's house early. We have family dinner on Saturday. Knowing Devin, it'll be an overdone affair so she can show off the new nursery, her cooking skills, and her very much alive husband."

"Bitter doesn't look good on you, babe. You know your sister isn't rubbing it in your face." She reaches across the sofa and puts her hand on my knee. "It's okay to still hurt. Just keep perspective, okay?"

She's right. She's always right. I nod.

"And I'll meet you at the Crunch no earlier than seven. That alone is a sin on Sundays."

I'm about to tell her it's a deal when my phone rings. The words *Simon Says MOVE* flash across my screen, and I groan. What do these guys want now? I answer the call, lift the phone to my ear, and grimace as I shift again. My whole leg burns with pins and needles.

"Miss Warren?"

"Yes."

"It's Mack."

"Oh." *You.* I shoot Mal a look and point at the phone dramatically, mouthing, '*It's him.*' "Yes?"

"Simon was going to call you, but it was my fuck up, so I thought I should be the one to tell you."

My organs drop all at once, and it feels like I'm on a rollercoaster. "What happened?"

"We missed a box that had to go to your storage locker. When I unloaded it at the end of the day, I dropped it. There are some broken items inside."

"You *opened* the box?"

He pauses for a moment before collecting his thoughts. "I wanted to see how much damage had been done. I hoped nothing had broken."

"I told you to be careful." Which box had he dropped? What had he broken? Oh, God. I'd meticulously kept every single item safe since Daniel died. I'd dusted the stupid bull statue he bought in New York, a tiny replica of the Charging Bull in the financial district. I'd kept working batteries in his watches. Adjusted them during every daylight savings change. I'd laminated and neatly packed all of his random pieces of artwork he liked to buy at garage sales in case the artist 'made it big someday' and we could sell them for a profit, or tell the story behind it as it hung on our wall. I'd poured hours of my soul into preserving everything of him I had left. "I told you to be careful," I say again, because no other words will come.

"I know."

Was he going to apologize? Did he even care? It sure didn't seem like it.

"I'm coming down there," I say.

CHAPTER FOUR

*Simon Says MOVE* looked exactly as I expected it to. Moving vans are parked in a small lot outside a duplex-style industrial building. On the right is a gated and secured storage locker facility that seems to be part of *Simon Says MOVE*.

My keys jab into my palm as I tighten my fist and glare at the front door of the moving company. I see movement inside, mostly just passing silhouettes. The sun shines too brightly for me to see much of anything through the windows that blast my own furious reflection back at me.

For a moment, I study myself.

Like every time I see myself in a mirror, I can't recognize the woman staring back at me. She's lost forty-seven pounds since Daniel died. Most of the weight came from her breasts and ass–his favorite physical attributes. Her face is hollow and tight. The natural fullness her cheeks used to have, their pink flush, is nonexistent. Her hair is still dark, but brittle and less shiny. She hasn't had it cut in at least a year and a half, and the last appointment was only at the merciless poking and prodding of her mother. Her jeans are too big. She looks like she should work for the damn moving company.

"You need to do better," I mutter to myself before plucking up the courage to walk inside with my head held high.

A bell chimes above my head as I pass over the threshold and pause to let my eyes adjust to the dim lighting. It smells like car tires and cheap surface cleaner in here. I scrunch up my nose and frown at a pathetic-looking coffee station with a sign that invites me to help myself to a cup. Packets of powdered milk sit in a Styrofoam cup.

*No, thank you.*

I move to the counter. It looks like it hasn't been updated since it was installed in 1986. The countertop itself is mint green, the same kind of stuff that used to be in all my friends' parents' kitchens–or dental offices. Someone has hand-painted a mural on the wall behind the front counter–a picture of a moving van and a smiling man who I assume is supposed to be Simon. He's waving, presumably, at me, the customer.

The very perturbed customer.

Nobody stands behind the desk, but I can hear voices through a door to the right, which must be the office. Someone laughs.

I clear my throat. "Hello? Excuse me?"

Looking around, I see no bell on the counter.

The laughing from the office only gets louder, so I lean over the counter and raise my voice, calling again. A few seconds pass, then thirty, and still, nobody comes to check the front.

My keys are probably drawing blood by now as I march around the counter, move to stand in the doorway, and glower at the three men crowded around with their hands in their pockets.

"Could one of you be bothered to help me, please?"

Simon, who is furthest away leaning against the wall behind his desk, pushes himself upright with a startled look. "Miss Warren! Apologies, I didn't hear you out there. What can we do for you?"

"One of your movers broke some of my items," I say, shooting Mack, who has his back to me, the dirtiest look I can muster. "I'd like to talk about reparations and see the damage for myself. Please," I add, even though I'm not feeling very up to being polite.

Simon casts Mack a wary look.

Clearly, this is a manager who doesn't like confrontation.

Mack sighs. It's a long, drawn out, tedious sound. He turns to face me. "Follow me."

"I'd rather deal with literally anyone else."

Dusty snorts.

Mack's eyebrows raise. "Suit yourself."

*At least he's consistent,* I think as I cross my arms and turn to Simon. I'm about to open my mouth and tell him just what I think about his humorless, grumpy, Levi-wearing, apathetic dickhead of an employee, but he beats me to the punch.

"Mack," Simon barks, snapping his fingers in annoyance. His tone drops and loses its initial sharpness. "We talked about this."

Dusty looks everywhere but at me, obviously wishing he could be anywhere else. He tucks his hands into a pair of khakis that are in such terrible condition that nobody could ever deem them wearable—not even as work clothes as a mover, painter, drywaller, insert-more-messy-trade-careers-here. His hair sticks out in a bunch of different directions, and his nose is in dire need of a wax or trim. I conclude without a shred of doubt that Dusty might be the most single man I've ever seen. It is simply inconceivable that a woman could put up with his messiness.

Mack lets out another one of those long, drawn-out sighs before brushing past me into the lobby. "Come with me, Miss Warren. I set the damaged items aside for you. You tell me the value, and I'll write you a personal check."

"A check?" I follow him, shooting Simon a look over my shoulder to let him know I'm not impressed with having to deal with Mack. "What is this, 1980?"

Mack acts like I never said a word and leads me outside and to the right, where we pass through a secure gate into the lot lined with rows upon rows of storage lockers. The doors are a hideous shade of pumpkin-orange, and the number on each unit has been done in a fresh shade of dark green. Clearly, nobody here has an eye for what looks good.

*Or how to give half-decent customer service,* I think as Mack stops at locker 77 and pulls a band of keys down from around his bicep. Those—the biceps, I mean–are perhaps the only thing in this forsaken business worth looking at.

So, I do.

Look, I mean.

His skin is tanned from working through the summer, and his muscles and tendons ripple beneath the surface as he slides the key in the lock, twists, and then bends to lift the storage door up by a handle near the ground. He heaves effortlessly, and the door slides up with an obnoxious rattle before locking loudly into place. He stands back, gesturing for me to take a look.

To their credit, the locker is organized. Heavy boxes are on the bottom, working their way up to smaller, lighter boxes. All of my hand-written labels face outward for easy sorting and finding. The unpacked items, like our side tables and other pieces of furniture, are stacked neatly against the wall to my right.

On top of one of said nightstands is an open box with a red X on it. I move to it instinctively, pull open the tabs, and peer inside. My stomach is in a tight knot as I gaze down into the depths of Daniel's memories.

A crystal vase lays in pieces next to two ceramic mugs–one I painted, and one he painted. We thought it would be a fun idea to paint my parents' Christmas village-themed mugs for Christmas the year we were engaged, but our artwork turned out so hideous that we kept them for ourselves. Under no circumstances could we present them to my classy, golf-club going mother, who spent hundreds, if not thousands, of dollars on our gifts every year. No way.

Every year that we pulled them out of the box on December first, we laughed our asses off remembering our shock when we picked them up after they were fired in the kiln.

I reach into the box and pick up a shard of Daniel's mug. His Christmas tree, which I joked looked like a green hedgehog taking a poop (the poop being the tree trunk), is still fully intact on the piece of ceramic. The knot in my stomach suddenly comes undone, and the release of pressure shoots upward and burns the back of my eyes until the tears blind me. I run a thumb up the side of the tree and hiss in pain when I slide my skin right across the sharp edge.

I recoil and drop the shard.

"No," I gasp, reaching for it.

Mack has reflexes like I've never seen, and he catches the shard in his palm. I didn't even see him moving toward me. Blinking away tears, I stick my thumb in my mouth to hide how much I'm bleeding while he offers me the broken piece of mug.

"Who was the artist?" he asks.

"What?"

He nods sheepishly at the pooping hedgehog tree. "You or him?"

*Is he making fun of me?*

I search his eyes. They're dark, deep, endless pools of brown, and his eyelashes are longer than mine. There is no hint of a joke in his stare, and yet, I start laughing.

"He painted it," I say. "He was so embarrassed when we picked it up. He wanted to throw it in the garbage, but I insisted we keep it forever." I laugh again, shaking my head as I recall how red his cheeks had turned when the employee at the ceramic studio lifted his mug out of the box. She'd valiantly told him how much she loved his 'attention to detail,' referring to a plaid scarf he'd attempted to paint on a snowman. I'm still smiling as I turn to the box, searching for the piece with the plaid scarf. It looks more like a busted caterpillar than anything else.

Mack steps back and slides his hands into his pockets. His lips turn down in a frown, and he looks away. "I'm sorry. I sort of fucked up the forever part for you."

I find the piece with the plaid scarf, but look up at him. I'm not sure what to say. So, I shrug. "Shit happens."

He blinks. "I thought you were going to skin me alive."

"Me too. But apologies go a long way with me."

He rubs the back of his neck. "Still feels flat to me. Let me make it up to you."

The broken piece of mug has a nice weight in my hand, and the edges aren't as sharp with this piece. I drop it into my purse and look back into the box. I rummage around, sifting through broken items that don't punch me in the gut the same way the Christmas mugs had. "It's fine," I say absently. "Maybe I needed something like this to happen to remind me they're just things, after all."

"Come out for a drink with me tonight."

My eyebrows raise, but I try to hide my surprise by closing up the box. "I don't know if that's a good idea."

"Why not?"

Try as I might, I can't think of a valid excuse. My mind goes blank, and my thoughts turn to static.

"I'm afraid I'm going to have to insist," he says. "I'm off in two hours. I'll pick you up at yours and take you to a place I like. Casual. Jeans and a T-shirt sort of digs."

"Digs?"

Mack gives me the first earnest smile I think I've seen from him. It crinkles the corners of his eyes, and his white teeth are a stark contrast to his dark stubble. He's one of those people who look totally different when he smiles. His handsome level shoots up to one hundred, and my ears start to burn.

"Yes, digs," he says, leading me out of the locker and closing it behind us. After he locks it, we start walking back toward the gate. "Are you a beer or cocktails sort of girl?"

"Both."

"Mysterious," he muses, holding the gate open for me. He turns to lock it behind us and shields his eyes against the sun when he scours the parking lot. He nods to the nearest vehicle, a sleek white Mercedes. "That yours?"

*How does he know that?*

"Yes."

Without asking, he walks me out to my car, and after I disarm it, he opens my driver's door for me.

I rest a hand on top of the door before getting in and open my mouth to ask him what happened to the rough and tough asshole from the other day. But I close my lips.

He cocks his head. "Yes?"

"Nothing. I'll see you in a couple hours, I guess?" I sit down and tuck my legs in.

He grins. "Don't get your hopes up. I'm no Christmas-mug painting heartthrob who can afford a car like this or a swanky condo in Port Moody."

"Oh, don't worry." My ass hits my leather seat, and I grab the door handle, flashing him a smile of my own. "My expectations are on the floor."

He laughs and closes my door, stepping back as I press the ignition and pull away.

For the first time in three years, the elephant of grief sitting on my chest shifts position, and I can breathe a little easier. I'm not sure if it's because the broken mugs didn't destroy me or because a handsome man wants to take me out for drinks. Either way, it feels good.

And that makes me feel immediately guilty.

The elephant settles back into place, and I grip the steering wheel, grasping at the fleeting glimmers of relief as they slip away.

# CHAPTER FIVE

MACK IS seven minutes late picking me up. While I wait on the curb for him, I speed-text Mal, complaining, and fretting, and wondering if he's stood me up. She texts back and tells me to be patient. A few moments later, he pulls up in a dark blue old Ford truck with a dent in the front fender and a noisy rattle in the engine. The thing has to be almost thirty years old.

Mack gets out and comes around the hood to open my door for me. He's wearing a clean shirt and dark blue jeans with boots that appear to be Blundstones, even though it's a hot summer evening. As he holds open my door, I catch his dark eyes looking me over, taking in my outfit.

His gaze makes me immediately insecure, and I wish I'd just worn my original outfit choice: a pair of old jeans and a white T-shirt. But I had to go and convince myself that getting dressed up was a good idea. Well, sort of dressed up. My red cotton summer dress and white sneakers aren't exactly fancy. But it's the nicest thing I've worn in a long time, and the closest thing I have in my closet to something that actually fits me. And, perhaps most importantly, it's new and not something Daniel has ever seen me wear. Although, dresses were his favorite on me, and if he had to pick a color, it would have been red.

I definitely should have worn the jeans.

The passenger door groans as Mack opens it. He grimaces. "Need to oil that. Nice dress."

"Should I change?" I blurt out, fidgeting with the strap of my crossbody purse. "You said this place was casual. I can run up really quick."

"No way," he says, smiling. "You look great."

I'm sure I'm as red as my dress as I step up into his truck and sit on the bench seat. He closes my door, and soon, he's in the cab with me and pulling away from the curb. I try to think of something to say to ease the awkwardness while Bob Seger plays on the radio. Is he feeling it the same way I am? What is he thinking about?

*Why do I care so much about what he's thinking?*

"How's your first couple nights at the new place been?" he asks as we brake for a red light.

*Lonely. Quiet.*

"Good." I shift in my seat. The metal buckle on the seatbelt bumps my forearm, and I flinch but play it off. I forgot how hot those things get in the summer sun, and this dang thing doesn't have AC. The last time I was in a vehicle this old, I was twenty-two or something like that, and Daniel picked me up from work in his old Bronco that broke down on the side of the road that same night. I'd lost my virginity to him in the back of that beat-up old monstrosity on a back road in the middle of July.

The light turns green, and Mack takes a left a few blocks down the street. We're heading down toward the inlet. The water dazzles under the setting sun, so I take my sunglasses out of my purse. Mack's truck rolls over a speed bump, and we pull into a parking lot outside an unassuming brewery with yellow patio umbrellas and sliding bay doors.

I hop out before he has a chance to come open my door. I appreciate chivalry, but I don't need a guy to overdo it. I'm capable of opening my own doors and kind of used to it now that Daniel is gone.

Mack closes my door behind me and gestures up at the sign above the bay doors. "Best brewery in town. I figure since you're new in these parts, you should start on the right foot."

The brewery is called The Folly.

"A lack of good sense or general foolishness," I say.

Mack looks down at me and quirks a dark eyebrow.

"Folly," I say. "That's what it means."

"Right."

*Don't be a smart ass, Charlie. Daniel might have found it endearing, but most people do not.*

Mack leads me inside. The brewery has a high ceiling, so the noise carries and echoes like a chamber. Three employees laugh behind the wood-top bar, and a fourth is out in the front, wiping down tables and collecting empty beer glasses. I read a chalkboard menu behind the counter displaying the night's features. I spy a citrusy lager that looks good, and when Mack asks me what I want, that's what I ask for.

He baulks.

"You don't approve?" I ask.

There's a couple in front of us in line. They're holding hands, and the woman, blonde-haired and slender, rests her chin on his shoulder and smiles up at her man. He must have just said something funny–something private and just for her–because she has a twinkle in her eyes that I'm immediately sure only appears for him. He dips his head to her and kisses her nose.

The intimacy of their moment hits me in the gut.

"Fruit doesn't belong in beer," Mack says, saving me before my thoughts have a chance to fully descend into anguish. He shifts his weight, shaking his head vigorously enough that a few dark locks fall over his eyes. He brushes them away. "I should have known you'd have bad taste."

My mouth falls open in mock incredulity. "Bad taste? Me?" I gesture down at my red dress. "Debatable."

He chuckles. It's a deep, warm, welcoming sound. "A dress isn't the same as a beer."

"Fine. Order for me."

He glances down at me. "The last time I did that for a woman, I got scolded to high heaven. Pass."

"The last time?"

He smirks. "Are you asking about my dating history?"

*Gosh. How does this man make me blush so easily? And why does he have a smart-ass comment for everything I ask him?*

I grip the strap of my purse to stop myself from fidgeting. "Do you usually bring up your dating history when you're out with someone else?" I counter.

"Are we 'out'? Is this a date, Miss Warren?"

The heat in my cheeks builds, and I can't make eye contact anymore. So, I nod up at the menu. "No, this isn't a date. And I changed my mind. I want the contaminated fruit beer."

Mack rubs his chin. The couple ahead of us finishes up their order and moves away from the counter to find a table outside.

We step forward, and Mack hooks a thumb in my direction. "She's gonna have the mandarin lager. I'll have the IPA."

I can't help but chuckle. He really had to specify that I was the one drinking the fruity beer and not him. He sees me smiling after he turns from the counter, tucking his wallet back in his jeans.

He arches an eyebrow. "What?"

"Nothing," I say over my shoulder as we head outside to pick a table.

The sun is low in the sky, but the evening is still hot. Across the street, children run from platform to platform on a tiered play-ground. Their squeals and laughter, and the occasional cry, make for easy background noise. I've always enjoyed the sound of children playing. While most of my friends, like Mal for example, find it grating, I find it cheerful and hopeful. It has always reminded me of Christmas.

Of course, when I had my struggles conceiving, the sound of their joy was a little less hopeful. But now, years later, I can sit and listen again.

A server brings out our beers, and we take a sip. Mine is delight-fully light and dances across my tongue. I nod approvingly, going back in for another sip, while Mack watches me darkly over the rim of his glass.

I lick my upper lip, paranoid there's foam clinging to it. "It's good," I say.

"I can tell."

"Thank you for bringing me here. I needed to get out of the house." I look around–at the park across the street, the maple trees, the ice cream parlor down the road. Port Moody is a nice, easygoing, comfortable place. Simple living. It moves at a much slower pace than Vancouver, and as I sit in the warm summer evening air, I am struck with a profound sense of being right where I'm supposed to be.

*Didn't see that one coming.*

"I can't imagine it's been easy," Mack says.

"What?"

He looks at me like I've just lost brain cells. "The move. You know. Doing it all alone. Navigating the… loss." He picks the word carefully, and his brow furrows before he shakes his head. "Sorry. I shouldn't have said anything."

"Why? Afraid you might remind me my husband is dead?" I manage a small, albeit sharp, smile. It's a smile I give the universe every now and then when I'm pissed instead of sad. A big "fuck you" smile. "Don't worry. There isn't a single moment when I forget he's gone. But I've had a lot of therapy, and I can talk about him. Although I'm sure I've given you the opposite impression."

Mack's lips press into a fine line, but he doesn't say anything.

"I'm a fun date, huh?" I ask, quirking my head to the side.

His easy smile returns. "So, this *is* a date then?"

# CHAPTER SIX

Forty-five minutes and two more mandarin lagers later…

"Did you grow up here?" I slide to the opposite side of the picnic table to escape the sunlight blasting under the umbrella as it dips toward the horizon. In the shade, I take a sip of my lager and find it empty. Oops.

Mack switched to water after his first drink. "Toronto."

"Boo."

He rubs his jaw and flashes me a disarming smile. "Don't tell me you're a Canucks fan?"

"I grew up watching hockey," I say. "And I'm loyal to my team."

He rocks back on his side of the picnic table bench like I've swung a right hook. He puts a hand on his chest, feigning dismay. "She drinks fruit-contaminated beer and cheers for the Canuckleheads." He pretends to check his phone and acts like an important call has just come in. "Who's in the hospital? Yeah, okay, I'm on my way."

I throw a balled-up paper napkin at him and laugh.

Mack slides his phone back into his pocket and rests his forearms on the table. "I assume this means you grew up here?"

"Born and raised in Squamish, then we moved to North Vancouver when my Dad's business took off. I was fourteen."

I still remember how jarring it had felt to move from Squamish, a small town nestled near the mountains with not much to do besides outdoor recreation, to Vancouver, where the noise, the bustle, and the vibe was a stark contrast to what I was used to. My high school was six times the size of my old school in Squamish, and getting my bearings had taken some time. I had issues with some mean girls, which was inevitable, a crush on a boy who I am pretty sure has a criminal record now, and I ate lunch by myself in the library for nine weeks straight.

Until I met Daniel.

"It's hard to picture a girl like you coming from Squamish," Mack says.

"Why?"

"The flashy car, arrogant attitude–"

"Excuse me?"

He laughs. "Look, you didn't make a great first impression, okay?"

"And you did?"

He hesitates. "Touché."

It is possible that Mack is right. Daniel had come from a middle-class, hardworking family, just like I had, but his drive and relentless pursuit of 'the best' had spurred us toward a life I never imagined for myself. We drove luxury vehicles, had a 2.5-million-dollar home, took two annual vacations, enjoyed spa and private golf club memberships, and were in the process of buying a second home on a lake in the interior to enjoy during the summer months.

From the outside looking in, we had everything.

"I can see where you might have thought I was a bit... spoiled," I say.

"What did he do for work?"

I know he's asking about Daniel. Normally, when people ask about him, I work hard to change the subject. But tonight, sitting in the waning sunlight with Mack, I don't feel like I need to run or find shelter.

"Concrete pouring for residential and commercial properties. He had a lot of city contracts. The new wharf in New Westminster was done by his company." I wish I had more of my drink left so I had something to do with my hands. "He liked the work, and it paid really well. But it wasn't his dream."

"What was his dream, then?" Mack looks me over, an eyebrow arched. "From where I'm sitting, it looks like the guy had it made."

"His dream?"

Mack nods and shifts in his seat. Behind him, the sun suddenly winks out and disappears on the horizon, plunging us into shade. Edison bulb string lights come to life above our heads. "Yeah," Mack says. "If concrete pouring wasn't his dream, what was?"

*Fatherhood.*

*Family.*

*Legacy.*

My stomach suddenly rolls over, and I grip the table when it feels like the whole world is swaying.

Mack notices and puts his hand over mine. "You good?"

I shake my head.

He looks around, gets smoothly to his feet, and comes around to my side of the table, where he helps me to my feet and steadies me with an arm wrapped around my waist. Even though I'm embarrassed, I lean on him for support, and he walks me off the patio, across the parking lot, and past his truck. We settle on cool grass in the park across the street from the brewery, and he stands, watching me with concern as I sit and lean back on my hands and take some deep breaths.

I want to lie and tell him I had too much to drink. I doubt he'd believe me.

"I shouldn't have asked so many questions about him," Mack says. "It's none of my business."

"It's okay."

He slides his hands into his jean pockets. They get stuck at the knuckles, thumb out, and I gaze up at his wrists and exposed forearms while he glowers across the street at the brewery like it's to blame for my sudden bout of... whatever this is. Guilt? Shame? Grief? Who knows at this point? In these past three years, I have become intimately acquainted with being uncomfortable and not in control of my body.

Mack lowers himself to the grass and sits beside me.

Should I reassure him more? I don't want him to be uneasy sitting here with me, wondering if he did something wrong.

He takes a deep breath. "My sister died when I was a kid."

I turn my head in his direction sharply. Perhaps too sharply.

He glances at me and gives me a quirk of his lips, a glimpse of a smile without mirth. "She was nine. I was eleven. Old enough to know what death meant, but too young to fully grasp the consequences of 'gone forever.'" He leans back on his hands just like me.

"Was she sick?"

He shakes his head once and keeps his unreadable brown gaze fixed on the inlet on the far side of the park.

I realize I'm holding my breath and let it go. This man has known grief and pain like I do. Air fills my lungs a little more easily than it did a few minutes ago.

I kick off my sneakers and wiggle my toes in their crisp white socks. "I'm sorry she died."

"Yeah."

His walls are going up, and I wonder why he mentioned her at all. But I'm not going to push. Maybe he was just trying to make me feel better by relating to my loss. I start telling him that I'm feeling better. "Why does touching grass fix so many problems?"

"She fell out of a third-story window."

My insides perform a stunt, and I feel like I'm the one falling. "Mack... I..." I close my mouth, trying to think of the right thing to say, but the right thing doesn't exist. Finding my resolve to use my words, I look at him. He doesn't meet my eyes. "Were you home when it happened?"

"No. I was at school. She stayed home because she had chicken pox."

A million questions rush to the foreground of my mind, but I let them die on my tongue. Asking questions isn't fair. In all my moments of letting down my defenses, questions *always* made me put them back up.

So, I play it safe. "I've never had the chicken pox."

Mack finally looks at me, and the furrow in his brow softens. "Probably because of how spoiled and soft your life has been."

I blink.

He chuckles. It's a deep, rumbling sound in his chest, and I know I'm imagining it, but I swear I can feel it vibrating the ground beneath me. He flashes me his white teeth in that smile of his that transforms him from ordinary man to *stunning* man.

Mack winks. "Careful, Miss Warren. I know what you're thinking. And no, I don't kiss on a first date."

My mouth falls open, and my cheeks burn furiously.

His chuckle blossoms into full-blown laughter at my expense, and I'm still trying to collect myself as he rises smoothly to his feet, turns to offer me his hand, and waits patiently while I put my sneakers back on. I take his hand and let him help me up before I brush grass off the back of my red dress.

"You're a piece of work," I tell him. "Simon should probably fire you. I can only guess how many bad reviews he has for his business because of you."

Mack just smirks. "It's part of my charm."

"Debatable."

He leads me back to his truck and opens the door for me once more, and as I watch him walk around the hood to his door, I push down the sense of disappointment in my chest. Our "date" seems to be coming to an abrupt end, and I'm not entirely sure why.

If I look at the facts, like my near panic-attack and dead husband, it's pretty clear that Mack has opted not to deal with my shit. With a smile like his and a body under his T-shirt that I know is chiseled to high heaven, he won't have any problems meeting a girl with less baggage.

He hops up behind the wheel, turns the ignition, and throws the truck into reverse. He smacks the radio hard when an Elton John song is interrupted by static. The impact solves the problem. We drive back to my condo in comfortable quiet, and he parks at the curb under the shade of a maple tree with burgundy-colored leaves.

He rests a hand on the wheel before turning to me. "I hate to call it early, but I have somewhere I need to be."

"I get it. This was fun. Thank you for taking me out." I open my door and pause to turn back to him. "Seriously. I needed it."

"I know." That radiant smile returns, crinkling the corners of his eyes. "Can I call you again sometime soon?"

"I didn't scare you off?"

He chuckles. "There is nothing scary about you, Miss Warren. Dead husband or not."

His brazen way of talking about Daniel doesn't piss me off. If someone else had spoken about him that way, I might have found it jarring, but for some reason, I appreciate how simply Mack looks at it. It's just a fact. No strings attached.

Not being handled like a baby is refreshing.

"I guess I'll have to work on sharpening my intimidation factor," I say as I slide out of his truck, fix my dress, and flip my hair over my shoulder.

"Good luck with that, sweetheart."

"Are you even going to walk me to my door?"

Mack glances down the short path that cuts across the manicured lawn in front of my condo. It's flanked on both sides by a colorful flower garden bursting with purple lavender, vibrant hostas, and crawling vines with little blue flowers I don't know the name of.

"I think you can make it there in one piece," he says. "See you soon, Miss Warren."

"See you soon, Mack. And hey," I add, "stop calling me that."

He puts the truck in drive. "As you wish, sweetheart."

I glower at him. "I prefer Charlie."

The words aren't even out of my mouth before I'm cut off by the rumble of his engine as he drives away.

# CHAPTER SEVEN

My sister's house stands proudly on the corner of the street. The front lawn was torn out last spring and replaced with artificial turf, so it's obnoxiously green and devoid of plant life. The first floor is all done in white-washed brick, and the second floor has white panelling. The large windows are trimmed in black, complemented by a black front door with stained glass windows all around it. Above the front door is a small but functional balcony off Devin and Brett's bedroom. I imagine they both like to sit out there in the mornings and sip their coffees made in their fancy espresso machine.

Sitting in my car parked across the street, I watch movement through the living room window. I can see my mother inside, holding a glass of white wine in one hand. She's wearing a bright pink outfit and standing with my father in his old gray polo shirt that she hates so much. My sister must be sitting on the couch because it seems like they're looking down and talking to someone. Being as pregnant as she is, I know she's been having a lot of swelling and trying to stay off her feet. Hosting a family dinner has probably left her feeling spent.

I'll offer to stay and help clean up while she soaks in a bath or something. That would be nice, wouldn't it?

My car chimes softly when a text comes through my phone. I smile when Mal's picture comes up on my caller ID on the screen console. It's a picture of her from a drunken night in Hawaii. She's wearing aviators and has her tongue out. At that time, she had vibrant blue hair slicked into a short mohawk and a nose ring.

**Mal:** *Good luck tonight. If you start feeling sorry for yourself, just remember Devin still can't eat cold cuts or sushi for another month. XO.*

I smile, but the weight that's been on my chest all day remains.

Devin and I used to be thicker than thieves. Now, in the debris of my shattered life, she's the most triggering person for me to be around. It's really fucking unfair.

"Fair," I grumble, turning off my car and getting out to grab the flowers I brought from the back seat. I think about what my therapist always says: fair is a word we use when we're trying to teach children to take turns. It's not applicable in real life. The sooner you accept that nothing is fair, the sooner you can shift your mindset from being a victim to being in control again.

I clutch the flowers and look up at the house. "I'm in control. I'm in control."

Who am I kidding?

Already exhausted by a night that hasn't even begun, I make my way across the street and up the steps to the front door. I knock twice and let myself in, calling hello, and am greeted moments later by Brett, who looks sharp in a light blue collared shirt and black jeans. His auburn hair is a bit longer than usual and swept back off his forehead. He takes the flowers from me and locks the door once I step inside.

"Glad you're here, Charlie," Brett says as I step out of my shoes. "Devin is up to her eyeballs in your mom's advice and could use a lifeline. The flowers will be a nice pick me up. Thanks for bringing them."

"On it," I say, hanging my purse on the hook by the door. "Give me three minutes, and then come into the living room and invite me into the kitchen to help you with something. I scratch your back, you scratch mine."

Brett laughs and gives me a sheepish nod. "Deal."

I follow him into the belly of the house. He splits off toward the kitchen to put the flowers in water while I make my way to the well-appointed living room, complete with blue velvet sofas, a Turkish rug, antique accent furniture, and a pile of gifts from the baby shower still in their gift bags and boxes, but clearly unwrapped.

Devin is sitting on the sofa, just as I expected. She's wearing a flowy yellow dress and fanning herself with a paper napkin. Mom is hovering over her, prattling on about the benefits of drinking raspberry leaf tea to induce labor.

"I read about it on a mommy blog," Mom says matter-of-factly. "Now, of course, there are some risks, and it's not professional medical advice, but sometimes you have to take matters into your own hands to make sure baby comes."

Dad gives Mom an imploring look. "No baby stays in their mother's womb forever, Deidra."

Mom waves him off. "I know that, darling. Don't be silly. Oh! And dates. Did you read about the benefits of dates in that article I sent you, Devin?"

Devin lights up when she sees me and practically screams my name. "Charlie!"

Everyone turns to me and greets me warmly. I accept hugs but tell Devin to stay where she is. I go to her, give her a hug, and whisper in her ear that Brett and I have a plan to save her.

Devin squeezes my hand as I sit down beside her. A silent thank you. I squeeze back and look everywhere but at the massive swell of her belly. I swear, it's bigger than last weekend at the baby shower.

I eye the pile of gifts. "Do you need help putting things away?"

Devin groans. "I can't find the will to get it done. Bending down is impossible."

"Mom," I say, "you've always had a knack for organization."

Mom lights up. "Yes, yes, that's true! I don't mind organizing your drawers and putting your things away in the nursery, Devin."

Easier than feeding a spoonful of peanut butter to a dog.

"Brett said dinner was still half an hour away," I say to nobody in particular.

Mom takes the bait though. She smacks my father excitedly on the arm before grabbing his wrist and hauling him toward the foyer and stairs to the second floor. "Come on, let's see how much we can get done. Grab the heavy bags."

The pair of them leave, the tissue paper in the gifts swishing gently as they disappear upstairs.

Devin lets her head fall against the back of the sofa. "You're an angel, Charlie. Seriously. She's been talking at me for over twenty-five minutes. You know what conversation I never wanted to have with Mom?" She lifts her head to give me a look that drips with disgust. "Perineal massages."

"Oh, no."

"Oh." Devin nods slowly. "Yes. She went into anatomically correct detail about how Brett could 'help me out down there,' and proceeded to show me in the air with her fingers by–"

"Nope," I say, cutting her off. "I don't need to know."

Devin pouts and looks down at her belly. "I just need this baby *out* of me. Like, yesterday."

Finally, I look directly down at her belly as she rubs it over the yellow cotton dress she's wearing. So round. So perfect.

Devin gives me a hopeful little smile. "The baby is kicking. Want to feel?"

Guilt gnaws at my insides when she notices me recoil like she asked *me* to touch her perineal. She turns pink, and I look away, fixating on a single loose thread on the corner of her Turkish rug.

"Sorry," I breathe.

"It's too much. I know."

A hundred things go unsaid between us.

*What will happen when the baby is here? How will I ever hold them and be a good auntie? Will they resent me because they can feel my jealousy? Will I be able to love them without feeling like I've been slighted? Will Devin forgive me for not showing up for her the way she probably always imagined?*

*Will I forgive myself?*

"Hey." Brett appears in the doorway with a kitchen towel over his shoulder. He looks a bit disheveled from cooking, but he's wearing an easy smile as he comes over and offers his wife a hand up from the sofa. She protests about not wanting to move unless food is ready.

"Dinner isn't ready yet," he says with an air of apology in his voice. "But I whipped up some cherry tomatoes with basil and bocconcini to hold you over."

"You glorious bastard," Devin murmurs.

Brett chuckles and glances over his shoulder at me as we follow a waddling Devin to the kitchen. "I think that was a compliment?"

"Flattery isn't her strong suit." I shrug one shoulder and get an itch to tease my sister. "Hey, Brett? Ever heard of a perineal massage?"

Devin has reached the island in the kitchen. She uses her teeth to pull a vibrant cherry tomato drizzled in balsamic glaze off a toothpick, which she throws at me. "Shut up, Charlie."

Brett slides the plate of tasty appetizers toward me, and I immediately smell the freshness of the basil. I grab one, take a bite, and savor the sweet and savory explosion on my tongue while I bend down and pick up the toothpick my sister threw at me.

"Is that some sort of new age massage technique?" Brett asks. "If you've got sore muscles, you should try acupuncture. Works great for me."

I snort.

Devin scowls at me. "Charlie is pulling your leg, Brett. It's a massage for your vagina so you don't tear when you deliver the baby. At least, you have to *hope* you don't tear."

Brett blinks a few times and looks back and forth between us. One eyebrow quirks up. "I can't tell if you're being serious."

I reach for another tomato. "Google it."

His lips press into a fine line, and he seems to consider it before shaking his head. "I've learned in these last few months that ignorance is bliss."

"You're not going to stay innocent," Devin promises, slowly lifting one hip so she can ease onto one of the barstools at the island. She grips the edge of the counter to adjust herself and find her center of gravity with her belly pulling her forward. "When this baby comes, you're going to have a front-row seat so you know exactly what it takes to bring them earthside." She gives him a sweet smile. "And then I can hold my suffering over your head until the day we die and get whatever I want."

Brett shoots me an imploring look.

"Don't look at me. You're the one who married her and knocked her up. Better buy her a nice push present," I warn.

"A what?" Brett asks, his voice thinning.

Devin hurls a toothpick in his direction this time. "If I don't get something shiny and expensive after this pregnancy, I'm selling your motorcycle and getting myself a sauna."

"A sauna?" Brett and I ask in unison.

Devin waggles her finger at us. "Don't knock it. Sauna therapy is great for your health, and I'm going to need all the help I can get to heal from this." She scowls at her belly.

I find myself looking down as well–but with longing. I would have given anything to have a "ruined" stomach, graffitied with stretch marks and loose skin. To have wider set hips. To not be able to see my feet or shave my legs with my belly in the way. Sometimes it scares me when I think about what I'd do to have a baby and be in Devin's shoes right now.

*And she thinks her body is being ruined. She's not grateful enough. She doesn't know how lucky she is. She doesn't deserve–*

"The nursery is just *darling*," my mother coos as she and Dad return from upstairs. She sweeps toward us at the island and helps herself to a tomato while Brett checks the dish in the oven. A rush of hot air passes us before he closes the oven and announces dinner is five minutes away. Mom perks up. "Just enough time to come take a peek at what I did, Devin. Come along."

Devin groans and hangs her head. "I don't want to walk up the stairs, Mom. This baby's massive head is pressing on my cervix."

"Okay, now," Dad says, holding up both hands. "Let's keep it PG."

"That *is* PG," Devin growls. "Cervices aren't sexual, Dad. Don't make it weird. God. Why do all men act like they're four when a woman talks about her body during pregnancy? I swear, the next man who–"

"Darling?" Brett interjects with a soft smile. "Deep breath."

Devin's scowl softens, and she inhales through her nose and exhales through her mouth. "Sorry, Daddy."

Dad looks like he wants to bury his face in his beer glass and breathe in so he can pass out and escape this conversation. He offers her a nonchalant nod while our mother takes Devin and me by the hand and hauls us toward the stairs to show off her work in the nursery.

I go up ahead while Mom helps Devin one step at a time. She still has a month to go, and I wonder how she'll survive it if she's already this uncomfortable.

At the landing, I hook a right and step into the pastel yellow nursery. I freeze as evening sunlight streams through sheer white curtains that fan out and settle every few seconds in the summer breeze coming through the cracked window. It smells fresh in here, like new carpet and cut grass.

Only halfway up the stairs, Devin snaps at our mother to give her a moment.

Time comes to a standstill as the nursery closes in on me.

A white bassinet stands beside a plush recliner, the perfect cozy spot for breastfeeding at any hour of the day. Beside the chair is a darling bookshelf that turns on its base. It's covered in bumblebees and honeycombs and is stocked full of books, as well as a couple of wicker baskets on some shelves that hold things like pacifiers, mittens to protect baby's face from scratching themselves with their fingernails, and wipes...

*It was supposed to be me.*

I look away, hating the way the resentment catches fire in my chest and threatens to engulf my lungs in smoke.

*This isn't fair.*

Under the window is a changing table that isn't fully organized yet. Neatly folded infant clothes sit neatly atop it in three piles. I assume Mom unpacked them from the gift bags and wasn't sure if Devin would prefer them in the dresser or the closet.

*This is everything Daniel wanted.*

A nightlight is plugged into one of the outlets near the recliner. It's a teddy bear holding a bundle of yellow balloons. A hand-painted mural, done by Devin's insufferable friend Stephanie, portrays a scene of woodland creatures against a backdrop of tree trunks and greenery. The ceiling is also painted; overhead, there is an expanse of blue sky and fluffy white clouds.

*Leave.*

The burn in my lungs floods the rest of my body and sets all my nerve endings to high alert. I know I'm triggered. I've had this conversation with my therapist a hundred times over. Sometimes, when the feeling comes, I'm able to hold it tight for a moment and then let it go. Not right now. The fire just keeps burning hotter, and I know if I don't leave, I'm going to say or do something I regret—something I can't take back.

Like scream.

Or trash the whole nursery.

Or sob into the bassinet like a psychopath.

Devin comes around the corner into the bedroom and pauses to hold the doorframe and catch her breath. "I don't care that walking up the stairs is good for me," she says to Mom. "I'm tired, and fat, and have you seen how swollen my feet are?" She sticks a puffy foot out from the hem of her yellow sundress. "They're not the only thing swollen, either."

"Devin," Mom scolds softly. Her tone brightens when she comes into the room, holds her arms up, and gestures all around in a big circle. "What do you think?"'

Devin scrutinizes the room with one hand on her tummy. "It looks the same."

Mom frowns.

I'm burning alive.

"I have to go," I blurt out.

Devin and Mom look at me. Devin's expression falls, but she recovers quickly and manages to smooth out the concern on her forehead and replace it with a smile.

"It's okay," she says.

"Go?" Mom cocks her head to the side. "We haven't even had dinner yet. You just got here. What's more important than this? It might be our last time all having dinner together before you-know-who arrives." She reaches over and pats Devin's stomach.

Devin swats Mom's hand away. "It's okay. You go. I'll text you later."

I owe her a hundred apologies and even more thank yous, but I can't get any of them out of my mouth, so I hurry past both of them, rush down the stairs, pass the kitchen, and throw on my shoes and light coat at the door.

Brett comes over. "You good, Charlie?"

I don't dare look at him. Tears blur my vision, and the grip I have on my control is slipping with every passing second. I just shake my head, open the door, and haul ass out of there. Brett calls after me, but he doesn't follow.

Thank God.

My hands shake as I get into my car. I push the ignition and drive about half a kilometer down the road before I have to pull over, open my door, and throw up.

As I sink deeper into the leather seat, the shaking in my hands subsides, and the burn in my chest begins to ebb away. I've had panic attacks like this before, but lately, I've been able to stop them before they get this intense. Not tonight. The nursery was too much. Too perfect. Too painful

A text message comes in on my phone and connects through my Bluetooth. It pops up on my navigation screen. It's from Mack.

**Mack:** *Just met another crackpot who likes grapefruit in their beer and thought of you. Let's try another brewery this week. You're buying this time.*

I stare at the screen before scrambling to find my phone in my purse.

I start texting. Delete it. Write it again. Delete it. Write it a third time. Stare at it, thumb hovering over the send button.

**Charlie:** *Come over.*

# CHAPTER EIGHT

THE FIRE IS BURNING on the outside now.

I lean forward, my chin resting on my hands atop my dining room table, and stare at the flickering flame of a vanilla scented candle burning in front of me. It dances, performing a bespoke routine just for me. As wax pools beneath the flame, I suddenly get cold feet and blow it out.

Mack isn't the sort of man a girl like me lights candles for.

And I didn't text him for romance.

I texted him for a distraction. Relief. Escape.

Every passing minute feels sharp and cruel until he arrives and buzzes up to my unit. I let him up, and my palms start sweating as I wait for his knock at the door. When it comes, I pretend to be busy and call out, "Just a second!" so I can fix my hair in the full-length mirror by my front door. I hate that I care what I look like, and what's worse, that I care how he thinks I look.

Nevertheless, I open the door.

Mack greets me with that lopsided, sheepish smile of his and a warm dark brown gaze. "Sorry I'm late." He holds up one hand, showing me a brown paper bag full of stains on the bottom. "I grabbed us something."

"Is it spoiled?" I let him in and lock the door behind him as he steps out of his boots. "Why is it leaking?"

"Hold your horses." He moves comfortably into my kitchen and places the bag on the island next to my bowl of fruit. He cracks open the bag, leans over it, and inhales deeply. His eyes close, and I'm powerless against the little topsy-turvy trick my stomach does as I regard him like that. His eyes flutter open, and he holds the bag toward me. "Look."

For some reason, I go on my tiptoes to peer into the bag, even though I don't need to. At the bottom of the bag, nestled in snug to each other, are two slices of cheesecake drizzled with a red jelly and absolutely smothered in fresh berries.

My mouth starts watering. "Wow."

"You have no idea." He tears the bag down the side in one sharp movement, exposing the cheesecakes, and looks around for a plate like one should materialize out of thin air for him. "Best cheesecake in the province."

"We'll see about that."

I grab us plates and forks, and Mack plates the cheesecake for us, making sure to pile mine up with all the berries that fell off. He licks his thumb, popping the whole digit in his mouth, and I pause with my fork halfway to my mouth, watching his cheeks pucker.

*Get a grip, Charlie.*

Mack goes in for a heaping bite, nods approvingly, and then slams his fist down on the counter.

I squeak in surprise and drop the fork.

"Fucking hell, that's good," he growls, his jaw flexing, his heated gaze falling on his plate before sweeping up to me. "You gonna try it or just stand there? Don't tell me you're one of those girls that won't eat sugar."

"Do I look like a girl who doesn't eat sugar?"

He seems to take this as an invitation to look at me with permission. His eyes do a full sweep of me from head to toe and back up again. He nods, somewhat approvingly, before shrugging one shoulder and taking another bite of cheesecake that he now has to speak around. "Yes."

I prickle, but I deserved it. Back when Daniel was still alive, I was nearly fifty pounds heavier. That girl knew how to eat and eat well—and she thrived. She ate sugar. She drank soda. She loved martinis. She loved life. This version of me? She often forgets meals several times in a row. Grief leaves imprints, and not feeling hunger was one it left on me.

To prove my point, I take a bite of the cheesecake and let it sit on my tongue for a moment. It melts slowly, deliciously, and fills my mouth with rich, tangy, cheesy sweetness.

"Oh, my God," I breathe.

"See?" Mack looks proud of himself. "What did I tell you?"

I go in for another bite. This might be the cure for my weight problem right here. "Where did you get this?"

"My sister made it. Not the dead one. My other one."

I take another bite, this one weighed down with as many berries as I can fit on the fork. While I chew, I push the plate away. It's rich as hell, and I need to go slowly.

"It's incredible," I say. "You'd better not have just introduced me to something I can't go buy. Is this a 'my sister makes this just for me' cheesecake? Or does she sell them somewhere?"

He chuckles. "She sells them out of her house. Online orders only. Unless you're family."

"I'm going to need her website."

He texts it to me, explaining that his sister is trying to grow her baking business, and she'll be thrilled about having a new customer. "Her name is Gia," he says before polishing off the last bite of his cheesecake. He licks his lips, folds his arms over his chest in a way that makes his forearms look as tasty as Gia's cheesecake, and leans on my counter. "So, why am I here?"

"Pardon?"

"You asked me to come over. I'm over." He lifts his chin a fraction, and his dark eyes narrow slightly. "Why?"

"I…"

*Shit.*

I didn't really think that through. A guy with an ego like Mack's was bound to ask such a direct question, and I should have anticipated it. There are lies I can tell, like I got spooked by a rowdy argument one of my neighbors in the condo was having, but Mack is staring at me with an edge that suggests he'll see right through an excuse.

"I had a shitty night," I say. Honesty is probably the best policy here. "I was invited to dinner at my sister's beautiful house with her and her perfect and very much *alive* husband." Pausing, I notice how resentful my voice sounds. I try again, this time softening my tone and taking calm breaths. "She's at the end of her pregnancy, and our parents were there, and it was just... a lot."

Mack's head tilts to the side just a bit. "You're going to be an aunt."

"Yes."

"That's exciting, right?"

"It's... complicated."

"How so?"

"Do you always ask this many questions?"

"Do you always act this cagey with a guest *you* invited over?"

Grumbling under my breath about how annoying he is, I grab a bottle of white wine from the fridge, pour a glass, and drink half of it while he watches me. I offer him a glass, and he nods once. His expression is unreadable as I pass him his glass, and we both take a sip. I wonder if he's judging me. I wouldn't blame him if he were. But a widow should be allowed to cope however she sees fit.

"I have to ask you again," he says slowly. "Why am I here?"

"Can't we just, I don't know, not do this?"

He frowns. "Maybe I should go."

"No," I say.

Fuck. I've played my hand. I've rolled over and showed him my belly, and now he has all the power in the situation, and I'm just the idiot with the dead husband drinking wine like it's water.

Not a cute look.

"Please stay. I invited you here because I had a bad night," I say.

"That's the truth. And I needed something or someone to take my mind off things for a bit. It's all gotten a little too heavy to carry, and I need help just…" I trail off, wishing I could find the right words to express to him what was going on in my head when I sent him that text.

"Letting it go?"

We lock eyes.

"Yes," I say. "Yes, exactly."

Mack puts his wine glass down. He takes a step toward me, and I stiffen but don't retreat. He moves closer, reaching for me, and puts a hand on my hip. The touch is gentle and respectful, but it's warm and wild to me. I haven't been touched by a man since Daniel. It's been three years since I felt any form of affection from someone I was attracted to. That's 1,095 days. But who's counting?

Mack's hand moves from my hip and travels up my side before slowly jumping to my elbow and following the line up my arm to my shoulder. As his palm comes up to cup my neck, I inhale sharply, and he gently presses his thumb to the base of my neck.

He goes still before trapping me with a destructive smile. "Your heart is racing, Charlie."

My stomach performs yet another acrobatic trick against my will.

"What's wrong?" he pushes. "No smart-ass comment to make?"

My mind has a hard time catching up to my body. I'm flooded with sensations that have been dormant for so long they feel foreign– the fluttery feeling in my chest, the heat coursing through my veins, the tingle in my lips as I lose myself staring at his mouth. His lips are turned up at the corners, and I can tell he's enjoying this position of power he's in. When he speaks, I catch glimpses of straight white teeth.

"There are a lot of ways to let go of a bad night," he says, his thumb sliding along the tendon in my neck and pausing at the top of the column, just below my jaw and over my pulse. "Drink wine into oblivion. Watch a movie until you fall asleep. Eat yourself to death." His gaze flicks to the cheesecake and dances with mirth before sliding back to me. The depth of his stare promises trouble, and his next words solidify that fact. "Fuck until you can't see straight."

My breath hitches. I quiver under his touch and wish I could at least play it cool. But his hand on my pulse guarantees he knows *exactly* what kind of reaction I'm having to his words.

Mack's smirk moves closer as he puts his mouth to my ear. "I'm not the sort of guy to make assumptions. So what's it gonna be, Charlie?" He nudges my cheek with his jaw, tilting my head back so he can drop his head and press a hot kiss to my throat. "I just need one little word, and I can make you feel better, even if it's just for tonight."

His teeth pinch at my skin, and I gasp, press both hands to his chest, and hesitate. I should push him away. This is way too much, too fast. The last time I had sex was with my husband, the night he finally got me pregnant after years and years of infertility. And the night he was killed. I thought I was going to die as well in those weeks after I lost him, and I swore I would be loyal to him forever. His whole life had been ripped away, and I owed him at least that for being the one who didn't drive to the store for ice cream that night.

In those early days after Daniel died, I thought I had his child to love. I thought I could pour everything I had into our baby, and that would fill up the broken parts of my soul that shattered the night the police knocked on my front door. While planning his funeral and settling life insurance policies and cancelling cell phone plans–all amongst the other blur of tasks one must do when a loved one dies–I spent hours researching the safest car seats, best swaddling methods, highest rated strollers, wearable breast pumps. I became obsessed with consuming as much information as I could. Our baby wouldn't have Daniel as a steady father figure or wealth of knowledge. They would only have me.

And I had to make sure I was enough for them.

But I wasn't. I lost our baby, too.

Suddenly, and almost impulsively, I push at Mack's chest. Hard.

Mack backs up a step, and he takes his hands off me. He gives me more space and slides his hands into his pockets. "Movie then?"

I shake my head and feel my insides starting to catch fire again.

Every second I have to spend looking at him adds kindling to the embers. The burn hurts, but there's also coursing waves of desire rippling through me that make me feel like a traitorous bitch.

Widow.

Failure as a mother.

Disloyal wife.

Cheat.

*Whore.*

"I'm sorry," I manage, despite my bottom lip beginning to tremble. "I'm sorry. I shouldn't have texted you. I shouldn't have…"

Mack shrugs one shoulder, pushes my plate of cheesecake toward me, and moves to the front door. "It's all good, Charlie. Eat the cheesecake. Go to bed. Scream into your pillow."

I stare at his back as he leaves and flinch when the door closes behind him.

"I'm sorry," I say again, but this time I'm not talking to Mack. I'm talking to Daniel as I clutch at my chest and sink to the floor with my back against my kitchen cabinets.

I draw my knees to my chest, hug them tightly, and sob into my knees.

# CHAPTER NINE

DR. FLAGSTAFF IS five years older than me. She wears her black hair in a blunt bob and is always meticulously dressed. Today, as she sits across from me on the velvet green chair in her therapy office, sporting wide-leg linen trousers, strappy sandals, a black pedicure, and a tight black shirt. Every move she makes sounds like jingle bells with all the bracelets on her wrists. She shifts often, adjusting the notepad balanced on her crossed knee as she regards me with a smile I have grown to understand.

Back when I first started my sessions with her two and a half years ago, I'd found Dr. Flagstaff intimidating. She didn't mince words, didn't shy away from confronting grief, and didn't give me an out whenever I tried to find one. She pushed me hard but compassionately, and without her, I'd never have survived after Daniel.

She'd mentioned a few times lately that one day I wouldn't need her anymore. I doubted that was true.

"So." Dr. Flagstaff tucks her black hair behind one ear, showing off an industrial piercing. "Mack."

"Mack," I say, nodding once.

"What's so crazy about him that it made you book an emergency session? It's been a long time since you needed one of these. Not that

I'm complaining," she adds with kindness in her voice. "Did something happen between you two?"

"No," I say before frowning, shaking my head, and fidgeting with the throw pillow on my lap. It has purple tassels on the corners, and stroking them always makes me feel a bit less exposed. I shift, trying to get comfortable, and the aches and pains in my legs from doing the Coquitlam Crunch earlier in the morning flare up. "I mean… yes. Sort of. I asked him to come over last night. And he did."

She waits patiently before prompting me. "And?"

"And… and I let him touch me. And he kind of…" I trail off as my cheeks grow hot. "Turned me on."

Dr. Flagstaff nods her most understanding nod. "And this has caused turmoil for you." It's not a question but a statement.

"Yes," I say, and then the rest of my thoughts start flooding out of me. "He's the first man I've felt any kind of way about since Daniel. He's ridiculously attractive, easy to talk to, and he makes me laugh. And he has the capacity to hold space for me when I talk about Daniel. He doesn't make me feel like damaged goods. He just sort of meets me where I'm at, and it doesn't feel like he has any expectations of me, whereas it feels like almost every other person in my life does—except for Mallory."

"He makes you feel seen."

"Yes," I say again, more animatedly this time. "And I got it in my head that it would be a good idea to invite him over and kiss him or let him do whatever he wanted to me. Touch me. Have sex with me." God, just saying it out loud gets me hot and bothered. "I thought I could handle it. But when it got right down to it, and his hands were on me, and he was asking permission–" I break off and grimace at the thought of how close I got to letting him kiss me on the lips. "I got scared. I started thinking about Daniel, but I wanted Mack to kiss me *so badly*. More than kiss me. I wanted him to take control and let me turn my mind off, but it all came to a grinding halt. I asked him to leave, and now I'm being eaten alive by all this guilt and shame. Every time I close my eyes, I see Daniel's face."

"Take a breath, Charlie," Dr. Flagstaff coaches me with her

soothing voice. I inhale with her, letting the breath fill my lungs and quiet the voice in my mind. We exhale together before she continues. "Would Daniel be upset with you for this, do you think?"

"Yes."

Dr. Flagstaff has no reaction. "Let me rephrase. If Daniel, knowing full well he was dead, had a chance to see you catch feelings for another man, do you think he would feel betrayed that you wanted to feel good?"

"I don't like that question."

"Why?"

*Because it's cruel,* I think. Because Daniel shouldn't have to know his widowed wife had a moment where she let another man put his hands on her—and that she liked it. Because it's unfair. Because it's betrayal. Because—

"Where's your head at right now, Charlie?" Dr. Flagstaff presses, uncrossing her legs and leaning forward to pick up her glass of water from the coffee table between us. She takes a slow sip and sets it back down beside a short vase of fresh cut yellow daisies. "You're disappearing on me."

My shoulders drop. Called out, I stare at the daisies. "I'm wondering if I can ever let someone love me again… or if I'll ever find someone who made me feel as safe as Daniel." My throat aches as I hold back tears. "I'm wondering if I'll ever feel like I can need someone as willingly as I needed my husband."

Dr. Flagstaff sits quietly. She never feels compelled to fill an uncomfortable silence. More often than not, she lets me sit in it when I speak words she knows have been weighing on me. She waits, patiently, until she thinks I've had a reasonable amount of time to digest my own thoughts.

"Let's do an exercise," she says.

"Really?"

"I know they're not your favorite," she says, smiling. "But this one is important. And difficult. I want you to pretend to be Daniel."

"I don't want to."

"I know you don't. But you can, and it's not real. I'm going to be you. I want you to respond the way you know in your heart of hearts he would respond if he could. Okay?"

*No, not okay.*

"Fine," I say, sitting up a little straighter and preparing for battle. "I'm Daniel."

Dr. Flagstaff sets her notebook aside and leans forward to rest her elbows on her knees. "Daniel, there are some things I need to tell you. Can you listen and respond when I'm done?"

I blink at her.

"Daniel?"

"Yes," I say. "I can listen."

She nods approvingly. "Okay. Well, I've met someone. You've been gone for three years, and I don't feel ready yet, but he makes me hopeful for something I thought I might never have again. It scares me. And it makes me feel guilty because I still love and miss you every day. You were my person for such a long time, and I just need to hear your thoughts. What should I do?"

I don't realize I'm crying until the tears are literally dripping off my jaw onto my thighs. I wipe them away as Dr. Flagstaff maintains her kind smile and eternal patience in the face of my grief.

"Charlie," I start, my voice croaking, "I miss you too." A sob wracks my chest. I clutch my hands together in front of my chest and squeeze. "I've been waiting for you to meet someone. I don't want you to be alone. We talked about that when I was alive."

"Keep going," Dr. Flagstaff says gently.

So I do. I lean into the memory of Daniel and me sitting on our patio set four summers ago. I close my eyes and picture it in my mind: my bare feet resting on his knees as he rubs them, the glass of whiskey sweating on the table in front of him, the first three buttons of his shirt undone exposing his chest, a robin chirping on the fence nearby. We talk in theoreticals about imaginary realities where one of us is gone, and the other is left behind.

Daniel insists he has to die first because he wouldn't survive losing me. I insist I won't survive losing him. Then, he looks me in the eyes and makes me promise that if something were to happen, I choose life, and I keep moving forward.

Opening my eyes, I find Dr. Flagstaff watching me. I clear my throat and wipe away fresh tears. "Charlie," I say, mostly to stay in character and ensure she doesn't accuse me of cutting corners in her exercise, "I can't rest knowing you're alone."

Another one of those potent silences stretches between us. I inhale slowly several times, trying to keep the tears at bay as I settle into a calmer state.

Dr. Flagstaff leans back in her chair and rests her hands on the armrests. "I don't think Daniel could have said it better himself."

"He could've," I smile. "He was better with words than me."

Dr. Flagstaff chuckles softly and runs her fingers over a sparkly bracelet on her left wrist. "So what are you going to do now?"

"Probably go home and cry some more."

She laughs in earnest. "Not a bad idea. This was a big session. You were very vulnerable. But I think you made some good progress here. You spoke some important truths aloud. I think you need to spend some time reflecting on Daniel and how he would give you permission to call Mack and see if there is something real between the two of you. Life will go on, Charlie. With or without you. You've spent the last three years standing still. But in a matter of the last few weeks, you've sold your home that you intended to fill with yours and Daniel's children, you've relocated to a new city, you've attended a triggering baby shower, and you've met someone who excites you. This is a lot after the kind of loss you experienced. Give yourself some credit. You're resilient, courageous, and deserving of love and attention from a man you're attracted to. It really is that simple."

I gnaw at the inside of my cheek until it hurts, and my mouth tastes like copper. "What if my baggage is too much for him?"

"Then he has the right to make the choice to walk away," she says simply. "But you don't have the right to make that choice for him. Mack gets to decide what's too much. Now," she adds just as I'm about to reach for my purse and call it a day, "let's talk about your family dinner at your sister's. You said you bailed before dinner. What happened?"

Nothing gets past Dr. Flagstaff.

I drop my purse strap and sigh. "And here I thought you were going to take mercy on me."

"Fat chance. We still have twenty minutes left." She leans back and picks her notebook back up. "Lay it on me."

Over the next ten minutes, I give her the nitty-gritty details of last night's dinner at Devin and Brett's house. She nods along but never interjects, even when I go on a rant about my overbearing mother and her control issues and how hard it's been for me to be around her while she's so hyped up on the baby train.

"She doesn't get it," I say, shaking my head. "She sees all the positives with Devin's pregnancy, and I want her to be happy, of course, but it would be nice if she showed a bit of compassion for how hard this has been for me. I was supposed to have the first grandchild. I was supposed to be painting my nursery yellow. I was supposed to be drowning in baby clothes and books and soothers and–" I break off and ball my hands into fists. I've cried enough tears for Daniel, for what we lost, for what was supposed to be and never will be. I refuse to cry for these petty feelings I have for my family. They deserve to feel this joy. "I'm not crying about this anymore."

"Have you ever told your mother or sister how difficult Devin's pregnancy has been? What can of worms it has opened for you?"

My silence is answer enough.

"Maybe it's worth considering opening up to Devin a bit. From everything you've told me, the pair of you have a strong sisterly bond. I bet she's been walking on eggshells,ot knowing what she can share about her pregnancy with you. Giving her some boundaries might actually really help her find her footing and help you both feel closer at this time. Strain like this can lead down bad paths if you don't address it. Resentment grows like a weed in the silence and all the things left unsaid."

"You should make your own bumper stickers, Dr. Flagstaff," I tell her as I glance at the clock on the wall. We have less than a minute remaining.

"You have two assignments this week, Charlie," Dr. Flagstaff decrees. "Talk to your sister, and talk to Mack. We'll regroup next week and figure out what the next right move is for you. Do we have a deal?"

Grudgingly, I nod. "Deal."

# CHAPTER TEN

"I'M NOT A CHEESECAKE GIRL," Mallory says from behind the steering wheel of her pickup truck. She drums her fingers on the horn as we wait in traffic. Up ahead, the light turns red, and she lifts her foot from the brake. "Ice cream? Sure. But cheesecake? How good can it be?"

"I've been thinking about it for days," I say. "It was like eating a slice of heaven."

"I can tell you all about eating heaven." Mallory winks.

"Don't be gross."

"I assure you, there is nothing gross about going down on a woman. A dick? Now *that's* gross. Veiny. Rude. Not to mention hideous."

"Rude?" I ask, laughing as she picks up speed and a summer breeze ruffles my hair through the open window. "How is a dick just existing *rude?*"

"Because it's attached to a man. Therefore, it's rude by default."

"Noted."

At the end of the street, Mallory takes a right turn and pulls over at the curb in front of a one-level yellow house. It has a white door with peeling paint, and an overgrown garden lines the path of broken paving stones up to the entrance.

She puts the truck in park. "Oof. This place looks rough. And you want to pick up food here? There's no way these people have a Food-safe certificate. I can smell the salmonella from here."

"Don't be so judgmental." I open the truck door and get out. "This cheesecake is going to help me fit into all my clothes again."

Mallory gets out, and we walk up the broken path together. Today she's wearing leopard print pants that look like they're painted on to her long legs. She has a crop top on with her red bra straps showing, which match her red sunglasses and lipstick. My best friend is the definition of bold and I-don't-give-a-fuck, and I've always loved her for it.

I knock on the front door just above the two signs that read 'No Solicitors' and 'Beware of Dog.' As soon as my knuckles rap on the surface, a dog starts barking inside. It's a deep, rumbling, gruff bark, and it makes me take a step back.

Mallory doesn't move an inch.

The door swings inward abruptly and bangs on the wall. A man in a white muscle shirt covered in beer stains stands at the threshold, peering out at us. He's massive—at least six-foot-three with a football player's build and the beginnings of a beer belly. He lifts a hand to shield his bloodshot eyes from the sun and lets out an unimpressed grunt. Without a word to us, he turns and hollers over his shoulder.

"Gia! Door!"

He abruptly turns and goes back inside, leaving the door ajar while the dog continues barking from somewhere in the house. We hear him let out a string of colorful curses at the dog.

Mallory and I share a look.

"Okay…" she says, leaning forward a bit to peer inside. "Hello?"

I give her elbow a tug and pull her back onto our side of the threshold. "Be patient. I'm sure she's coming."

"Uh huh." Mallory pushes her sunglasses on top of her head and crosses her arms. "Who do you think Handsome was?"

"Hopefully not the guy who bakes the cheesecake," I mutter.

Perhaps Mack gave me the wrong address. But no, he said his sister's name was Gia, and that's the name on the business card, which matches the address, and the name the drunk big-boy yelled. This is the place. The jarring feeling in my chest is probably just because it's not exactly what I was expecting. Based on the sensational flavor and texture of the cheesecake, I figured the confectionist's home would be as perfect and dreamy as her product. This place? It was a far cry from dreamy.

The longer we stand at the front door, the stronger the scent of stale beer and wet dog becomes.

Mallory slides her sunglasses back over her eyes and turns on her heel, stepping back onto the path. "Well, I'm calling it. No cheesecake for you. Let's go."

"Give her one more minute," I say.

"To poison your dessert?" Mallory shakes her head. "I don't think so. Somebody around here has to have some sense. I guess I'm her."

I'm about to follow Mallory down the overgrown path when a short, dark-haired young woman appears in the doorway. She has rosy cheeks, and her hair is piled in a mess on her head. A pink bandana with little bananas on it holds loose strands at bay. She's wearing disco ball earrings, a pink apron, and loungewear underneath.

"Hi," the young woman beams. She thrusts a flour-dusted hand at me. "I'm Gia. Are you here to put in an order?"

I shake her hand and get lost staring into her eyes for a moment. They're as endless and dark as Mack's and rimmed in the thickest, darkest lashes I've ever seen.

Mallory steps up beside me and pokes me in the ribs, making me yelp.

"She's here for cheesecake, yes," Mallory supplies. "Don't mind her. Her brain stops working at random intervals of the day. She says it's to delete unnecessary information she no longer needs so she can make room for more." Mallory grins wide and looks Gia up and down. "Was that your husband who answered the door?"

"You're shameless," I whisper out of the corner of my mouth. Only my best friend would blatantly check out and investigate the relationship status of a complete stranger so boldly while her husband–assumedly–drinks beers in the other room.

Mallory just shrugs and feasts her eyes on Gia's cleavage as the young woman laughs and claps her hands together. She's well endowed, that's for sure, and her boobs do a little dance that I know Mallory is enjoying.

"Yes, that was Clayton." Gia wipes the flour off her hands onto her apron, undoes it, and hangs it on a hook in the small entranceway of the house. The hook is somehow crooked. It seems like most things in this house are in some state of disrepair.

Gia certainly doesn't look like she belongs here. She looks like she belongs behind the counter of a quaint little bakery in downtown Port Moody, with little pink and gold accents everywhere.

"Don't mind him," Gia says as she steps outside with us and closes her front door. A piece of paint literally breaks off and floats in a zigzag pattern between us to land on the sun-faded welcome mat. Gia steps on it as she heads down the path and hooks a left toward their driveway and garage. "Come with me," she chimes. "I have some cheesecakes already prepared and chilled, or we can do a custom order together."

Mallory and I share a brief look, but then we're following Gia, who bends down in front of her garage door, grabs the handle, and hoists it up with effortless grace that I'm surprised her petite body can perform.

Mallory fans herself and pumps her eyebrows at me. Just out of earshot of Gia, she leans over and says, "My literal dream girl."

"Shush." I clear my throat. "I'm sorry, should I have ordered ahead?"

"Nope, I have plenty of stock." Gia spins to us and expands her arms wide, showing off what is clearly her pride and joy in the single-car garage behind her. There is a row of mismatching fridges against the back wall and two deep freezes. All are neatly labelled with flavors of cheesecakes. There are tables, storage shelves, and a desk with a computer, notebooks, and what appears to be a cash register. The floor is clean, and black back-support mats have been laid down over the concrete. A fan is running, pushing a gentle breeze through the space, which is significantly hotter than the outside air with all the appliances running.

"She's not much," Gia apologizes, "but she's my baby. If I keep getting orders, and my brother keeps hyping me up the way he has been, I might be able to open my own shop sooner rather than later. Now–" She claps her hands together eagerly and spins to me. "What would you like? Strawberry shortcake cheesecake? Peaches and cream? Mango madness? Butter ripple?"

"Erm," I stammer, trying to think about the one Mack brought to my place the other night. "I tried one that was smothered in this red jelly and covered in berries. It was so good, and fresh, and sweet... Oh, gosh. I'm sorry, this isn't a good description. But Mack was the one who made me try it."

"You should have led with that!" Gia goes to the largest fridge of four at the back of the garage, opens the door, and holds it there with one hip while she peers inside. Every shelf is full of cheesecake boxes. She gently slides one out, lets the door fall closed behind her, and brings it over to her desk. She sets it down and lifts the lid, exposing the very same cheesecake Mack brought to my condo. Except instead of two slices, there is a whole pie. Gia puts a fist on her hip. "This is my top selling cake. Mack's Favorite."

"What's it called so I can order it next time?" I ask, my mouth already watering.

"Mack's Favorite," she giggles. "Seriously, that's what I named it. He eats one a week." She delicately closes the box and slides it to me across the desk. "He's always been able to burn calories faster than I burn through cream."

Mallory clears her throat to remind us she's still there. "Which one is *your* favorite, Gia?"

Oh, my God, my best friend is *such* a fuckboy.

Gia, oblivious to Mallory's flirting, floats to another fridge and pulls out a smaller box. She brings it back, opens it up, and reveals a dark cheesecake smothered in raspberries and chocolate drizzle. Mallory and I peer down like we're glimpsing the depths of Pandora's Box.

"I call this one the Sinner," Gia boasts. "Dark chocolate, shaved almonds, and a reduced raspberry glaze made with port and muddled berries."

"Fuck me," Mallory breathes.

Gia giggles. "Everybody says that when they try it. Here." She bustles over to a drawer in her desk, withdraws a fork, and brings it to Mallory. "Try it."

"Oh, Mal doesn't like cheesecake," I say.

Mallory looks like she wants to slap me.

Gia shrugs and offers me the fork instead. "That's okay. Different strokes for different folks, right?"

"Exactly," I say, offering her the fork back. "I can't take a bite of your perfect cheesecake. You can sell it, can't you?"

"Not this one," Gia says. "Don't worry, I need help getting rid of it, really. Go for it."

Feeling a bit odd about taking a bite of a perfect cheesecake I'm not buying, that could easily sell for forty or fifty bucks, I plunge my fork into the smooth chocolate, which has no resistance. When I bring it to my mouth, I can smell the rich chocolate and the raspberries, and when it touches my tongue, I steady myself with a hand on Mallory's shoulder.

"This should be illegal," I say.

Gia does a little bounce up and down, sending her boobs north and south rapidly. Mallory shrugs out from under my hand.

"I'm glad you like it! You can have it. Consider it a first-time customer gift." Gia goes behind her desk and closes the boxes of cheesecake. "Do you just need the one?"

"I can't take it for free."

"Please do," Gia says. "To be honest, it was a custom order, and then the event fell through that the customer ordered it for. Kind of sad. She got it for her mother's birthday, but her mother had a stroke, so obviously, the party is postponed. And now I have a cheesecake I need to get rid of before it goes bad."

"Well, I'd still like to pay for it," I tell her. "Their loss is my gain. And I have just the person I can share it with."

Gia beams, rings me up, and takes my cash with gratitude. "I hope I'll see you again."

"You're never going to get rid of me now that I've tried your baking," I tell her.

Mallory sees her chance to get even with me and takes it without remorse. "She's also got the hots for your brother," she says with a wink, "so maybe y'all will have a double date or something soon."

Gia blinks at me. "Really?"

"What? No! I mean, yes, I think he's attractive. Sorry if that's weird, him being your brother and all, but–" I throw my hands in the air. "Ugh! Mal! You ass."

Mallory laughs like Lucifer, throwing her head back and shaking her shoulders. "You poked the bear, Charlie."

Gia's head snaps to me. "Your name is Charlie?"

"Yes, why?"

"No reason," she says hurriedly. "A friend of Mack's is a friend of mine. Any time you want to order, shoot me a text or call me. I'll make whatever you need."

"Will do, Gia," I say. "Thank you for these."

Gia waves us goodbye, and we head to Mallory's truck. As I scold her for putting me on the spot, and she hisses back about me spoiling her chances–with a married woman, no less–we hear Gia closing the garage behind us.

Mallory looks over her shoulder and pouts. "She even has a nice butt."

"She's *married*, Mallory. Stop being so horny."

"Maybe if you eat both those cheesecakes by yourself, you'll get your butt back." She smacks my ass. "It used to be magnificently perky. And round. Daniel and I talked about it all the time."

"How dare you."
"He was a lucky man."
"Mal!"
She throws her head back and laughs again as she opens the door of her truck and slides in.

# CHAPTER ELEVEN

The Sinner cheesecake is balanced on my open palm as I struggle with my oversized bag hanging from my other elbow. I knock on the front door of my sister's house and reposition everything in my arms as I hear heavy footsteps approaching. I think it's going to be Brett who opens the door, but instead, I'm greeted by Devin, whose ponytail is as loose as the oversized gray pajama set she's wearing.

"Hi," I say, holding up my bag and the cheesecake box. "I come bearing gifts to apologize for leaving dinner the other night."

Her eyes flick from the bag to the box and then back to me. "What's in the box?"

"The kind of peace offering nobody in their right mind can reject. Can I come in?"

She blows a loose strand of hair out of her face before stepping back and inviting me in with a wave of her hand. She's barefoot, and her pink pedicure is chipped. I notice a stain on her shirt and bags under her eyes.

She might have needed this more than I realized.

Devin leads me into her kitchen, where I unveil the cheesecake with the same enthusiasm Gia and Mack shared for it. Devin is instantly intrigued, grabs us some plates, cuts us some slices, and pours us each a glass of milk. We bring our treat into her living room, curl up in our respective corners of her sofa (which takes her significantly more effort than me), and dig in.

Devin's eyes roll back in her head. "There are still good things in the world."

"Hard day?"

"Hard week," she says, going in for another massive bite. She tries to talk around it, gives up, chews, swallows, and continues. "Brett has been working like crazy trying to make sure he's good to take some time off once the baby comes, and Mom has been up my ass for the last three days. You want to know what she told me when she called me this morning for our first check-in call of the day?"

I frown. "First?"

"Yeah. Exactly. She calls me three times a day, Charlie. She's losing her damn mind."

"That sounds… horrific."

"Yeah, you're telling me." She stabs her cheesecake with more gusto, swoons over another bite, drinks some milk, and shifts in her spot. "She said that she was reading an article about how important it is for grandmothers to bond with their newborn grandbabies, *especially* the grandmother on the maternal side. Why? Beats the shit out of me, but she drove that point into the ground for fifteen minutes before I got her back on track enough to get to the point. Which was, wait for it–" She pauses for dramatic effect. "So that she can feel like this is *her* baby too."

"Ew."

"Yeah. Precisely. Fucking ew. So I asked her, 'Did you fuck Brett to make this baby, Mom?'"

I laugh. "And what did she say?"

"She told me I was being inappropriate, that I was probably exhausted and should take a nap, and that she would call me back around lunchtime to make sure I was drinking enough water and avoiding anything with high sodium."

I stare at my sister. "I'm sorry, Devin. I didn't realize she was being that overbearing. What does she mean *her* baby?"

"Great fucking question." Devin shovels more cheesecake into her mouth. We sit quietly for a moment before she exhales, and her bottom lip starts trembling. A whimper escapes her as she holds back tears. "This is really good cheesecake."

"Oh, Devin." I slide across the sofa and wrap her up in a big hug. Her belly gets in the way, but I don't care, and as I hold her, I become acutely aware of the fact that I haven't done this for my baby sister in quite some time.

Just over seven and a half months, I would guess. The length of her pregnancy.

*You've been a shit older sister,* I think sharply. More than anything, I just want to let go. Create space. Slide back to my corner of the sofa, grab a throw pillow, clutch it to my stomach, and hope the moment passes quickly.

But a mini Dr. Flagstaff sits on my shoulder, looking as good as ever with her blunt black bob and an encouraging nod. So I squeeze Devin harder.

She melts into my arms and lets out a shaky breath.

"Brett has gently asked her to back off a hundred times," she says, letting go of me and sitting cross-legged while wiping at her tears with the sleeves of her pajamas. "But every time he tries, Mom acts like she agrees with everything he's saying, promises to give us some breathing room, but then just keeps smothering us the next time we see her!" Devin takes a venomous bite of cheesecake and glares out her living room window as she chews. Outside, on the perfectly manicured lawn across the street, her neighbor is getting into a Lexus while his wife yells at him from the open front door. "Could be worse, I guess," Devin sighs. "I could hate my husband as much as Lucy hates Darrel."

"Isn't Darrel the guy who yelled 'hot dog eating contest' at your block party last year and then proceeded to eat the hot dogs that were for everybody to eat?"

"Yup." Devin nods. "That's him."

"Everyone hates Darrel, not just Lucy."

Devin cracks a smile. "He got so drunk, at the end of the night, he rode his son's bike into the back of that Lexus."

We watch as Darrel nears the stop sign at the end of the street in said Lexus. I spot a giant dent in the rear fender and burst out laughing.

"Karma." We giggle in unison.

Still amused by ourselves and a little less tearful, we both slide back to our corners of the sofa, maintaining our smiles as we look thoughtfully at each other.

"I've missed you, Charlie."

"I've missed you too," I say. Dr. Flagstaff is back on my shoulder, a hopeful smile on her face as she ushers me to keep talking with little waves of her hands. I could have left it at that, but I force the words out of my mouth. "I'm sorry I've been such a shit sister lately, Devin. It's been really hard for me to be around you. Like, *really* hard," I add, breathless as I try to hold on to my emotions. There is too much still to say for me to fall apart already. "And it's been so confusing because I'm so happy for you and Brett, and I know in my very being that you guys are going to be the best parents for this little person, whoever they are. But holy fucking hell, Dev, am I ever *furious* that I don't get to do this with Daniel, too."

The water behind the dam I've constructed in my chest crashes against my ribs, but I hold fast.

Devin's mouth works, but no words come out as her eyes grow glassy and then brim with tears. "I–" She clears her throat and looks away. When she closes her eyes, the tears spill free and roll all the way down her cheeks to drip off her chin. She hurriedly wipes them away, and her brow furrows as if she's angry with herself. "It's not fair for me to be the one crying right now."

I'm not sure how to respond to that, so I just shake my head. "I haven't given you the chance to know what's been going on in my head. Don't be mad at yourself. I kept you at arm's length."

"I knew though," she whispers. "Of course I knew. And I've been a shit sister too because I didn't push you to come around more often, or call you when I felt sick in my first trimester, or all the other things sisters do. What we were supposed to do," she adds. "I'm furious too, you know."

I nod. "I know."

Devin looks back out her living room window. I follow her gaze, and we watch some neighborhood kids go past on skateboards. I didn't even know kids still rode skateboards. In my chest, the water behind the dam is growing less wild. Less destructive.

"I'll understand if you don't want to be around the baby," Devin says after a few minutes.

"What?"

She looks at me. "If it's too much, and it hurts, I get it. I won't be upset." She shakes her head. "That's not true. Of course, I'll be upset. But I won't be mad at you. Charlie?" She turns to face me directly and shimmies onto the middle cushion of the couch. Her knees are touching my thigh as I stay facing forward in my corner of the sofa. Devin puts both her hands on my forearm. "Don't try to protect me from your feelings anymore, okay? I can handle it. Even if it hurts my feelings. I want to know what you're carrying, and maybe together we can make it a bit lighter."

Now I'm the one wiping away tears.

I swipe at them angrily, like they're being little shit narcs for selling me out for being a softie.

"Damn it," I sniffle as I try to pull myself together. The dam didn't break as I expected it to. Instead, I'm left feeling like I can breathe better. *Dr. Flagstaff was right.*

Devin puts her hand behind her and rises from the couch, belly first. With a hand pressed to her lower back, she begins waddling to the kitchen. "Can I get you another drink? I've gotten hooked on Poppi sodas. All I want is an ice-cold beer, but for now, those things do the trick."

"I'll try one of those," I say. Then I get to thinking about what Devin said. "Hey, that whole 'want to know what you're carrying' line was pretty smooth. Did you read that in a book somewhere?"

"No."

"See it on Instagram?"

She's reached the kitchen now, and she laughs at me. "No! You brat. You're not the only one who goes to therapy, you know."

I stand and hurry into the kitchen with her. "Excuse me? You? In therapy? Actively?"

She opens her fridge, grabs us each a soda, and fetches glasses and ice. "Yes, Charlie. Why is that so hard to believe? I have shit to work through with this pregnancy, okay? And you haven't been around for me to talk to, and I'm definitely not going to ask Mom."

"What about Stephanie?"

"Please." Devin cracks our sodas and pours them generously. "Stephanie is the best friend to laugh with, have fun with, relax with. She's my ride or die, yes. But she doesn't know me like you know me. And she's incapable of letting me share anything without making it about her motherhood experiences."

I take my freshly poured soda, and hesitate. "Yeah, that tracks."

Devin sips her drink and starts heading back to her living room. She pauses and switches gears, and we end up on her back patio instead. We settle onto a cushioned patio set under a striped umbrella.

"Stephanie just wants to be part of the action. I don't know how well we're going to do once the baby comes." Her gaze slides over to meet mine. "Or how you and I will do, either."

"My therapist expressed concern about that too. She encouraged me to tell you how I am feeling about all this."

Devin snorts. "Same."

"Look at us, out here wildin' in 2025."

"Don't say wildin'."

We both fall into comfortable silence again and sip our sodas. Devin has a beautiful backyard with a messy wildflower explosion along her back fence line. To the right, there's a gazebo over a fire pit. To the left is the perfect spot for a playground for my soon-to-be niece or nephew. Directly in the middle is wide open green grass, where I've spent many a summer night playing beer pong, bocce ball, badminton–you name it.

"So how do we start?" I ask finally.

Devin shakes her head. "Honestly? I have no idea."

I nod. "One step at a time?"

"Deal."

# CHAPTER TWELVE

My room is dark when my alarm goes off, which makes no sense. My alarm is set for seven o'clock in the morning. In the summer, it's already daylight by then. So why is it so dark?

I fumble around blindly, reaching with one hand for my phone somewhere on my nightstand. I knock it off, hiss a string of curses, and finally manage to snatch it up off the floor. My vision is a blurry mess, and the glare of my phone only makes it worse. Squinting doesn't even help.

But I can make out the red and green circles on the bottom of my phone. Answer or decline. This isn't my alarm; this is someone calling me in the middle of the night.

And middle-of-the-night calls are never good.

My pulse sky rockets as I hit the green button. "Hello?"

"Charlie, don't freak out," a man says. It's Brett. I recognize his voice instantly. "Devin is at the hospital. Your mom knows, and I wanted to be the one to tell you because your mom is kind of hysterical right now."

"What happened?"

"She's okay," he says, his tone reassuring and smooth. "She was feeling light-headed before bed tonight, so we stayed up and got her some juice and sat down to see if it would pass. But it continued to get worse. So I called an ambulance, and they didn't mess around. We're out of emergency and in the maternity ward for monitoring."

My heart thuds hard and fast against my ribs. When I speak, my voice sounds like it's a hundred miles away. "Okay."

"She has a fever and an infection. They're running tests, and they're treating the infection. She's going to be here a couple of nights most likely, but all the doctors are telling us that she and baby are going to be just fine. This is a blip. Nothing to panic about, okay?"

"Okay," I say again, gathering a breath. "Okay. Devin's okay?"

"Yes," Brett says. "I promise. But… we could use a favor."

"Anything."

"Can you grab some stuff from the house for us? We didn't bring anything and could use some pajamas and–"

"Say no more, Brett. I'm on it. Give me an hour, and text me what hospital room she's in. Also, what did you say about Mom being hysterical?" A mental image of my mother in the canary yellow house robe she used to wear when Devin and I were kids flashes in my mind. She's yelling bloody murder over some milk Devin spilled on the living room rug. Our mom does hysterical better than anyone else I know. "Is she with you guys?"

"No, she's trying to get here. But your dad won't drive her."

"Why not? Not that it's a bad thing. But usually he caves."

Mom has her license, but she's never quick to drive herself anywhere. It's only a last resort, and she never drives at night, in the rain, or over a bridge. Living where we do, it's almost always raining, and bridges are a dime a dozen. Not to mention that in the fall and winter it's dark before five P.M.

Brett chuckles. "Not this time. Devin told her mom not to come. Begged her not to. Your dad heard, and he doesn't want to go against her wishes and stress her out more. But I've been instructed to bar the door if she shows up here at the hospital. Pray for me."

"Prayers can't help you, Brett."

He chuckles again. "Thanks, Charlie. See you soon."

As soon as I hang up the phone, I dial Mallory. My hands are still shaking, and I'm in no state to drive to Devin and Brett's house and then the hospital. All adrenaline-spiked like this, the last thing I need is to be behind the wheel of a car. After Daniel, driving has become something I avoid whenever possible. I can still do it, but not when my nerves are shot like this.

I'd have a panic attack and drive into oncoming traffic.

Mallory doesn't answer.

I hit redial multiple times while I also get dressed. She still hasn't answered by the time I have my socks on and my ponytail tightened. My palms start to sweat. Minutes tick by, so I pace and wait for her to call back. She doesn't.

*What if Mallory was in an accident?*

*Oh, fuck.*

*Oh, fuck.*

Heat blazes through me. White hot, merciless, and full of crippling terror. I clutch at my chest and suck in a ragged breath that won't come as panic skewers me.

"It's not real," I mumble to myself. "It's just a thought. Not a fact. It's not real."

*I need to get to the hospital.*

If it weren't the middle of the night, I would call Dr. Flagstaff to talk me off the ledge. She'd know all the right things to say, and she'd reassure me that all these feelings are normal considering what I've gone through. I tell myself that over and over, but the fire in my chest won't go away, and my hands are starting to cramp.

I've been on the verge of a full-blown panic attack like this multiple times, but I've only ever lost control three times and let the panic win.

I could call an Uber.

My hand is shaking as I try to navigate the app and input my address. My inner voice whispers something that brings a rush of clarity.

Just call *him.*

Without thinking, I dial Mack's number. The act is one thousand percent crossing a line. It's inappropriate. It's unfair. I kicked him out of my house a few nights ago, and now I'm going to call him at prime booty call hours… to ask for a ride to the hospital.

Better a man I know than a stranger behind the wheel of an Uber.

Despite the knot forming in my stomach, I dial.

Mack answers on the third ring with a thick and scratchy voice. "Don't tell me it took you this long to change your mind?"

"Huh?"

His smooth, deep rumble of a chuckle fills the line and does things to me that I refuse to acknowledge. "If you're ready for me to kiss you, I can come over."

*Oh. My. God.*

"No," I say. "No, thank you," I add, trying to be polite. But that just sounds weird coming out of my mouth. I shake my head at myself. Why is he so hard to talk to all of a sudden? His company was so easy and effortless at the brewery. Now, talking to him is like walking on pins and needles. "This is totally out of pocket for me to ask, but my sister is in the hospital, and I need a ride into Vancouver. I'm freaking out. Otherwise, I'd drive myself, and I don't have anyone local I can call who could get me there as fast as you could." I suck in a breath of air and hold my breath, waiting for him to tell me to kick rocks.

Driving all the way to Vancouver General is definitely a letdown if he thought this was a booty call.

"Give me ten minutes, and I'll be there," he says.

"We have to make a stop at my sister's house on the way."

"All right. See you soon, Charlie."

Mack shows up at my condo within the ten minutes he promised, which kind of surprises me. He must live really close by.

Or he was crashing at some other woman's house nearby.

*And if he was, it's none of your business,* I chastise myself.

He waits patiently at the open passenger door of his dark blue Ford pickup, watching as I rummage through my purse, double checking that I have everything I need. Which I suppose I do. I'm not the one spending the night at the hospital. But I'm scattered and coming down from the anxiety that nearly claws my insides apart.

"Good?" he asks.

I nod and climb up into the truck. A few minutes later, we're on the highway heading downtown to my sister and Brett's house. I bring Mack up to speed on my sister's situation and the dynamic with my mother potentially showing up at the hospital.

He shoots me a wary glance. "Your mom sounds like a real peach."

"She's a good person," I say. "But she has her flaws. She poured her whole self into raising Devin and me, and once we both moved out, Mom sort of collapsed in on herself like an imploding star. Now that a grandbaby is finally on the horizon, it's amplified her… less desirable traits."

He laughs. "What a gracious way of calling someone an asshole."

I tense for a moment. That's my mom he's talking about. But on the other hand, he's not wrong. Suddenly, I laugh so hard it turns into a snort. I clamp a hand over my mouth.

Mack grins broadly. "Come on. Just say it. Your mom can be an asshole."

"I can't."

He rolls all the windows down and proclaims at the top of his lungs, "Charlie's mom is an asshole!"

"Mack!" I reach over the console and smack him on the shoulder.

He just pumps his eyebrows at me.

Throwing caution to the wind, I follow suit, turn my face out the window, and yell, "My mom is a raging asshole!"

"Raging?" he muses with a smirk. "Nice."

Grinning from ear to ear, I let go of the final effects the anxiety had on me. Laughing felt good—insanely good—and now, I can settle a little deeper into the bench seat of his truck and enjoy the cool wind in my hair and the heat pumping through the vents.

Mack turns on the radio, cranks the volume, and we listen to seventies rock all the way to Devin's.

When Daniel and I used to take drives together, we would listen to podcasts or audiobooks. This is a much different pace.

Mack comes inside Brett and Devin's house with me, whistling as he steps into the foyer. "Nice joint."

He follows me upstairs and waits at the top of the landing, seeming a little uncomfortable at the prospect of going into their bedroom. I know where Devin keeps all her things, and I have an easy time locating some comfortable clothes, pajamas, socks, and sneakers. I pack some items for Brett as well before going into their bathroom and packing a small bag of toiletries. We head back downstairs, where I grab some snacks from their pantry and drinks from their fridge.

When I turn to leave and head for the front door, I find Mack standing in their living room with his hands in the front pockets of his jeans. His attention is out the sliding doors at their perfectly landscaped and illuminated backyard. It's completely private back there, so they often leave the blinds open. He's in jeans and a gray shirt that's a bit stretched out around the hem. Probably from lounging at home. I notice his socks don't match, either. One is white, and the other is gray. He likely didn't put much thought into what he was wearing when my phone call jarred him out of bed. His back is to me, and he hasn't noticed that I'm not packing food anymore, so I steal a private moment to just… look at him.

His shoulder blades leave two sharp lines beneath the fabric of his shirt. There's more stubble on his neck than the last time I saw him when he almost kissed me. I bet it's hit that spot where the growth is no longer scratchy but soft. He should shave. His jawline is too handsome to conceal behind a beard.

Mack glances over his shoulder and catches me looking right before my gaze was about to drop to his ass.

*Thank goodness.*

"Ready?" he asks with a flick of his chin toward the front door.

Twenty minutes later, we're parked at the curb in front of the main entrance of Vancouver General Hospital. The sun will be up in less than two hours, around five-thirty, but the city is still sleeping. Restless but still, all at once. That's Vancouver at night for you.

Mack rests a hand on his steering wheel. "Are you sure you don't want me to park and help you carry all that inside? Her room might be in one of the towers. That's a trek. And you're loaded down."

"I've got it." I slide out of the passenger seat and open his back door to haul the bags I packed out of his back seat. They weigh me down more than a little. There's a good chance I over-packed. Rolling my lips between my teeth and grunting with a bit of effort, I swing one of the bags over my shoulder. It pulls me backward a bit, and I sway on the spot to regain my balance.

"Do you?"

I look over at Mack, who is smirking. How unsurprising.

"Yes," I manage, and I force myself to stand up straighter. I've lost muscle along with weight, and sometimes I still forget I'm not as strong and sturdy as I used to be. "I've got this. Thank you so much for the ride. And for picking up the phone at two in the morning. I really appreciate it."

"Anytime, Charlie."

*Anytime?* Really?

A pair of headlights swing over us and glint off the metal bumper of Mack's truck. I shield my eyes as the car pulls a U-turn to circle up behind us and park at the curb as well. As soon as I see the Mercedes emblem on the hood when the headlights wink out, I know the other shoe has just dropped.

"Oh, no," I breathe.

Mack, still behind the wheel, twists to look over his shoulder. "What is it? You know them?"

The passenger door opens, and my mother hurls herself out onto the sidewalk. Her head snaps left, then right, and then her wide and wild eyes land right on me.

"Charlie!" She throws her arms wide, the sleeves of her billowy shirt catching the air like kites as she rushes toward me. Her bedazzled sandals slap against the soles of her feet. "Thank goodness you're here! Devin *needs* us."

The hug she consumes me with reminds me of how an octopus eats its prey.

I squirm out of her grasp just as my dad catches up to her. His mustache is wild and busy–ungroomed, unlike usual–and he looks like a man far too tired to have been behind the wheel of their car.

"Dad," I say with a curt nod before looking back and forth between them. "I was under the impression you weren't supposed to come here, Mom. And that Devin is just fine. She just needs some breathing room, and I'm sure Brett will keep us in the loop."

My mother plants her fists on her hips. "If I'm not supposed to be here, why are *you* here?"

I bite my tongue.

"Morning."

All of us snap our heads in Mack's direction. He's still in the driver's seat and lifts a couple of fingers of the hand resting on the wheel to wave at my folks. He's wearing an easy-going smile, but I can tell it's not genuine. The corners of his eyes aren't crinkled like usual.

Mom's head swivels back to me. "Who's this?"

"Nobody," I blurt.

"Ouch," Mack says.

"A friend," I amend, desperately hoping Mack leaves it at that. He has no idea just how complicated my family dynamics are at this very moment. I have an objective, which is to maintain the peace and keep my mother from going King Kong on Vancouver General.

Mom's eyes narrow on Mack, whose easy smile stays in place even as he gets out of the truck, walks around the hood, and comes up onto the sidewalk to shake my dad's hand and then offer to shake my mother's. She takes it after a moment.

"I'm Mack," he says. "I helped Charlie move house and showed her some local spots around Port Moody where she can meet some new people."

"Nice to meet you, Mack. I'm Lee, and this is my wife, Deidra." My dad puts his hand on my mother's shoulder. "Deidra, we really should head home."

She shrugs out from under his hand. "Our daughter is in the

hospital. What sort of mother would I be if I sat at home while our baby was suffering, all alone, without answers–"

"Mom," I interject, a tickle of irritation forming in my brain, "Devin isn't alone. She has Brett. You know, her husband? The father of their child? The man who literally knocked a guy out in a grocery store for grabbing Devin's elbow when he asked for her number, and she said no? Remember him?" I'm aware that my temper is starting to bloom, and I don't want to lose it right now. Brett and Devin are counting on me to keep a level head. "He's got her. She's safe. And they are right where they're supposed to be right now. And, most importantly, they want to be left *alone*. None of us are exceptions to that. I'm literally dropping this stuff off and going right back home."

*Unless Devin tells me to stay.*

Mom looks like she's about to stomp her foot. She gazes across the street at someone on a pedal bike who is probably making a long and early commute to work. Her attention returns to me, and she catches me off guard by trying to take one of the bags from my hands.

"You two go home. I'll deliver the bags," she says.

"No." I pull back.

Dad groans.

Mom yanks harder. "Charlie, for God's sake, give me the bag. Do you understand how stressful this is for me? I just want to see Devin with my own eyes and make sure she's okay!"

"I'll send you a picture," I say.

"The last time I had a daughter in the hospital, she nearly died!" Mom lets go of the bag, and I go stumbling backward. "And her baby *did* die. So, forgive me for feeling extra paranoid and needing some reassurance right now. Devin should understand how difficult it is for me to sit on my hands and not be able to do anything!"

Her words are a sharp, electric, furious attack on my heart.

My cheeks burn with shame, and I lock eyes with my father, who no longer looks exhausted but wide awake and just as ashamed as I am.

"Enough, Deidra," he says, gently turning her away from me. "That wasn't fair. It's time to go home."

Mom sniffles and starts to cry. As she wipes at her tears, she mutters something to my father that I can't hear, but I know it's laced with self-pity and victim language. My father nods reassuringly and begins rubbing her back in slow circles as he walks her back to the Mercedes.

*Enabler.*

I adore my father, but the way he coddles her at whatever cost to my relationship with him hurts deeply. It always has. He might be willing to let her get away with it, but I'm not.

The words fall from my tongue before my brain has a chance to catch and squash them. "Fuck you."

My parents stop in their tracks.

Mack, who I didn't even realize had his hand in the small of my back ever since the moment my mother grabbed one of the bags, tenses.

Mom turns her wide, tearful eyes on me. "Excuse me?"

With a trembling chin and shame rioting in my chest, I turn and walk up the hospital steps. Mack only hesitates for half a second before he follows me.

# CHAPTER THIRTEEN

MACK and I stand shoulder to shoulder in the hospital elevator.

"That was something," he says after we pass the first three floors. He's carrying all my bags. He insisted on it.

"My mother?"

"Sure. Your mother."

The elevator stops on the fifth floor, and a nurse gets in. She's carrying a massive water bottle that matches her pastel green scrubs. She jabs the button for floor eight, the same place we're going, and pulls her phone out of her pocket without glancing at either of us. Her pants are worn so high up on her waist that the outline of her ass is truly the peach emoji.

"She's self-absorbed," I say finally.

He grunts.

"What? You disagree?" I face him directly and cross my arms over my chest. The nurse scrolls through her Instagram feed. Mack studies me with a sidelong glance and leans up against the railing behind him. His hair, I notice, is a wild mess and sticking out every which way. Was it like that when he picked me up? Did the wind blowing through the open truck windows mess it up? Why am I fixating on his hair so much? And why do I want to run my fingers through it?

I snap back to the conversation and put my guard back up. "By all means, share your opinion about my mother based on the ninety-second interaction you just saw."

"You were the one who told *her* to fuck off. Not the other way around."

Scoffing, I roll my eyes. "It's been a long time coming."

The doors open on the eighth floor, and the nurse leaves. We step out next, but right before we reach the nurses' station, Mack catches my elbow and gently pulls me closer to him. I'm so close I could lean three inches to my right and find myself right up against his chest. I can smell the lingering scent of his cologne–cedar and musk. His eyes, pitch black in the dim after-hours lighting of the hospital, shift slowly back and forth between mine as he speaks.

"Was she talking about you?" he asks softly. "Did you…"

"Lose a baby?"

His lips press into a fine line, and his eyes darken even more. He nods once.

"I did," I say, instantly putting more space between us. "And for some reason, my mother has treated *my* loss like it was the worst possible thing that could have happened to *her*, not me. And now Devin is having her first child, and everything I thought my mom and I had squashed is bubbling to the surface again, and I *can't* do this all over. I *can't*," I say again because there is no possibility of survival if I have to relive my nightmare from three years ago. "I barely survived the first time."

Mack just keeps looking at me.

Just looking.

His unnerving eye contact makes me self-conscious, so I yank one of Devin's bags from its perch on Mack's shoulder. I'm too flustered for my own good and end up grabbing a fistful of his shirt as well, and with that one yank, I manage to literally tear the shirt open from collar to arm pit, exposing rounded shoulder muscle and the outer twenty percent of his pec.

*Oops.*

Now, I'm not just self-conscious. I'm melting in a puddle of my own embarrassment. Right on cue, the elevator doors open again and deliver a fresh group of nurses, who have to scoot around us. While I make hurried apologies to them, Mack rips off the hanging piece of fabric and drops it in the waste basket near the elevator door.

"Shit." I hiss between my teeth. "I'm sorry. I didn't mean to."

"It's fine."

"It's so not fine," I mutter.

Mack puts his hand gently on my upper back and suggests we go see my sister. I've never been so thankful for someone showing me mercy. He easily could have snapped back at me that he'd just done me a huge favor, and I'd just gone and ripped his shirt in gratitude. That's undoubtedly the kind of attitude I'd have if our roles were reversed. But not Mack. He is cool as a cucumber as I tell the nurse the name and room number we are looking for. He leans on the counter with one arm, his full, firm, impressive chest muscle totally on display.

I catch the nurse noticing and staring, her eyes widening by a fraction. She abruptly looks away and at me before she turns neon pink.

"I get it," I tell her.

She gives me a shaky smile.

"Get what?" Mack asks, his attention sliding back to me.

"Nothing," the nurse and I say in unison.

His eyes narrow. "Uh huh. Sure."

Giggling, the nurse stands from her desk and motions for us to follow her around the U-shaped nurses' station. Her short blonde ponytail bounces with every step in her pristine white Sketchers. She leans over the counter and points down the hall. "She's in room eight, just at the end of the hall on your right there. I was just in there with them, and she let me know to expect you."

"But to be on the lookout for a Bohemian-dressed woman with pink and blue streaks in her hair?" I ask.

"And a timid husband over her shoulder," the nurse adds with a dimpled smile.

*Gosh, she's pretty,* I think. *And she didn't just rip Mack's shirt or jump down his throat for asking obvious questions.*

"Thank you," I say, hurrying off down the hall with Mack on my heels. Devin's bag thumps against my hip with each step I take, and I kind of wish I'd let Mack carry it the rest of the way. Packing for three nights might have been overkill.

Daniel used to say I'd make a great prepper.

I have to stop and move to the side when a nurse comes by rolling ultrasound equipment. Tucking in between two unused beds, I let her pass and wonder why I was struck with the thought of the nurse at the desk being pretty. Did I feel threatened by her? No. Did someone like her make a lot more sense for Mack to pay attention to instead of me?

The grieving childless widow?

Yeah. A heck of a lot more sense. After what just happened, and how thoughtful and kind he's been to me tonight, he's got to be ready to run the other way.

*I've been a pill,* I think.

I treated him poorly the first day we met, when he first set foot in the house I shared with Daniel. I got cold feet the night he kissed me and kicked him out of my condo.

I called him in the middle of the night asking for help—when I had no business doing so. We aren't friends. We're barely acquaintances. And yet, he came.

And then I go and bite his head off and trauma-dump my shit on him all because I was triggered by my mother.

*After tonight, you probably won't ever see him again,* I think.

There's a pit in my stomach when we finally reach Devin's room. It's dimly lit, but there is a touch-activated lamp on a rolling table beside a hospital bed, where my sister is lying on her side with a pregnancy pillow wrapped around her whole body like an anaconda. She has her Kindle propped up in one hand and is reading while she sips water from a massive water bottle, never taking her lips off the straw.

Brett is on a chair by the window. His chin rests on his chest, and he's snoring quietly.

"Dev," I whisper, lingering at the threshold of the room.

She glances over her shoulder, perks up, and smiles with relief.

"Charlie! You're here." Her eyes snap to the bags Mack and I are carrying. "Please God, tell me you brought the biggest drawstring pajamas you could find."

I reach into the bag over my shoulder and pull out a powder blue pajama pants covered in strawberries. "These ones?"

She looks like she's about to cry. "I need to get this hospital gown off. Stat."

Brett wakes from what might have been the only few minutes of rest he's had all night. He rises from his chair with a hand in the small of his back and a grimace on his face.

But soon enough, he gives me a warm smile, comes over, and hugs me. "Glad you're here, Charlie. Any problems?"

I nod. "We don't have to get into it right now. Let's just say the Eagle landed, but I spun her around and sent her north."

He taps the side of his nose. "Ah. Good."

Mack clears his throat. I turn and find him still standing in the doorway. I go over and lead him into the room.

"Dev, Brett, this is my friend, Mack." The word 'friend' may not be accurate, but it's the best I can do considering the circumstances. Dr. Flagstaff, who always encourages me to confront the truth of things, would probably give me an exercise to narrow in on the right feeling, not word. And if I had to describe what Mack is to me on those terms, I'd probably call him my *first-crush-since-my-husband-died-and-the-first-person-who-hasn't-made-me-feel-like-I'm-damaged-goods-who-I-kind-of-want-to-make-out-with-and-smell-him-all-the-time.*

Yeah.

Totally succinct.

"Mack, this is my sister Devin and her husband, Brett," I continue.

Mack and Brett shake hands. Devin waves over her shoulder at him as she gets herself into a seated position and attempts to untangle herself from her snake-pillow. Brett notices she's struggling and hurries to help her.

She waddles past me and snatches the strawberry-printed pajamas out of my hand on her way to the bathroom. "I'll be back."

Brett gestures at the two chairs by the window and invites Mack and me to sit and have a quick visit. When I push back and say we should just go, he drops his voice so Devin can't hear him while she's in the bathroom. "Just ten minutes? She only just calmed down from all this when she heard you were coming, Charlie. She needs rest, too. Don't get me wrong. But ten minutes with her sister will make that rest easier to come by."

"Of course," I say without thinking. If Devin needs me, I'm here. No questions asked.

"Is the cafeteria open?" Mack asks. "I can run down and get you guys some sandwiches, or tea, or... whatever pregnant women eat at three-thirty in the morning."

Brett laughs. "She'll eat just about anything these days. Don't tell her I said that," he adds hastily, shooting me a panicked look.

"I won't tell her. I'll hold on to that and blackmail you in the future," I say.

Brett laughs again. He's always been an easy laugher. I like that about him. My sister needs someone with a glass-half-full attitude. And one thing is for sure about Brett—he's going to be an incredible dad.

Mack gets to his feet and says he'll be back before heading out for the cafeteria. Moments after he leaves, Devin comes out of the bathroom in her pajama set. She tells me all about how scary it's been being in the hospital while Brett lifts the bags we brought onto the bed and starts unpacking them. She tells me about how important it is in this final stretch of her pregnancy to keep her mental game strong. The hospital gown was corrupting that, she tells me, emphasizing how it made her feel like a patient and like something was wrong with her.

*I know exactly what you mean, Dev,* I think but don't say out loud. The last thing Devin needs right now is me making her feel like I need her to make me feel okay.

"Luckily, everything is fine," Devin finishes. "I just have to take it easy, and I'm going to extra appointments with my OBGYN leading up to delivery. Just to keep on top of things." She places her hand lovingly on her belly. "We're almost there. Just a little longer."

Without thinking, and for the first time since Devin's pregnancy, I reach out and place my hand on her stomach, too. She stills and looks up at me, but all I can look at is her round belly and the sight of my hand upon the stretched strawberry-printed fabric. Beneath my palm, her belly button protrudes. I smile. That's a feeling I have been wondering about for three years, and a sight I knew I would never look down and see on myself.

"I'm so relieved you're both okay," I whisper.

Devin doesn't say anything. She just nods and wipes away tears that keep flowing. Brett wordlessly comes over, wraps both of us up in a big bear hug, and kisses the top of her head. I'm not sure how long we all stay there for, but I am sure all three of us are crying, and nobody wants to let go. Finally, Brett releases us and guides Devin back to the bed. I follow, and Brett moves the bags aside so my sister and I can curl up together on her bed and cry.

*Add 'sixth sense' to the list of reasons why Brett is wonderful for Devin.*

I give my sister a squeeze and close my eyes. This all could have ended so much differently. The way it all ended for me. Abruptly. With no warning. No kindness. No mercy.

Just emptiness.

# CHAPTER FOURTEEN

MACK INSISTS on walking me to the front door of my condo when he drops me off at five in the morning. Birds chirp in the maple trees that line the street. A dog barks a few houses down but goes quiet after the owner bellows at them to shut up and slams their screen door.

Before I go inside, I turn to Mack. "Thank you for helping me tonight. I was desperate, and you came through, and I did a shitty job showing my appreciation." I nod at his torn T-shirt sleeve. "I'll replace it."

He glances down at his chest like he forgot he's been walking around like a damn playgirl ad. He shrugs one shoulder. "It's just a shirt."

"Exactly. Easy for me to replace it. Please? It will make me feel better."

"Suit yourself. Size large. Long fit. No white."

I try to stop myself from grinning but fail. Maybe it's the exhaustion. "You had those specifications locked and loaded."

"I know what I like."

I lick my lips. And just what *does* Mack like? Pretty blonde nurses with bouncy ponytails and perky butts from walking around in

Sketchers all day getting twenty thousand steps? Or underweight grieving housewives with absolutely *zero* physical attributes she can describe as perky?

"Well, anyway, thanks again," I say. "And don't worry. I won't call you in the middle of the night again needing a crazy favor. And I won't expose you to my mother, either. Jesus. So embarrassing. You saw me acting like such an ass." I shake my head and slide my key in the front door. "Family is a mess sometimes, right?"

"Always," he says nonchalantly.

I open the door and keep it ajar with my hip. I manage a smile that feels like goodbye.

He slides his hands in the pockets of his jeans and starts heading back to his truck. "For the record, I act like an ass sometimes too. More often than not, actually. I have the history to prove it."

"Oh, I know."

His easygoing smile returns. He pauses when he's a few feet from his truck and calls back to me. "Hey, Charlie?"

"Yes?"

"It would be a damn shame if you never called again. Dumb favor or not. I'll pick up."

He gets in his truck and drives away, and I stare after him, a stupid smile stretching my cheeks so big it hurts.

My smile is gone when I'm awakened by my phone ringing less than three hours later. Squinting one eye open, I scowl at it buzzing on my nightstand. My room is bright with morning sunlight, so there won't be any going back to sleep now. I roll over and look at the screen.

I'm not at all surprised to see that it's my mother calling.

I let it go to voicemail.

She continues calling throughout the morning as I go about my normal routine of watering my plants outside, pruning them, and turning them to make sure they get the proper amount of sun. I wipe down my patio furniture and brew some tea, which I sip outside while I write in my journal.

Dr. Flagstaff would be very impressed. If only I managed to do this every day, not sporadically a handful of times a month. But with everything that happened last night, I feel called to put my thoughts onto paper. I write about how terrified I was when Brett called me. How desperate I was to get to my sister as quickly as possible. How my thoughts spiraled to worst-case scenarios.

And then I keep writing about how Mack swooped in and got me from point A to point B. No complaining. No judgment. No hesitation. Upon reflection, one thing becomes startling clear: my spiraling thoughts calmed the moment I got into his truck last night. Yes, I was still deeply worried for my sister as I packed the bags and made for the hospital, but the panic had ebbed away and all but disappeared.

Because of him.

I close my journal and stare out at the sunrise to the east. The sky is nearly neon, burning with pinks and oranges so vibrant it could be a painting. Sinking a little deeper into the cushion of my chair, I admire the view as the reflection of the sun dazzles across the still water of the inlet. It's too early for boat traffic or disturbances. No rush hour traffic inches down the street below. No neighbors stir in their units. No children holler in the park across the street.

This is the definition of peace.

*I wonder if Mack is watching the sunrise, too.*

The thought catches me a little off guard, and I shake my head at myself. "Not likely, Charlie," I murmur. He was up with me until the ass crack of dawn. If he has any sense, he's face down in his pillow right now.

When I step inside to take a shower and get ready for my day, my phone is ringing once again, and I swipe it angrily from where it's sitting face-down on the kitchen counter and lift it to my ear.

"Mom, it's early, and I'm running on about two hours of sleep. We can talk about this later, okay?"

"Mom?" Mallory's voice fills the line. "Talk about what later?"

"You are never going to believe the night I had." I fall into the corner of my sofa in the living room, shower forgotten, and launch into the tale of everything that unfolded last night, starting with the call from Brett and ending with what Mack said to me when he dropped me off. My thoughts are pretty organized for once, probably because of the three-page journal diary I just vomited from the tip of my pen.

Mal is silent for a beat on the other end. "Listen, I'm gay as can be, but Mack sounds hotter and hotter every time you tell me about him."

I gush about how he held space for me last night. How he let me have my feelings, never shamed me, never lectured me, never tried to steer me away from having my own reactions to things unfolding in real time. "Hell, he let me use him as a punching bag and then still told me to call him," I finish.

"I think he likes you. Like, *likes* likes you."

"No, come on-"

"And I think you *like* like him."

"Mal, what is this, high school?"

"Charlie," she says firmly. "There is nothing wrong with catching feelings for this man. He sounds great. And you know I don't say that about men. Ever. Even Daniel had to bust his ass to earn it. You should call him and go on a real date."

The thought of calling Mack and asking him out for dinner makes my pulse spike. "Absolutely not."

"Chicken shit."

"No," I press. "I just think that ball should be in his court."

"Ah, yes, internalized misogyny at its finest. It's okay. It's not your fault. Society did this to you. You need liberation! You don't need a man to ask you out, Charlie. You're a desirable, beautiful, powerful, intelligent woman, and you can go after what you want when you want it. Mack would be lucky to have-"

"Stop," I say, loving her fierceness but knowing this is where Mallory and I differ. "Every interaction I have with Mack teaches me something new about him. I'm really happy taking things super slow. I'm into him. I can admit that. But if we're going to go on a date, I want him to initiate it. I want to know while I'm sitting there with him that he wanted to be there with me, so he made it happen. I like when a man takes steps. Daniel was always so good at that. Actions are language. I have to give him room to communicate who he is."

Mallory is quiet for a moment. "Damn."

"Too much?"

"Nope, not at all. I'm proud of you." I can hear her smiling on the other end of the line as she says that. It makes me smile, too. She lets out a devious little chuckle. "This is a big deal. You're healing, Charlie. Let's celebrate."

"Charcuterie and reality TV?"

"Dixie's."

"Are you high? No *way!*"

"I'll call the girls and see if they want to come."

"No," I say. "I don't have the energy for the crowds or the noise. Or the strange men on the dance floor. Can't we just stay in?"

"I know one of the servers. She can get us in with no cover charge," Mallory says. "I made out with her after hours and apparently rocked her world. She always gets me in for free."

"Yeah, you've told me like a hundred times."

"She was a good kisser."

"Mal, can we just stay in? The bar isn't my vibe anymore. I don't even have jeans that fit me, let alone a cute going-out top."

"I'll bring you an outfit and pick you up at nine. This is happening. Buckle up, cowgirl. We're going dancing at Dixie's."

# CHAPTER FIFTEEN

Dixie's is lit up like a Christmas tree even though it's the middle of July. Colorful lights line every inch of trim around the windows, roof, doors, and down the posts and edges of the covered patio. By the time we pull up in a cab, it's dark out, and light is spilling out of the bar into the gravel parking lot where clusters of people smoke cigarettes and joints while they laugh and talk. Cars pull up and spit out groups of people who have already been pre-drinking somewhere else. Most are in their early twenties. Some might even have fake IDs. Devin and I had our fair share of underage nights at Dixie's when we were seventeen and eighteen. Our parents would have had a hairy fit if they had known that was the real reason why we went for sleepovers with our cousin out in Port Moody when we were kids.

When I step out of the cab in Mallory's black cowboy boots, black low-cut top, and denim shorts, I'm hit with the smell of beer, tequila, and weed.

Mallory loops her arm through mine and inhales deeply. "Oh, yeah. That's the stuff right there. No inhibitions, no regrets. Let's have fun tonight."

"Castles in the Sky" by Joseph David-Jones is playing from inside the bar as our boots crunch on the gravel. My layered bracelets jingle, and my hoop earrings bounce against both sides of my neck as I walk. I haven't dressed like this in ages, and I feel like everyone is looking at me–like I'm too old, too fragile, and too out of the loop to be here. Mallory, on the other hand, has a strut in her step, and her chin is held high like every person in the bar is waiting for her to arrive.

We spot a couple of our friends in line, women we've collected from different corners of our lives.

There's Heather, the guitar-playing free spirit Mallory and I met on a camping trip eight years ago. Now, she lives and works out here, and she's always down for a night out dancing.

There's Chelsea, the southern ray of sunshine who moved here to marry her now-husband, who both Mallory and I went to high school with and still see at Christmas parties and such.

And then there's Analise, the preppy and beautiful brainiac who develops security software for some big tech company that earns her over three hundred grand a year. We actually met her through Daniel, who went to business school with her.

The girls see us coming and get giddy, jumping up and down and waving us over to join them in line. Nobody complains that we're budging as we crash into our friends for hugs, laughter, and promises of a good night ahead.

Chelsea loops her arm over my shoulders and leans into me. She smells like the spearmint gum she's chewing, and she looks cute in her denim shorts, boots, large buckled belt, and denim vest that shows off her lean stomach. "I hear we're out celebrating," she says, her southern accent making her voice sound like honey. "I want to hear all about this Mack character. Do you have pictures?"

"No," I say, shaking my head and blushing. I jab Mallory in the ribs with my elbow. "Did you really have to tell everyone about him?"

Mallory just grins.

Heather takes her rust-colored hair out of its ponytail only to pull it back up. "Describe him to us."

"Erm…" I trail off.

Mallory gives me an encouraging nod as we inch closer in line to the front door, where bouncers are checking ID. They're dressed in jeans and black T-shirts that say 'security' in yellow block letters across their chests. Their arms are thick, and so are their necks, and their trap muscles are nearly up to their earlobes, so they look like they're permanently shrugging. Dixie's is as fun as it is wild. On occasion, things can get a bit rough around here. I've been lucky and have never been around on a bad night.

"Mack is tall," I say.

The girls nod encouragingly.

"He's got dark hair," I continue, "and *really* dark eyes."

"Girl, give us the goods!" Heather cries.

Analise opens her small crossbody bag to apply some lip gloss. "Yeah, what's his demeanor like?"

His demeanor?

I've never really thought too hard about it, but I try to put it into words for them to paint a broader picture of Mack. "He's easy-going and relaxed, but he has an undercurrent I haven't quite put my finger on yet. Like, when he's looking at me, he's calm, cool, and collected on the outside. But inside? I feel like there's some turmoil. Like something is always rumbling inside him."

The women all share a look.

Analise fans herself and giggles. "He sounds like a bad boy."

"He's not," I say.

Her eyebrows shoot up. "You sure?"

Frowning, I think about it. "I think I'm sure."

"That's an oxymoron," Mallory says.

"Nerd," Chelsea says.

"Coming from you?" Mallory scoffs. "Please."

It's our turn next, and we all pull out our IDs to proudly flash them at the bouncers, who barely glance at them and wave us through. We're not in our twenties anymore. We're not passing for under nineteen. Not by a long shot.

As soon as we're inside, Mallory flashes her pearly whites at a girl collecting cover fees, and we're waved past and head for the bar. The place is packed, as it always is, and we find ourselves in line again. The girls keep poking me about Mack, so I give them the best I can.

"He's fit. And not the kind of fit you get at a gym. He earned his strength. He's got broad shoulders, and his jaw is insane, and he walks with this easy... authority? I don't know how to describe it. But he just seems very self-assured. And he never fills silence with words. He's content to just sit, and he listens really well, even if I'm sort of verbally attacking him."

"Or physically attacking," Mallory adds for good measure.

The other three girls blink at me as we inch closer to the bar to order our drinks. I roll my eyes and scan the menu overhead as I respond. "I may have ripped part of his shirt off in the middle of the night last night."

"You hooked up with him?" Chelsea cries.

"What? No!"

"Define 'middle of the night,'" Heather says.

"Three A.M.," Mallory announces like the shit disturber she is.

"Stop!" I hold up both hands, and all the women look at me. "Mallory is sabotaging me on purpose. It wasn't kinky. It was quite literally the polar opposite. I was yelling at him on a hospital elevator because my mom got under my skin, and he was the only person there I could take it out on."

"So you physically attacked him?" Analise frowns and looks at the others before taking my hand. "Charlie, I think maybe this is a problem we shouldn't be poking jokes at."

Mallory throws her head back and laughs movie-villain style.

Gritting my teeth, I say, "I took a bag off his shoulder with a bit too much gusto and didn't realize I also had hold of his shirt. It's not a big deal."

We finally reach the front of the line just as our bartender is about to step off the floor for his break. He holds up a hand to tell us our order will be taken in a moment before taking off his apron and slipping away. Meanwhile, the music is cut off as the DJ is replaced with a live rock band from the local area. The lead singer starts to sing "Jolene" into the microphone, which she cradles on its stand like it's her hot date for the night. Her voice isn't as heavenly as Dolly's, but it has power, and she holds her own with the band.

Heather drums the rhythm with one hand on her bare thigh. Chelsea taps her foot. Analise sways her hips. Mallory stretches to the tips of her toes to peer over the bar, no doubt looking for the cute server she hooked up with in the past who got us in for free.

We all have our backs to the bar when a smooth, deep voice asks what we're ordering. "Tequila shots are on special, or if you want to get wild, you–" He breaks off mid-sentence when I turn, recognizing his voice, and lock eyes with him.

"Mack?" I say.

All the women zone in on him like crows spotting something shiny on the sidewalk.

He straightens with a grin. "What are you doing here?"

"Me?" I gesture at the bar. "You never told me you worked at Dixie's."

He tosses a towel over his shoulder and braces both hands on the bar. "You never asked."

*He has an infuriating way of communicating sometimes,* I think. *If 'communicating' is what you can even call it.*

He raps his knuckles on the bar three times. "What are you drinking, ladies? I have to keep this line moving."

We order our drinks, and Mack slyly gets away with not charging us. We leave the bar so other patrons can order and find a table close to the dance floor where we can sip our drinks and work up the nerve to step out there together.

It's going to take me more than one drink–especially considering that Mack is in the building and apparently an employee. Everybody knows Dixie's. It's kind of a big deal and one of the most popular bars outside of Vancouver. With its country and rock 'n' roll edge, it has a laid-back atmosphere that draws good vibes. There are no little black dresses and high heels to be seen. Women wear jeans, shorts, sneakers, and sandals. Men wear jeans and boots with T-shirts. The drinks are decent and cheap. The music is good. And the dance floor is always packed. What else could you ask for?

"He's *extremely* good looking," Heather says as we settle into our booth. "I know you said he was hot, but I mean, come on. Men who look like that don't walk around places like Port Moody."

"What do the kids say?" Chelsea presses a manicured finger to her chin, feigning thoughtfulness. "He has 'rizz.'"

Mallory cringes into her beer. "Stop that right now. Never say that again."

The night continues, and by the time we order our third round, we're starting to itch for the dance floor. Analise gets up to request a song. Heather and Chelsea go to get shots.

I lean close to Mallory. "Why do I feel weird about not knowing Mack works here?"

Mallory shrugs. "I don't know. He isn't obligated to tell you. Maybe it just didn't come up, you know?"

I chew away at my bottom lip.

Mack is a stranger to me. This encounter has made that abundantly clear. This morning, I was almost entertaining the idea of letting him take me on a date, but now my brain is spinning in circles trying to riddle out why I feel like running. I grew up with Daniel. I knew every corner of his past, present, and future before I married him. Every single stop on the road trip of our lives had been mapped out in my head.

But Mack?

He's foreign. Unpredictable. Un-mappable.

Should I really be entertaining the foolish idea that he and I might have something?

# CHAPTER SIXTEEN

Sweat rolls down the back of my neck and disappears beneath the fabric of the black top Mallory brought for me. Standing in front of the mirror in the bathroom, I draw my hair up off my back and hold it in a mess on top of my head with one hand so I can fan the back of my neck with the other. It's hotter than sin in Dixie's–probably because I'd been catching Mack shooting glances at me from behind the bar when I was dancing with my friends.

Did I put an extra sway in my hips? Maybe.

I kind of like how he watched me.

But I also kind of don't trust him now.

*Maybe I'm the problem,* I think as I let my hair fall back down. The curls have mostly fallen out. It's flat, a bit tangled, and dull from the hairspray, but who cares? I haven't had shiny hair in three years.

Mallory comes out of the stall directly behind me with a drunken swagger to her step. She sidles up beside me to wash her hands and tells me she needs water. Stat.

So we head out to the bar, where Mack gives us each a bottle of cold water. He watches my throat as I tip my head back and chug. I can feel the heat of his stare trickle down to the low-cut top of Mallory's that I'm wearing.

Abruptly, he hollers at one of the other bartenders that he's taking five. The bartender quips back that he can have two minutes. They're too slammed. Mack plants a hand on the bar and uses it to effortlessly hoist himself over and land in front of me.

I blink up at him in surprise.

He doesn't say a word. Just takes my hand and leads me out to the dance floor, where he plucks the water from my hand and slides it into the back pocket of his jeans. He leads me wide before tugging sharply and spinning me into him. He catches me tight against his side, his arm wrapped around me like a cage, and looks down at me, a cocky smirk playing on his lips.

"If I were the jealous type," he says, "it would piss me off knowing you came to a place like this… in an outfit like that." His gaze rakes me up and down. "But I'm not the jealous type."

"You sure?"

"I'm just grateful to fucking be here." He grins, reaching down with his free hand and startling me by grabbing a handful of my ass.

I squeak.

And then he's spinning me out, around, and back in. His feet move quickly, and his confidence is graceful as he dips me, pulls me back up, and holds me close for a quick combo where I try to follow the fluid motion of his hips. The dopamine starts to hit as I catch up.

"You've got it," he says. "Just like that, baby girl."

*Baby what?*

My heart starts to pitter patter, and I know it's not from the effort of dancing. His words have pushed a boulder off me, and the way he looks at me is just making it pick up speed.

When he holds me close, our lips are mere inches from each other.

"If you weren't here with your friends," he breathes.

*Tell me what you'd do.*

"You'd what?" I dare him to continue.

"I'd take you somewhere away from prying eyes so I could kiss you how I want to."

"How do you want to?" I manage, my breath fluttering, alcohol coursing through my veins, my nerves fraying at the ends with excitement. I'm playing a dangerous game. On one hand, he's made me nervous tonight by reminding me that there is so much about him I don't know.

So much that could sneak up on me. Scare me. Change my mind about him. Send me hurtling back to isolation and survival mode. The list goes on.

But the dancing redeems him.

Daniel liked to dance, but not like this. We danced to slow songs where he could sway and give me a twirl or two and look like he knew what he was doing, but really, the man had two left feet. He still deserved credit for trying, though.

But Mack dances like he owns the place–like every step is right. I find myself looking up at him, counting all the differences between him and Daniel.

The scruff on his jaw and neck compared to Daniel's always clean-shaven jaw.

The dark mysterious stare instead of Daniel's inviting blue eyes.

Mack's broad shoulders and Daniel's narrower, leaner build.

The way Mack makes my heart race, while Daniel used to make me feel at ease. Always.

Mack startles me by closing the space between us and suddenly pressing his lips to mine. The kiss is soft and brief and ends with his deep voice rumbling by my ear as he leans in close.

"Against a wall. All to myself. Begging me for more."

My cheeks burn. "Mack..."

"Tell me no."

I should, but I don't want to. I want to scream *yes.* So I say nothing, and he takes my silence for the answer it is: permission. He grabs my hand and steals me away from the dance floor. We weave through dancing bodies, emerge by the stage, and hook a right down a dimly lit hallway past what appear to be break rooms and the management office. We push out a back door illuminated by a red exit sign and spill out into the back parking lot of Dixie's, which has a canopy to the right with benches for employees who smoke.

I assume that's where we're going, but Mack leads me across the lot to his truck, and we take cover behind it for privacy.

There, he pushes me against the driver's side door and doesn't hesitate. He takes my face with both of his hands and kisses me like I'm the first big breath he's taken all day–like every breath before this kiss was shallow and unsatisfying.

I relax into his kiss, letting his tongue slip past my defenses and start untying all the knots in my brain about why I shouldn't do this. Because *this* feels so damn good.

I run my hands up his chest and over his shoulders. Soon, my fingers are at the nape of his neck and sliding into his hair–something I've wanted to do for what feels like ages. He smiles against my lips and presses his tongue deeper, exploring me with steady and controlled curiosity. A soft chuckle rumbles in his chest that has me coming untethered as he holds me more firmly against the truck and wedges his knee between my thighs.

*Fast,* I think. *Is this too fast? What happens after this? Do we go in his truck? Does he try to get in my pants? Does he expect something from me? Do I have to put out now? What the hell does 'putting out' entail these days?*

"Stop thinking so much, Charlie," he mutters against my lips.

Right. Stop thinking.

*How?*

Daniel never would have kissed me like this. Yes, we were passionate, but not in public. And not so hot and heavy. And I swear, I never had this thrill in my stomach when Daniel kissed me.

*What does that mean?* I wonder as the kiss deepens, and I find myself stretching to the tips of my toes so I can meet his height better and kiss him more deeply. I can feel my mind numbing to the lust.

I cling to him and hook one leg around his. Mack lets out a low growling sigh before tearing his lips from mine and trailing kisses down the side of my neck and down, down, down, until his breath dances across the top of my breasts that nearly spill out of my low-cut top. His teeth pinch, and I gasp as every muscle tenses.

He glances up at me with a devilish smile. "Steady."

His hands slide up the back of my shirt. His fingers dip under my bra and trace vulnerable, sensitive skin all the way around until they're pinched between my underwire and my ribs. He finds the front clasp between my breasts, with an ease that makes me wonder just how many times he's done this, before he flicks it open with his thumb and forefinger. It pops open, and my breasts spill free for him to cup them under my shirt, push them up, and devour the milky tops with kisses and suckles.

It feels so damn good I could pass out right there on the asphalt beside his truck.

To be touched like this after so long feels like someone lifted an invisible weighted blanket off me. His touch lights tiny fires across my skin. His mouth comes back up to meet mine, and he withdraws his hands from my shirt to grab my hips and draw me firmly against him.

I can feel him through his pants, rock hard, ready, and intimidating.

*Ask him to stop. Tell him it's too much too fast. Tell him you're not ready.*

But the words never form, and I give up trying to convince myself to make him stop. I don't want him to. I want him to keep going. I want him to carry me into oblivion, because right now, for the first time in three years, I have both feet out of the realities that almost crushed me. I'm just Charlie. Not the widow. Not the woman who lost her baby.

Just.

Charlie.

Being kissed by a hot guy in the Dixie's parking lot.

"More," I hear myself say before I slip my hand up under the hem of his shirt. His lower stomach briefly flinches in when my fingertips touch him, but then he wedges me more firmly against the truck and consumes my mouth with even more fire. I feel the hair below his navel that disappears beneath his jeans, but I'm not ready to follow that yet, so I let my hand wander up, and I explore every ridge of his muscled abdomen until my panties are quite literally waterlogged.

I'm about to make a wild suggestion that we get in his truck when someone yells his name across the parking lot. Our kiss ends abruptly, and Mack lifts his head to look over the hood of his truck at whoever hollered for him.

I stare breathlessly up at him, silently pleading for him to tell them to kick rocks so he can drop his head back to me and kiss me again, but I get a strong feeling that isn't going to happen when his eyes narrow, and his mouth presses into a firm line.

Mack abruptly steps back from me. "Go back inside, Charlie."

Curious, I move to stand beside him so I can see who ruined such a good moment. Two men walk across the gravel lot toward us. The Christmas lights around Dixie's shimmer behind them but don't make them look jolly. In fact, they look downright pissed.

And scary.

They're both built like linebackers with broad shoulders and wide, muscled torsos that make it impossible for them to rest their arms flush at their sides. Kind of ridiculous, if you ask me. But not the funny kind.

The scary kind.

I glance over at Mack. "Who are they?"

He doesn't so much as look at me. "Go back inside. Now."

# CHAPTER SEVENTEEN

BEING TOLD what to do has never really been my strong suit. Daniel used to say to our friends and family that I had to be led toward something and never explicitly told to do it. It's why all my jobs working for someone else failed. I didn't like to be managed. A flaw? Probably.

But also a defining pillar of my personality.

And Mack telling me what to do after practically fucking my throat with his tongue?

I don't like it.

"Charlie," he says, his hard stare burning into me. "Why are you still standing here?"

"Who the hell do you think you are?" I challenge.

His eyes widen for a brief millisecond before his jaw flexes, and he takes a step toward me that is full of masculine energy. I retreat a step.

He pauses, drops his shoulders, and softens his voice.

"You're not safe here." His brow creases, and he doesn't meet my eye. "I need you to go inside so I can deal with this."

I don't like him bossing me around, but I also don't like being told I'm not safe—and believing him. My attention snaps back to the two approaching men, who are more than halfway to us, and I'm hit with

131

a pang of fear. Can I leave Mack here in good conscience? Who are these guys? Are they going to hurt him?

Are they going to hurt me if I try to leave?

"Go," Mack says, nodding toward Dixie's. "I'll meet you back inside."

That eases enough of my worry to force my feet to move. I walk away, giving the two men a wide berth as I pass. They barely spare me a glance as they continue their beeline toward Mack, who I glance at over my shoulder as I struggle to get my bra done up. He's come out behind the tailgate of the truck to meet them and shows no trace of the kind of fear that's unfurling in my gut with every step.

When I reach the back door, I pause and watch, fixing my shirt.

One of the men is in Mack's face. He doesn't back down. The other begins walking around his truck and must say something Mack doesn't like because Mack's attention snaps to him, and he says something sharp that brings all three of them back together in a tight-quarters confrontation.

My adrenaline starts circulating.

*Are they going to hurt him?*

*Does he need my help?*

*Am I even capable of helping?*

*Should I tell someone?*

Yes.

Clarity splashes cold water on the spiking adrenaline. I march inside and head for the first employee I see–a bouncer in one of those black T-shirts with the yellow 'security' on the front. I tell him Mack is in trouble out back, and he flags down another bouncer, and the pair of them disappear out the back door.

My next course of action is finding my friends, who are spread out. Mallory is at the bar flirting with the server she has a crush on. Heather is dancing with a guy in a backward ball cap and Levi's. Chelsea and Analise are at our table sipping drinks that look like they might be Long Island iced teas. I go straight to Mallory, who notices I'm on edge before I even reach the bar. Her attention immediately leaves the bombshell server.

"You good?" Mallory asks.

I shake my head and quickly bring her up to speed.

The server overhears and clicks her tongue. "That's just Mack for you, baby doll. He's got friends in low places, and they turn up here looking for him every now and again. Let him handle it. He always does. Under the radar style so the boss doesn't find out, you know?"

"Oops," I grimace. Perhaps I shouldn't have told the security guys to go help him.

The server collects some drinks from the bartender and slips out from behind the bar. "I'll be back," she says to Mallory. With her free hand, she points at the floor. "Stay right here."

Mallory draws a little cross over her heart. As soon as the server is out of earshot, she leans over to rest an elbow on the bar and pretends to melt into the floor. "I think I'm in love."

"Stop it," I tell her. "You barely know her. You just think you're in love because she has freckles and blue eyes."

Mallory blinks. "Who shit in your cocktail?"

I manage a grumbling apology. "I'm mad at Mack, not you. I'm sorry. I literally just had the best kiss of my life, and now I find out he has unsavory people tracking him down at work every now and again? What the hell is that?"

"Best kiss of your life? Really?"

"I didn't say that."

"You *literally* just said that, Charlie. Verbatim."

*Shit. Did I?*

"I didn't mean it," I say hurriedly. "Obviously, I have had better kisses with Daniel."

*Right?*

I start searching through my memory files of all the best kisses I've shared with my husband. Some of the top of the list happened that last night we were together. Others happened during our honeymoon. Our first kiss was pretty up there, too.

But had any of them topped the rush I'd just felt outside with Mack?

I'm not willing to answer that. Not even just to myself.

"I think I need to go home," I say.

"Charlie, hold on a second. You don't have to run. Give him a chance to explain what's going on. Maybe it's an innocent mix up."

"No," I say, shaking my head.

She doesn't understand. She *can't*. She doesn't have a dead husband. She doesn't know what this kind of guilt feels like, and as I stand here talking with her, it's eating me alive. I try to think of what Dr. Flagstaff would tell me, but she's not on my shoulder when I need her this time. I've probably had too many drinks.

"I'm okay," I reassure Mallory. "Tell the girls I love them and to have a fun rest of the night. Seriously." I nod across the room at the blonde server. "Don't let me ruin this for you, okay? This is just one of those things. I need to be alone."

Mallory pulls me in for a quick hug. "Okay. I'll check on you tomorrow morning. If you need me, call me, okay?"

"Promise."

And with that, I make my escape, hurrying out the front doors and into the gravel parking lot. A line up of cabs has already formed, knowing this is the start of peak time to drive intoxicated patrons home. I flag down a ride and head back home, where my condo welcomes me with silence.

I climb into bed still feeling the heat of Mack's body against mine. The burn of his lips. The pinch of his teeth. The wildness of my desire for him.

But in the back of my head, a tiny voice cautions me.

*He's trouble.*

I've had enough trouble to last me my lifetime. The very last thing I need is a man making my life and my healing more complicated than it needs to be. I don't fall for men who get into altercations with muscled ex-con-looking assholes in country bar parking lots.

I sigh up at my bedroom ceiling. "You need to do something with your time."

Otherwise?

I'd find myself back in Mack's arms. Under him. Around him.

I swallow and press the heels of my hands into my eyes. "He's off limits. No looking. No touching. No talking. No more." I fluff my pillow and roll onto my side, trying to believe myself that I can walk away from this thing with Mack so easily.

Sleep doesn't bring reprieve. He may be off limits in the waking world, but in my dreams?

Mack is everywhere.

# CHAPTER EIGHTEEN

"I got a job," I tell Dr. Flagstaff as I settle into the corner of the sofa in her office a week after my night out at Dixie's. I drop my purse on the cushion beside me and accept the bottle of water she grabbed from her mini fridge. "Thanks."

"Interesting." Dr. Flagstaff takes her seat across from me in her usual green velvet chair. She presses her fingertips together, the many rings on her right-hand glinting in the sunlight streaming through her window. On the table beside her, an essential oil diffuser emits a cloud of eucalyptus-scented steam. "I didn't know you were trying to find a job."

"I wasn't. But recent developments made it clear that I needed to find something to do with my time. Be productive."

"Developments?" She gives me a sly smile and tucks her bob haircut behind both ears to show off lobes studded with sparkly jewelry. "Such as?"

I launch into the harrowing tale of my week–my sister's emergency hospital visit, Mack giving me a ride, me ripping his head and shirt off at the hospital, my confrontation with my mother and how I've been avoiding her calls all week, and everything that transpired at Dixie's over the last weekend.

"You went to Dixie's the night after you visited your sister?" Dr. Flagstaff purses her lips. "You were running on fumes. Mack must have been too if he was out all night with you the night before."

I nod. "Yes."

She lets this go, but speaking it into existence paints a clearer picture for me I haven't considered: perhaps I wasn't operating as my best self that night.

To compensate and earn a gold star, I blurt out, "I talked to my sister like you wanted me to. It went well. We're good now."

"And did you talk to Mack?"

A long pause proceeds to stretch between us as I deliberate how to answer. I mean, technically, yes, I did. And technically, I told him things that I hadn't planned on letting out of the bag at all. Like losing my baby.

And he still didn't bail.

He did the opposite of bail, really.

"So that's a no." Dr. Flagstaff crosses one leg over the other and bounces one foot. "You told him about your losses and your relationship with your mother and sister, but you never talked to him about, well, him?"

"No, I didn't."

"How come?"

"It's pretty obvious, isn't it? I chickened out."

She gives me a knowing smile. "I don't know if I'd call it that. You did something pretty brave, Charlie. You danced with him. Let him lead you somewhere private. Let him kiss you with what sounds like some pretty serious passion. That all takes considerable vulnerability. If you asked me, which you have, because you pay me a pretty penny for my opinions," she adds with a cheeky wink, "you took some big steps last weekend. I'm impressed."

And here I thought she was going to scold me for acting like a reckless teenager and following my heart and desire, not my head.

I gnaw on the inside of my cheek. "I can't stop thinking about him."

"In what context?"

"Kissing him. Being mad that he lied about working at Dixie's. Wondering over and over what the hell happened in the parking lot when I went inside…" I trail off, letting my mind wander back to that night–to the multi-colored lights casting a dim glow over the gravel lot while the dangerous-looking men approached us and confronted Mack. And how I hurried inside and left him there. Did I have any right to be angry? "Wanting to see him again. Wanting to *never* see him again. I'm so confused."

"What's the worst-case scenario for what might have happened between Mack and those men?"

I shrug. "They fought?"

Dr. Flagstaff gives me an encouraging nod that I recognize as an invitation to let my thought process take me further than that.

I let my imagination guide me for a moment–I let the anxiety take the lead like Mack took the lead on the dance floor.

"He could have bought drugs," I say.

Dr. Flagstaff doesn't laugh or judge me. She just nods. "He could have."

"Or sold drugs," I continue. "I don't know what scary-looking guys like that do in parking lots. I know what men like Daniel do when they see people who look like those men. They get the hell out of Dodge to make sure everyone stays safe. Daniel never would have put me in a position like that. He would never have a reason for men like that to want to approach him at night in the middle of an empty parking lot. He would never–" I break off and close my mouth.

Dr. Flagstaff offers the words we both know need to be said aloud. "Mack isn't Daniel."

"No. He's not."

A rush of grief hits me like a kick to the abdomen. I wrap my arms around myself and try to fight the way my throat begins to tighten.

"It's okay for that to make you sad, Charlie," she says softly. "Feelings like this are normal. Wanting the next man you have feelings for to be more like Daniel than not makes logical sense. Daniel was safe and familiar. Mack is–"

"Rough, and unsophisticated, and trouble," I finish. "Big trouble."

*Huge, sexy, intimidating, gruff, cedar-smelling trouble.*

*Oof.*

"Charlie?"

"Sorry?"

Dr. Flagstaff giggles. Actually giggles. "Listen, this is not my place to say as your psychiatrist, but girl, it's written all over you. You're smitten."

I groan and sink deeper into her sofa cushions.

Her giggle morphs into real laughter. "Charlie, I'm proud of you. This isn't bad news. I'm sorry. I need to get it together. Normally, I don't get to be part of things like this."

"Like this?"

"Meet cutes. Giddy feelings. It's a nice change of pace."

"Oh." I consider this for a moment and realize it's true. Most, if not all, of our interactions for the past three years have been centered around my trauma and my grief.

*This* is *a nice change of pace,* I find myself thinking.

She proceeds to tell me that she thinks me getting a job is a good idea, and that maybe taking a bit of space from Mack is in order so I can figure out what I actually want, and if I should be wary of him now. I don't tell her about his sister in the rough and tumble house with the drunken caricature of a husband to round out the image she has of Mack. I don't tell her about the way I think about him every night when I go to bed. And I definitely don't tell her about the white-hot dreams I've been having about him, either.

I leave the appointment with a reminder to take things slow, go at my own pace, and be gentle with myself. I'm wading into uncharted territory, and there is one guarantee: discomfort.

*The best things happen outside of our comfort zone,* I remind myself later that afternoon as I drive in for my first day on the job as a barista. As a thirty-six-year-old woman with no formal training or education, I'm not qualified for many jobs. When I was married to Daniel, he covered all of our living expenses, and I pursued passion projects like trying my hand at flipping furniture. Not my thing. Everything I touched turned from bad to worse. I tried ceramics and pottery, which was even worse. I wrote poetry, decorated our home with every changing season and holiday, and became fairly skilled in the kitchen.

But nobody was going to pay me for any of that.

I'd always been able to make a decent cup of coffee. How hard could steaming a latte really be?

Hard, as it turns out.

My first day has me on edge. One minute I'm taking cash from a customer and trying to count out their change, and the next I'm behind the biggest espresso machine I've ever seen trying to froth milk without burning it. Six drinks are returned to be remade over the course of the next hour and a half, and my new boss, a redheaded and perky middle-aged woman named Sheila, pulls me aside to give me a pep talk when she sees me crumbling.

"Everybody was new at some point," she assures me. "You're doing great. Just smile, keep trying, and push through the first three weeks. It will all become muscle memory, I promise."

I want to ask her why she even took a chance on me, but I just tighten my apron and get back to work. Hours pass, and then a couple of days pass, and by the time I'm on my fourth shift, I feel somewhat capable. Not good, but capable.

I can warm paninis in the industrial oven, brew drip coffee on a rotation schedule by timers, and froth milk without burning it. I can't, however, seem to remember when to use sugar-free syrups or how to not burn myself every time I wash a steaming pitcher.

In the final hour of my fourth shift, around eight thirty in the evening, I look up from the register to find my mother blinking back at me.

"Mom?"

"Charlie," she says, her voice thin and controlled. "Do you have time to talk?"

Talk? Oh great. Just what I want to do. My brain is already full trying to juggle my feelings about Mack, my fears, and all the new information that comes with my role as a barista-in-training. But Mom has been calling me for days on end, and I know I can't ignore her forever. Perhaps it's best to rip the band aid off sooner rather than later.

"I'm off in half an hour," I tell her.

At the end of my shift, I meet my mother outside, and we walk around the block a few times. I haven't spoken to her since our encounter outside the hospital, and even though I've had time to digest what happened, I haven't figured out what I want to say to her.

We take a seat on a bench under a maple tree. A street lamp shines down on us, and we sip teas I brought us when I finished closing the coffee shop.

"Do you like the job?" she asks.

I shrug. "It's okay. The people are nice enough. Some of the customers are a bit annoying. But I'm going to stick with it. I think it's good for me. It gets me out of the condo a few days a week, and I think it will be a good place for me to meet some new local people. Connect. Plug back in," I finish.

She nods and picks at a piece of lint on her rose-colored pants. "That's good. I'm glad for you."

"How did you know I worked here?"

"I didn't. I take a Pilates class down the block and saw your car."

"Oh."

A quiet moment stretches between us. Then she breaks it. "I want to talk about your sister."

*Here we go.*

"Okay."

She doesn't look at me. "Devin invited me over yesterday afternoon for lunch. We had a good, long conversation, and she told me about how the two of you talked a couple of weeks ago. About her pregnancy and how it's made you feel. About how scared you are."

I try not to crush my paper cup of tea. "Uh huh. And?"

She turns sideways on the bench to face me more directly. "Don't you think that was terribly unfair of you, Charlie? You've gotten in her head. She's terrified of saying the wrong thing in front of you. She doesn't want to bring up old memories. But she deserves this. She deserves a normal delivery and a normal motherhood experience without the dark cloud of what happened to you hanging over her shoulder all the time."

Every muscle in my body tightens like I'm about to go to war.

It takes a beat for me to notice that my mouth is hanging open. I close it. The gears in my head turn.

*What. The. Fuck?*

Mom keeps talking. "I don't say any of this to hurt you, sweetheart. You and Devin are the two most precious people in my life. And what you went through was a horrific tragedy. I think about Daniel and what should have been every single day, and I know you do too. We all do. But that was three years ago. This is now. Devin's baby is *now*. We have to rally around her and move forward."

"What should have been?" I repeat.

She puts her hand on my knee. "You should have had him by your side forever. Until you were both old and gray, and he had arthritis in his hands from all the knuckle-cracking he used to do. Until you had grown children who would come sit around your table when life got hard, and you and Daniel could pour all your love into them. Like your father and I were able to do. Until–"

"Please stop."

She squeezes my knee, and a sob bubbles out of her. "I can't, Charlie. I love you so much. And I see how broken you still are. And I want to help, but I don't know how to. And Devin has everything ahead of her, and it scares me to think that what happened to Daniel and your baby is going to taint the best thing to ever happen to your sister."

I nod slowly.

She lets out a sigh of relief. "You understand, don't you? Please say something."

"I... understand."

She wraps her arms around me in a fierce hug that sloshes the tea out of the little hole in my lid. It burns my hand, but I barely notice. All of my feelings are racing out from the rugs I've brushed them under. My anger. My hurt. My betrayal. My anger at Daniel for leaving me. My anger at myself for letting him get in the car that night. My hatred for everyone who still has their husband. My jealousy for mothers everywhere. My disdain for people who take their families for granted.

"We have to be strong for your sister now," Mom says softly, rubbing my back. "She deserves that."

I inhale and close my eyes. The shadows rush back under the carpet, and I use a staple gun in my mind to secure all the edges down.

So be it.

# CHAPTER NINETEEN

When the sun comes up the next morning, I call in sick to work. Sheila's voice is thin, and I can tell she's disappointed and frazzled, and now she has to work four extra hours to cover me.

But I can't get out of bed.

Grief has clawed its way back into every corner of my soul and made a home there. It's heavy, dark, and damp. My own bones feel like they're weighing me to the bed, trapping me there, and I don't have the strength to fight the good fight today.

Today, the grief wins.

My thoughts have been racing since my mother told me her concerns for Devin. I'm full of doubts and questions, wondering if Dr. Flagstaff led me astray by encouraging me to be honest with my sister about where her pregnancy had put me emotionally. I'd thought Devin and I both walked away from that conversation on the same page. I never wanted to burden her.

But it seems I have.

Guilt settles in with the grief.

My stomach rolls with nausea I've been fighting all night long. Curling up on my side, I wrap my arms around myself and close my eyes. When Daniel's smiling face flashes behind my eyelids, I snap them open again.

There is no escaping this kind of punishment. It follows me everywhere.

It hasn't been this bad in a long time. Paralyzing episodes like this have become less frequent. The day I signed the paperwork to sell the house had been the last time I was consumed by the darkness. There'd been the occasional speed bump, like my moment at the brewery with Mack, or the turmoil of moving day, but this was next level.

That was dangerous.

What if I can't shake it this time?

What if this is who I've become? Permanently.

What if Devin gets pregnant again, and I have to face this a second time? What is going to happen when my friends start having children? Who am I going to be when I am fifty and alone and have no family at my Christmas dinner table? Will Devin always have to be responsible for dragging her spinster older sister out of the house and into the daylight?

My vision blurs with tears that soak my pillowcase. I have been crying for hours. I'm exhausted. Hungry. Thirsty. All the things.

But I still don't get out of bed.

Morning gives way to afternoon, and the sun cooks my room to an insufferable and stifling heat. Sweat mingles with tears as I lay in salty, damp sheets. When the hottest point of the afternoon wanes, and the sun shifts out of view of my bedroom window, the temperature decreases, and the relief brings a flicker of temptation to get up and have a cool shower.

But I don't.

I want ice cold water.

But I don't go get it.

Writing in my journal might help.

But I don't try.

I just rot. Like I deserve. Like I should.

***

I wake to a knock on my door and sit up, rubbing at my eyes and catching a whiff of something unpleasant. Myself. Grimacing, I glance at the time and see that it's eight-thirty at night. The sun is low in the purple and blue sky. A cool breeze blows through my window and dances across my skin.

The knock comes again.

Grumbling, I throw the blankets off, swing my legs over the side of the bed, and manage to step into a pair of sweatpants. I'm wearing an oversized T-shirt--one of Daniel's I couldn't bring myself to put in storage—and I tuck it into the waistband of my sweatpants as I make for the door.

I yank it open, expecting an Amazon delivery driver or a strata board member.

But it's neither of those people.

It's Mack.

"How did you get in?" I ask skeptically, looking back and forth down the hall like the culprit might be close by.

"Someone left the front door propped open," he says before looking me up and down. One dark eyebrow arches slightly, and his eyes dart back up to meet my gaze. "I was in the neighborhood and thought I would drop in. I haven't seen you since Dixie's."

"Uh huh."

His eyes narrow so minimally I almost miss it. "Are you going to invite me in, or should I go?"

*You should go.*

*I'm not fit to be seen by anyone.*

"Now isn't a good time," I tell him.

"Are you okay?"

"I'm fine."

His lips press into that thin, uneasy, unconvinced smile of his. "I can go. But I can also come in and make us something to eat, and we can watch a shitty movie. I don't want to be an ass, but you look like you could use some company."

I look down at myself. I'm a mess. I'm sure my face and my hair are infinitely worse than my outfit. I lick my dry lips. "I..."

"Come on," he says softly, offering me a warm smile. "You can kick me out any time you want to. No harm, no foul."

Despite the desperate ache to return to my bed, I let Mack into the condo, where he kicks off his boots and moves to my kitchen, opens my fridge, and starts rummaging through my things. He pulls out some vegetables, finds a cutting board, and begins chopping things up.

"What are you doing?" I ask.

"Making you something to eat." He pauses cutting, fills a glass of water from the dispenser in my fridge door, and hands it to me. "Drink."

I stare at the cold glass of water and involuntarily lift it to my lips and drink greedily. Mack watches out of the corner of his eye as he returns to cutting vegetables. When I look down at the cutting board, I notice something wrong with his hands.

His knuckles are busted and bruised.

"You should see the other guy." Mack chuckles softly, but when I don't, he puts two and two together and senses that I'm uneasy. "The other guy was a punching bag, Charlie. At the gym."

I look him in the eyes. Can I trust that?

He keeps talking. "I had some anger I needed to work out. Sometimes hitting a bag without gloves does the trick. I pay for it in the end," he adds, holding up his right hand and wiggling his fingers. "But it's better than punching a wall. Or someone's face."

Well, I suppose I can't argue with that. But I'm also not sure I can believe him. I think about the men in the parking lot and the confrontation. What are the odds he has bruised and split knuckles after that from a *punching bag*? Does he think I'm naïve?

"You don't believe me," he says.

"No. I don't."

He nods and pushes the cut-up vegetables to me.

"I'm confused," I tell him.

He just stares at me, waiting for me to continue.

"Why are you here acting like my mom? I don't need vegetables. I don't need someone to come in and save me, least of all you."

"You look exactly like someone who needs saving, Charlie."

His words sting. I grab the tray of vegetables, march them to my kitchen sink, cram them all down the garbage disposal, and turn them to bits and pieces down the drain while I glare daggers at Mack.

He folds his arms over his chest. "Cute."

I let go of the garbage disposal button and fill the silence with a demand. "Tell me what happened at Dixie's last weekend."

He leans on my counter. "I worked a closing shift, danced with a pretty girl, had a kiss with her I can't stop thinking about, and went home alone for some bizarre fucking reason because she wasn't there when I went back inside."

"No shit, I wasn't there." My voice is all barbs and razors. "That scared me, Mack. Who were those men? What did they want to talk to you about? Why did I have to go inside?"

He stares at me coolly. "They're assholes who got what they deserved."

"So you *did* get in a fight." I let out an exasperated laugh. "Of course you did. It only makes sense that I *finally* let my walls down with someone, and then right when I start to think I can trust him, the other shoe drops, and it turns out he's an unsophisticated loser who brawls in parking lots with ex-cons and then lies about it." I lift my chin. "You should go."

"No."

I blink. "Excuse me?"

He shrugs one shoulder. "No."

"You said I could tell you to go anytime and that you would leave," I seethe. Who the fuck does he think he is?

"That was before you decided to pick a fight with me and make a bunch of assumptions."

"So you didn't get in a fight with them?" It's my turn to cross my arms as I scoff dramatically. "What did you think was going to happen? That you could tell me to scram, and I would go back inside scared with my tail between my legs and actually wait for you to come get me? I don't know you, Mack! And I'm not in a position to take any risks because–because–" I search for the right way to try to explain to him what I'm feeling. "Because I'm so paper-thin that I feel like a paper cut will make me bleed out."

His jaw works, but he says nothing.

"I can't be around someone who makes me feel unsafe," I whisper. Dr. Flagstaff would give me a gold star for spilling my guts like this, consequences be damned.

He grimaces and looks away.

I walk to my door to let him out, but he stays rooted to the spot in my kitchen. I put my hand out to open the door.

"Those men were there because of Gia," he says.

I pause and look over my shoulder at him. "Your sister? Why?"

Mack takes a long, steadying sigh and rakes his fingers through his hair. Looking a bit disheveled, he pushes off the counter and comes toward me. "Because she's married to an asshole who likes to keep me in line."

"You're being vague." My body is taut. Wound tight like a spring. He's close enough that I can smell that cedar cologne of his. I wonder if he can smell my sweat and tears, too. "Just tell it to me straight. Why were those men at Dixie's?"

"To rough me up because I broke the restraining order Gia's husband has against me."

That isn't what I expected. And it's not what I want to hear, either.

"Restraining order?" I repeat, my voice sounding like it's coming from someone else's mouth as I try to make sense of what he just said. I picture Gia in my mind's eye, standing in her garage surrounded by cheesecakes and refrigerators. Then I think about her drunken husband, who'd answered the door in the stained muscle shirt.

What was his name again?

Clayton.

"Why did he take out a restraining order against you?"

Mack looks suddenly tired. He nods at my sofas in the living room. "Should we sit?"

We settle into opposite ends of my sofa. I curl my legs up under myself and sit facing Mack, who rests an arm on the armrest beside him, his wrist slack, hand hanging.

"Gia started dating Clayton when she was only nineteen. Clayton was twenty-eight. It already put a bad taste in my mouth, but my little sister isn't the sort you can tell what to do. She has to make her own choices. And her own mistakes," he adds grimly. "And Clayton was just that. A mistake. He whittled his way between Gia and me, creating separation and distance and convincing her that I was trying to sabotage her happiness or independence or whatever. Over time, and masterfully, he succeeded in driving a wedge between us."

I can hear the tension and anger in his voice.

"Her friends tried to step in and help. They tried to get her to see that Clayton wasn't good for her. That he was manipulative, cunning, and hellbent on having her all to himself. But Gia couldn't turn her back on him. She saw a man who needed saving, and she's always been the sort to believe in second chances. Hell, she'll give someone a hundred chances if she thinks there's an ounce of goodness in them. And Clayton… let's just say whatever goodness might have lived in him is long gone."

I think about the state of the house Gia and Clayton share. The way he'd answered the door, imposing and wasted, dirty and physically huge. Then there was Gia—petite, sweet, soft, and, for lack of a better word, weak in comparison to her husband.

"Does he hurt her?" I hear myself ask.

Mack's face abruptly contorts into a mask of fury before he gets his emotions under control and regains neutrality. "Yes."

My stomach rolls over. "Badly?"

His gaze slides to me, and he gives a slight inclination of his head. *Yes.*

"Why haven't the police done anything?"

"Because she won't press charges."

"Why?"

Mack laughs without humor. "Because she loves the fucking asshole. Because she's terrified of what he'll do. So she protects him at all costs."

I mentally take a step back so I can get a broader picture of the scenario between Mack and his sister. I think of the men in the parking lot, the restraining order, Clayton, and Gia's desire to get her cheesecake business off the ground. I think about the cheesecake Mack brought me a couple of weeks ago and frown.

"When did you break the restraining order?" I ask.

Mack gives me a knowing look.

"When you brought the cheesecake here for me?" I whisper.

He nods. "Clayton wasn't supposed to be around. Just Gia. She told me to come get some slices. We do that often. Clayton just never knew about it. But he came home early from the bar that night and saw me driving away, apparently. So he sent his buddies to send a message and make sure I stayed away. And I knocked their teeth in."

Now I feel anger simmering beneath the surface as Mack flexes his fingers, stretching the busted skin on his knuckles.

"I'm sorry," I say softly. "That's not how things should be between a brother and sister."

"No. It's not."

"I can't imagine how Gia must feel."

*Trapped. Scared. Alone.*

"I don't pretend to know," Mack says, "but her relationship has cost her a hell of a lot. Cost *us*."

I wait for him to continue, a sinking feeling growing in my stomach when he meets my gaze directly.

"You should know," he says slowly, "that I've had some... run-ins with the law."

The sinking feeling in my stomach becomes a full plunge into oblivion. My fingertips are suddenly cold. My breath hitches. The nausea I'd kept at bay all day comes back to life in my gut.

Mack looks away like he's ashamed. "Four years ago, I was there when Clayton put his hands on my sister, and I lost it. She had to pull me off him. I... I nearly killed him."

My heart starts to race.

Mack rubs the back of his neck and closes his eyes like he can see the memory playing in his head. "I don't even remember half of it. One minute, Clayton is in her face, and he has his hand on her neck, and the next, he's unconscious beneath me, and Gia is screaming at me to stop. Neighbors called the cops."

I swallow past the lump in my throat and try to take a calming breath. "You hate him. Would you have killed him?"

Mack looks everywhere but at me and clears his throat. "Yes."

The answer should scare me, but it doesn't. His situation is devastating, especially considering he has already buried a little sister when he was a kid. To wake up every day knowing his other sister is in danger and he can't do anything about it?

Unimaginable.

The air in my condo is hot and thin. I can't stop my racing thoughts, so I narrow in on one pressing question. "Why are you telling me all this now?"

Mack doesn't look away this time. "Because you're unravelling, and I know how it feels to lose every ounce of control you have. I don't want you to have to do it alone, Charlie. I see you."

My breath hitches. There's nowhere to hide. Nowhere to run.

*I see you.*

# CHAPTER TWENTY

My gut churns like the current at the bottom of a waterfall, and all I can think about is how terrified I am. Mack is right. I am unravelling. Ever since my mother told me all her fears about Devin, I've become a ball of yarn coming undone a little more with every passing minute.

And I've only just managed to finally roll the yarn back up after Daniel.

Mack watches me closely, his dark, intense, all-seeing gaze stripping me naked. He never says a word; he just lets this silence linger between us as my body and mind desperately try to connect to each other and make sense of everything.

*Impossible.*

I've been trying to make sense of all of this for three years. Trying to make sense of Daniel dying because he went to buy his wife ice cream. Trying to make sense of Daniel's final minutes, upside down in his Porsche, bleeding out from his injuries, trying to grab for his phone just out of reach on the half-collapsed roof of the passenger side.

The seat where I always used to kick my bare feet up on the dash-something Daniel always said was terribly unsafe-and sing at the top of my lungs to Brooks and Dunn while we drove open back roads when we went to visit family in the valley.

Trying to make sense of what he would have told me if he'd been able to reach his phone and call me that night while I read my book in the bath. I know that's what he would've wanted in those final moments. He'd deserved it, and it had been fucking stolen from him. From *us*. No goodbye. No closure. Just cold death, upside down on the asphalt, headlights shining on him from other people pulling up and trying to help.

In the weeks after he died, the police told me that Daniel wasn't killed on impact—something I believed all the way up until a few days after his funeral. And God, do I wish I could still believe that. Easier wasn't the right word, but it had been more manageable believing he didn't have to wait for death to come. He didn't have to grapple with that unflinching *knowing* that it was over for him.

No dream-fulfilling future of becoming a dad. No first days of school, of graduation, of fights with a rowdy teenager, of dropping them off at university, of growing old, of retirement, of our golden years—of the privilege of dying old and well-lived.

I knew Daniel better than I know myself, and in the months after his passing, I became consumed with his final moments. It was all I thought about. All I dreamed about. All I knew. I found some peace in the fact that, knowing him, he'd have accepted his fate by the end and probably found a fraction of a moment to close his own book before his heart stopped. To let it all go.

Me included.

I hated to think that he fought it tooth-and-nail and drew his last breath raging against the cold truth and unfairness of it all.

"Charlie," Mack says softly, pulling me back to the present moment with him in my quiet living room. The lights are dim. Night has fallen outside. Mack is half in shadow from the low lighting, but I can see the way the storm in him crashes against the shore. "Stay here."

I don't know what he's talking about until I realize I'm crying. Sobbing. Breaking into all the pieces I've held together for as long as I could. *Stay here.* As in, don't go back to that place. Don't leave my body. Don't leave him.

But staying here means letting it all unravel fully.

Right to the end.

And feeling *all of it.*

I suck in a ragged, desperate, shaking breath and shake my head. "I can't."

"Just let it out."

"Stop telling me what to do," I say, clawing at the ends of yarn and trying to cram them back into my chest. Brush the shadows back under the rug. Put everything back on the shelves. "You don't know me. You didn't know Daniel or who we were. You're not anything like him!" My voice is raised, and I'm on my feet now. My hands are balled into such tight fists that my knuckles ache, and my palms sting from my fingernails. Then, I scream at him. "He's dead!"

Mack is on his feet now, too. He closes the space between us in two quick strides, already reaching for me, and even though I hate him in this moment for dragging me to this horrific place, I let him catch me when I fall.

We fold to the ground, and he gathers me in his arms with a fierceness that makes me feel like I can suddenly breathe. When I inhale, it's only to let out another scream. It shocks me. My ears ring. My apartment echoes in protest of the cracking silence. Mack wraps his legs around mine, settles in behind me, and makes me hug myself with my arms before sealing me in with his embrace. I let out another scream that steals all my air and leaves me sagging in his grasp, sobbing uncontrollably.

The yarn is fully undone. Everything on the shelves is smashed to pieces, and the shadows have run as far as they can from me.

Mack inhales deeply behind me. "I've got you."

The sobs start slow, and soon, I'm just weeping and sniffling, and I feel like a tiny child as I turn in his arms so I can curl up against his chest and listen to his heartbeat. It's a steady drum that brings me back to a baseline that doesn't make me feel like I'm dying.

My fingers curl in his shirt. "I'm sorry."

He hasn't let me go and gives no indication that he intends to. "I know."

"I didn't realize…"

*That it was all still so raw. That I was this fragile. That my mother, and Devin's pregnancy, could bring all of this rushing right back to the surface. That I couldn't win this battle anymore.*

"I did," Mack says. "I've felt it on you since the day we were in your storage locker with the Christmas mug."

"How?" I croak.

"I told you, Charlie. I see you. And–" He pauses, frowns.

I lift my cheek from his chest so I can look up at him. *Yes?*

He absently strokes my cheek and brushes his thumb along my jaw and then my lower lip. His brow furrows, and he lets his hand fall. "I feel like you need rest."

My eyes flutter with exhaustion. He's not wrong. But God, I don't want to be alone. He helps me to my feet, paying attention to every move I make as we walk down my hall together. I cast a longing look at the shower, wondering if I have the energy to take a quick shower before I collapse into bed.

And my dirty sheets.

*Shit.*

Mack moves into my bedroom ahead of me, and I start apologizing for the messy bed. I tell him I want to change the sheets, and he watches me like I've sprouted a second head as I go on a ramble about everything I *should* and *need* to do right now before I can lie down. I tell him I need to shower as I begin stripping the sheets off my bed. I tell him that I've been decaying in my own bodily fluids all day. That he showed up at just the right time to save me from myself.

"I'll run you a bath," he offers.

Mid-strip of a pillowcase, I freeze.

"Not a bath kind of girl?" he asks.

My nervous system transports me back to the night Daniel ran my bath for me. It was the last time I was in a tub. Unwilling to let myself slip away into the insanity of grief all over again, I yank my thoughts back to my messy bedroom and drop the pillow out of the case. "I prefer showers."

He disappears into my bathroom, and I continue stripping the bed. I hear the shower turn on. My blood runs cold even as hot steam pours out the open door.

*Maybe this is a bad idea.*

"Actually," I call over the sound of the water hitting the bottom of my marble-tiled shower, "I think maybe I'll just crash on the sofa and forgo the shower. I can–"

Mack comes out of the bathroom with no shirt on.

"What the…?" I breathe.

*Does he think he's about to get lucky right now?!*

He looks down at himself and quickly back up at me. "I've never tried to operate such a fancy shower with so many faucets and switches. I got soaked."

I was too preoccupied with the sight of his abs, swollen chest muscles, round and defined shoulders, and the dark hair spread across his chest to notice that his hair is wet and so are parts of his jeans.

I smile–something I never imagined possible after the breakdown I just had. "It's a bit obnoxious, isn't it? I thought I'd be obsessed with the custom features when I put an offer in on this place, but really, it's more trouble than it's worth. I never use half of them."

"Hop in," he says, hooking his thumb toward the bathroom. "I'll take over here."

I look down at my salty sheets. "Erm. I'd rather you not."

"Fine." He shrugs and leans against the doorframe to the bathroom. "I'll watch you strip and get in the shower, then."

My cheeks burn furiously. "You will not."

"Then I suggest you let me make your bed."

Grudgingly, I let him nudge me out of my own bedroom, and I slip into the bathroom, where I undress and get under the spray of hot and perfectly pressured water. I scrub myself relentlessly, like I can wash away the grit of my sweat, and tears, *and* the thrumming emotions still running through my body. I can't, but it's worth a shot anyway.

Once I'm dry, I wrap myself up in the robe I keep in my bathroom and return to my bedroom, where I find my bed decently made in fresh sheets from my linen closet. It's not as precise a job as I'd have done, but for a guy like Mack, it's impressive. He's not in the bedroom, so I move down the hall to the kitchen, where I find him on the phone talking under his breath.

"I can't tonight," he says gruffly. "You'll have to get somebody else."

There is a moment of pause where someone says something on the other end.

Mack just grunts.

They say something else.

"Look, I don't really give a damn what you're going to have to do to cover for me," Mack says. "I can't come in."

He hangs up the phone and turns to find me standing there in my robe. He looks me over slowly, his eyes taking slow account of my bare legs and the sash around my waist.

Part of me feels obligated to tell him he can go. If someone else needs him, presumably work, he doesn't owe it to me to stay here in my doom-and-gloom condo. But the thought of him leaving makes me feel like I've been run through. After bursting open like I did, I still feel like I need him here to help hold me together while my wounds heal.

Or at least start to close.

Mack moves to me and stops when he's mere inches away. I breathe him in, all cedar, and musk, and comfort. Perhaps he's not as foreign or off-limits as I have let myself believe. Perhaps he is as safe as it gets.

Perhaps.

He offers me a lopsided smile. "Do you want me to tuck you in?"

# CHAPTER TWENTY-ONE

WHEN I OPEN MY EYES, my bedroom is bright. Birds chirp outside. My room smells like clean laundry and my shampoo.

And cedar.

I swallow and become more aware of my body in the seconds that pass. Mack is asleep behind me. At least, I'm pretty sure he's asleep. His hand is draped over my hip, his touch warm and still. I can hear him breathing, a slow and steady rhythm of someone still in a dream world.

While I get my bearings, I take stock of the night after I showered. Mack came with me to my room and teasingly put me to bed like I was a child. He pulled the blankets up to my chin and crammed them around my shoulders, effectively trapping me in my own bed. He made me laugh; I'll give him that. Then he sat on the edge of my bed and told me his courtesy stops here, and he would not, in fact, be reading me a bedtime story.

I close my eyes and smile at the fuzzy memory of him sitting there, looking down at me, grinning like a fool. He looked so hand-some. If I wasn't on the verge of falling asleep, I might have tried to kiss him.

When he went to leave, I asked him not to. He silently agreed and laid down beside me so he could wrap me up in his arms and let me drift off to sleep. There was no drifting. I fell into oblivion within seconds.

I have no clue what time that was. Or what time it is now. The brightness of my bedroom suggests it might be close to eight or so in the morning. There are neighborhood sounds outside. The dog down the street is barking, like always. People are awake and going about their morning.

Except for us.

My phone suddenly buzzes from somewhere in my bedroom. Not my nightstand, where I usually keep it. Mack stirs and lifts his hand from my hip.

"Shit," I say sourly, throwing the blankets off and looking through my room to find my phone.

Mack rolls onto his back with a deep, content moan. "What time is it?"

"Not sure." I lift clothes from my floor to try to find my phone "Where the hell is it?"

He lifts his head from the pillow. "Your robe is open."

"What?!"

I look down at myself, discover I'm almost hanging out of my robe, and quickly wrap it up tighter. Luckily, no titty popped out. Or my lady bits. For fuck's sake.

Mack grins and lays his head back down. "This is a nice way to start the morning."

Scowling and holding my robe closed, I continue my search and find my phone on the bathroom counter. My boss is calling me. And it's ten in the morning, not eight. I should have been at work half an hour ago.

"Fuck, fuck, fuck!"

Mack lifts his head again.

I answer the phone. "Sheila. I'm so sorry. I overslept. I can be there in–"

"Don't worry about it, Charlie. I'm sorry, this isn't working out. I'm going to have to let you go. I can't have people on my team who

I need to cover shifts for like this. It's not fair to my other employees."

"Fair?" I echo. Sheila has no idea what unfair is. I do. Intimately. But that's not her burden to bear. So, I take a deep breath. "I understand. I wish you all the best. I'll drop my apron off later today."

"That would be great."

She ends the call.

Mack clasps his hands behind his head. His biceps stand at attention, and I pray to gods I don't believe in that an unnatural force might sweep in and rip the covers off so I can get a good look at the body he's hiding under the blankets. He never put his shirt back on last night. He'd gotten into bed with me half-naked. That stirs something to life just below my navel.

"That didn't sound good," he says.

"I just got fired, so no, not really."

He gestures around my bedroom. Sure, it's a bit of a mess, thank you, manic-depressive episode, but I know the mess isn't what he's pointing at. "You're not hurting for money," he says. "Who cares if you can't pour lattes anymore?"

I toss my phone onto the bed. "It was a good way for me to get my mind off things. Step back into society. Try to live like a normal person." I pick up my pillow and throw it at him, smiling. "Not that a guy like you knows anything about being a *normal* person."

He scoffs. "Boring."

Mack rolls out of bed abruptly, and my gaze catches on his back muscles as he turns away from me.

And then I look down at his ass.

He's wearing briefs. Tight. Black. Leaving little to the imagination.

When he turns to look at me, he catches me staring, looks down at his own ass over his shoulder, and hits me with a panty-dropping smile. "I'm not a piece of meat, Charlie."

My laugh catches me off guard.

Mack chuckles, grabs his jeans from the floor, and then goes to my bathroom to get his shirt. When he returns, he's fully dressed.

And I'm disappointed. His ass was just as perky as the pretty blonde nurse's at the hospital.

"Breakfast?" he asks.

***

Twenty minutes later, we sit across from each other on a sun washed patio, sipping lattes and studying the breakfast menu of a trendy spot down by the water. The day is already hot, and out in the inlet, people are taking to the water in their kayaks or on their paddleboards Children run around in neon bathing suits at the water park up the shoreline in the grassy area flanked by cypress and maple trees while their parents are hot on their heels, pleading with them to put sunscreen on.

Music pours out of speakers mounted on the exterior of the restaurant, and the server who checks on us bops her head to the beat of a Beach Boys song while she takes our eggs Benny orders.

Across from me, Mack looks like a man who didn't just suffer a horrible night with a woman he's not even getting lucky with. I hate the way the insecure thought ripples through me and leaves me fidgeting with the corner of the white tablecloth. I mean, what is a guy like him sticking around with a girl like me for? No matter which way I look at this, it's impossible to convince myself that he's genuinely into me. In our first weeks of knowing each other, I'd figuratively grabbed a fistful of red flags and smacked him on the nose with them.

*Whap. Whap. Whap.*

He leans back in his chair, reaches his arms up over his head, and cracks his back. The motion lifts the hemline of his shirt up, up, and up a tiny bit more, exposing abs that are impossible not to look at. And here I am, sitting in a loose top that used to hug all my curves, with pale skin practically untouched by the summer sun, with messy hair piled in a bun because I fell asleep with it wet last night.

So sexy.

Mack's attention drifts down to the inlet as he settles back in his chair. The sunlight sets his dark gaze ablaze in the most vibrant shade of brown I've ever seen as he drapes an arm over the back of the empty chair beside him.

"So what are you going to do about all this?" he asks.

I set my latte down after taking a delightful sip of espresso-flavored foam. "All what?"

"Your mom. Your sister. The baby." He stares at me blankly. "And how you're clearly not at a point where you can fake it till you make it. What's the plan?"

"Survive one day at a time until it all feels normal again?"

Mack arches an eyebrow.

"I don't know what else I can do, okay? My mom is right. Devin deserves better than to have her Wednesday Addams sister hanging over the happiest moment of her life. I don't want to ruin this for her. I don't want her to feel like she has to make me feel better all the time, or like she's on eggshells with me. I don't know." I rest my chin in my palm and watch children run through water features at the spray park. "Maybe I should keep my distance for the last month of her pregnancy and the first few weeks after the baby is here."

He shakes his head.

"You disagree?" I ask.

"Your sister lit up like a kid on Christmas morning when you showed up at the hospital. There's no way she feels like you're a burden or a downer. Not if she's reacting that way to you."

Okay. Well, I haven't thought of it like that.

"From where I was standing, it's pretty obvious she needs you," Mack says. "Is it possible the message is getting twisted by your mom? I'm not saying she's trying to cause a rift. But some people don't communicate well. Maybe Devin said something, and your mother heard it or interpreted it wrong."

"Are you trying to get a job as my shrink? I already have one of those, and she's very good at what she does."

He chuckles. "I'm just saying. Bailing on your sister now would probably do more harm than good. To both of you. As soon as you saw her, you chilled out too."

His objective view of the situation holds merit. Brett often tells me similar things about Devin and me, and he was her rock when Daniel died, and she didn't know how to show up for me. The loss of her brother-in-law broke her, too.

But nobody really knew how to grieve because he wasn't their husband. He was mine.

Maybe she and I need to have another conversation.

*Ugh.*

Our meals arrive, and Mack and I dig in. While we eat, we talk about things that don't matter–like how Simon has Mack booked all week long on grueling moving jobs with Dusty that are going to cripple him by the weekend. He tells me how he's also picked up some closing shifts at Dixie's to make up for the riffraff the night I was there. Apparently, he's walking on thin ice with that gig. The disappointment I feel at possibly not seeing much of him this week surprises me.

"What did you used to do for work before the restraining order?" I ask once our plates are gone, and we've paid the bill. Neither of us is inclined to leave yet.

He eyes me over the rim of his coffee mug as he takes a sip. Then, he sets it down. "What? You don't think I worked as a residential mover before my shiny reputation got tarnished?"

"No, I don't. And I don't think you were a bartender, either."

He shrugs. "You're not wrong."

I wait for him to answer and wonder if he's not going to.

Finally, he says, "I worked in security."

"Okay," I say slowly, waiting for him to elaborate when I know full-well he's not going to give me any more details than the bare minimum. So, I tighten the reins on my patience. "What kind of security? Cyber? Residential? Commercial?"

"Personal."

"For who?"

"Whoever was willing to pay for it."

I roll my eyes. "Having a conversation with you is like pulling teeth."

He sees my mug is empty and pushes up from the table. I follow him off the patio and down a poured concrete path that leads away from the restaurant and down to the inlet. We pass the children, the water park, and a pop-up lemonade stand.

"I worked as a private security detail for hire on a contract-by-contract basis. But that didn't sit right with my clients once my restraining order started showing up on background checks, so booking jobs became impossible. I moved on."

"What made you get into that line of work?"

"Why all the questions?"

"Why the resistance to answering them?" I push back.

He slides his hands in his pockets as we pass under the shade of a large maple with low branches that brush his hair. "It was a natural role for me," he explains. "I didn't have to answer to anyone, I took the jobs I wanted, and I had the chance to help people who didn't feel safe moving around Vancouver for whatever reason."

My mind snags on his final words. "*Whatever* reason?"

"I didn't ask a lot of questions. If they thought they needed protection getting from point A to point B, who was I to question them? The world is fucked up. Everyone could probably benefit from someone being paid to have their back these days."

I consider his words as we hook a left and find ourselves on the rocky shore of Burrard Inlet. Up ahead, a dock stretches out across the water like an arm trying to reach the other side of the inlet. Men throw fishing lines, children rush to the end in a game of tag, and couples stand at the railing admiring the view.

*He's wired to help people,* I think to myself as Mack picks up a rock and slingshots it across the water. Ripples fan out and jostle two ducks floating on the surface. One lets out a perturbed *squawk,* while the other tucks its beak into its back feathers and closes its eyes.

He tried to help his sister, and that cost him the lifestyle he'd built for himself.

He tried to help strangers, and they wouldn't take his help *because* he went to bat for Gia.

Now, he's trying to help me.

What price is there going to be for that good deed?

Maybe I need to stop worrying so much about what he wants and why he's choosing to spend his time with me. Maybe I need to focus on what choosing me might cost him.

Because, if history has proven anything, nobody cares about me without getting burned.

# CHAPTER TWENTY-TWO

A WEEK LATER, I sit with Mallory at the drive-in theater in the back of her pickup truck. They're playing *Grease*, and the music bops out of the speakers through the sliding window behind us as we lounge in the bed on an air mattress. We're loaded up with blankets, snacks, pillows, and pop, and I've filled her in on everything that happened with Mack.

And how I've been avoiding him all week.

"Poor fool," Mallory sighs.

"He's not a fool."

"Of course he is."

"By what metric?"

She lolls her head toward me instead of lifting it from her pillow. Her brow furrows, and her eyebrows seem to turn to liquid as they paint squiggly lines above her eyes. "Don't ask questions you already know the answers to."

Right. He's a man.

Smiling, I sink deeper into my pillows and reach for a bag of Reese's cups. I pop one in my mouth. "When I met him, I thought I was too good for him. Now, it's pretty obvious that it's the other way around. He's already had some pretty unfair setbacks in his life. I don't want to pile on and be another red mark on the list."

"Oh, shut up, Charlie. Not good enough for him? What's in that chocolate, delulu acid?"

"What's delulu?"

"You." Mallory shakes her head and watches the screen as Danny struts across it. "Delulu is believing that a basic man like Mack–no offense–could possibly be out of *your* league. He should be kissing the ground you walk upon. He should be on his knees every time he sees you. He should–"

"I get it."

"Do you? Because from where I'm sitting, I've been listening to a whole heck of a lot of bullshit over the last hour about how lowly my bestie thinks of herself. What's your therapist's name again?"

"Dr. Flagstaff. Why?"

"Because, clearly, she's not doing her job if you're having thoughts like this."

I smile and hand her the bag of chocolate, which she digs into. "She's not a hothead like someone I know. I talked to her about all of this the day before yesterday, and she thinks I'm being reasonable in stepping back from him."

Mallory rolls her eyes. "Screw reasonable. It's pretty obvious what you need, Charlie. And it's not space."

"Oh? Well, if you're so brilliant, do tell me what will cure me."

"Mack. And his dick. Inside you."

"Mallory!"

Someone in a vehicle next to us shushes me loudly. I shrink down so they can't see me over the box of the truck.

"Sex complicates everything," I hiss. "I'm too confused to have sex with him. I need to sort out how I feel, what I want, and what pace I want to go before I can take that plunge. And he's going to need to wait. I've only ever been with Daniel. I can't just give that to the next guy after him to show a little interest."

"You are the polar opposite of an orgasm, Charlie."

I wasn't sure what that meant, but I felt offended anyway, so I snatched the chocolate back. "Mine."

"Rip it off like a band aid. Call him. Fuck him. Wait, no, let him fuck you, see what he's really made of. And then you can decide if you want space or not. What if you spend weeks or months trying to figure out if you even like the guy, and after all that time and anticipation, he turns out to be a lame lay?"

"Sex isn't everything."

"Pfft. Yeah. Sure. Okay."

"I'm not ready," I press.

"You're never going to be. It's going to be like losing your virginity all over again. But you've done it before, and it only means something if you want it to. Maybe for once in your life you shouldn't overthink something, and you should just go for it. What's the worst that could happen?"

"I regret it."

"Okay. So what? You regret it. And you move on."

It all sounds so simple when she puts it like that, like sex isn't a soul-bonding experience to be shared between two people who love and trust each other. Like it doesn't belong only to lovers. Like it can be as casual and impulsive as going through a drive-thru when that burger craving hits.

But what happens if the craving never stops?

***

We drive home at two in the morning with the windows down and the cool summer air filling our lungs. Mallory cranks a Green Day song, and I close my eyes and tip my head back, trying to be as present as possible, but thoughts of Mack keep sneaking past my defenses.

Mack's ass in his boxer briefs last weekend.

Mack's abs when he lifts his arms over his head.

Mack's grip around my body when I was crumbling.

His scent. His strength. His unwavering patience.

But then all the reasons to continue avoiding him crash against me.

He's tangled up in trouble with his sister's husband, has mediocre employment, a traumatic history with a dead little sister, and he has a restraining order out on him. Is that really something I want to entertain?

I have my own baggage, and it's pretty damn heavy. I can't carry any more.

And yet…

My body aches for him. All of Mallory's talk made me blush, for sure, but it also planted seeds in my head that I can't shake. As we head down the highway for home, all I can think about is kissing Mack, telling him I trust him, and letting him take the lead.

Because it's true, I realize.

I do trust him.

"Mal," I hear myself say.

"Mm?"

"Can you take me to Dixie's?"

Mallory grins like the devil just settled into her bones. "Fuck yes, I can."

***

Mallory pulls around to the back lot of Dixie's, and lo and behold, Mack's truck is parked in the exact same spot it was last time.

Like fate.

I hop out of the passenger side and pause to shoot her a wink. "Wish me luck?"

"I wish you orgasms and bruises. No more. No less. Low stakes sex, babe. Just have fun!"

*Low stakes sex. Right. I can do that. Can't I?*

I close her door and hurry around to the front of the bar, where I flash my ID to a security guard and get in with no problems. The place isn't all that busy on a Tuesday evening, but there are some older couples on the dance floor showing off their moves to some Chris Stapleton song. I make my way to the bar, but there is no sign of Mack.

There is a sign of the pretty server Mallory has the hots for though, so I ask if she's seen him.

"He's in the back," she says. "Should I get him for you?"

"Can you tell him to meet me at his truck?"

She nods. "Can do."

I'm back outside and leaning against Mack's truck in less than two minutes. The music changes to something more upbeat and pop inside, and it gets a little louder when the back door swings open, and Mack strides out. He has a towel over one shoulder, and he's wearing black jeans and a black shirt with the sleeves rolled up. As per always, he has his Blundstones on, and he walks toward me with purpose. When he gets close enough for me to make out his features, I can see he's smirking at me.

"Where have you been?" he asks, stopping a few feet away and hooking his thumb into the pocket of his jeans. "Avoiding me?"

"No." I wet my lips. "Maybe."

"Last weekend was intense. I figured maybe you needed some space."

"I did. And now I don't."

Mack's gaze rakes over me, and for the first time I realize I've come all the way here for sexy times... and I'm wearing sweatpants with a missing draw string and an oversized T-shirt.

Oops.

I feel my cheeks getting hot, and what felt like a good idea twenty minutes ago is now paralyzingly embarrassing. I'm like a yo-yo bouncing from one impulse to the other. On one hand, I feel like I should cut him off completely to protect myself *and* to protect him from the fatal car accident that getting into a relationship with me would become; on the other, I want to throw myself into his arms right this second and beg him to kiss me like he did the last time we stood in this very spot.

Like he needed me.

Like every second without his hands on my body was torture.

Like he owned me.

"Erm." I brush at my sweatpants and try to think of a good excuse as to why I'm wearing them. Nothing comes to mind. "I was at the drive-in theater with Mallory. That's why I look like a schmuck."

"You'd have to try a hell of a lot harder to look like a schmuck, Charlie."

Is he into this?

I fidget with the stretched-out waistband. "How much time do you have before you have to go back inside?"

"Enough."

"Enough to what?"

His gaze darkens, and he closes the space between us in two strides. "To do what you came here for."

There is no time to come up with a witty or flirty answer—not that I could have if I tried. His lips seal on mine, and with another step forward, he pins me against the truck. Without thinking, I lift one leg, and he hooks his hand under my knee and holds me to him.

"This is the part where we got interrupted last time," he says, breaking our kiss and looking down at me with heat burning in his eyes. "If you want me to stop, you just have to say so."

"No. I want this."

*I want you.*

He waits a beat, as if he's giving me a moment to change my mind, or to see if my resolve will crack. When I stand firm, he devours my mouth with another kiss. His tongue explores me ravenously, and I yield, clinging to his shirt as my senses buzz and hum, and the gravel parking lot around us fades to white noise.

He grazes the top of my sweatpants with his fingers. When his hand disappears beneath the fabric, I let out a gasp, but he doesn't stop to give me any time to think. This time, he's pushing forward, and I'm along for the ride as he rubs me over my panties. I'm already wet and aching all over, and he's barely touched me.

"This is exactly what I need," I whisper, letting my head rest against his truck as he tugs my panties aside. The panicked voice I expect might scream at me about betraying Daniel in this moment stays quiet. I'm grateful for that because this feels too damn good to stop.

My pulse quickens as he runs his fingers over my clit. My whole body trembles, and he smiles like the devil as he teases me.

"Tell me what you need," he purrs.

And then he presses a finger inside me.

I gasp and clutch at his shoulders to hold myself up. It has been *so* long since I felt any sort of pleasure like this. I'd let myself believe I didn't deserve this kind of sensation anymore–that my time feeling the heat of desire had ended when Daniel's life did.

But this euphoria sets all those resignations ablaze, and they turn to ash in my mind.

*This. Is. Divine.*

His finger presses into every part of me, exploring, gentle and steady, until he finds a rhythm that makes me squirm on the tips of my toes. He seems to like it because a soft chuckle rumbles out of him.

"I said," he growls, "tell me what you need."

He wants me to talk? Now? How can I?

His fingers still. "Tell me."

Chasing the high of the pleasure, and yearning for him to continue, I find my voice. "I need *this*. I need to go for it. Rip it off." I gasp as he fills me with another finger. *Oh God.* "I need you to fuck me so I can get it over with."

Suddenly, I'm empty.

Mack steps back. "Get it over with?"

I slump against his truck with a lust-drunk smile. "I have to stop overthinking it. I just need you to fuck me. Right here. In your truck. I don't even care. I have to stop being so precious about it."

He frowns.

"What?" I push off the truck and reach for his fly. "Are you going to play hard to get now? Haven't I done enough of that for the both of us?"

"Charlie," he says, pushing my hand away.

"What?"

He shakes his head. "Never mind. I should get back inside."

I blink several times. "Wait, what?"

"You should go home."

Home?

Just like that?

*Shit.*

"Fine." I march past him, clipping his shoulder with mine. "This was a one-time offer. You can bet your ass–" his perfect, firm, perky ass– "that I will not be coming back and throwing myself at you like this again."

I hear his boot crunch as he turns around, but he's not following me. "I'm not interested in fucking you like ripping a band aid off," he calls after me. Employees who are smoking in the covered section near the emergency exit sign look up, the embers on the end of their cigarettes illuminating their faces as they take drags and watch the show. "Stop right there, Charlie."

His voice is a command.

I turn and look over my shoulder, my blood pressure spiking, my vision tunneling in on him.

He points at me. "You can get the stick out of your ass and stop acting like a brat who didn't get what she wanted. You think you can use me to fix whatever is fucked up inside you? Not happening." He marches toward me. "When I fuck you, it's going to be on my terms, and I sure as hell am not going to accept anything other than complete and total submission from you. Do you fucking understand?"

This is a version of Mack that's new to me.

And it's pissing me off.

I laugh in his face. "Submission? Who do you think you are?"

"I was good enough to have my fingers inside you two seconds ago." He glares down his nose at me. "What's wrong, princess? Is this how you act when you don't get what you want?"

What I want is to hit him. Right in the bridge of the nose. *Hard.* But I just bite my tongue and seethe in silence with my shoulders inching closer to my ears. Every muscle in my body is tense and humming for release. An orgasm, a scream, a punch–any of the three would work.

But all three are totally inappropriate right now.

"You're an asshole," I say.

He just shrugs. "Fine by me. I'm not the one who tried to use someone to get off. Or as a distraction."

His words sting.

Mostly because they're true.

I flee before I dig a deeper hole and embarrass myself further. The shame closes in on me as I skirt around the side of Dixie's, too humiliated to walk past the smoking employees.

A single thought turns the shame up higher.

*What would Daniel think if he could see me right now?*

# CHAPTER TWENTY-THREE

MOM DELICATELY PICKS up her buttered corn on the cob with her pinkies sticking up in the air. In front of her, her plate of barbecued chicken skewers and vegetables steams. She takes a bite of corn and promptly drops it back on her plate, cursing how hot it is and sticking her finger in her mouth to try to suck away the burn.

Across from her, Dad shakes his head. "It just came off the grill, Deidra."

She sips her icy cold lemonade. "I know that, Lee."

I push my vegetables around on my plate with my fork. Across from me, Devin is inhaling her food regardless of the burn. She has to lean over her own belly to try to hold her food over her plate so as not to make a mess. When that fails, she ends up placing the plate on her stomach and using it as a table.

Beside her, Brett catches my eye and gives me the most minuscule shake of his head possible.

I know exactly what he's trying to tell me: *Don't say a word.*

I smile and look down, leaving Devin to eat her meal like a bear after a long season of hibernation.

Brett clears his throat. "Thanks for the impromptu dinner invite. Saved us having to grocery shop today."

Devin nods with a mouthful of corn.

Mom tips her head at Brett. "Our pleasure. We only have so many evenings like this left before we have another family member at the table with us." She makes a sound in the back of her throat that sounds like a rodent being squeezed really tightly. "I just can't wait. I know you're uncomfortable, honey," she adds when Devin shifts in her chair, "but as soon as baby is here, you'll forget all about the aches and pains, and all you'll feel is love."

"Right now, all I feel is pressure." Devin licks her lips and puts her now empty plate back on the table. "And the never-ending need to pee."

"Okay," Dad chuckles softly. "Maybe not appropriate dinner talk."

"Don't be a prude," I say.

Everyone looks at me.

"What?" I ask.

Ever since Mom told me I needed to reel it in with Devin, it feels like my whole family has been walking on eggshells. I briefly entertained talking to Devin like Mack suggested I should, but after our dismal encounter in the Dixie's parking lot, I started questioning if I really wanted to take advice from a guy who wanted me to be 'submissive.' Yuck. What did he know about sisterly relationships, anyway? Or motherhood? Or miscarriage?

Nothing. That's what.

Mack and I haven't spoken since that night, which was well over a week ago. Devin's due date is three days away, but she isn't showing any signs of going into labor yet, much to her dismay. Brett has been her saving grace through it all. As her patience thins instead of her cervix, he's been doing everything he can to keep her spirits up. His paternity leave won't be effective until the day she goes into labor, but he's cashed in on some vacation days to take this past week off and help get the house ready.

I've said it once, and I'll say it again. Brett is one of the good ones.

The best ones, actually. Like Daniel.

God. What I would give for him to be sitting at this dinner table with us. He'd be beside me in the empty spot that haunts me every time I sit at a table. His hand would probably be on my thigh or the back of my chair, and he'd easily enjoy the conversation as it shifts from one topic to the other. He'd take the heat off me and Devin by laughing at Mom's stupid jokes and acting engrossed in conversations with my dad about work. When our meal was done, he and I would clear the table so we could gossip in the kitchen while we did the dishes. He called it a sanity break.

I need one of those now more than ever.

As Mom unloads all her excitement on my fatigued sister, I collect the dishes and do them by myself. I scrape scraps into the food waste bin under the sink, rinse the plates, and line them up in my parent's dishwasher. I scrub the pots and pans and set them on a drying rack on the counter and rinse the sink out before wiping down the counters. Then, alone in the kitchen of the house I grew up in, I gaze out the window to the patio where my family sits.

Where they laugh.

Where they make plans for their futures.

*Where do I fit into all of this now?*

Back outside, I top up everyone's lemonade from the pitcher in the middle of the table. Mom is gushing over a picture Devin is showing her of the outfit she bought for baby to come home from the hospital in. It's gender neutral, apparently–yellow, by the sounds of it.

Devin doesn't ask if I want to see it, and I don't ask her to show it to me.

I'm not sure if that's strange or not.

Sighing, I return to the kitchen, a safer place than the patio right now, and get distracted by photos trapped under magnets on the refrigerator. I pause to inspect them and find myself smiling at photos of Daniel on our wedding day. He has a cigar hanging out the side of his mouth, and his arms are draped over my dad's shoulders and my uncle Gary's, Dad's brother. Daniel never liked the picture, or hardly any of our wedding pictures, because his barber botched his haircut three days before the wedding. He thought the cut made him look boyish. But I don't see the haircut. I just see three huge smiles. All three of them were well into their drinks by that point of the evening, and I can see by their eyes that they're drunk, but they're all pretty damn happy, too.

Best night of my life.

"Are you good in here?"

I yelp and spin to find Devin waddling through the sliding patio door. She gives me an apologetic smile. "I didn't mean to scare you."

"I'm fine. Just..."

She looks at the fridge and waddles over to look at Daniel. She puts her fingers gently on the corner of the photo. "I think this was taken a few minutes before Uncle Gary tripped over one of the power cords for the DJ booth and knocked over your whole champagne tower."

Laughter bubbles out of me at the memory of poor Uncle Gary lying on his back on the dance floor covered in champagne. Daniel keeled over and nearly broke a rib, he was laughing so hard. There is a photo somewhere in the ether of the aftermath, but I've long since lost it. Some extended family member or another probably has it on their Facebook.

Devin lets her hand fall from the picture, and she shifts her weight from one foot to the other.

I look down at her belly. "How are you feeling?"

"Fat. Pregnant. Swollen. Hungry all the time but also feeling too full to eat more than a few bites at once. Irritable. Impatient. Tired." She turns away from the fridge so she can lean against it. "And everyone keeps telling me to get my sleep now because it will be impossible once the baby comes. Why do people say shit like that?"

"Because people are garbage."

"Straight up."

I lean on the island across from her. "How's Brett? Any jitters?"

"He's cool as a cucumber, which shouldn't annoy me, but it does. Where does he get off being so chill about everything? I'm about to push a watermelon out of my coochie, and he's playing whale sounds at night to try to help me get into a 'Zen state.'"

I burst out laughing and let out a snort. "You're not a whale sounds kind of girl."

"Precisely. I'm an impenetrable silence kind of girl. And blackout curtains. And not being touched."

"Poor Brett."

"Poor Brett nothing," she says. "He doesn't have the most daunting task ahead of him. I'm shit scared, Charlie. What if I can't do it?"

"Give birth?"

Devin nods, and for the first time since we were literal children, I see fear in her eyes.

"Oh, Dev," I say softly, reaching for her and wrapping her in a hug. "You'd be a true freak if you *weren't* scared. You're about to bring life into the world. It's terrifying! But you're the strongest person I know, and there isn't a doubt in my mind that you can do this. And you're going to be wonderful at it. *Way* better than Mom, at least." I wink.

Devin laughs.

And then her eyes widen in surprise.

"What? Is she behind me?" I look over my shoulder to make sure my mother didn't hear the jab I just took at her, but nobody is there. So I turn back to Devin, who is now looking down at the floor. I frown and follow her gaze down. "What's the matter? Oh... shit."

A puddle of water is between her feet, and more water is continuing to drip from under her dress.

Devin grabs hold of both my upper arms and holds on for dear life. "Charlie," she whimpers. "The doctor said it never happens like this in real life!"

"It's okay," I say, more to myself than to her. "It's better than okay. It's perfect. Dev, you're going to have your baby soon. Hello deli cuts and sushi!"

She lets out a shaky laugh and holds me tighter. "I need Brett."

I turn my head over my shoulder again and yell Brett's name at the top of my lungs.

"Subtle, Charlie, real subtle," Devin says, and then she winces.

"You good?"

She takes a deep breath with her eyes closed. "I think I just felt a contraction."

Brett comes stumbling through the sliding doors. "Is someone hurt?"

"Nope," I say, my stomach rolling with anticipation, my palms sweating with nerves. "But your wife is in labor."

Brett stands there like a deer in the headlights. "But it's not even her due date yet. We have more time."

"You sure don't," I say. "You get her to the hospital; I'll go to your place and get your hospital bags. *Again,*" I add.

"They're in the trunk already," Brett says. "We don't go anywhere without them. Okay. Okay. Breathe, Dev." He takes my place in front of my sister and holds her face in his hands with so much love in his eyes, the tidal wave of joy I feel for my sister threatens to wash me all the way out of the kitchen and back onto the patio. He strokes her cheeks with his thumbs, and his eyes fill with tears. "We're going to have our baby today."

Devin is shaky but smiling as she turns to me. "Charlie, I need you to do me one last favor. Please? It's important."

"Of course."

"Don't try to keep it together for my sake, okay? If this hurts you, then it hurts you. And that's okay. Like I said. I'm strong. I can feel the joy and the grief of this at the same time. You believe me, right?"

I search her eyes. "I..."

My parents burst inside, and chaos descends upon us. Amidst the rush of my mother bombarding Devin and everyone starting to hustle her out to the car, my sister reaches between Brett and our dad to grab my hand and squeeze. I squeeze back before letting go, and I wait at the front door while Brett gets her in the car, and they drive off, leaving my parents frantically trying to figure out their next steps in the driveway.

*You've got this, Dev,* I think.

And then I pray to a God I don't even believe in that my sister and her baby stay safe.

# CHAPTER TWENTY-FOUR

Elton John plays softly through someone's headphones in the hospital waiting room. Powder-green walls clash with muted magenta chairs with peeling plastic seats that stick to my bare legs every time I move. It smells like stale coffee and cleaning products, but this section of the hospital has a pleasant buzz of excitement to it. It's not an ICU or NICU.

It's just a waiting room for families ready to meet their next family member.

My knee bounces restlessly as I wait. I've been here for three hours. Maybe four? Mom and Dad are down at the cafeteria grabbing us sandwiches and tea. Brett came out to update us once, but he was like the Flash, here one second and gone the next. He reported that Devin was in good spirits and still hadn't opted for her epidural. He grinned like an idiot and told us she was a powerhouse and doing great. Then he rushed back to her side–as he should.

This is the first time I've been alone.

I don't like it.

My thoughts get the better of me every thirty or so seconds, and I have to fight tooth and nail to bring them back to reality.

Devin will be okay. There will be no more funerals.

Just life.

Attempting to ground myself within my body, I do a few things Dr. Flagstaff taught me to stay present. I close my eyes and inhale deeply several times, filling my lungs and releasing as I pull focus on what I can smell–the stale coffee, cleaning products, and someone's perfume in the waiting room that reminds me of how my grandmother always used to smell at Christmas when she doused herself in clove essential oils. I pay attention to the chair at my back and how it's stuck to the back of my thighs. My sweaty feet in my sandals. My pulse in my ears. The murmur of conversation around me. The clacking of someone typing at the nearest nurses' desk.

Feeling a bit more centered, I open my eyes just as Mom and Dad return. They're carrying cups of piping hot tea and a little bag of goodies from the cafeteria. Dad looks tired but happy, and Mom is as high-strung as she was when they left. She sets the bag down on the chair beside me and opens it up to pull things out and offer them to me one at a time.

"I wasn't sure what you'd want, sweetheart." She hands me a tuna sandwich. "There's also egg salad, chicken salad, turkey and swiss, ham and cheddar… I thought there was one more in here."

"Tuna is fine. Thank you."

She gives me a thin-lipped smile and meets my eyes. Then she piles everything back in the bag and sits beside me. She puts her hand on mine. "I love you, Charlie."

Dad sits down on my other side. He says nothing, but he puts his hand on my other one.

I feel my walls shooting up. There's no doubt in my mind they spent their entire walk to the cafeteria, their time in line, and their walk back talking about me and how I am feeling. How they can manage me. How they can keep the pain and the grief at bay long enough to make this moment the perfect picture they've had in their heads all these years. I get it. I had the same picture too.

"I love you guys too," I say.

We eat our sandwiches and wait.

And wait.

And wait some more.

The clock near the vending machines clicks and clicks until the hour hand has gone around several times over. By two in the morning, my niece or nephew still hasn't made their debut, and I've chewed off every bit of nail possible, leaving nothing but raw and puffy fingertips in the wake of my anxiety.

So I call Mallory.

Her voice is thick on the other end as I step out into the cool air of the summer night.

"Charlie? What's wrong? Did something happen?"

"Hey," I say, pacing back and forth in front of the main entrance of the hospital. "I'm sorry I woke you up. I just need to talk to someone who isn't my mom or dad for a minute. Can you give me a few?"

"Of course." I hear her shift in bed, the sheets rustling, and then the echoes in the background change, and I assume she's leaving her room. I wonder why, and then it occurs to me she might not be alone. Oops.

"Actually, it can wait. I can call you back in the morning when—"

"Don't be silly, Charlie. It's fine. I can talk. I'm just going to get some water and go sit on my porch. Tell me what's happening."

I share everything from the moment Devin's water broke, including every paralyzing fear that has coursed through my system since that moment. By the time I've word-vomited everything I can think of onto her, another fifteen or so minutes have passed.

"This is so exciting," Mallory says.

Okay. Not what I was expecting.

"Um, yes, it is," I say.

"That doesn't mean it's not scary, too. All your feelings sound perfectly reasonable to me."

"You're my best friend. You're supposed to say that. Especially when I'm in it."

"Do you want me to tell you something different?"

I look up at the night sky above. Stars are twinkling like they're putting on a show for my sister and her big night. Have they always sparkled like that? I hope Devin has a room with a window, and she can see how magical this night is.

Not that she'd care with the pain I'm sure she's in.

For some reason, I take the phone from my ear so I can snap a quick picture of the night sky above.

Then, I place the phone back to my ear. "No. I don't know. Maybe I don't need you to tell me anything. I just…"

"I can sit here with you as long as you need."

The walls I've kept up all night start to come down, piece by piece, like I'm gently laying them on the ground rather than letting them get knocked over. "Thanks."

"Do you want a distraction or quiet?"

"A distraction might help."

Mallory snickers. "Well, in that case, do I have a story for you." She launches into a tale about how she took the server at Dixie's out for dinner. "Her name is Sally–how cute is that? Anyway, I took her out for all-you-can-eat seafood, and she threw down like the good girl she is. We went for a walk, talked about all our hopes and dreams for our future, and I took her back to my place. I think I might be in love, Charlie."

Despite the tension and nerves still clinging to some of the corners of my insides, I manage a genuine smile. "Love, huh? And here I thought you'd be an eternal player knocking down chicks like bowling pins until you were looking at retirement homes in Florida."

"I would pull in a retirement home and you know it."

I burst out laughing. "I fucking love you, Mal."

"Anyone who has the pleasure of knowing me loves me, but not many get the honor of me loving them back. I love you too, Charlie. Now, serious question time. Do I tell Sally how I feel, or do I play a little hard to get?"

"Don't tell her you love her, you psychopath. It's too soon. You need to practice taking your time. It's not a bad thing to stretch the anticipation out. I know you're not precious about sex like I am, but maybe when your heart is involved, you could benefit from slowing down."

"Boo." Mallory chuckles softly. "Hey, speaking of sex... what ever happened when you went to Dixie's to climb Mack like a tree?"

I hesitate. It's too embarrassing to relive in my head, let alone say it all out loud. I kind of naively hoped I'd be able to pretend it hadn't happened. I'd been repressing the exchange all week long. Now, it feels like a distant memory, but I know that is only because Devin having her baby is taking up every ounce of real estate in my brain. Once things return to baseline and the baby is here, and I know my sister will be okay, I know Mack will come crawling back into my thoughts.

"Uh oh," Mallory says as my silence continues filling the line. "That bad, huh? Was he a bad lay? He didn't strike me as the sort of man who couldn't get down in a good way, you know? You just weren't into it? Did I push too hard? I'm sorry. I thought–"

"It wasn't your fault. I threw myself at him, and he rejected me."

Mallory gasps dramatically. "How dare he."

I explain how it all went down, filling her in on the ludicrous things he said about making me be submissive.

Mallory is quiet for a moment.

"Say whatever you're thinking, Mal."

"I've said it once, and I'll say it again... it's kind of hot, Charlie. In a really confusing way because fuck a man telling you to be submissive. But also... *fuck* a man who makes you *want* to be submissive."

"You're a freak."

"Sally agrees."

It's impossible to have a serious conversation with Mallory without smiling, so even talking about one of my most humiliating moments of all time, my cheeks are hurting. "He's an ass. I think I'm officially done with him. It was a fun glimpse at what could be, and that maybe I do have room to catch feelings after Daniel. But with someone who isn't Mack."

"Fair enough."

*Yeah, if only it* felt *fair.*

The hospital door opens behind me, and I glance over my shoulder out of reflex more than anything. My dad stands there, grinning so big I can see almost all his teeth. His cheeks are rosy, his eyes glassy, and I can tell he's been crying.

"Baby's here," he breathes. "You coming, or what?"

My heart leaps into my throat. "Mal, I have to go."

"Give that baby a snuggle for me, Charlie. Call me back if you need to. I love you. You've got this. Go be in the moment. *This* moment. Promise?"

My dad's smile is contagious, and I find myself grinning too. "I promise."

# CHAPTER TWENTY-FIVE

THE MATERNITY WARD is eerily quiet as Dad and I hurry down the hall, past the nurses' desk, past other rooms of fresh parents, and stop outside Devin and Brett's room. There is a sink outside their door, and we both wash our hands diligently before Dad steps into the room ahead of me.

I catch myself at the threshold like I've walked into an invisible wall.

*You can do this,* I tell myself. *Everyone is okay. Everyone is healthy. There are no bad vibes in this room. Just life. Just life. Just life.*

I step in.

A small fan propped in the corner hums. It's pointed at the hospital bed, where my sister lays propped up with a pillow she brought from home. The case is decorated in tiny embroidered flowers; roses, daisies, and tulips. My sister's hair is a tangled mess pulled into the messiest bun I've ever seen on top of her head. Some strands are sticking out and greasy with dried sweat from all the work she just did. She's wearing a mint-colored robe, and she's puffy and swollen as she looks down at the sleeping bundle in her arms.

Brett sits beside her, his chair drawn up to the bed as close as he can get it. His knees look crushed, but if he's uncomfortable, I can't tell, because he's smiling and weeping like a little boy on Christmas morning who just got the best gift of all. His hand rests on the bundle in Devin's arms, and I watch, entranced, as he lifts his pinky finger. Tiny little fingers are wrapped around his digit.

Mom turns into a puddle of tears at the sight.

Beside me, Dad wraps his arm around my shoulder and holds on with fierce strength. It catches me a little off guard. He hasn't held me like this in well over a year. After Daniel died, Dad used to hug me like he was holding all my pieces together. But life moves on, and the fierceness fades as people return to their normal routines.

I haven't realized how much his hugs ease the chaos in me.

"We're on the other side of it now," Dad says softly, just to me and me alone. "They're all right. We're all right." He looks down at me. "Right?"

I rest my head on his shoulder. "I think so."

Devin manages to tear her eyes off her child long enough to notice I've come into the room. She beams, radiant and exhausted all at once, and reaches one hand out to me. "Are you ready?"

*No.*

*Yes.*

*I want to be.*

I inch toward the bed. Devin shifts, preparing to hold her baby out to me. I'm almost at her side. On the other side of the bed, Mom and Brett watch, and time seems to slow down.

*This is going to hurt so bad.*

At my sister's side, I look down into the bundle of blankets. Nestled amongst the soft blue fabric is the most precious child I've ever seen, with shocking dark hair, deep reddish-purple skin, tiny fingers and toes, and the tiniest upturned nose I've ever seen.

Something inside me fractures but doesn't break.

I hold my breath as Devin holds her baby out to me. Slowly, carefully, and with full knowledge that I am taking the most precious thing in the world into my arms, I accept the offer, scoop the baby up, gather them close, and stare into their perfect face.

I hear myself speak. "Who are you?"

Devin wipes tears from her cheeks. "Auntie Charlie, this is your nephew, Jameson Charlie Warren."

Mom's head snaps to Devin. "Charlie?"

Devin sniffles and nods, the tears flowing freely now. "We wanted to give him the name of the strongest person we know. It was an easy choice."

Brett nods, gets to his feet, and comes to my side to look down into the face of his perfect son. "We know you never really liked your name," he says, speaking to me like I'm the only person in the room. "Maybe this changes that?"

The fracture in my chest continues to grow.

My parents were under the impression through their entire pregnancy with me that I was a boy. They painted my nursery blue, bought dinosaur-patterned onesies, and daydreamed about what raising a son might be like. My father fantasized about throwing a baseball around the backyard and teaching me to ride my bike. My mother imagined a son who would grow into a man she could call whenever she needed help–and he would come running.

But they got me instead.

Dad and I still played catch in the yard, he still taught me to ride a bike, and they never made me feel like I was a letdown compared to the son they thought they were going to have.

But they never changed my name. They kept the boy name they'd fallen in love with when Mom was six months pregnant.

Now, my nephew shares the name that has always felt like it never really belonged to me. Not fully.

"Jameson," I breathe, gently tracing one of his puffy cheeks and running my finger into his hair. "You are perfect."

The fracture keeps spreading. Fraying. Cracking. I want to glue it all back together, but I know I can't–not when I'm looking into the face of a little boy who is going to have a life full of love, of hopes and dreams, of chances, of heartbreaks, of firsts, of lasts... of everything my child didn't get.

I hate the claws of resentment that sink into me. They're sharp, and curved, and they belong to a predator I'm all too familiar with that has been eating little pieces of me for three years. It's an angry creature. It feels like smoke is filling up my organs as the claws dig in deeper, and the beast takes a bite out of my heart. It's hard to breathe, and the hospital room feels intensely hot all of a sudden.

Devin's eyes widen with surprise as I push her baby back into her hands.

"Charlie?"

I'm not sure who spoke to me–one of my parents, my sister, or Brett. All I know is that all four of them are staring at me. They have no idea that at any moment the monster inside me is going to open its jaws wide and try to swallow them all whole.

I have to get out.

*Run.*

Before I can get a word out, my mother is at my side with a steady hand on my arm. "Sit down, Charlie."

Sitting means I have to stay. I shake my head.

"*Sit,*" she says sternly.

A chair appears behind me, thanks to my dad, and I collapse into it.

On the other side of the bed, Brett watches me with a furrowed brow and white knuckles as he holds the bed rail. Can he see the beast inside? Can he feel it? Does he know it's about to take over?

I don't want to implode. Not here. Devin doesn't deserve it. I would lose so much progress she and I have made. I can't risk that. So, I meet Brett's eyes, and I hope he can feel my desperation as he stares back at me.

He gets to his feet. "Charlie?"

"Yes?" My voice is a plea. Pathetic. Weak. Desperate.

*Please save me.*

"Can I talk to you in the hall for a minute?"

"Yes," I say again, standing.

My mother reaches for me, but Brett grabs my hand and leads me out into the hallway. It's several degrees cooler out here. There isn't a baby in sight. The only people watching us are strangers, and I've gotten quite used to letting strangers think whatever the hell they're going to think about me. Meltdowns in grocery stores or my own front lawn over the last three years have made sure of that.

Brett puts his hand between my shoulders and encourages me to keep walking when I stop a few feet outside the door.

"Where are we going?" I ask.

He has his phone out and is typing away with one hand. "I'm calling you an Uber, and you're going home."

"Brett, I'm sorry, I didn't want to ruin anything. I didn't mean to be the Debbie Downer. I… fuck."

He stops, slides his phone back in his pocket, holds me at arm's length, and looks me dead in the eyes. "Listen, I say this with all the love in the world, okay? I need you to hear it. Can you hear something hard right now?"

I search his eyes. I trust this man. I always have. "Yes."

"You don't have the power to ruin this, Charlie. This is bigger than all of us. You don't have to put on a brave face for me or Devin. I don't give a damn what your mother has told you, or what she's told Devin, or what perfect picture she's trying to create. Perfect isn't real. This? Your broken heart? *That's* real." His jaw is tight, and his resolve is evident. "Devin's and my joy is real, too. You don't have to be on the same page as us to be part of this. It's okay to need to leave. It's okay to cry. It's okay to rage against how fucking unfair this is. I'm still raging with you. Daniel was my friend." His voice cracks, and his mouth twists before he can draw his emotions back under control.

I want to look away because it would be easier, but I don't. His hold on me is grounding.

"I miss him every fucking day, not just for you, but for me, too. He would be all hands on deck tonight. He'd be right in there, teasing me as a new dad, bringing Devin some ridiculous push present that would piss me off because he spent more money than I did–" he breaks off, chuckling at the conjurings of his own daydream. "Daniel would be the light in the room that we all need right now. But he's gone. So, we need to find new ways to let the light in. And if we can't, it's okay to step back and catch our breath. So please, don't feel bad.

This is a lot. We understand. I'll tell your parents you left. But I'll give you a head start," he adds with a classic Brett smile.

I crumble and throw my arms around him.

It catches him off guard, and he stands stone-still for a moment before wrapping his arms around me. His hug is brotherly and warm. Safe.

"Thank you," I whisper. He has no idea the gift he just gave me. The permission to leave without guilt, and to be seen for how badly I'm hurting, makes the monster inside a little quieter. The claws withdraw. The jaws close. And I can breathe again.

"Go," he says, breaking the hug. "Before your mom comes out here and says something we can't unhear."

I go.

# CHAPTER TWENTY-SIX

T HE BAR IS a far cry from the kind of place I would usually go.

But the places I would usually go are all closed. And for good reason. It's three-thirty in the morning. Functioning adults are in bed, where they should be, not at dingy hole-in-the-wall bars drinking beer out of dirty sleeves and eating peanuts out of silver bowls that everyone has had their hands in.

I shift on the uncomfortable barstool and order another martini. They taste like shit in this bar. They're not cold, but they're strong enough to take the edge off the night.

Instead of going home, I told the Uber Brett ordered for me to take me somewhere I could get drunk. When we pulled up outside the Lion, I almost changed my mind. A girl like me isn't built for a place like this. Bars like the Lion are reserved for bikers, rejects, assholes, and men with poor hygiene.

It doesn't matter. I'm not here to make friends. I'm here to keep the monster at bay.

Four martinis does the trick.

Midway through ordering my fifth drink, I spot a familiar man near one of the pool tables. He has a puffed-up chest, broad shoulders, a receding hairline, phase one of a beer belly, and he looks like he smells of nicotine.

I remember who he is.

Clayton.

Gia's husband.

He paces around the pool table to scope out his next shot. The big oaf calls a pocket before swaying drunkenly on the spot and leaning into the wall for support. Clayton pushes off, aims his shot with his pool cue, and strikes the ball clean off the table and onto the floor. He lets out a bellow of a curse before bursting into booming laughter that has almost everyone glancing in his direction.

Clayton throws both hands in the air, accidentally dropping the pool cue with a clatter. "I win, fuckers!"

The disgruntled pushback from the other men near the table suggests Clayton did not, in fact, win.

I continue watching Clayton and his little charade while I sip my fifth martini. It's unpleasant, but effective, and the bar begins to get a little murky, like I'm seeing everything under water. The dulling of my senses is welcome because I'm finally not picturing Jameson in my mind anymore and wondering if my baby would have looked like him or not.

The door to the bar opens, and I'm stunned when morning light trickles in before it promptly swings closed again. It's morning already?

A petite young woman with short hair walks in, and I do a double take.

It's Gia.

She's wearing pajama pants and a tank top, and she walks in like she's been here a thousand times over. Which, I suppose with an alcoholic asshole husband, she probably has been. She marches over to Clayton, who lifts up his nose when he spots her, and she says something to him that is probably along the lines of, "It's time to go home."

Whatever it is she says, it pisses him off.

He shoos her off with a wave of his hand. "Piss off, bitch. Can't you see I'm in the middle of a game?"

Gia flinches.

Clayton seems to find this amusing, and he gets in her space even more. She's so small compared to him. Her nose is level with his chest.

"Go wait in the car," he tells her.

Gia looks around at the men watching her. Then her gaze lands on me, and her eyes widen in surprise. I freeze with my martini halfway to my lips, and she frowns at me—like she has any right judging me for being in a skeezy place like this when her husband probably spends more time here than he does at home.

She turns back to Clayton. This time, I can hear her words as she speaks. "I'm going home. You can stay, but if you need a ride, you'll need to call a taxi."

She steps away from him to leave.

Clayton catches her upper arm. "The fuck did you just say to me, woman?"

She looks down at his hand on her arm.

He pulls her in closer. "I asked you a fucking question."

She looks away. "I'll wait in the car."

"Good whore."

My pulse races. The monster is back, but this time, I don't feel like I need to keep it locked in a cage. I feel like I can open the door, bare my fangs, and finally let the anger out all the way.

I slide off my barstool.

Gia pulls her arm free of Clayton's grasp. His fingers leave red imprints on her skin. She sees me coming and makes a dash for the door. She's gone.

"Hey, you," I call, walking in what I hope is a straight line but knowing in my heart of hearts I'm probably all over the place. My martini is still in my hand, so I take a sip.

Clayton spots me coming. He looks me up and down. I'm still in the jean shorts, sneakers, and plain T-shirt I wore to my parents' house for the barbecue last night.

"What do you want?" he demands.

The other men around the pool table are watching with drunken interest.

"You shouldn't talk to her like that," I tell him matter-of-factly.

He studies me a bit longer before his lips peel off his teeth in a jeering smile. "Why? You want me to talk to *you* like that instead? Are you the kind of girl who likes a man with a… firm hand?"

Bile climbs up the back of my throat.

Clayton keeps talking as he takes a few steps toward me. "Usually, I like 'em with a bit more meat on their bones, but you've got a pretty face. I can work with that."

I look around the bar. "Is this where you come to get away from yourself?"

He cocks his head.

"As far as shitholes go, this is about as bad as it gets," I say. "I bet everyone here pretends to be happy to see you when you walk in demanding drinks. I bet they all talk about you behind your back as soon as you leave. I bet you're known around here as the fat drunk asshole who beats the shit out of his wife. But a place like this is full of cowards. And lowlifes. And men who would never call you out to your face. But me? I will, you ugly, dirty, disgusting, pathetic excuse of a man."

The bar is silent except for the sound of the dishwasher running behind the bar and an old rock song on the speakers–half of which are not working.

Clayton just stares at me.

One of the men on the other side of the pool table snorts and starts laughing. "I think she has the hots for you, man."

Clayton glares daggers at me, but I just glare right back. What's he going to do? Hit me? Fine. I'll get a black eye and a huge payout. Fuck him. Fuck any man like him. Fuck the universe for letting an asshole like Clayton keep drinking himself into oblivion while a good man like Daniel gets killed by a drunk driver just like him.

"Karma already got you for all your sins," I tell Clayton, feeling brazen and unafraid and… inspired. It feels good to lash out. To hurt. And he deserves it, so what do I care? If there is one person I can take my anger out on and not feel any guilt about, it's this guy. "You think you can do whatever you want to whoever you want because you're a bully, but your life is sad and lonely, just like you deserve. Your wife is afraid of you. She doesn't obey you because she loves you. She obeys because she has no choice. You're not powerful. You're weak. The only way you can get a woman to touch you is to force her. To intimidate her. To make her feel like you're all she has when that is so not true."

"Shut up," he spits.

"No," I say simply. "You may be able to tell your wife to be quiet. But me?" I grin right back at him, just like how he smiled at me with that menacing sneer. "Nobody owns me. I have nothing to lose."

I don't know who this devil-may-care woman is, but right now, I kind of like her.

Clayton, on the other hand? He hates her with everything he has.

So I poke him again.

"Your daddy must have *hated* you," I say.

The bar explodes.

Clayton hurls his cue stick at me, and it misses my head by an inch. The bartender leaps into action and gets between me and Clayton, who comes barreling toward me with surprising speed for such a big man. Perhaps it was only surprising because I'm hammered. I don't flinch, I don't run, I just stay there like I've grown roots, watching as multiple men pile on Clayton's back to hold him back from getting to me.

It takes five of them to bring him down.

One of them glares over his shoulder at me. The bartender. "Get the hell out of here, and don't come back."

I shrug one shoulder, set my glass on the nearest table, turn, and walk out.

I feel nothing. No monster. No storm. No pain. No grief. No anger. Nothing.

And it feels fucking wonderful. So wonderful, I have half a mind to walk right back into the chaos and kick Clayton right in his fucking face. He deserves it. I mean, why shouldn't I? Justice comes in all shapes and forms. Why not in the shape of my sneaker leaving the form of the sole on his forehead?

A tiny voice of reason tells me to just go outside, and I listen, pushing out onto the sidewalk into the dim light of dusk, where I find Gia sobbing in the front seat of a burgundy Toyota Tercel.

I stop short.

The window is open, so I call her name softly. She peers at me between her fingers, quickly wipes away snot and tears, and wipes her hands on her pajama pants. I didn't notice when she was inside, but they're not in the nicest condition. Rips, holes, stains everywhere.

A loud yell sounds from inside, and glass smashes.

Gia goes rigid, and her eyes widen like a baby deer. "Did something happen?"

I give her a shit-eating grin. "I gave Clayton a taste of his own medicine."

All the color drains from her face. "Get in."

"I think I'll walk. I need to get this alcohol out of my system and–"

"Get in. Now!"

Another yell comes from inside, followed by more broken glass, and a full-blown brawl breaks out. Gia starts her engine, which rattles and groans, and black smoke plumes out of the exhaust pipe. She leans across the center console and throws open the passenger door.

I step off the curb to get in just as the bar door is thrown open, and Clayton is tossed out on his face.

Gia looks like she's just stepped into her own horror film.

He lifts his head slowly, sporting a bloody nose, split lip, and redness around his right eye. "*You,*" he growls. "Stay right where the fuck you are."

"Get in the car!" Gia practically screams.

Her terror cuts through my drunken haze, and a moment of clarity washes over me. I just provoked a diabolically abusive man, and now there is nothing between us but twelve feet of asphalt.

He pushes up to his knees, and I leap into the passenger seat. Gia hits the gas and pulls away from the curb, tires screeching, before I even have a chance to close my door. When I do, I look over my shoulder as Clayton runs out onto the street after us, shaking his fist in the air and cursing at us. He disappears when Gia takes a sharp right.

I grip the oh-shit handle on the roof and shoot her a lopsided smile. "You could get a job as a getaway driver. I bet you'd make enough money to open your cheesecake bakery."

Gia glares at the road ahead and white-knuckle the steering wheel.

I tell her the directions to my apartment, but she drives right past it.

"Where are we going?" I ask, rubbing at my eyes. Five martinis is *definitely* too many.

"Thanks to you, I can't go home now," she says. "And thanks to you, when I finally *do* go home, my garage is probably going to be trashed, and all my orders will be smashed on the ground. Why did you do that?" She turns her imploring gaze to me. "What did I do to you?"

# CHAPTER TWENTY-SEVEN

"I can't believe you."

Gia has said this to me at least fourteen times in the last twenty minutes. We're stopped at a red light in an empty intersection, and she keeps checking her rear-view mirrors like Clayton is going to catch up to us on foot.

Not likely. Not with that much alcohol in his system, and what is likely serious liver disease.

But she's scared.

And it's my fault.

"Now I can't go home," she says again as the light turns green.

"Why would you even want to?"

Her head snaps to me. "Excuse me?"

"Why would you want to go home to that asshole? Why not pack up your shit and leave him?"

I'm saying a lot of things I know I wouldn't say if I was sober.

Gia takes a left turn, and we end up on a residential street in Port Moody, about a ten-minute drive from my place. It's farther up the hill from the inlet and more densely crowded by trees than the lower section of the city near my apartment. There are no shopping districts here, just street after street of houses built in the eighties and nineties with large front lawns, fences in need of repair, and financed shiny cars in the driveways. It must be garbage pick-up day because dozens of bins are already out on the curb, even though it's barely six o'clock in the morning.

"You have a lot of nerve," Gia mutters. "You don't know me. You bought one cheesecake from me, and you think you know my whole life story?"

"I talked to Mack."

Her cheeks burn neon pink. "Well, Mack doesn't know what he's talking about, either."

"No? So he's got Clayton all wrong? He's a nice guy who treats you right and never lays a hand on you?"

Her cheeks redden further, and her lips form a straight, puckered line.

She pulls into a driveway and puts her car in park. In front of us is an attached carport with a large, old, dark blue truck parked in it. Mack's truck.

*Shit.*

Gia kills the engine and gets out of the car. I sit inside, hesitating to follow, and decide it would probably be best if I just wait here and let them talk. But that apparently isn't an option because Gia storms around the hood to my door, yanks it open, and points at the ground like she's speaking to a toddler.

"Out," she says. She jabs her finger at the ground again. "Now."

Slinking out of her Tercel like a scolded border collie, I wonder if the nausea rolling in my stomach is a symptom of my nerves for finding myself in Mack's driveway at the ass crack of dawn, or if it's all the martinis catching up to me in a bad way. I swallow a burp that tastes like gin and olives.

*Blah.*

Gia slams the passenger door behind me. I nearly jump out of my skin. She grabs my wrist and marches me up to Mack's front door, which is tidy and plain. The door itself is black, as is the handle and the number pad, and there is a coiled-up hose lying on the ground in a puddle of water, presumably from watering his green lawn yesterday evening.

Gia knocks aggressively. She still has a vice grip on my wrist. She waits twenty seconds or so before pounding her fist on the door again. After another ten or so seconds, I hear footsteps from inside, and Mack yelling that he's coming. We hear him mumbling on the other side, and when he yanks the door open, it's on the final note of his string of curses.

"Son of a…" He trails off when he spots us. At first, when he sees his sister, he looks confused and shocked. Then his gaze slides to me, narrows, and darts back to Gia. "Why is she here?"

Gia leads me by the wrist, forcing me to step forward. "Go ahead and tell him, Charlie."

Mack folds his arms over his chest.

"Erm," I stammer. Where do I start? What did I do wrong again? How did I fuck up my most recent social interaction? Oh, yeah. Clayton the dick. "I was at a bar," I start.

Gia throws her arms up in frustration. "She's hammered, and she happened to be at the same bar I was supposed to pick Clayton up at this morning, and she got it in her head that it would be a *great* idea to confront him and call him an asshole."

"That's not true," I say.

Gia snaps her head to me.

"I told him he was a weak bully and that his dad must have hated him."

Gia's mouth falls open.

Mack arches a dark eyebrow and lets out a grunt that is indiscernible.

"To be fair," I add, "I was five martinis in."

"At this hour?" Mack asks.

"Don't judge me."

He looks me up and down, taking in my denim shorts and sneakers. He looks like he's putting two and two together and coming to the conclusion that I didn't go home last night. Maybe he thinks I was out getting laid or something–seeing as how he refused to take me to bed. Let him think that. Let him think I got lucky with someone else.

*Why do I want to provoke him so bad? Why do I want to make him feel as shitty as I do? What's wrong with me?*

Mack sighs, opens his door further, and invites us both inside. Gia kicks off her shoes–slippers, I realize–and trudges down the hall and disappears around a corner into the kitchen. I hear water running seconds later as I try to get my sneakers off without falling over.

Mack watches me struggle as he closes the front door and leans against it. "Need help?"

"No." I sway on the spot as I try to bend down and untie my shoelace. Unwilling to let him win, I sit down on the cool tile floor of his entranceway and unlace my shoes like a child would. "I can do it."

"Sure you can, princess."

"Don't call me that."

"Are we back to you hating me?"

"Maybe I never stopped."

"Ha." He barks a laugh without humor. "Is that why you came to Dixie's? For a hate fuck? Sure didn't seem like that."

"Stop saying that word."

"What word?"

"Fuck. I don't want to think about you and that word in a sentence together again. You had your chance, and you decided not to take it. That's just fine." I manage to get unsteadily to my feet, where I have to brace myself on his wall, my hand beneath a framed picture of a black-and-white image of an old model motorcycle of some kind. Typical dude decor.

"Maybe you should wait in Gia's car," Mack says.

"No," Gia calls from his kitchen. "She just torpedoed my life. She's not setting foot in my car again. Or eating a single bite of one of my cheesecakes." She pokes her head out from behind the corner of the kitchen, and she wags a disciplinary finger at me. "I mean it. Not one bite. Not even a sniff."

I roll my eyes. "Someone had to tell that clown of a husband of yours to kick rocks eventually. Why not me?"

Gia's face flushes red yet again. "Mack, make her stop talking."

He gently guides me by my upper arm to his living room, which is a comfortable, dimly lit, dark-walled room. The blinds on the windows are closed, and a single standing lamp behind the sectional sofa is on. There's a large stone fireplace, a small TV in the corner, an old coffee table that has seen better days, and a bookshelf full of random magazines and books. He brings me a glass of water and encourages me to drink. A few minutes later, he delivers me a slice of toast with butter, which is perhaps the most wonderful thing I've ever put in my mouth.

He sits across from me, and eventually, Gia comes into the room and plops down beside her brother.

He leans forward with his elbows on his knees and turns to look at Gia. "I guess you're crashing here for a bit?"

She gives him a defeated nod.

"Will Clayton be out of the house tonight?"

"I'm sure he'll be drinking himself into oblivion, yes," she says.

Mack nods. "I'll go to your place and grab your things. I'll take pictures if he's damaged your garage. You may need them."

Gia wrings her hands. "He was so mad, Mack... I haven't seen him that unhinged in a really, really long time."

My insides start squirming unpleasantly.

Mack reaches over and closes his hand over both her tiny ones to stop her fidgeting. She stills immediately, like his touch is a dock on rough waters. He draws a deep breath, his chest rising, shoulders dropping, and exhales. "I'm going to take Charlie home, and then you and I will plan the next steps," he tells his sister. "This may be the end of the road, Gia. I know you've fought for a long time to try to hold this thing together, but if this is the last straw, you know I'll stand by you through it all, right?"

Her bottom lip trembles. "Someone is going to get hurt."

Mack's expression darkens. "Someone already has. You. A hundred times over."

She looks down at their hands.

"I'm sorry," I blurt out.

Mack looks up at me, but Gia doesn't. It's like she didn't even hear me.

But God, do I need her to hear me.

"I didn't mean to do this to you," I say. "I didn't mean to poke the bear and make a bigger mess for you. I thought–I thought I could hurt *him*. I thought he deserved it. And I thought I would be the one he'd lash out at. I didn't think–"

"Precisely," Mack interjects. "You didn't think. You're good at that, Charlie. You have an intimate understanding of pain, and yet you give no second thought to inflicting it on someone else. It's fucked up."

His words strike right where they were intended. I try to breathe, but the hurt is deep, and my lungs feel stuck. I don't have the right to cry after the mess I've made, but I want to. I want to fall apart right here.

Instead, I get to my feet. "I'll call a cab. You don't have to drive me. You're right."

Gia cries silent tears.

Her brother stares up at me. "I'm not sending you home in a cab in this state. You could barely take your own shoes off. You good here for fifteen minutes, Gia?"

She nods and wipes her tears.

Mack rises, says he just needs a minute to change, and disappears down another hall, presumably to his bedroom. I wonder what that room looks like. His house isn't what I expected, that's for sure. It has a much more lived-in feel than I expected from a bachelor pad. It's tidy, organized, full of little things only collected by living–like his books, his framed artwork, and his furniture. None of it appears to be a hand-me-down. He chose it all.

Gia and I sit in the humming silence of his living room and wait for him to return.

When he does, he's wearing his usual uniform: dark jeans, black T-shirt, and a black ball cap. His hair sticks out at the back, and I think of the time at Dixie's where I had the chance to run my fingers through it–to feel how soft it was, and to be the lucky woman who had the chance to get so close.

I grit my teeth against the burn of regret.

We head to the front door. Mack steps into his Blundstones, and I struggle to put my sneakers back on. The dizziness reduces me to having to sit on his floor and slide them on one at a time. I don't bother tying them. I just cram the laces under the tongue of each shoe and get to my feet.

Mack opens his front door, and I *almost* step out.

And there, grinning at me, is him.

Clayton.

The sight of him sobers me up *instantly.* I'm not looking into the face of a man. I'm looking into the face of a monster with unbridled wrath clutched in his fists at his sides. Anger radiates off him and sets off every alarm bell in my system that wasn't ringing back in the bar.

"Found you," Clayton snarls.

And then he lunges at me.

# CHAPTER TWENTY-EIGHT

I DON'T EVEN HAVE the chance to scream before I'm on the ground, dazed and dumbstruck. Clayton never put a hand on me. I was down before he even made it over the threshold. I prop myself up on one hand just as Mack steps over me after knocking me out of the way of Clayton's lunge. Frowning, I take stock of what just happened.

Clayton is on his ass holding his jaw.

Mack bends down to grab him by the front of his shirt.

Gia hollers my name and hurries down the hall to yank me to my feet. "Get up!"

My balance is wobbly as I look on in awe as Mack somehow manages to haul Clayton to his feet. Every muscle in his arm is standing at attention, veins straining, shoulders swelling.

He winds back and strikes Clayton again.

Clayton goes down like a sack of potatoes.

And there, in the hazy moment of Clayton trying to get his bearings, all of my senses come hurtling back to me.

"Stop." I wrench free of Gia and grab Mack before he has a chance to unleash more fury on his sister's abuser. I grip his elbow and dig in my heels, using every ounce of strength I have to drag him back inside. But Mack is rooted to the spot, and it's as if he doesn't even know I'm there. He shakes me off like I'm nothing but a leaf clinging to a branch in mid-November. "Mack! Please!"

Mack just rolls his shoulders.

Clayton is on his hands and knees now, trying to stand up. He lifts his head, showing off his bloody nose, and spits blood. His smile is red and hideous as he puts a hand on one knee and gets back up.

Gia retreats behind me.

This is bad. This is really, really, *really* bad.

Mack has a restraining order against him. I don't know what sort of ramifications there are going to be for this, but I know they won't be good, and I know they're going to involve the law.

What if Clayton presses charges? *Can* he press charges if he was the one who broke the order? What grounds does he have to stand on? He didn't show up with a weapon… but Gia did. I am so out of my depth; my brain feels like it's being swallowed by quicksand.

What if Mack gets arrested?

Who will protect Gia?

Where will she go?

Is she going to be in trouble, too?

What will happen if Clayton has her all to himself in that dingy house?

*What have I done?*

"Come on, pretty boy," Clayton spits. He lifts both hands and curls his fingers in a come-hither motion at Mack, inviting him to move closer. I notice the grit under his nails, the scarring on his knuckles, the coarse hair on each digit, the copper stains settled into them. Those hands have hurt people. People like Gia. "Let's see what you're really made of. I've wanted to kick your teeth in for fucking years."

Across the street, a neighbor comes out of their house. He's middle-aged, average height, and is wearing khakis and a white button-up. He crosses his lawn and walks with purpose. He's on his cell phone.

"Cops are on the way," the neighbor shouts.

Clayton looks over his shoulder at the neighbor and then turns all the way, setting his sights on his next target. The neighbor pauses halfway across the street, realizing he's just caught the attention of a rabid dog.

Mack starts laughing.

It's enough to bring Clayton's focus back to him. Mack takes his ball cap off and throws it on the ground.

"You've been waiting for this for years?" Mack taunts. "Let's see it then. Hit me like you hit my sister, you coward."

Clayton snarls.

The neighbor is still in the middle of the street, unsure whether he should continue his approach or not. Hell, I'm not sure if he should either, and in his shoes, I'm not sure I'd want to get any closer. Mack radiates years of pent-up fury and justice. Clayton is nothing but insanity and malice poured into a large body built for causing hurt.

"Please," I hear myself say.

But neither of them are listening.

Mack and Clayton crash together, two titans of hatred, and the impact is jarring to my senses.

Daniel only ever had one fight in his entire life, and that was in high school, and it barely counted because it was on a football field. He never would have found himself in a situation like this. Daniel was a peacekeeper by nature, and that had always made me feel safe.

I feel anything but safe right now. And it is my own doing.

*I hate you, Charlie.*

The thought isn't foreign. It's cold but familiar, and I curl myself around the mantra until I can disappear from this torture. My mind goes somewhere else. I don't see the blood on the grass. I don't hear the sirens wailing. I don't hear Clayton pleading for mercy.

Until Gia comes running past me with a damn baseball bat over her shoulder like a hardcore psychopath. The sight doesn't line up. Sweet, petite, pretty-in-pink Gia wields the bat, marches right up to the men, and swings.

I hear the impact.

A cop car rounds the bend and hurtles right up onto the front lawn, kicking up grass and leaving torn lines in the wake of the tires. Clayton falls flat on his back, unconscious–hopefully not dead. Mack stumbles backward, stunned by the sudden end of the fight, and turns to look at his sister with wide eyes and slack hands. All the fight is out of him now as he stares at her. She pants heavily and drops the bat as the cops come rushing up the lawn yelling at all of us to get down on our knees and put our hands on our heads.

How did we get here?

How did *I* get here?

My mind transports me back to simpler times and stir-fry dinners with Daniel on TV tables while we watch reruns of our favorite shows. Of lazy Sunday mornings, stepping into a hot shower with him to ease into the day on the right foot. Of lounging in the waning evening light on our back porch, talking about our future children, and how we hoped they didn't play soccer because neither of us could stand to watch the sport. Of local pop-up markets and buying fresh produce. Of baking cookies together for him to bring into the office. Of New Year's Eve parties. Of how we fit together in our bed and how he always wanted to be the big spoon. Of how he smelled like rain and evergreen trees.

The police yelling at me jars me back to the present moment. Dew in the grass soaks my bare knees.

An officer cuffs Mack, hauls him up, and marches him to their cruiser. They throw him in the back before going to Clayton and checking his vitals. An ambulance arrives next, and the paramedics waste no time tending to Clayton and brushing the officers off.

So they turn their attention to Gia and me.

My tongue is thick as one of them, a buzz-cut, broad-shouldered, blue-eyed brick house of a man stares down at me with his fists planted on his hips.

"Which one of you is going to tell me what happened?"

Gia licks her lips. "That's my husband. The one in your cruiser is my brother."

"And?" he pushes.

Gia explains everything like this isn't her first rodeo. And of course, I know it isn't, but her level head in such a situation feels *wrong.* I can barely catch my breath as I watch a cop lean over the open door and talk to Mack in the back seat. They offer him a towel and an ice pack, which he holds to his jaw.

Is he hurt?

How many licks did Clayton get in?

*It all happened so fast.*

"Excuse me," I say.

The cop doesn't blink. His attention remains on Gia, who is now bringing the cop up to speed on the restraining order and how Mack didn't violate it–she came here with me and didn't realize Clayton was following her, and Clayton started the whole altercation.

"Excuse me," I say again.

They continue ignoring me, but my body does not. My own blood cells are trying to escape my veins in order to get to Mack and make sure he's okay.

"My brother has cameras," Gia says, pointing at the front door. "You can review the footage yourself."

"Excuse me," I say again, more forcefully this time.

The cop turns his head and slow-blinks at me. "Yes?"

I nod toward his cruiser. "Can I see him and make sure he's okay?"

The cop twists to look back at the other officer talking with Mack. I can barely see him because the cop is a bit on the wider side. All I can see is that he has one leg out of the car, his boot resting on the grass, and the cop is doing all the talking. It doesn't look tense, and clearly, the cuffs they put on have been taken off.

That's a good sign.

The cop with Gia and me nods. "Go ahead. Martinez!" he calls to the other officer. "Sending one over to you."

Martinez, the cop with Mack, backs up as I hurry to my feet and rush across the grass to get to Mack. When I reach him, I take quick stock of his injuries: a split eyebrow that's bleeding only a little, a bruised jaw, swollen lip, and a bit of blood on his knuckles.

I drop to a knee and grab the ice pack so I can hold it for him.

Mack catches my wrist but doesn't force me away. "I'm fine."

"Like hell you're fine. Nobody is fine. I just set everything on fire.

I'm sorry. I'm so sorry. I wasn't thinking. I just… I don't know what's wrong with me."

"You made a bad judgment call. It happens."

"Stop forgiving me for treating you like shit, Mack."

He frowns.

"I think…" I trail off and shake my head.

"What?"

"I think I need help. Real help. When I insulted Clayton at the bar it felt *good*. I wanted to hurt him. I wanted to make him mad. I didn't care if he hurt me back. I almost… wanted him to."

Mack's expression darkens. "If he'd laid a finger on you, I would have–"

"I know."

His jaw flexes, and he lets my wrist go so he can pull my hand against his chest and hold it there. "We're all okay. Clayton has a thick skull. He'll be fine, too. Concussed, most likely. Maybe a little dumber than he already is. But fine. And you?"

I let my palm soften against his chest as he takes the ice pack from me.

*What about me?*

Mack cups my cheek. "You're going to be fine too. With help. There's no shame in that. And there's no shame in confronting a bully, either. That was brave, Charlie. Batshit crazy, but brave."

"It was stupid."

"That too." His hand falls from my cheek, and so does the warmth of his touch. "But one good thing came of all this."

"If you can find a silver lining, do tell."

He manages a grin despite his swollen lip. "I got to lay him out. Finally."

# CHAPTER TWENTY-NINE

MY KNEE IS BOUNCING at the police station as I give my full report to a female officer. She has strawberry-blonde hair that is cut short and is slicked back. It curls out at the bottom and the back, and she kind of looks like she's from the future. Her features are angular and a bit severe, but the assault of freckles across her nose and cheeks softens her a bit. And when she smiles, I feel like I'm still talking to a human, not a robot.

"I think I have everything I need, Ms. Warren." She clacks away on her keyboard a few more times before pushing her chair back and smiling at me. "If you'd like, can I arrange for an officer to take you home? You look exhausted."

I am.

This is a level of tired I haven't felt in, oh, gosh, three years. Holy hell, am I getting sick of the timeline of events of my life. It's like I have my own reference of before or after Christ. Except it's before or after Daniel.

"Um," is all I manage to say.

Then Mack is there with a hand on my shoulder. "I can take you home, Charlie."

His touch soothes me, and if it weren't for him offering his hand to help me to my feet, I could have fallen asleep right there in the precinct. We collect Gia on our way out, who finished her report shortly before me, and all three of us step out into the bright light of day in the parking lot. It's just past noon, and it's hot as hell crossing the black asphalt to the shade of a maple tree across the street. I sink onto a park bench under the tree while Mack orders the three of us an Uber. Gia's hands had been shaking too much to drive us here, and the police drove Mack in the back seat of their cruiser.

"What happens now?" I ask.

Mack and Gia exchange a look.

"With Clayton," I clarify.

Mack continues to stare at his sister. I glance up at her as well, finding her fretting with her hands in the shade. A light breeze ruffles the leaves above, and sunlight trickles through, dancing across her features.

"I…" she says, her voice weak. Soon, it gains some power. "I'm going to talk to a lawyer and figure out my options. I have a history of reports with no charges, but I think… I think I'm ready. I can't do this anymore. He could have killed you," she says to Mack.

He arches an eyebrow.

Gia glares at him. "Don't be a tough guy. He could've, and you know it. He was absolutely wasted and didn't feel a single hit you landed on him. If he'd managed to get one good one on you, and you lost your footing for even a second, he would've–"

"Enough."

Gia looks away and crosses her arms.

"The car will be here in five," Mack says. "And for the record, I took it easy on him, because I didn't think you'd forgive me for murdering your husband in front of you. Like he deserved."

His words stun me. Not because they're harsh, or crude, but because I *believe* them.

Gia still won't look at her brother. "I know. I'm a fuck up. I get it, okay?"

"Don't put words in my mouth," Mack says. "He's lucky I–"

A sudden wave of nausea rolls over me, and I barely have time to lean forward and put my head between my knees before I hurl all over the dirt beneath the park bench. Gia gasps and rushes to put her hand on my back and hold my hair up. I suck in a ragged breath of air and vomit again, clutching at the bench seat to stop the dizziness that came out of nowhere.

"Adrenaline," Gia says compassionately. "It's normal."

"Or all the martinis," I hiccup.

Her voice softens. "Or that."

My phone starts buzzing in my back pocket. It feels like a fever dream to pull it out and see my sister's smiling face from her wedding day fill my screen. I don't think I have the presence of mind to have a conversation with her right now, and the last thing I want to do is to make her worry about me when she's still in recovery at the hospital, so I let it go to voicemail. I'm in the middle of writing her a text when she calls again.

Which means I have to answer.

Two calls back-to-back from Devin means I'm going to suffer the consequences for not answering.

I hold it to my ear. "Hey, Dev. Everything okay? How are you feeling?"

"Mom is driving me *fucking* crazy, Charlie."

Groaning, I manage to sit upright. Gia still has her hand on my back, but she lets go of my hair. Mack stands in front of me wearing a mask of concern. My focus is on my sister, though. "Is she at the hospital?"

"She never left! Dad went home, but she slept in the waiting room like a legitimate sociopath so she could be in my room at the ass crack of dawn. Do you know what she asked to do, Charlie? Take a wild guess. The *fucking* audacity!"

My sister never speaks like this. Normally, she's the vision of beauty and class. This is a new level of angry. Brett must be making a food run or attempting to get my mother to leave the waiting room; otherwise I'd hear him trying to soothe his wife.

"I don't know, Dev. What did she do?"

"She asked to give Jameson his first bath." A bitter laugh tears out of my sister. "Can you imagine? The *nerve* it takes to ask a new mother to bathe her baby? When she knows *full well* that we're waiting to bathe Jameson for as long as we can because I read all about how good vernix is for a baby's immune system, and all the health benefits of not having a bath right away. Mom keeps calling me 'hippy dippy' and saying how she wants to kiss him but won't with the vernix on him. *Ugh!*"

I chew on the inside of my cheek and force my tired brain to say something helpful. "Can you ask one of the nurses to kick her out? I heard they'll do that subtly if need be. Something about asking them for pineapple juice."

"Pineapple juice?" Devin pauses. "Charlie, what are you talking about? Where are you right now?"

I look across the street at the police station. "Outside getting some fresh air. Why?"

"You sound… I don't know… weird."

"I'm just tired."

"*You're* tired? I just pushed a watermelon out of my fucking vagina, and for some God forsaken reason, our mother is still here at the hospital when she should be literally anywhere else!" Her voice is raised in pitch now. "I need her gone. Now."

I rub at both eyes and drop my phone. How did I forget it was even in my hand? Cursing, I scoop it up and check the screen. Not broken.

When I bring it back to my ear, Devin is saying my name over and over.

"I'm here," I tell her. "And I can come kick Mom out. I just need–"

Suddenly, Mack snatches my phone out of my hand. I scramble to my feet and try to take it back, but he holds me at arm's length and addresses my sister.

"Hey Devin, congrats on having the baby. That's wild. I hope your recovery is going well." He grunts when I kick him in the shin, but he still doesn't give me the phone back. "Listen, Charlie wants to come help you, but she would probably make everything worse. She hasn't slept all night and had a bit of drama this morning. Don't worry, she's fine, but she needs to go to bed. Having her at the hospital would probably set fire to the tiny thread keeping her and her mother connected, and then you'd be trying to worship your new baby *and* play therapist."

"Mack!" I seethe. "Give. Me. My. Phone!"

He nods to something Devin says. "Yeah, that sounds really fucking annoying. And this is probably going to annoy you and Charlie, but I'm not going to let her come to the hospital."

"*Let?*" I hiss.

I have a feeling my sister said the same thing because he holds the phone away from his ear, and I hear her tiny voice raise as she starts yelling bloody murder at him.

Serves him right.

He rides out the first wave of verbal assault before talking to her again. "I got it. You're pissed. And I don't blame you. But when the dust settles, maybe you'll both thank me. I have to get your sister home. She can fill you in later."

He hangs up.

On my *sister.*

"Mack," Gia scolds. "That wasn't very nice."

He shrugs. "Nice is overrated. Now come on. Let's get out of here."
***

Gia gasps loudly as I let her and Mack into my apartment. Sunlight breaks through every window and glints on the marble floors of my kitchen. Fresh flowers bloom in vases on the island, and an unlit vetiver and cherry blossom candle fills the air with a breezy aroma. I kick off my sneakers and let the solace of home fill my lungs as I drag my feet down the hall to my bedroom.

Mack follows. Gia explores the condo.

My bed greets me with a hug as I collapse face-first into it.

Mack clears his throat.

I peek one eye open and peer at him standing in my doorway. "What?"

"What's your door code?"

"Like I'd tell you."

"I want to come check on you later tonight." He pushes into the room and sits on the edge of my bed. "Somebody has to make sure you don't do something stupid. Again," he adds with a wry grin.

Against my better judgement, I give him the codes to get up to and inside my condo. Out in the hall, I can hear Gia muttering under her breath about how nice my place is and how she'd never leave if she got to live here.

"You can stay here if you want." My voice is half-muffled in my pillow. I draw in a deep yawn and snuggle in tighter. "I have a guest bedroom down the hall. It's all yours if you want. I've been living alone for a long time. It would be nice to have some company."

Mack's hand rests on my back and moves in a slow circle.

I smile into my pillow. "That's nice." Somewhere along the way, delirium has set in. The exhaustion, the adrenaline, and the martinis were a cocktail made for an inevitable crash and burn. "Daniel used to rub my back like this, too."

Mack's hand stills for a moment, but then he keeps going. "My mother used to do this for me when I was a kid."

Why have I never thought to ask Mack about his mother before?

"What was she like?"

His deep chuckle sends a pleasant vibration through the mattress. I settle into it more deeply and listen to the lull of his voice.

"She was hell on wheels. Like me. Restless, messy, stubborn. She worked as a real estate assistant by day and tended bar on Friday and Saturday nights. Gia and I would stay with our aunt and cousins on those nights. Big, wild, out-of-control childhood."

He keeps talking, and I want to hear every word, but sleep settles in, and so do dreams about Mack in the back of a cop car.

Mack kissing me in the rain.

Mack throwing his head back and laughing at a joke I don't remember making.

Mack standing on a sun-washed patio with my new nephew in his arms.

# CHAPTER THIRTY

THE SOUND of rustling sheets wakes me. The frame creaks softly, and
the mattress dips out from under me and toward the other person in
my bed. It's dark, fully night, and I sigh contently, feeling safe and
settled beneath my feather duvet.

"Hi," I murmur.

Warmth presses up against me. The heat of a man's body, firm and
strong, and a hand on my hip. His touch moves up to my waist and
slides under my shirt. I let out a soft moan and stretch, arching my
back and pressing my ass into Daniel's crotch. He's rock hard. I love
that I can do that to him so easily. Drunk on fatigue and power, I
reach back and rub him over his jeans.

*This must be a dream,* I think as a rush of arousal courses through
me. Daniel doesn't visit my dreams as frequently as he used to, but his
touch is welcome, even if it isn't real.

"Where've you been?" I ask.

His lips press soft kisses to my bare shoulder. He gently moves my
hair away from my neck to trail more kisses up to my ear. He nips at
my earlobe, and I giggle, tucking my chin to my chest to fend him off.

The hand he has up my shirt slides under my bralette. I moan as he cups my breast in one hand and squeezes. He pulls me harder against him when I try to unzip his fly.

"Playing hard to get?"

His breath on my neck is hot, but he doesn't answer me. I'm not inclined to stop him, though. A quiet fuck sounds perfect. All my senses are pricked to him and every move he makes. My insides are hooked and being drawn down to the deep part of my core where lust blossoms. I feel the weight of it growing as he removes his hand from my breast and lowers it to my hip, and then my stomach, where he flicks open the button of my jean shorts and then draws my fly down slowly.

For a dream, this all feels pretty damn real.

I wiggle my ass against his groin, teasing him. A soft sound escapes him; not a moan, not a growl, not a sigh. Something primal, low, and full of need.

My panties are officially wet.

Daniel guides my shorts down, and I lift my hip from the mattress to help him. He stops when they're midway down my thighs, trapping my knees together, and surprises me when he slides his hand between my thighs.

His fingers slide through my pussy, gently massaging from clit to perineum. The pressure is exquisite. My fingers curl in the duvet as a desperate whimper escapes me.

"Tease," I manage between short breaths.

His fingers swirl over my clit and stay there. Every passing second builds the pressure in my core, and I will my body to be patient. He'll give me what I need. To show my appreciation, I arch my back further, and he responds by sliding his other hand under my pillow and gripping my neck–which is something Daniel has never done before.

I freeze in his grip, startled.

He leans in close behind me and kisses the back of my neck. "You're going to be worth the wait. I can tell."

My pulse spikes.

That was *not* Daniel's voice.

"Wait," I gasp as reality comes crashing down around me.

But Mack already has his fingers inside me. And this is definitely not a dream.

*Oh, God.*

This is so wrong.

But *so* good.

"Yes," I breathe, trying to turn and face him. But he has a hold of my neck, and he keeps me in place so he can fuck me with his fingers and press his teeth into my shoulder as I writhe against him. I'm filled with a deep sense of knowing that we shouldn't do this, and that the regret and guilt that is going to follow in the wake of my pleasure will be crippling, but I don't want to tell him to stop. I feel full for the first time in three years.

I feel liberated.

All because the man I'm falling for has finally taken the initiative to take me.

Mack lets me go and rips my shorts off. Stitching tears. Denim digs into my thighs. Then they hit the floor, and I'm in bed with Mack in nothing but my shirt, bralette, and panties. He nudges my panties to the side to press his fingers in deeper. Unrestrained by the shorts, he has better control, and he takes advantage, pressing against my clit with the pad of his thumb while he stretches me with his fingers.

I claw at the blanket and pillow like I need to escape—but that's the very last thing I want.

Mack rolls me onto my back and leans over me. His fingers still work their magic, and I'm a breathless puddle of lust beneath him. I lift my ass from the mattress in a silent plea for him to give me more. Fuck me harder.

*Make me forget everything for just a little while longer.*

He obliges. As his fingers find the sweet spot inside me, he lowers himself down the bed and settles on his stomach between my thighs. I'm hooked by the sight of his handsome face disappearing behind my mound as he licks my slit from bottom to top, and then dances his tongue over my clit while he fucks me with his fingers.

My control begins to slip.

Mack must sense it, because a smile curls his glistening lips. "Good girl."

*Oh fuck.*

I've read that line in books a hundred times over, and it always got me a little hot and heavy. But hearing it in real life? His words masterfully open a trapdoor in my mind full of all the lust, desire, and unfulfilled needs I've denied for three years. They come rushing out like demons from hell, untethered, unashamed, and manifest in my core as my orgasm builds. Mack seals his lips over my clit and suckles, his tongue still swirling over the tip, until my hips buck and the final threads of control snap.

I cry out.

I don't mean to, but the sound tears out of me as I come undone. He holds my hips down and thrusts his fingers deep inside me. I come on the sheets, messy and wet, and stare down in amazement as he laps at my juices.

He rises to his knees with my legs resting on top of his strong thighs. I watch, mesmerized by the flex and strain of the tendons in his hands and forearms as he undoes his fly. My awe turns into shock when he pulls his dick free from his boxers.

Oh.

Oh, *no.*

He holds himself in one hand, stroking his length, and I consider trying to flee. He's huge. Too huge. My insides hurt already just thinking about trying to take him inside me. But the thought of *not* taking him hurts more. I need all of him, pain or no pain, and I need him now.

So, I spread my legs for him.

Mack drops over me, planting a hand on the pillow beside my head, and lowers himself further to meet my lips with his own. His kiss is patient and gentle. Tender, even. I whimper against his lips and reach up to slide my hands up under his shirt. I trace taut muscle and find that delicious trail of dark hair below his navel. I'd wondered what it led to the first time I saw it, and now I know. And tonight, it's mine.

I guide his shirt over his head and throw it on the floor. Then, I let my hands wander lower, and lower, until my fingers trail over the cut of his hips and down to his dick. I take him in one hand and hope he doesn't feel how much I'm trembling. The truth of what I am about to do isn't lost on me, even if I want it.

Once I do this, I can't take it back.

Once I do this, the last man I made love to will no longer be my husband.

Once I do this…

Mack seems to be reading my mind. "We can stop."

I search the depths of his dark, steely gaze. This man would stop if I ask. I know that. He would do everything to make sure I don't feel bad, too. But I think…

"I think I'm ready," I whisper.

He cups my cheek in one hand. The touch is so gentle, so reassuring, that it makes my eyes well with tears. He brushes one away with his thumb as his brow furrows. "Are you sure?"

I nod, pressing my cheek into the warmth of his palm. "Yes."

The next kiss he gives me starts off slow, but it builds, and so does his hunger as he presses between my lips and explores my mouth with his tongue. He tastes like *me*, and as the kiss deepens, I continue working him in one hand, relishing his length, imagining what it will feel like to take him inside me. Gently, I guide his tip down so he's pressing against my opening. He lets out a groan into my mouth. Then his fingers fill me again. I gasp, and he gives me another finger.

It's almost too much.

"I'll get a condom," he offers.

"You don't need one." My words come out clipped and choppy. "I can't. Get. Pregnant."

"There are other reasons to wear one."

His offer only turns me on more. A man who cares about sexual health? Okay. I love that. But I love the feel of his bare flesh against mine more, and I know I'm not bringing anything to the table that could put him in danger. I'd have to have had sex recently in order for that to be the case, and, well, *widow.*

"I trust you," I say.

He kisses me again with rekindled fire; his tongue fucks my mouth while his fingers fuck my pussy. I'm hurtling toward oblivion with every passing second, and it scares the hell out of me to know that this is just the beginning.

He drops his hips a little, removes his fingers, and leaves me momentarily empty so he can step off the bed and strip his jeans and boxers off the rest of the way. I admire the sight of him in all his glory as he comes back to me. He gently cups my neck with one hand as he leans over me and the tip of his dick presses against me. The pressure builds until he drops a little lower, and then the head of his dick slides in.

And there's no going back.

He gives me a couple more inches. Slow and steady. My body takes the reins and my brain takes a back seat. My legs fall open a little wider, and everything begins to relax. Tense muscles ease, and he presses in deeper. Deeper. Until I feel like I'm going to burst.

I flinch when I can't take anymore and am about to tell him to stop, but he already knows.

He reaches down with one hand and massages my clit. I prop myself up on my elbows and watch, panting, as he gives me another full inch. And then another.

My head falls back. Stars burst behind my eyes. A moan rolls out of me.

Mack pulls out and slides back in.

I grip the sheets under me.

*More.*

"Fuck," Mack growls, gripping my thighs and dragging me closer to him. I pull the sheets with me, unhooking them from the corner of the mattress, and admire every cut line of his labor-chiseled body. The built shoulders, powerful traps, swollen chest, and mouth-watering abs that flex and ripple with every thrust of his hips. No human being has any right looking this good, and yet here he is, looking like the cover of a men's health magazine while he's nine inches deep inside me.

Maybe ten. I've never been good with measurements.

His speed quickens, and he pushes my thighs back so he can press in deeper. It's *too* deep, and I yelp when pain blends with pleasure. He slows his rhythm but still buries himself up to the hilt, demanding I make more room for him. My body complies, and soon, all I am is *sex*. His thrusts quicken, his control mounts, and I lose myself to it all as he drives in and out, pumping me until I can hear how wet I am. The sound is proof of my arousal, and for some reason, it turns me on even more.

"That's it," Mack practically purrs. "Take it."

*Yes.*

"I'm yours," I whimper. "Don't stop."

My words do something to him. He rolls his shoulders and lets out a growl that almost scares me. Almost. Then he pulls out, steps off the edge of the bed, flips me onto my stomach, and drags me to the edge. I spread my legs, perched on the edge of the mattress on my knees, and lean forward to rest on my elbows, my ass in the air for him. Mack presses inside. His length feels even bigger at this angle. I bury my face in the mattress and muffle a cry as he stretches me.

He grabs a fistful of my hair and pulls me back up. The flash of pain in my scalp startles and surprises me. I've never been manhandled in bed before. He yanks me up so that my back is pressed to his chest. Then he grabs my jaw, turns my face to the side, and devours my mouth with his while he fucks me with slow, deep thrusts. I can barely breathe, let alone stay upright like this. But for him, I do it. My legs cramp. My pussy aches. Every cell in my body screams for release.

"This is what I meant," he says, resting his cheek against mine, his voice full of gravel and need. "I knew you would submit. I knew you'd fucking love it. I can see it in your eyes."

All I can do is take it.

His dick inside me. His strong hands all over me. His eyes on me. I'm more exposed than I've ever been—and I know full well in this moment that I will let him do anything he wants to me. I want to show him that. I want him to know how much I trust him.

And how much I want him.

So I arch my back, taking him even deeper until I can't catch my breath. I'm more vulnerable than I've ever been with another person, including Daniel, and I'm about to come. It's not what I ever imagined would turn me on, but the proof is in the pudding.

Or the cum that's running down the inside of my thigh.

Mack chuckles before kissing me fiercely, stealing any chance I have at filling my lungs, and drives into me as I give in to the most intense orgasm of my life. My toes curl, my mind implodes like an atom bomb, and the animal inside me takes over as Mack throws me down on the bed, holds me there with a hand against the back of my neck, and fucks me until he loses control and fills me with silky warmth.

My whole body quivers in the aftermath of the most intense orgasm I've ever had as I brace myself for the guilt, shame, and regret.

As soon as Mack pulls out, those feelings fill me up with force.

# CHAPTER THIRTY-ONE

While Mack washes up in my bathroom, I stare at the ceiling. The guilt is present, and so is the shame.

But the regret?

It's already starting to fade. I feel fully present in my body and am aware of a hundred micro-details all at once. The damp sheets beneath me. The wetness between my thighs. The ache inside me that hurts but also feels wonderful at the same time. The taste of Mack's kiss and his fingers on my tongue. The dull burn from his stubble scratching against my cheek. The smell of sex in the air. The cool breeze coming through the open window. The chatter of someone outside who may or may not have heard us fucking. The hum of my refrigerator down the hall. My own pulse still thrumming in my clit. Mack turning the bathroom sink off.

He returns, fully naked, and lingers in the doorway to stare at me. "I'd like to do that again. Soon."

"I think I'm going to be walking funny tomorrow. You're going to have to hold your horses."

He lets out that carefree and rare laugh of his. "That so?"

I nod and invite him to come back to bed with me. He does, and we curl up together with ease.

"What does this mean?" I ask after a few minutes of comfortable silence.

"That you have a delicious pussy."

Giggling, I shake my head. "I'm trying to be serious. What does this mean for us?"

He traces a lazy figure-eight pattern on my shoulder. "What do you want it to mean?"

"There you go, answering my questions with more questions. You don't have to play hard to get anymore, Mack. In case you haven't noticed, I got you already."

His smile is devil-may-care and sin. "And I got you."

"So are we… a thing?"

"I'm not seeing anyone else. I want to see where this goes." He stops tracing the figure eight, and we stare into each other's eyes. "I care about you, Charlie. I want to fuck you again," he teases with a playful smile, "but I also just want *you*."

"I want to see where this goes, too."

"Then it's settled. We're exclusive. You're mine."

"Hold on, cowboy, I–"

He silences me and pulls me in close by pressing a kiss to my lips. His hand wanders down my stomach and settles once more between my legs. I try to squeeze my thighs shut, more out of playful defiance than anything else, but he's stronger than me. He teases my still very sensitive clit. "Mine."

I reach down, take his wrist, and encourage him to do more than just tease me.

"Yours," I whisper.

***

That evening, Mack and I sit on my living room floor and eat Thai takeout. He fails miserably with chopsticks, which is perhaps the funniest thing I've ever seen, and when I descend into a fit of laughter, he throws a pork wonton at me.

"Ew!" I run my fingers through my hair. "You got grease in my hair!"

"We can shower together later."

"You've got solutions for everything, huh?"

"I'm a problem solver by nature. And a giver." He flashes me a smile before trying once more to pick up some of the pad thai with his chopsticks. His thumb moves in an aimless circle.

I snort. "I think this might be the only thing I've ever watched you do that *wasn't* sexy."

His brows shoot up. "Not a bad track record. So long as I don't give you the ick."

I shrug one shoulder. "It remains to be seen."

Mack puts the chopsticks down in favor of the wrapped-up plastic cutlery that had been tossed in the bag. "In that case, I'll play it safe."

The rest of the meal is filled with this kind of exchange–playful jabs, quick one-liners, the occasional thrown wonton or stolen kiss. I catch him looking down my shirt nearly every time I lean over, and I feel like a teenage girl caught up in a whirlwind romance. But those youthful love stories are always so tragic because they end. Like how mine did with Daniel. But with Mack, things feel different. Today has given me something precious that I had long since given up on.

Hope.

Hope that it might get better, that love isn't off the table for me, and that I do still have a chance to find someone I can grow old and gray with. Someone who will keep me young by keeping me laughing. Who will fill my life with good memories and moments. Who will remind me how to live again and who will make me proud that I never gave up in the darkest of moments. Who, just by choosing me, might help Daniel rest more peacefully.

That someone might be the man in front of me trying yet again to use his chopsticks to pick up three noodles. *There's that stubbornness he said his mother possessed,* I think as a smile stretches my cheeks to the point of aching.

He glances up. "Stop."

I grin, twirl a chopstick in one hand, and scoop up a generous bite of pad thai. I drop it in my mouth and chew, making sure to visibly savor it while he scowls.

"Show off."

More giggles ensue, and I revel in how happy I am. Truly happy. I haven't felt like this—like myself—in ages. It's refreshing. Invigorating. If I start feeling like this too much, I worry I'll become obsessed with it. And with him.

Maybe I already am.

"Hey," I say. "I never told you why I was out at the bar so late in the first place and in the mood to pick that fight with Clayton."

"I was wondering when we'd talk about it."

"Were you waiting for me to bring it up?"

His mouth presses into a fine line when he captures the noodles after several minutes of effort. Slowly, with tedious care, he begins raising them to his lips. "I didn't want to push." He's halfway there. "But I assume it had to do with Devin having her baby." The noodles fall from the trembling hold he has on them. "Shit."

I watch the show and lean back on my hands. "I thought I would handle it better, but I kind of fell apart and spiraled."

His attention slides from the chopsticks to me. "It explains a lot."

"The half dozen martinis and poor judgment calls? Yeah, I guess so."

"She had a boy?"

"Yep. His name is Jameson. And his middle name is Charlie."

Mack gives me a boyish grin. "Shit name."

"Hey!"

He throws his head back and laughs with a hand on his chest. I adore the sight of him in this moment. When he recovers, he abandons his chopsticks on the edge of the take-out container of pad thai. "Okay, okay, in all seriousness, that must have been really tough for you. How did it feel?"

"Wonderful. Horrible. Exciting. Terrifying. And like I was looking down a wormhole in time at the baby Daniel and I could have had."

Mack nods slowly. "That... makes sense."

"Does that bother you?"

"That you held your nephew for the first time and thought about the baby you lost?" His features pinch together, and he shakes his head. "No. Not in the slightest."

"No, that I still think about him all the time. That I probably will forever. Maybe. I don't know." I frown, feeling that giddiness that had been so ripe a minute ago start to rot. "This morning, when you got into bed with me and started touching me…" I trail off, unsure if I should reveal this or not, but decide to keep going. "At first I thought you were him."

Mack waits like there's more he's waiting for me to say. When I stay silent, he takes a deep breath and says, "When did you remember it couldn't be him?"

"When you said I would be worth the wait."

The muscles in his jaw flex, and he looks away. I wonder if the flicker I just saw in his eyes was shame. "I'm sorry, Charlie. I wouldn't have touched you like that if I knew–"

"Please," I say, my voice soft. "Don't. When I realized it was you, I didn't want to stop. And I'm glad we didn't. And," I add, "I'm sorry for the other night when I made you feel like I was using you. I didn't want the first time we had sex to be like ripping a band aid off. But I've been so scared to take that next step. You're the first person I've trusted since Daniel died, and the first person I've felt something for. I didn't know how to take the next steps with you without self-imploding. If you haven't noticed already, that's kind of my MO." I wince and count off the next steps on my fingers. "Get in over my head, have a huge reaction, say shit I can't take back, and then regret it all when the sun comes up."

He's quiet for half a moment. "Not a deal breaker for me."

My smile is involuntary. "Darn."

# CHAPTER THIRTY-TWO

MACK and I wake up together in my bed the next morning. We're both naked, and Gia is at a meeting with her lawyer. I'm sore from the sex we had the night before, but not sore enough to deny him when he gives me a morning treat. We fuck in my bed, and then again in my shower, and then again in the kitchen while I make us scrambled eggs and smoothies. After all the exercise, we both need the protein. They are perhaps the worst I've ever made, but Mack gives me grace and says he doesn't blame me for fucking up the eggs with his dick inside me.

And that thought plays on a loop in my head all the way into the later afternoon, when I find myself in Devin and Brett's living room picking up diapers, empty bottles, pacifiers, and discarded receiving blankets.

*Never thought I'd be horny while cleaning up baby stuff,* I think as I put away the last of the mess and begin straightening out the sofa cushions.

Devin is sleeping upstairs while Jameson also sleeps. Brett is at the store trying to sort out an issue they're having with their brand new, and quite expensive, baby monitor. And I—auntie extraordinaire—am doing everything I can to simplify their lives for the night shift.

A quick-to-put-together casserole is baking in the oven. The fridge is restocked with fresh produce and a few ready-to-bake meals for the next two days, including an overnight brunch wifesaver breakfast that I grew up eating every Christmas morning. All their favorite drinks are there, and as I look at the catch-all pile of junk on my sister's dining room table, I decide to also prep and organize her breastfeeding cart.

I had a vision in my head for all the things I was going to do post-partum. A breastfeeding cart had been at the top of my list so I could roll it around our massive house and not have to haul everything around with me or have a stash in every room. Based on resources from doulas, I'd done my own research to figure out what kinds of items belonged on a breastfeeding cart, and it is as I am going about putting it together that Brett comes home flustered and annoyed.

"They couldn't fix it?" I tuck some of my sister's favorite protein bars into a little basket on the top shelf of the cart next to a bottle of iced water and some burp cloths.

He slips off his sneakers and rubs at his eyes. "Nope. It's a warranty claim issue, so I have to call the manufacturer, and if it checks out, they can send a replacement, but the sales guy warned me the process can take a couple of weeks. So I just bought a new one. Don't tell Devin."

"Why?"

"Because she needs a win, and letting her think that *I* won at the store is as close as she's going to get to that today. It's been a rough start."

"Cluster feeding?" I ask.

He drags his feet into the living room and collapses onto the sofa. "How'd you know that?"

"Daniel and I were obsessed with conceiving for years. I read everything I could get my hands on."

"Right. In that case, any tips on how she gets through it?"

"Not really." I tuck some nursing pads into the second shelf of the cart beside Devin's wearable breast pumps. "Although, one thing that could help is if you sit with her for those middle-of-the-night-feeds.

Even if there is one every hour, and it feels like you're going to fall asleep standing up. It can be really lonely and daunting, and when the exhaustion settles in mixed with the hormones, it's like the Wild West for a new mom. Company will help her sanity. And remind her you're a team."

"Noted."

"How's she doing besides that?" I stack the bottom of the cart with extra towels, snacks, diapers, pads, and wipes. "Have you seen anything we should keep an eye on?"

Brett shakes his head. "She's adjusting well. She's happy. Cries at the drop of a hat, but happy. I catch her on the couch with Jameson just staring at him with so much love in her eyes. It makes me a little jealous. She's never looked at me like that."

I laugh. "And she probably never will. I bet you look at him the same way."

He rubs the back of his neck a little bashfully. "He's got me wrapped around his finger already. The joy is as overwhelming as the exhaustion."

I wish I understood, but I smile like I do.

"Hey, Charlie? Can I ask you something? It might... rub you the wrong way."

I slide the cart against the corner of the sofa where Devin usually sits before taking the armchair by the window and facing him. "Sure."

He rubs his hands on his thighs before leaning forward and resting his elbows on his knees. "You seem unusually happy. After the way you left the hospital, I thought you might be struggling. And understandably so. But this is kind of making me worried. Is something going on?"

"Oh."

"I know, I know," he says hurriedly, showing his palms as if in surrender and shaking his head. "I'm sorry. It's not my business, and I know you don't like when people go poking around. I just care about you, and I know how hard this has been, and how much harder your mother has made it for you. I need to make sure you're okay. Not for Devin's sake. But for my own. And for yours."

I consider his words, and they make me smile. "You're a good person, Brett."

He looks a bit pale. "This isn't reassuring me at all. I thought you'd tell me to kick rocks."

"Am I really that much of an asshole?"

"No, but you can be... reactive."

Fair enough.

I sigh and consider telling him I'm better adjusted because my therapy is finally paying off, but I decide to just be honest.

"I'm starting to... ugh, no, that's not right. I think I'm falling for someone."

He blinks. "Pardon?"

It's my turn to hold up both hands. "It's crazy. I hear what you're thinking. And I was thinking it too. But I mean it. I'm seeing someone."

His mouth falls open.

"Oh, come on, don't act that surprised!"

"Who?"

My sister, who has just come down the stairs, emerging from her midafternoon nap in an oversized pink nightgown, answers for me. "Mack?"

Brett turns to his wife and smiles. She goes to him and sits on his lap. I love the way he wraps his arms around her and holds her close.

While they sit pretzeled up together, I tell them all about Mack and me deciding to make things official. I leave out all the juicy details about me picking a fight with a man I know is violent in a bar after their baby was born. And I absolutely have no intention of telling them about the restraining order. That would probably add some unnecessary doubt and distract from the takeaway, which is Mack and I finally coming together and acknowledging this thing between us.

"Wow." Devin nods along well after I've stopped talking. "Wow."

"Good wow or bad wow?" I ask.

"Good," they blurt out at the same time.

"Just unexpected," Devin adds.

*Tell me about it.*

"I think it all happened right when I needed it the most," I tell them. "I mean, Mack has been around since moving day. You know how much I'd been struggling in that big house. Everything–every corner–reminded me of Daniel. But Mack was there on the hardest day for me when I had to close the door on all of that. He's been there, quiet and steady, ready when I needed him. I can breathe because of him."

"That's what scares me," Devin says softly.

"Why?"

Devin looks like she wants to take back what she said, but she continues anyway. "What if this is all just the perfect distraction for you to avoid how you're feeling? I mean, it makes sense that Jameson would pull all those memories right back up for you. Maybe you should sit in them and feel them, not bury them with Mack."

"I don't bury them with him. I talk to him about it all."

"Just... be careful, okay? And go slow. I want this to be a good thing for you."

"It is."

This isn't what I was expecting. I sort of thought they'd both be really happy for me and that they would see what I feel–lighter, brighter, and softer. Mack choosing me has sanded down some of my still-rough edges. No, I'm not fully healed, but there is light on the horizon.

Baby Jameson starts crying upstairs.

Devin gets up to go get him, but Brett insists and goes on his own. Seconds after he leaves, we hear Jameson go quiet, and Devin smiles contently as she listens. It's as if she's forgotten I'm there.

*Do they think I've forgotten Daniel because I'm finally letting myself live a little?*

Devin spots the breastfeeding cart beside her favorite corner of the sofa. She lights up and goes over to inspect it. "Did you do this?"

"Yes." I stand up. "I think I should go."

"Oh. Okay." Devin peeks at the second row of the cart and tucks her hair behind her ears before coming to me. "I'll walk you out."

She stands in the open door, the summer breeze tugging at her nightgown, while I bend down and do up the ankle straps of my leather sandals.

"You should bring Mack to Mom and Dad's for Brett's birthday."

I look up at her. "Do you think that's a good idea?"

"Why not? If you like him, and you're exclusive, he should be there. He's already met us at the hospital. Dad can show him how bad he is on the grill, and Brett can save his dinner from being ruined. Maybe Mack will be the wingman Brett needs."

*Since his other one died,* I think.

"I'll think about it." I straighten and step outside into the midsummer afternoon. Brett and Devin's neighborhood has always smelled floral. Perhaps it's all the hydrangeas in everyone's yards.

Devin catches my arm. "I'm sorry I didn't react how you wanted. I'm not judging. If you're happy, I'm happy, and I know you're not impulsive, and you've thought this through." She squeezes me. "Thank you for coming over and helping get the house in order today. I'm grateful."

I smile. "I'll be back in a few days to restock your fridge."

"You don't have–"

"Shut up, Devin. I want to." I wink and hop-step down her front steps and toward my car in the driveway. "I'm going to bring you the most life-changing cheesecake you've ever had in your life."

# CHAPTER THIRTY-THREE

MALLORY OPENS the door to her apartment and greets Mack and me with a beaming grin. "Welcome, sir and lady. Come in, come in." She waves us inside with a little bow, and I brush past her with a suspicious look over my shoulder.

"Why are you being so weird?"

"I picked out an outfit for you."

"What? Why?" I look down at my clothes. Simple white linen pants, a coral short sleeve top, and gold sandals. "What's wrong with this?"

Mallory looks at Mack. "Hey man, beer?"

"Sure," he says.

I gape after them as they head into her small, but nicely appointed, kitchen. She fought tooth and nail with her landlord for him to let her paint the cabinetry purple. When she first told me that was her plan, I tried to talk her out of it, but once Mallory has her mind set on something, it's very challenging to un-set it. It turned out that the landlord loved the color, and I had to admit, it added charm to the builder grade apartment. The gold hardware added a bit of texture and lux, and her patiently acquired collection of eclectic decor pulled it all together; the blue and white floral teapot, the picture frame fridge magnets full of photos of all her friends, the boob-shaped salt and pepper shakers, the oil painting of a lesbian couple fucking hanging on the pantry door.

It is all very Mal.

Mack notices the picture as he takes his first sip of beer. "Huh."

Mal pumps her eyebrows. "Nice, right?"

He agrees with a quiet nod before taking another sip of his beer.

"Um, hello? I'm still standing here," I interject. "What's wrong with my outfit?"

Mallory looks me up and down and grimaces. "You look like a fifty-year-old sales associate manager at a jewelry store counter."

Mack coughs and sputters into his beer.

I glower at them both. "I do not."

"At least wear something that you fill out," Mallory says. "Those pants are doing your ass zero favors. Right Mack?"

Mack clears his throat and shakes his head. "I'm not stepping in that."

"Wise," I say.

"Coward," Mallory scoffs as she struts down the hall to her bedroom. She encourages me to follow with a wave of her hand.

When I round the corner of her bedroom, I find two outfits laid out on her bed. One is a tennis dress. It's royal blue with crisscrossing straps on the back, and it looks like it would be pretty tight. And not at all the kind of thing Mallory would be caught dead wearing. She very obviously went out and bought this stuff specifically for me when I told her I was bringing Mack to Brett's birthday dinner.

Sneaky little bitch.

I love the hell out of her.

The second option is a white vest-style top and a floral printed skirt. I gravitate toward it immediately, but I'm not quite sure I have the nerve to show up in something so... nice. It's been three years since I cared about how I look, and if I show up in that, everyone will see it written all over me.

Effort.

Care.

Life.

Am I ready to make that kind of declaration at a family dinner?

"Sporty cute," Mallory says, pointing at the tennis dress, "or simple feminine. We could also switch the skirt out for shorts if you prefer. Or pair it with sneakers to tone it down."

"Mal," I say, "I don't know if–"

Mack walks up behind me. "The blue dress. Easy choice."

Mallory spins Mack around and shoves him out into the hall. She follows him out and tells me to get changed. She and Mack will wait for me in the kitchen.

I do as I'm told. Partly because it's not worth arguing with Mallory when she decides something is happening, and partly because I want to walk out there and see the heat in his eyes when Mack sees me in the blue dress.

I hesitate to put it on when I see that it's an extra small on the label. I'm not an extra small. That's just ridiculous. But I try it on anyway, and it fits like a glove, hugging my curves and pushing my tits up to a place they haven't been in a long time. Gravity who?

Mallory has a full-length mirror on the back of her bedroom door. I pause to check myself out in it, noticing yet again how thin I am, and how the sight doesn't match the image I have of myself in my head. My legs used to look muscular, and I spent almost five days a week back when I was with Daniel going to the gym and lifting heavy. I had the time, the will, and the desire to be strong.

I miss her.

But as it turns out, the dress does something for me. Way more than my linen pants. Mallory is, unfortunately, right.

Which she reminds me of as soon as I walk into the kitchen. Luckily, it's easy to drown her out because Mack is looking at me the way I hoped he would. With intensity, a locked jaw, and a firm grip on his beer bottle.

He whistles.

I do a little twirl. "You like it?"

He moves toward me, wraps his arm around my waist, and pulls me in for a kiss that tastes like Mallory's beer.

"Bleh. Girl on guy PDA." Mallory pretends to gag. "I have to sanitize everything now."

Mack breaks the kiss when he starts to laugh. "Is she always like this?"

"Oh, no," I assure him. "She's usually much worse."

MACK PARKS HIS TRUCK ACROSS THE STREET FROM MY PARENTS' HOUSE in the very same spot Mallory parked when we arrived for Devin's baby shower a month and a half ago. The sun has disappeared behind some clouds, but blue skies are on the horizon. We get out, grab the six-pack of beer and bottle of wine from the back seat, and cross the street with Mallory narrating her predictions of how the night is going to go, and who's going to be there.

"So long as I don't have to make small talk with Stephanie, it will be a good night," Mallory concludes as we cross the path to the porch steps.

"Who's Stephanie?" Mack asks.

"My sister's best friend," I say.

"A witch," Mallory adds.

"Shush," I hiss. "The windows are all open."

"If she's a witch, she can hear me anyway. Or feel my loathing for her."

I roll my eyes. "Don't listen to her. Stephanie isn't that bad. She's just–"

"Horrific," Mallory says.

The front door swings open, and Brett greets us with a giant grin and a cocktail sporting a neon yellow paper umbrella in one hand. "Heyo!"

Mallory talks to me out of the corner of her mouth. "He's *hammered.*"

"Yup," I say.

"Buddy!" Brett comes out of the house to throw an arm around

Mack's shoulders. "I'm glad you came. Good to see you again." He smacks Mack on the chest. Hard.

Mack grunts. "Thanks for having me."

"Let's get you a drink. Come on. Kitchen is this way. And you have to meet my kid."

Mallory and I share a look out on the porch.

"This is gonna go one of two ways," she says. "Bad. Or really bad."

"Don't be such a pessimist."

"Says the literal widow whose whole personality for three years has been doom and gloom."

"Exactly," I say as we step into the house. "You're the sunlight. Don't steal my schtick."

She lifts her chin and smirks down at me. "I've missed this version of you."

"Same. Now let's go find Mack before Brett drags him into the garage to look at my dad's old Thunderbird."

The party is in full swing.

Men are gathered outside around the grill, where my dad is teaching his version of a master class on how to grill the perfect steak. It smells heavenly, and we find a spread of appetizers that my mother is flitting around and tending to like a mother to her baby birds. There's potato salad, watermelon and feta salad, pasta salad, and Caesar salad. On colorful platters at the far end of the table are wings, mini sandwiches, fresh veggies, and corn on the cob. Mini chocolate cakes, chocolate-dipped Oreos, rice crispy squares, and brownies are displayed on a tiered platter. Guests mill about the yard snacking on little morsels from their paper plates while music plays from the speakers mounted on the back of the house. Kids splash in the pool while some of the mothers hover close by to keep an eye on the littlest ones.

Among those mothers is Devin. She has baby Jameson cradled in her arms, and she already looks like a natural, even though he's only ten days old. She bounces him gently and maintains conversation with one of the mothers with luscious blonde locks and a killer body.

Stephanie, of course.

Mallory spots a group of men; husbands, cousins, brothers. "I'm going to go ask if any of them have cute lesbian friends."

"Are you and the bartender done?" I call after her. "Sally?"

"Sally who?" Mallory calls back.

Laughing, I roll my eyes and head over to say hi to Devin, who has retreated to a shady corner of the yard on her own with Jameson. She greets me with a big hug and shows me sleeping Jameson, who somehow continues to get cuter with every passing day. His cheeks have taken on a rosy hue as they've gotten bigger, and they pucker in and out as he sucks on his pacifier.

"Hi, sweet boy," I say softly, not wanting to wake him. "Come get me when he wakes up; I want cuddles."

"Yeah?" Devin asks, eyes lighting up.

"Definitely."

She looks around. "Did Mack come?"

"He did. Brett whisked him away somewhere. Hopefully, not the garage. Otherwise, we won't see them for the rest of the night."

One of the kids sends a bunch of water over the edge of the pool, and we both leap back and out of the line of fire.

"Close call," I say, looking down at the splash marks on my blue dress.

Devin looks down and notices it. "You look good, Charlie."

"Thanks."

"No, seriously. You do. You look happy. And healthy. And just... like yourself, I guess."

"I don't want to jinx it," I say under my breath, "but I think I'm actually starting to feel like myself, too."

"Charlie!"

I flinch when Stephanie spots me. She throws her arms open and rushes forward to engulf me in a massive and obnoxiously tight hug. Devin gives me an apologetic smile as Stephanie holds on for about ten seconds too long.

I pat her back. "Nice to see you. Been a while."

She stands back, holding me at arm's length. "Oh my gosh, hasn't it? Devin's baby shower, I think. Wow, Charlie." She looks me up and down. "You look *so* good. It's nice to see you putting your best foot forward like this. Last time I saw you, I was kind of worried. You were so thin."

Devin makes a weird shushing sound that kind of sounds like a hiss. "Stephanie, that's not nice."

"It's okay," I interject. "I wasn't in a great place the last time we saw each other, and I don't think I was doing as good of a job hiding it as I thought I was. But you don't have to worry about me. I have plenty of people in my corner, and I'm going to be okay."

Devin blinks at me like I just teleported.

Stephanie nods sympathetically. "That is so good to hear. Oh." She pauses, looking past me. "And you brought Mallory. How nice to see her, too."

I can tell she doesn't mean it, but I grin anyway. "Yep, she's known Brett just as long as I have. He invited her."

Stephanie suddenly perks up. "Who's that hunk she's talking to? He knows she's gay, right?"

Devin groans.

I look over my shoulder at Mallory and find her laughing hysterically with Mack, who has an arm over his ribs as he laughs, too. God, what a beautiful sight.

"He's *so* hot," Stephanie gushes. "Devin? Is he one of Brett's friends from work? Is he single?"

"Jesus, Stephanie. Chill out. No, he's not single. And no, he's not Brett's friend. And even if he did happen to be single, it wouldn't matter, because you're happily married with three children." Devin shoots me an exasperated look. "He's Charlie's boyfriend."

Stephanie's head whips to me.

Satisfaction tickles my spine. "You should see him with his shirt off."

Stephanie turns pink. "Lucky girl. Excuse me. I need to get some food into my feral children." She spins on her heel to face the pool. "*Boys!* Out. Now. Let's get some veggies and ask Uncle Lee if he'll put those vegan hotdogs on the grill for you."

She stalks off, leaving Devin and me staring after her.

Devin bursts out laughing first, and I descend into maniacal giggles with her.

"I love her," she says. "We have a great history, but sometimes I wonder if we'd be friends if we met today."

"You don't have to wonder. I can promise you that you wouldn't be. She's so vapid."

"She's complicated," Devin says.

"If you say so. Come on, let's go see what those losers were laughing at."

"Oh, hold up," Devin says, her voice dropping into a loving coo as her attention drifts down to Jameson, who is starting to stir and make sweet little grunting noises. "Auntie is here and wants to see you, sweetheart."

Devin pours Jameson in his swaddle into my arms, and I cradle him close to my chest and stroke his head with my fingers. He nuzzles his cheek into my touch and reaches out of the blanket to wrap his tiny fingers around my pinky. He might as well have reached right into my chest and grabbed hold of my heart.

As I follow my sister toward the men and Mallory, I drop my head close to Jameson and breathe him in. "You and me? We're going to be thick as thieves, kiddo. Just wait and see."

# CHAPTER THIRTY-FOUR

UNSURPRISINGLY, Jameson is a chick magnet, and Mallory puts two and two together *fast*. She's not much of a baby person, but when she spots a flock of single women–a collection of Devin and Brett's friends–she pops up out of nowhere and starts laying the charm on thick.

Mallory eyes a pretty brunette with a massive thigh tattoo of a dragon and flowers. "Let me take him." She nudges me and starts slipping her hands under the swaddled baby. "Just for a few minutes."

"No." I pull Jameson away. "I'm not letting you use my nephew as a lure."

"Oh, don't be like that," she says.

After a bit of back and forth, Mallory wins, and she scoops my nephew up and manages to look like she sort of likes babies as the brunette with the tattoo closes in and coos down at Jameson.

Mack sidles up behind me. "She's got moves."

"She's a con artist."

He chuckles and hands me a glass of chilled sangria. "Have you and your mom had a chance to talk?"

I sip the refreshing drink and manage to slurp a raspberry out of the glass. It's loaded with brandy and wine and makes my cheeks pucker. "No," I manage. "She keeps flitting away every time we're in the same vicinity. But she's been watching you since we got here."

Mack and I talked about how stretched my relationship with my mother feels after everything that has happened between us leading up to Jameson's birth. I can sense that friction waning, at least on my end, but closure is needed. I want to wipe the slate clean and move forward on better terms for all our sakes. I have a *boyfriend*, which is a wild statement for me to make, even in the silence of my own mind, and I want her to see me doing well.

Mack nods across the perfect green lawn to the gazebo my dad built when Devin and I were kids. It's trimmed with white lattice and flanked by tomato and basil plants. Beneath the structure is a lounge area with an outdoor carpet full of mandalas in vibrant shades of yellow, turquoise, pink, and purple. The furniture is sleek and modern, and there are lit lanterns on the ground that will create the perfect ambiance once the sun goes down.

Mom is under there speaking with Brett's mother.

Now might be the best chance we have to chat, so I take Mack's hand and walk him over and introduce him to Kathy, Brett's mother. I've always found her to be patient and kind, with a steady temperament and a welcoming aura. Today is no different. She greets Mack with a one-armed hug while keeping her other arm outstretched, maintaining her hold on her glass of white wine. She's wearing a pink summer set of capris and a matching sleeveless shirt. She's a heavy-set woman with a large chest that she always decorates with long necklaces. Today she's wearing long gold necklaces with turquoise pendants that match her sandals.

"It's so good to see you, darling," Kathy says as she turns her attention to me. "I saw you with Jameson earlier. Isn't he such a doll?"

"He looks like your son," I tell her.

She smiles proudly. "Doesn't he, though? All cheek, no neck. Brett was exactly the same."

I laugh. "I'll make sure to tell him that every time his ego gets a little too big."

"You do that, dear. Tell me, what's the scoop with you two?"

Kathy's green eyes shift back and forth between Mack and me. "Are you an item?"

My mother shoots Kathy an incredulous look for asking such a bold question. I suppose I can't blame my mother for thinking a question like that might set me off. But it doesn't.

I take Mack's hand. "We are, as of very recently."

Kathy beams even brighter. "Splendid! Just splendid! You look dashing together."

Mack straightens. "Dashing, huh? I like the sound of that."

Kathy winks at him. "Take care of our girl, now. You hear? She's a special one."

Mack looks down at me as he answers. "She is. A handful. And a bit bratty," he adds with a devilish grin in Kathy's direction. "But special."

Kathy bursts out laughing and nudges my mother with her elbow. "He's a riot, Deidra!"

My mother gives Mack an unreadable look. "He is."

*Oof.*

Even Kathy seemed to feel the inauthenticity of the response, and she makes herself scarce, saying she needs to go "smell the baby". I call after her that she'll have to fight Mallory for him, which turns out to be a rather quick battle because Mallory relinquishes Jameson to his grandmother rather quickly, only to steer the tattooed brunette to the punch bowl and get her a drink.

"So how long has this been official?" Mom asks.

"A few days," I tell her.

Mack slides his hands into his jean pockets. "I got tired of her begging me to date her and caved."

I smack him on the chest. "Shut up. You did not."

He snorts and rubs at his chest. "Ow."

Mom watches us with the sharpened interest of a private detective. Not liking how she's scrutinizing us, I switch gears and try to make small talk with her. I compliment the decor and all her hard work on Brett's party. If Devin weren't freshly postpartum, I know she would have handled all this, but it was nice of Mom to step up and make it happen for him. Both Brett and Devin were going a little stir-crazy at home, so being out with their friends and having a nice time is good for them. And with all the extra hands, they have support with Jameson.

"They won't let me babysit," Mom says abruptly. It's off topic, but not off brand for her to bring things right to herself. "But they'll pass him around to people they haven't even seen in a year without a second thought."

"I don't really think those two things are the same," I say.

"Don't you know how hurtful that is? I'm his grandmother. When am I going to get my chance to bond?"

Frowning, I try to think of the right thing to say that will squash this here and now and not ruin the evening. "Have you told Devin how you feel?"

"Of course I have," Mom snaps. "She won't listen. She says it's too soon for her to be apart from him. But I can do everything she can for him."

"Well, not everything," I say. "Devin literally just became a mother. Give her a bit of time to wrap her head around it. When she's ready, I'm sure she'll reach out and set up a time for you to watch Jameson on your own. She's going to need her own time, too. Mom," I pause and put my hand on her shoulder, sensing her putting up walls and trying to push down what I'm saying. "Devin is going to need you. But it's so soon. Don't you want the time you get with Jameson to be time Devin can use to breathe? If she's worried about her son and feeling guilty, then what's the point?"

"You don't understand."

*Why do I even try?*

Beside me, Mack shifts his weight to his other foot and looks longingly at the men gathering around the grill.

I shrug. "Guess not."

"Some sympathy would be nice, Charlie."

I open my mouth and close it again. Every encounter I've had with my mother over the last six or so months has proven that there is no right thing to say–not when she has her mind made up, and she's decided that her feelings trump everyone else's. Including her daughter's, who has just become a mother, and who is in the literal eye of the storm trying to get her footing. It pisses me off.

A lot.

But I'm not going to ruin this for Devin and Brett. I've ruined enough.

*High road,* I tell myself.

"It's big of you to still throw this party and put a smile on when you're feeling this way," I tell my mother.

She finally looks at me and meets my eye, and the harshness of her glare softens. Her furrowed brow relaxes, and she gives me a small, but gracious, nod.

"Thank you, Charlie."

All my instincts want me to flee, but I wrap an arm around her and rest my head on hers for a moment. Mack watches, the faintest glimmer of a smile playing on his lips, as I give my mom a peck on the forehead and tell her to keep her chin up. Then, I take Mack's hand and lead him away from the gazebo to a quiet corner of the garden full of hydrangeas and bumblebees.

"I think I figured out your problem." Mack places his hands on my hips and draws me in close. If people are watching us, he doesn't seem to care.

"Oh, this ought to be good." I let myself lean against his chest, placing both hands flat against him. "What's my problem?"

"All this bad attitude and tension? You just needed to get laid."

I feign being insulted and pull away. "Excuse me? You're an asshole, Mack…" I trail off and realize I don't even know his last name. After all this time, how can I not know his full name?

He pulls me back with a delicious smirk. "Carver."

"Mack Carver." I roll his name around in my head and like the sound of it. It suits him with his sharp edges and mysterious undercurrent. "I like it."

He chuckles. "And if you didn't?"

"Then I'd have kept that to myself. I wouldn't want to hurt your feelings."

"There's that attitude. Do I need to lay you on your back and fuck you senseless again so soon?"

His words melt my insides, and I squirm in his grasp, looking around at all the people around. "Hush. Someone will hear."

He just leans in close. "Hear what? Me saying how I can't stop thinking about how good it felt to be inside you?"

"Mack," I plead. "Don't do this to me here."

"Then perhaps we should go."

"I have to say my goodbyes. They haven't even served the cake yet." I swallow and try to keep my head in the game–in the present moment at a *family* event–not in fantasyland with Mack. "I can't go yet."

He scans the yard quickly, taking stock of everyone present, and noting that a good chunk of them are watching us. He makes a low noise in the back of his throat. "Damn. Good thing I didn't feel you up. We're drawing a lot of attention."

I don't want to look. They're all staring, and I know why. I'm flirting with a man for the first time after Daniel. Some of them are probably judging me. Maybe some are happy for me. Maybe others are jealous because they want Mack for themselves. I can't blame them.

He's pretty spectacular.

*So why the hell are you not letting him take you home right now?*

I look up at him with a fire in my belly. "Let's go."

# CHAPTER THIRTY-FIVE

MALLORY HURRIES AHEAD of us across the street to Mack's truck and jumps in the air to click her heels together.

"Hurry up, you two," she calls over her shoulder. "Let's get the hell out of here before Stephanie realizes we're gone and tries to drag us into that group photo she won't shut up about."

Mack, walking beside me, reaches down and squeezes my ass. "As soon as she's out of my truck, you're mine."

My panties are soup.

My brain is mush.

And my anticipation is at an all-time high. Now that I know what fucking Mack feels like, I can't wait to have him all to myself. I have half a mind to leave Mallory here to fend for herself.

But only half. The other half knows we have to get her home before we can have our own fun.

Mallory chats our ears off in the back seat on the drive from my parents' place to hers. Even parked outside her townhouse, she's still yapping, telling us all about the two phone numbers she snagged from single ladies at the party, and how she knows one of them is a hundred percent straight but would make a great hook-up with no strings attached.

"Hey, Mal," I say, turning in the passenger seat to smile sweetly at her. "Get out."

Mallory blinks and lets her mouth fall open incredulously. "Um, rude."

Mack shifts in his seat behind the wheel and discretely tries to adjust his jeans, which look exceedingly tight around his crotch. Poor guy has had a hard-on for almost forty straight minutes. He needs relief, and I know just how to give it to him.

But step one?

Evict the best friend.

Mallory catches on quickly, gives me a knowing smile, and slides out of the back seat to come around to my open window. She raps her knuckles on the door. "You two kids have fun. Don't do anything I wouldn't do."

I shoo her away. "Bye, Mal."

She flips us both the bird and heads up to her front door. As soon as she's safely inside, Mack pulls away from the curb and navigates the narrow residential street to cross the city and hit the highway back to Port Moody.

It's dark, and the cab of the truck is higher than surrounding traffic, minus the occasional semi truck. That's not enough to deter me from sliding across the bench seat of his truck and unzipping his fly.

"Hold up," he says huskily.

I rub him over his boxers. He's rock hard and ready. Hold up? I don't think so.

The cab lights up briefly when we pass under an illuminated overpass. I pull him free of his boxers and stroke him while he keeps his eyes on the road. As I lean down, his grip on the wheel tightens, and his knuckles turn white. A rush of lust breaks over me as I press my lips to his tip and draw him into my mouth slowly, teasing him by rolling my tongue over his tip. His cock flexes in my hand, and I love how sensitive he is to my touch. I take him deeper, slowly working my way down his length and letting my tongue rest against his length.

"Charlie," he groans. "Jesus Christ. We shouldn't–"

I take more of him, as much as I can handle, and forgo breathing. Then I start bobbing on his dick, fucking my throat with his length until my eyes start to water. Every thought is gone from my mind. All that exists is his dick and the thrilling knowledge of how good it's going to feel when he finally has his chance to fuck me.

He switches lanes.

I devour him.

He pulls off the highway, his jaw flexing, his hips shifting as I suck him off. Another groan escapes him as he hits the brakes, and we come to a slow stop somewhere that isn't lit. I don't bother looking up to see where we are. I'm too busy suffocating and loving every second of it.

He yanks the emergency brake, grabs me by my hair, jerks his hips up, and drives his cock even deeper into my throat.

I grip the edge of the seat beneath me. I would moan, but I can't make a sound around him. He thrusts in and out, taking my mouth just like he took my pussy last weekend. I'm wetter than I've ever been, and if we keep going like this, I'm going to ruin his seats.

Mack slows his rhythm, and I take every inch, worshipping him, until he pulls me off and drags me into his lap. My back is against his chest when he pushes my legs open, his steering wheel between my knees, and runs his hand up the inside of my thigh. He stills when he discovers that the tennis dress has shorts built into it.

"The fuck is this?"

"Skort," I pant.

"That sounds like a shitty candy bar." He searches for the top of the shorts, but they're all sewn together in one piece with the dress, which makes him growl. With one quick jerk, he tears a hole in the seam down the crotch.

His fingers find my wetness, and he doesn't bother teasing me this time. I let my head fall back against his shoulder and sigh as he fills me up. I shift up and down, gently jostling in his lap as he fucks me deep and *right*.

Through the windshield, I see we're at a truck stop on the side of the highway. Headlights and brake lights pass us by about a hundred feet away. We're cloaked in shadow, hopefully invisible–but even if we aren't, it feels too good to care.

Mack shifts me in his lap, pulling my hips back and forcing me to sit up a little straighter. My head hits the roof of the cab, and I have to lean to the side as he lifts my ass up. I don't expect him to slide his cock in, but when he does, I relish the pleasure. He pushes in deep, dragging me all the way down on his length, and he holds me there as I squirm and roll my hips, feeling him press into all my deepest places.

"That's it," he purrs behind me. He reaches around in front of me to rub my clit.

I start bouncing, my ass slapping against his thighs, and I don't stop even when another car pulls into the truck stop area. The guy who gets out doesn't see us as he steps over the median and takes a piss in the grassy area on the other side.

Mack grabs my face and turns my head to the side so he can kiss me on an angle. He drags me back, arching my spine, and starts fucking me relentlessly as I descend into madness. My muscles turn to liquid, and I slump against his shoulder and the driver's door as he makes me come in his lap. The handle on the door digs into my hip. The lock mechanism stabs my elbow. But all of that is background noise to the crescendo of pleasure as Mack comes inside me.

We both pant for breath, and he holds me in his lap to kiss me tenderly, stroke my cheek, and run his fingers teasingly up and down the inside of my thigh.

"I never expected you'd be such a freak," he says.

"Honestly?" It's hard to talk. His dick is still inside me. But I don't want to move. "Me neither."

"So this is all just for me?" His hand stills on my inner thigh, his fingers reaching out to swirl over my clit as he slowly pulls his cock out and replaces it with his digits.

I moan and grip the door handle. His cum drips out of me, but he doesn't seem to care. He looks down over my shoulder, his eyes burning at the sight of me, swollen and pink, well-fucked, and ready for more.

Yes, I shudder. *It's all for you, Mack Carver.*

# CHAPTER THIRTY-SIX



"You got rid of the green velvet chairs," I tell Dr. Flagstaff as she sits across from me in a new armchair. It's a much simpler design than her old matching set; instead of lux velvet, these chairs are done in a floral-printed linen with pastel petals of yellow, blue, and pink. To me, they feel like Easter.

Dr. Flagstaff, on the other hand, looks like All Hallows Eve.

She's cut her black hair shorter since the last time I saw her. When was that? A month ago? Longer? Shoot, I can't recall. Gone is her blunt bob, and in its place is an adorable pixie that's longer on top, a bit shaggy, and wispy around her ears and eyes. The shorter cut shows off the earrings all the way up her cartilage and the defined line of her jaw above her sleek neck.

*She really is a beautiful woman,* I think for the first time in the three plus years that I've been coming to sit and talk to her.

"I did–a couple of weeks ago," she says, running both hands over the thick armrests on either side of her. She drums her fingers along the edges and gives me a warm berry-lipstick smile. "It took me a bit to warm up to them. The green felt a bit more romantic and my style, but this is growing on me. I think I might paint and put some wall-paper up, too."

My therapist and I don't usually do small talk, but this is nice. So I ask some more questions, collecting answers about how she wants the wallpaper to feel like Mykonos, how change is good, and how she might even change her light fixtures to something more opulent.

"I don't want it to feel like an office," she concludes. "I want my patients to come in and feel like they're somewhere that was curated for all the different versions of them. The versions pining for more, for less, for space, for closeness–all the things." She blushes–another first–and runs her fingers through her hair in a way that looks like she is surprised to find how short it is. She clasps her hands together in her lap. "Anyway. You're on the clock. Why are we talking about interior design?"

"It's nice to hear some things about you that are personal. I feel like I've known you forever. But all we do is talk about my problems."

"That's what you pay me for."

"Yeah, I know, but still." I flash her a smile. "I like you."

Her head cocks ever so slightly as she regards me. "Hmm."

"What?"

"Something's different since the last time you were here."

"It's been a while." I count on my fingers. "Two weeks?"

"Five, actually."

"Five?!"

She nods and leans back, settling deeply into her floral armchair. She looks so elegant with her long purple manicure and dainty ankles on display in her strappy sandals. For three years I have coveted how put together she is and ached to be able to get back to that myself. "I hope you've cancelled your last two appointments because things have been going well and not because you were avoiding me."

For the first time *ever*, I feel giddy sitting in my therapy appointment. I had half a mind to cancel again this morning when I woke up in Mack's bed to a hot coffee on the night-stand and him getting ready for work in front of the mirror on the back of his door. I'd sipped my coffee and watched his every move, appreciating the view as he zipped up his fly.

*Yum.*

"Things have been good," I tell Dr. Flagstaff. Then I giggle and feel my cheeks get hot. "Like... *really* good. Freaky good. Better than I thought I could ever get again."

Her eyebrows raise. "Is that so?"

I burst into a monologue, telling her every gritty detail of everything that has happened over these past weeks. How things got dicey with Mack and me, and how I thought it was all over, only for us to come back together after I pulled that ridiculous stunt with Clayton at the bar. Her eyebrows shoot up even higher at that. But by the time I circle all the way around to bringing Mack to Brett's birthday, to sleeping with him and spending the night with him nearly five nights a week, to his sister crashing in my guest room as of a few days ago after staying with Mack, her expression has settled into one of unreadable neutrality.

And that makes my stomach a little queasy.

"What is it?" I ask.

Dr. Flagstaff assumes her normal position of crossing one leg over the other. "Nothing. I'm happy for you, Charlie. It sounds like Mack has been a very positive addition to your life and that you two have something really positive between you."

"Yes, we do. But why do I feel like you're telling me what I want to hear right now?"

"I'm not. I'm acknowledging some truths. Of which there are more."

"Okay," I say slowly.

Whatever comes next, I'm not sure I'm ready for it. The last few weeks have been nothing short of blissful. I've been having the best sex of my life, I no longer sleep alone, and I'm pretty sure I'm falling in love all over again–a luxury and a privilege I had written off ever having.

Mack has proven me wrong on so many fronts and in all the best ways. Since meeting him, he's saved me from myself. From my past. From everything I lost and refused to let myself have. He'd come inside and turned all the lights on and made it impossible for me to keep living in the corners and the shadows.

"You're moving very quickly," Dr. Flagstaff says. "Sometimes, and perhaps in this case, it's not a big deal because both parties are equally invested and have the same objective. They're open and honest, striving to move forward and build a life together. If that's what they want, of course. Do you and Mack ever talk about where you want this to go?"

"We're taking it day by day and enjoying the ride."

"Have you been honest with yourself about what you want and need, Charlie?"

"I…" I trail off and think hard. "I think so."

"And what is that?"

Well, I should have seen that question coming. Dr. Flagstaff isn't in the business of letting her patients off the hook easily. If accountability had a sheriff, it would be her.

She sees me struggling, so she prompts me further. "Do you want another marriage? Do you specifically *not* want marriage? Do you want to move in with a partner one day again? Do you want to live alone always? Do you have expectations of this partner?"

I lick my lips.

"You don't have to answer me right now," she says graciously. "But I think it's important to consider those things, and when you're ready, sit down with Mack and talk about them together. He may not realize that you're blowing past all these important talking points that will help you both have clarity about where you're going. If you two want to build a life together, does he know what sort of history you bring to the table and how that can affect your life? You loved another man first–enough to marry him and go through all these steps together. Will that make Mack insecure at some point in the future?"

Well, fuck me.

"I don't know," I say softly.

*Giddiness officially snuffed.*

Dr. Flagstaff lets me sit in my discomfort and the truth of her words for a moment. Not only is accountability her thing, but so is sitting in silence and letting a moment breathe. She never rushes anything. She just holds space.

Finally, I take a deep breath and exhale slowly.

She takes this as her cue to shift gears. "This is your path to carve, but it might be wise to consider living in the moment, enjoying every wild, fun, unexpected second with Mack, but keeping it in the back of your mind that these conversations should probably happen at some point. Even if that's months down the road. Everyone moves at their own speed. Continue getting to know him. When the door to that conversation opens, have some thoughts already formed so you can be truthful about where you're at and where you want to go."

Another silence fills the room as I digest her words.

"Maybe we should have just kept talking about your new wallpaper," I say.

She laughs, bright and airy. "If you want to pay me to do that, by all means."

"Not really."

She nods, her smile honest. "For what it's worth, Charlie, I can see growth in you. Your posture is more relaxed, your shoulders are down, and your eyes are softer. You smile more easily. Your complexion is brighter. Even your clothes are different."

I look down at the new jeans I bought that fit me like a glove and the cute red shirt with little white daisies all over it that Mack loves because I wore it and a thong around his house a few nights ago and drove him wild.

"Thank you," I say.

"Either you're doing the work, or Mack is healing you in more ways than one," she says. "Just make sure that, if it's the latter, you have a contingency plan in place to keep moving forward if it's not with him."

Not with him?

That thought feels vile. Mack is mine, and I am his, and he

deserves more than for me to be talking about him in therapy like he's replaceable.

"I want to show him that I want him to stay," I tell her. "I want to bring him fully into my life and show him every crack and crevice of who I am. Good and bad. And then, if he leaves, so be it. If he stays?" I stop and think of Daniel. Of him smiling at me on Christmas morning. Of the way he kissed me on our wedding day. How he cried as he helped me take my dress off because of how lucky he felt to have me as his wife. How he pumped my gas every Sunday evening. How he made sure the fridge was stocked with my favorite snacks when PMS hit hard. How tenderly he gave me my fertility injections before I gave up. "If he stays, then I'll know I've found someone who loves me as much as Daniel did."

"As long as you've found someone you love as much as you loved Daniel," she says, a serious note in her tone. "Mack deserves that."

*Of course he does,* I think, wondering why she said it.

Our time ends, and as I drive home, I wonder over that final comment. Instead of heading back to my condo, I make for the highway, back to my old stomping grounds, and back to the church a few blocks away from the house Daniel and me were supposed to spend forever in. I stop at the house first, shocked to see the new owners have painted the red front door blue. They've poured more concrete to expand the driveway. A swing set is visible in the backyard over the fence.

The house is everything Daniel dreamed it could be for us.

I lurch away from the curb and make for the church, where I pull into the nearly empty lot and get out. I cross the grounds, the insoles of my sandals sticking and unsticking to the soles of my feet with every step. When I reach a marble wall that rises up out of the earth, I step in close and trail my fingers over the plaques until my touch settles on his.

HERE LIES DANIEL HALE.
Loving Husband and Son.

1984 - 2022
*"Gone but with us, eternally."*

271

CLOSING MY EYES, I lean in and rest my forehead on the plaque, the cool marble the only thing between me and the ashes of Daniel.

"Hey," I say softly. "I haven't been here in a while. There's a lot we need to talk about."

# CHAPTER THIRTY-SEVEN

"I THINK YOU'D LIKE HIM." I've lost track of how much time I've spent with Daniel. The sun has gone down, and the mosquitos are out, but I'm content sitting on the ground with my back against the marble talking to my dead husband. "He'd probably have rubbed you the wrong way the first time you met him. He definitely did me. He pissed me off, actually, and was kind of an asshole." I smile at the memory of meeting Mack when he showed up with *Simon Says MOVE*. "He broke your Christmas mug in the move. I thought I was going to break too." I tip my head back and look up at the sky. The stars are just starting to glimmer against the blue. "But I didn't."

*Maybe I should have. Maybe the grief should still be eating me alive. Maybe Daniel deserves more than three years. Don't Italian widows have an obligatory mourning period where they wear black and grieve their husbands? Maybe I should Google that.*

I smile when I hear Daniel's voice in my head. *"Don't you dare get rid of the color in your wardrobe, sweetheart."*

The cemetery is calm and still. I wrap my arms around myself. "I miss you."

Somewhere nearby, a cricket starts singing.

"I miss you so much, and falling in love with Mack is making me feel like you're further from me now more than ever. I don't know if that's a good thing or a bad thing. I don't know if it's going to catch up to me and ruin me. All I know is it's true. Daniel... I'm... I think I might be in love with him."

The cricket goes quiet.

"Are you mad?" I whisper into the night.

The silence is excruciating. I hang my head and close my eyes, wishing I could hear Daniel's voice one last time–wishing he could give me permission to love Mack recklessly and wildly, the way my heart wants to. But my mind is so scared. My body remembers the pain of everything I've gone through after Daniel. I can't live through that again.

"I feel like I'm in purgatory," I say, picturing Daniel in my mind's eye. We're in the kitchen of our dream house. It smells like the onions and peppers frying for the dinner I was making the night he died. I pretend the marble at my back is Daniel standing behind me while I run my burnt wrist under the cold water at the kitchen sink. "I feel like part of me died with you that night, and I've been a corpse walking around trying to pretend I'm still alive. Trying to pretend I still belong with everyone else. At the birthday parties, the baby showers, the family dinners, the cafes with strangers... After you were gone, nowhere felt right. Until him."

I ache for the marble to morph into my husband–to grow warm against me, to envelope me, to promise never to leave me again.

But the cold is sharp and raw.

"Mack has given so much of myself back to me. I can't lose her again. But I can't use him to keep me held together, either. I don't know how to walk this line, Daniel. I don't know how to love, and miss, and honor you, while loving and building a life with him that was supposed to be *ours*."

The cricket starts up again.

"If he even wants that with me," I whisper.

*"He'd be a fool not to want a life with you, Charlie,"* Daniel's voice says in my head. *"All I want for you is a second chance. Don't be too scared to take it on my account."*

Sniffling, I turn my attention to the stars, which bring me back to a night a long time ago, at the tail end of summer when I was nineteen years old, and Daniel rowed me out in a canoe to the middle of Rolley Lake. We laid under the stars wrapped in blankets and talked about our hopes and dreams for the future.

Baby names.

Wedding color schemes and guest lists.

The neighborhood we would live in.

The college fund we would build for our kids.

The hot mom car he would buy me.

The passionate sex.

The slow romance of our golden years.

The inevitable end. Together.

"If we could go all the way back to the beginning," I tell him, "I wouldn't change a thing. Would you?"

More crickets are chirping. The moon is starting to rise. The night is blooming.

*"Just my wedding haircut."*

I laugh until I cry, and then I cry until I laugh, and I cling tightly to the warmth in my chest.

# CHAPTER THIRTY-EIGHT

MACK LEANS against his counter in his kitchen. Beside him, a pot of noodles boils. I'm on the other side of the kitchen island chopping vegetables and dropping them into a bowl.

"What do you mean you talked to Daniel last night?"

We didn't cross paths last night. I went home after spending a couple of hours at the cemetery, and then Mack worked an early shift this morning, so we are catching up on the last forty-eight hours while we prepare dinner at his house. Gia is on her way over to join us after crashing at my condo for the last several weeks. Clayton is right where he should be, in jail, but she doesn't feel comfortable being in her house all alone, and I can't blame her. With all the time Mack and I have been spending together at his place, it feels wrong not to offer my condo to her. She'd been enamored by it the day they brought me home. Someone should at least enjoy it.

"I mean, I went to the cemetery, and I sat by his memorial, and I talked to him," I say.

"About what?"

"Everything. Us."

"Elaborate." Mack turns and checks the noodles, giving them a little stir. "Shit. I think I forgot to set a timer. How long have I had these in the water for?"

"Don't ask me. Daniel was the cook. I was the cute commentator."

Mack stops stirring for the briefest second before continuing. "Right."

"I know I sound crazy, but after my session with Dr. Flagstaff, I had this compulsion to spill my guts to him and tell him about you and me. About how I'm feeling, where this might be going, and, well, yeah."

Mack looks over his shoulder at me. "Where this is going, huh?"

I nod. "I'd like to talk about that sometime soon, if you're open to it."

He turns fully to face me, his lips curling up at the corners. "I am."

"Good."

"Good," he agrees. "Perhaps I should talk to him, too."

I toss some oil over the bowl of veggies and pause. "You would want to?"

"Why not? It's not like I can say the wrong thing and piss him off and have him punch me or something." He gives me a wicked little grin that shouldn't make me smile but does anyway. Then he offers an apologetic wince. "Too soon?"

"You're on thin ice, buddy."

He chuckles. "You can introduce us. I'll play nice, I promise. I'm sure he'd like to hear what my intentions are."

I roll my eyes and sprinkle the veggies with salt and pepper. "You think you're *so* funny."

"When I have a good audience, I'm hilarious."

"So it's my fault your jokes don't land?"

"Definitely."

Laughing, I pour the veggies onto a sheet pan and spread them out using a spatula. I bring them over to the preheated oven, hip bump Mack out of my way, open the door, and slide the pan in before closing it and obnoxiously setting a timer in front of him.

He chuckles. "If Gia weren't on her way over, I'd take you into the bedroom right now and punish you for being a brat."

Brat?

Oh, he has no idea.

I stick my tongue out, reach down, and grab his dick and balls.

His eyes widen in surprise, which gives me a rush of endorphins that makes me feel high. Laughing like a hyena, I take off running when he tries to smack my ass. He yanks the hand towel off the handle of the oven and chases after me, catching up to me in the living room, tackling me around the waist and throwing me down on the sofa, where he lifts my leg and gets a good three whips at my ass with the towel.

"Ouch!" I squeal-laugh, trying to wriggle and escape, but he's too strong, so I change tactics and grab him by the front of his shirt so I can haul him down and kiss him.

He eases into the kiss, leaning over me on the couch, and I reach down again and rub him over his pants. It's a much gentler approach than when I man-handled him, and this time I'm not being bratty, so he rewards me by pushing me against the back of the sofa and kissing me more deeply.

Then his sister knocks on his front door.

"We'll pick up where we left off later," he murmurs against my lips.

Pouting, I hold on to his shirt when he tries to leave to answer the door. "One more kiss?"

He gives me a reckless smile and another kiss that leaves me breathless when he manages to pull away and go to the door. I hear Gia's sing-songy voice as she comes inside, and I take a minute to regroup, fix my hair, and fan my cheeks. She doesn't need to know I'm all fired up and wish I could take her brother down the hall to his room. There may not be time for that tonight though, because he has a closing shift at Dixie's to get to by nine o'clock.

A real bummer.

I meet them in the kitchen, where Mack pours each of us a glass of red wine, and I put out the bruschetta appetizer I made. We sit with Gia on Mack's back deck while dinner simmers on the stove, the noodles set aside while the spices in the sauce mingle. A humming-bird flits from a maple tree in the neighbor's yard to a birdbath in the garden. Gia lights up when she sees it and slumps when it disappears as quickly as it came.

"Has Clayton tried reaching out to you at all from jail?" Mack asks, shifting the light-heartedness of the summer evening to something heavier.

Gia shakes her head. "No. But I expect he will soon."

"What makes you say that?" he asks.

She takes three large gulps of wine. "I'm serving him with divorce papers this week."

Mack's eyebrows shoot up.

"Really?" I ask.

This is something she's talked about before, but neither Mack nor I were totally convinced she'd go through with it.

Gia nods. "Really. I'm done. I have a safe place to stay because of you, and he's behind bars, so there is no safer time for me to cut all ties than now."

Mack lifts his glass. "Here's to that."

Gia and I clink our glasses against his.

"We should celebrate," I say. "I could call some of my girlfriends, you call yours, and we all head out to Dixie's tonight? Mack can pour us shots. We can dance the night away. What do you think?"

Gia giggles nervously. "I haven't gone out dancing in *years*. Clayton lived to go out, but never dancing, and he didn't want me going without him, either."

"Well, he can suck an egg," I say. "We're going to dress up, throw on some outfits that make us feel sexy, and go dancing. I'll call in the cavalry."

Mack grimaces. "Be warned, Gia. The cavalry includes a spicy lesbian with a foul mouth and a big appetite for cute girls."

Gia blinks at her brother. "I've met Mallory, and she was lovely."

He arches an eyebrow. "Wonderful? Really?"

"Watch it," I warn him, and the three of us chuckle.

Sitting with him and his sister, I notice a bunch of little things all at once; the deliciousness of the meal, the ambiance of the candles and the wine, the eighties rock playlist playing on the stereo in the living room. Little things that I've been blind to for such a long time because I've been so caught up in my head, my grief, and my longing for the life I lost.

But here, in this moment, I'm acutely aware that I'm living again.

~

MALLORY DUCKS BEHIND ME AS WE STAND IN LINE AT THE BAR AT Dixie's. She's hoping the pretty server she had that fling with isn't working. She hasn't shared too many details, but I know they ended on bad terms, just not bad enough to keep her out of our favorite bar.

On my other side, Gia bounces to the beat of a catchy pop song the DJ plays while the band rests their vocals. She has her hair done up in a cute little pinned updo; it's too short for hair ties or clips. The shorter pieces around her face are gently curled, framing her round features and big brown eyes beautifully. She wasn't too keen on Mallory's attempt to totally do her up, but she did accept the swipe of glitter on her eyelids and the plumping lip gloss.

And she looks fabulous.

So does Mallory, like always. She's dyed her hair dark blue since the last time I saw her at Brett's birthday, and she's wearing dagger-shaped earrings, distressed jeans, and a cropped black shirt with a lightning bolt on it. Under the jeans are fishnets studded with tiny glittery jewels. She looks like a punk rocker and stands out in the sea of country-bar loving hicks.

Like Heather, who was the only one of our friends who could swing a night out with such short notice. She was up for it as soon as Mal called her, saying she needs to get out and let loose for a bit to shake off how many hours of work she's been putting in. She's wearing cut-off shorts, cowgirl boots, and a tube top. She looks like she's straight out of a nineties poster some thirteen-year-old boy would have had taped to his ceiling.

In a good way.

When we get to the front of the line, Mack spots me. He's tending bar with wicked speed, pouring drinks, taking orders, and having his tip jar filled to the brim by pretty women who think his smile is just for them.

But it's not, of course.

He looks me up and down as he pours the four of us a row of tequila shots. "Damn, girl. You look good."

I do a little turn for him, showing off that same red summer dress I wore the first time I let him take me out to the brewery on the inlet. This time, I've paired it with cowgirl boots, and I have a bandana tied up in my hair, holding most of the dark mass up in a messy, curly knot on top of my head with loose strands pulled out, and dangly gold hoop earrings peeking through.

Mallory gives a little clap. "Doesn't she, though?"

He slides the shots to us, and we toast to a fun night out before throwing them back.

Gia almost spits hers back into the glass before managing to swallow it and wiping her mouth with the back of her hand. "That's horrible."

"It'll put some hair on your chest," her brother tells her as he takes the empty shot glass from her hand.

Gia scrunches her nose at the aftertaste. "I need something to wash that out of my mouth."

He fixes her a bright pink cocktail of some sort, which she seems pleased with when she takes a sip through a short red straw. He makes each of us one, tells us it's on the house, and shoos us away from the bar so he can serve the other customers in line.

We find a standing table near the edge of the dance floor to set our drinks down and chitchat. Heather tells us about how much she's been working and how woefully sad her romantic life is. Mallory, as one would expect, encourages her to find a hot guy here at Dixie's. Heather asks if Gia is on the prowl, and she goes a little quiet.

I put an arm around her. "Gia has just gotten out of a long-term relationship and is taking things slow. Unless a perfect gentleman should appear tonight, she's here to have fun with us gals. Right?"

She gives me an appreciative smile. "Right."

The DJ booth goes quiet, and the band takes to the stage. The main vocalist is a woman I've never seen here before with long blonde hair and the kind of body that brings men to their knees. She's wearing a rhinestone-studded belt, pink boots, and a short denim romper with fringe here and there. She takes the microphone in one hand and wins the favor of all the women in Dixie's with one question.

"Who's in the mood for some Shania?"

Gia chugs her drink, grabs my hand, and drags me out onto the dance floor. Heather and Mallory are quick to follow, along with every woman in the place, and soon, our feet are stomping to the same rhythm as a line dance breaks out that has me tripping over my own feet. Heather gets it right away, and soon she has a man beside her doing each step in beat with hers, and they're laughing together.

I'm struck with a wave of joy that is quickly followed by the sound of my own voice in my head.

*Am I really lucky enough that I get to have nights like this again?*

The hours pass, but they feel like short moments. We make friends with other women in the bathroom—trading lip stain, gloss, mascara, and giving out tampons and advice to dump their deadbeat boyfriends. We reconnect on the dance floor and stop men from dancing with girls who look uncomfortable. We buy each other rounds at the bar and step outside to hold our hair off the back of our neck and cool off before rushing back in when the band comes back on. We talk to strangers outside who offer us puffs of their cigarettes. For some reason, we try them, hack up a lung, laugh at how stupid it is, and chase away the taste of nicotine with a fresh drink.

Mack and I catch passing glances, and I love having his eyes on me when I dance, but I miss him, and I crave his touch like nothing I've ever experienced by the time I'm six drinks into my night.

Maybe I can steal him away for five minutes. That's all I need.

I break away from my girls on the dance floor and tell them I'm going to talk to Mack really quick. They're in conversation with new friends we've made and barely notice me slip away. On my way to the bar, I notice that Mack isn't there, when I only just saw him there a few minutes ago.

Is he on break?

I stretch to the tips of my toes to peer over the heads in the crowd, but he's nowhere to be seen. He must be outside, so I take that same exit he led me out all those weeks ago and push into the back parking lot of Dixie's. Several employees are in the smoke pit, along with some customers who are shit-faced and messy.

And that's when I hear it.

Yelling.

It's a man's voice–not Mack's. But I hurry toward it anyway, knowing in my gut that something is wrong. I find them along the backside of the smoke pit, secluded in a poorly lit spot. Mack has his back against the wall and his fists clenched at his sides. Another man, wearing a sports jacket and jeans, is pointing in his face and yelling at him.

"You're a fucking liar, Carver. Now I have these assholes knocking on my door before I open up for the night trying to track you down so they can 'have a word with you.' I'm sick of this shit at my establishment. I can't have a guy with a criminal record like yours on my payroll anymore. I tried to make this work. I really did, but you're a target for trouble. You told me you only had a restraining order. You never said you served time."

Mack hands it right back to him. "Are you telling me you wouldn't have done the same thing in my shoes? What was I supposed to do? Let him get away with it? Fuck that."

"Not trying to kill him with your bare hands might have been a better option than beating him to a pulp."

Mack lets out a frustrated growl. "I need this job."

"Yeah, and I need my employees to be safe. You're fired, Carver. Get your shit and get out."

The boss turns and walks off, right past me.

And that's when Mack sees me. He lifts his head, his eyes wide, and reaches for me.

But I'm already running.

*No.*

This isn't happening. This isn't real.

*Run.*

I make it back inside before Mack catches up, the exit door banging hard against the wall in his wake. He catches my wrist, but I yank free, sharp and furious, and round on him.

"How dare you." My heart is aching, rioting against the truth of what I just heard, and all the while the music of the bar is pounding in my skull. "You lied to me."

"No, Charlie, just listen, I–"

"I was listening. After everything, all this time, all these conversations… and you've been keeping this from me? Don't you think that's something you should tell someone when you tell them you want to be exclusive with them? We've been playing house! We've been talking about the future. I thought…" Anger coils around my insides. When was he planning on telling me this? How dare he. *How dare he.*

My pain makes my voice shake. "Don't you think I deserve to know you're a felon?"

He rakes his fingers through his hair, his jaw flexing, his eyes flashing with anger. "Don't call me that."

A bouncer comes out of one of the offices in the hallway and puts his hand on Mack's shoulder. "The boss wants you out, man. Now."

Mack shrugs out from under the man's grasp. "Charlie, I know how bad this looks, but I can explain. Just give me–"

"No."

His face contorts, furious.

*Is he mad at me?* He has no fucking right to be pissed at me. I didn't do anything wrong. He's the liar. He's the fraud. He's the imposter.

*He's not who I thought he was.*

The walls of the narrow and dimly lit hallway start closing in on me.

The bouncer gets hold of Mack again. "I'm not asking again, man. Turn around, and get out. You and your girl can sort this out another time."

The boss comes out of the office. "Take your bullshit and your girl out of my fucking bar, Carver. She's right to want nothing to do with your ass."

Mack's shoulders tense. His eyes darken. The hallway grows smaller still, pressing in, darkening at the edges. Shadows feel like they're reaching out and trying to cover my mouth and nose, making it harder for me to breathe. It's hot. Painfully hot. The base of the music thrums in the soles of my boots and beats like a drum building up to an explosion I don't think I can survive.

Mack turns on his boss. "Say that again."

The boss pales ever so slightly then retreats a step back into his office. "I said get out. Bruce. Take his ass outside. Fuck him up if you have to. Send a message."

Mack rolls up his sleeves.

The bouncer, apparently named Bruce, shakes his head. "Come on, man. We're friends. Let's not do this, okay?" He leans in and says something to Mack that I can't hear, but whatever it is, it's effective because Mack's shoulders drop, he nods once, and then he brushes past Bruce and the owner and storms out the back door, leaving me in the rubble.

Bruce sighs. "You going after him?"

I shake my head as numbness closes in.

He nods toward one of the offices. "Come on. I'll get you some water and find your friends. Then, you ladies can take a cab and get out of here. Yeah?"

I wish I had enough of a grasp on my mind to thank him, but all I manage is a small nod. He steers me into an office with a desk and two chairs. There are no windows, but two lamps provide ambient light. There's a mini fridge under the desk where he grabs me a bottle of water and twists the cap off. He hands it to me and watches as I take a few sips, my hand shaking around the bottle.

"Don't worry about Mack," Bruce says. "He's tough. He'll shake a night like this off in no time and be on his feet."

"Screw him."

# CHAPTER THIRTY-NINE

THREE DAYS LATER, Mallory brings me soup and a fresh-baked croissant from a bakery just down the road from my condo. She sits at the foot of my bed while I eat in my lap, feeling sorry for myself, telling her all about how Gia packed up the guest room and left yesterday because she felt like she was betraying her brother by staying with his ex.

*Ex.*

The word stings to say out loud.

"Have you spoken with your therapist about all this yet?" Mallory asks gently.

I shake my head as I soak a bite of my croissant in my tomato soup. "No. I know what she'll say."

"Is that a reason not to talk to her?"

"It is for right now. She'll tell me everything I already know. I went too fast. I didn't know enough about him before I jumped all in. I didn't ask the right questions. I didn't listen to my intuition. I let myself get distracted by his good looks, his charm, and his... well, how good he is in bed." I grimace. "And now he's taken something from me that I can never get back."

"And what's that?"

"It's stupid when I say it out loud."

"So what? It's just me. Stupid is my specialty. I have six tattoos for former girlfriends." She flashes me a supportive smile. "Come on. Lay it on me."

I can't look at her as I answer. The shame is too much. So I stare down at my bowl of soup. "Up until Mack, Daniel was the last man to touch me. To love me. And now I don't even have that anymore."

Mallory sits with that for a moment. "I'm sorry, Charlie."

Nodding, I wipe away fresh tears. "Me too. I feel like such an ass. Devin wants to kill him. My mom is telling me I should have known better, and men who look like him are no good for women like me. Whatever that means."

"Honestly, dude, your mom doesn't really get a vote. She lives in her own reality."

"It just hurts so bad. I... I was falling for him. Maybe more than falling. I might have been all the way there." I can't bring myself to say that four letter word. Not even to Mallory. I can't acknowledge that my feelings for Mack were–and still are–that incredible. He doesn't deserve it. How much of what he told me is true? How many other secrets is he keeping? Who is he really? Behind all the guarded looks, cagey answers, and blatant disregard for being honest with me... is a man I simply do not know. "Daniel never lied to me. He never made me question him. He never made me feel unsafe. Why did I let myself think a random guy who works for a moving company could hold a candle to my husband?"

Mallory stares down at her feet. "Charlie..."

"I'm so mad at myself."

"That's not fair."

"I can't help it. I should have seen the red flags. I should have–"

"No," she interjects, a little sharply. "Comparing Mack to Daniel. It's not fair. They're two different people. They had different histories. Upbringings. Traumas. Daniel was lucky and born into an upper middle-class family, just like you. Mack? I don't think he can say the same. People make choices based on their experiences. Daniel's choices were made from a place without struggle. Mack's were made with a much more jaded perspective of the world."

I study the creases in the corners of my best friend's eyes, the wariness in her posture as she hangs her head. I see turmoil there and feel like an ass.

"I didn't mean it like that," I say, even though that's a bald-faced lie, and we both know it.

She just nods. "Growing up gay in an all-girls Catholic school wasn't easy. Having a mom who wanted me to marry an Italian jock with a six-figure salary wasn't easy. Being pushed out by half of my extended family *wasn't easy*." Her lips press into a fine line. "I had a lot of obstacles, and people like me recognize that in other people. Mack had obstacles, Charlie. Big ones. One of his sisters died when he was just a kid. His other sister married an abusive asshole. Women don't do that unless their experience has shaped them to accept that kind of treatment. They grew up together. Whatever pushed Gia to choose a man like Clayton pushed Mack to where he is, too."

I wish I could suck all my words back in and hold them close. I feel like a scolded child, and I deserve it.

"Mack isn't Daniel," she says again, finally looking at me. "If that's who you wanted him to be, you were doomed from the start, and it wouldn't matter what kinds of secrets he was keeping. Maybe he sensed that Daniel was this pillar of perfection for you, and he knew if he told you the truth about his jail time, you would judge him and bail before you really got to know him. If he was catching feelings as strong as you, can you blame him for wanting to keep his guard up a little longer? You guys moved fast. Like, really fast."

"It felt right in the moment."

"So do tequila shots."

I set my soup and half-eaten croissant on the nightstand. "Touché."

Mallory sighs, tucks her legs up onto the bed, and turns fully to face me. "This probably isn't helpful right now, but I think in the long run, this will end up being a positive thing for you. You grew a lot because of Mack. He pushed you out of the hole you'd been living in for three years and helped you start backfilling it. I know you probably feel like you're slipping back into it, but you don't have to. You can stay up here." She gives me a smile that's full of hope, but her eyes are starting to tear up. "It's felt so good to have you back, Charlie."

Shit.

Now I'm crying.

I wipe at my tears as Mallory starts up too, swiping at the wetness on her cheeks and cursing herself for losing her cool. She has never been an especially emotional person. She likes to keep her feelings close to the vest. I don't blame her. I know how badly it can burn to let someone see you with no protection.

"I don't want to disappear again," I whisper.

"I know you don't."

"But if I do, it's not personal."

Her chin puckers, and she nods as more tears fall. "I know that, too. But I really fucking missed you, and I haven't known how to tell you that. Where do I get off being broken-hearted over losing a friend when she's lost her husband and her child?"

I had no idea Mallory felt this way and that she'd been keeping it to herself for such a long time. But of course, it all makes sense. We've led a one-sided friendship for three years. I barely managed to feed myself some days, let alone check in with her and show any semblance of curiosity about her life—her dates, her work, her health, her family, her woes, her wins. None of it. My own pain and grief were so consuming that every second of every day revolved around how I felt. What I'd lost. What I was going to miss out on for the rest of my life.

"I'm sorry," Mallory sniffles, "I shouldn't have said that."

"No, I'm glad you did. Don't be sorry. I've been a shit friend. A shit sister, too. And probably a shit daughter."

"Mm, the last one is a stretch. No offense to your parents."

I manage a small smile. "Thanks."

Mallory shimmies up the bed and props herself up on the pillows beside me. She crosses her ankles, her black pedicure matching her black and gold anklet. She draws in a deep breath and lets it out slowly. "What are you going to do now?"

It's my turn to sigh. "Make a therapy appointment, I guess? Spend my free time supporting Devin and Brett and getting to know Jameson. Hang out with you more."

"Coquitlam Crunch this weekend?"

I balk. "No."

Mallory manages a laugh through her final tears, which don't reappear after she wipes her eyes with her thumbs. "Come on. Exercise is good for you. Get strong with me."

"I'll think about it."

"Boo."

"I almost died the last time you took me."

"It gets easier every time."

"I don't believe you."

She falls sideways to rest her head on my shoulder. I rest my cheek on top of her head. Her hair smells like coconut.

"We'll be okay," Mallory says, perhaps more to herself than to me. "I know we will. I just won't let you disappear on me again. Even if you get mad at me for dragging you out into the world. Deal?"

My mind transports me back to the three years of hell after Daniel. I'd been alone on a life raft in a storm with thirty-foot waves. The weight on my chest carries a deep sense of knowing that I can't survive that kind of loneliness again. It would destroy me, and if I let it, destroy connections with everyone I care about. I'd almost imploded all of my most precious relationships over those three years, and again in these past eight weeks with everything mounting before Jameson was born. If I let the grief drag me back down into the icy depths, I could lose everyone who still cares enough to show up for me. Like Mallory and Devin. Like Brett. Like my parents, in their own fucked up way.

Mack was one man. Losing him doesn't give me permission to let go of everyone. I have to dig in deeper. Hold on tighter. Show up in whatever capacity I can. They all deserve that.

"Deal," I say finally, mentally pushing the weight off my chest.

*I can do this. I have* to *do this.*

Mallory reaches across me and grabs the TV remote from my

nightstand. She turns the TV on that's mounted on the wall above the dresser at the end of my bed. "Today, though, we can disappear. Fuck the world. Fuck showing up. And fuck Mack." She flicks through some apps before settling on Netflix, where she selects *Schitt's Creek* and hits play. As the episode starts, she pulls her phone out of her back pocket and opens a food delivery app. "I think we need snacks."

"I love you, Mal."

She flashes me a grin and looks at me, seeing the tears coming back in my eyes. She tosses her phone on the bed and throws her arms around me.

"I love you too, Charlie. It's going to be okay."

*It has to be,* I think as I squeeze my best friend tightly.

# CHAPTER FORTY



My mother sits with Jameson in her lap. It's a comfortable early September evening, and the family is together for Sunday dinner. Brett is in the house with Dad, watching a football game, and Devin is with us, sipping contently on a steeped tea and wearing breast pumps in her nursing bra that make a suction sound every three or so seconds. With all the time I've been spending with my sister, I've gotten used to it. Our mother, on the other hand, thinks the pumps are "cheating", and that Devin should strictly breastfeed, like how she did for both of us.

Devin has gotten to a great place of not caring what Mom has to say. I'm proud of her for that. Postpartum is something I have read infinitely about, but seeing it up close and personal with my sister is a whole different ball game than reading about it in books or blogs. When I was pregnant and preparing to have my baby by myself, I wanted to make sure I was prepared for any and all possible scenarios because Daniel wouldn't be there to do late-night bottle feeds or diaper changes. He wouldn't be there to talk me off the ledge when I was touched out, overstimulated, and spinning out from hormones. But all that prep work? It was nothing in the face of the reality of

"""

being a brand-new mom in a foreign body that seems to be doing everything it can to work *against* you.

Devin has handled it all beautifully.

Her first week was tumultuous, but once she and Brett found their rhythm, the following month was newborn bliss. Now, Jameson is two months old, and they're back in the thick of it, dealing with five wakes a night and the challenges of a tongue tie that have made latching damn near impossible.

Devin broke down to me three nights ago on the phone about how devastating it was to have a picture in her mind of how her breast-feeding journey would look, only to have it all come crashing down because of something out of her control. I'd done my best to listen, hold space, and not offer advice or tell her what to do. I knew from all my reading that that wasn't actually helpful. But I did follow up the next day with some resources of experts who deal with tongue ties and left her a hopeful voice note that perhaps her breastfeeding journey was not over, just taking a detour, and if they could resolve the tie, she might be able to get sweet Jameson to latch.

They've already gone to their first appointment, and as of this evening, things are looking up for Devin.

She removes her pumps once they're done and pours the milk into bottles with caps, not nipples. She tightens them and drops them gently in a cooler she brings everywhere with her to store her milk. Meanwhile, Jameson coos in our mother's arms as she tucks him in a little tighter with the plush blanket our aunt knit for him.

"Brett already wants another one," Devin says, holding her tea in both hands.

"No way," I say.

"Way. He's head over heels for Jameson. If it was up to him, we'd have a house full of six kids."

"Your poor vagina."

"Charlie," my mother says, her eyes narrowing in judgement.

Devin laughs. "Right? I told him he'd get three if all the stars aligned, two if he's lucky, and one if I continue feeling like I'm losing my mind."

"Three would be darling," Mom says.

*Three reminders of the one I couldn't have,* I think. But simultaneously, I also think that three would be a lot of fun. Three children to spoil and to be the 'cool auntie' to. I could show up with all kinds of treats that would make Devin's eye twitch and buy them toys that make ungodly amounts of noise. I could afford to take them on cool trips when they're older. Buy them cars for graduation–if Devin and Brett let me, of course. They might tell me I'm overcompensating, which would be true, but hey, so what? Daniel left me a couple million to burn, and our investments just keep growing.

"Three would be fun," I agree. "But if you guys stick with one? Jameson is more than enough. He's perfect."

Devin beams like the proud mother she has gracefully become. "Isn't he, though?"

The last four weeks have been challenging for me, but one thing I am infinitely grateful for is how my bond has developed with my nephew. Before he was born, nothing scared me more than thinking about the impending reality of there being a brand-new baby in the family at every event, every coffee outing with my sister, and every future family memory yet to be fulfilled. I believed that he would be a constant reminder of what I'd lost–but he is a far cry from that.

Jameson is nothing but joy for me. Having him in my life has brushed the dust off parts of my heart that I thought were long dead. Loving him? Easy. Missing him as soon as I say goodbye? Torture. Thinking about his future? A blessing.

Dr. Flagstaff and I are meeting two to three times a week. At first, it felt like overkill, but she keeps me accountable as I wade through the murky waters of my breakup with Mack. Thinking of him still hurts, and sometimes when I'm home alone, I ache horribly for him, but I have come to accept that we aren't right for each other. He was a great way for me to dip my toes back into the dating pool. He hurt me, and I hurt myself, but in the last few days, I've come to believe that maybe, in another six or so months, I'll be ready to try again.

Along with speaking with Dr. Flagstaff, I have been speaking with Daniel. I visit his memorial and resting place two times a week, bringing his favorite beer and drinking it even though I hate it. It makes me feel closer to him. Sometimes, I give him sports updates or tell him about the new hobbies I've started–like knitting–and about the new job I got working as a part-time receptionist for a real estate firm. It gets me out of the house, keeps my mind busy, and connects me with other people a few days a week, and has helped me practice building relationships and connections.

On other nights, I tell him how much I miss him. I tell him about Jameson, and how good of a dad his best friend Brett is. I tell him about Devin growing into her own as a mother and me growing into being an aunt. I complain about our mother relentlessly sometimes, knowing Daniel would just tell me to leave her be.

And, on occasion, I talk about Mack.

How much I miss him. How I hope he's doing okay. How I had to delete all his contact info to stop myself from reaching out to him and opening that door back up. How I wish he could come over for one last wild night in bed. It might be a weird thing to tell Daniel about, but my conversations with my dead husband have become something like journal entries to me, and I always leave the cemetery with a clearer mind than when I arrived.

After dinner with my family, I have every intention of going straight home, but since I'm in the city, I head for the church and cemetery and tell Daniel all about dinner and how Brett wants six kids.

"It's just obnoxious. Six?" I ask, smiling as I lean against the marble wall. "Classic Brett. Devin seems content with one for now, but I won't be surprised if they end up buying a bigger house and raising a whole soccer team. Those would be some lucky kids, don't you think?"

Sometimes, I hear Daniel respond in my mind, but lately, our conversations are a little more one-sided.

Sighing, I wrap my sweater more tightly around myself. "It's getting colder at night again. Mallory is talking about having an old-school Halloween party at her place. Bobbing for apples. Costumes. Pumpkin carving." A memory of Daniel and me at a Halloween party when we were nineteen pops up in my mind and makes me smile. "Remember when Sadie Pixon had that party when her parents were in the Maldives, and the cops came and busted it? We were hiding in the closet under her stairs. You were dressed as Superman and I was Lois Lane?"

An owl hoots nearby. A slow rolling fog creeps over the rise of the property, where tombstones and plaques disappear over the edge and beyond.

"Daniel?"

I close my eyes and listen for his voice in my head. It doesn't come.

"We made out the whole time," I recall. "You had my lipstick all over your face when we finally snuck out after the cops left. We walked back to your parents' house and stopped on the swing set at the park down the road. You told me you loved me. And that you always would."

Smiling, I start to giggle.

"That year for your birthday, I put the Lois Lane costume back on, and you just about lost your damn mind. If only my legs still looked like that, huh?"

The cemetery is silent, and so is Daniel.

"Why aren't you talking to me anymore?" I whisper.

Nothing.

Frowning, I push up to my feet and turn to face his plaque on the marble wall. I trace his name with my fingers and chew the inside of my cheek.

"I still need you, you know."

When his voice still doesn't press into my mind, I rest my forehead against the marble. It's cold as hell. Unforgiving. Barren.

Daniel is gone.

# CHAPTER FORTY-ONE

My head is down as I walk down the hallway after stepping off the elevator in my condo building. I'm looking for my phone in my purse, wondering if I left it at my parents' place, when someone clears their throat. I startle and look up.

Gia is leaning against my front door. She's holding a white paper shopping bag and has a crossbody purse that's bright pink and looks new. "Hey."

"Oh, hey." I find my phone and shut my purse. "What are you doing here?"

She sidesteps out of my way so I can punch the keypad into my door lock. "Can we talk?"

"If it's about your brother? No." The door unlocks, and I push inside, turning to invite her in. "But we can sit and have a glass of wine and talk about other things, if you like."

She fidgets with her purse strap. "Look, I… I know you don't want to talk about Mack. And I don't blame you. But this isn't for him. This is for me. Please?"

Her big brown pleading eyes are pretty hard to say no to.

Gia in general is hard to say no to. She's sweet, and a bit naïve, and the most generous person I've ever met. She'd let me in to talk about whatever I needed to. I know that for a fact.

Groaning, I invite her in. "Fine. Come on. What's he done now?"

"Nothing."

I pour us glasses of red wine in my kitchen, and we go sit in my living room. In a few weeks, it will be time to turn my pilot light on and enjoy my fireplace for the first time in my new condo. In the old house, I missed the past three years of decorating for the changing seasons and holidays, but this year, I have the itch to decorate my condo for autumn. I've already wandered around Homesense several times and picked out some garland and accent pillows.

Gia leans against one of said pillows–a burnt orange rectangle with fringe. "I'm worried about him."

"Okay. Why? Did he try to kill someone else?"

Gia flinches. "He's not like that. That night was a one-off. He had good reason to–" She shakes her head. "Never mind. I'm not here to talk about the past. I'm here to talk about right now." She lifts her chin. "I'm moving."

"You got your own place?"

"I found a place to rent."

"Nice. You deserve to have something that's just yours. Is it set up for your baking?"

Gia gives me a small smile. "Yes, it is. But there's a catch."

"Okay. Spill."

"It's in Jasper."

I pause with my wine halfway to my lips. "That's a whole different province. Like, a fifteen-hour drive from here."

"Or a short flight. Yeah. I need to start over, Charlie. I need a brand new, clean slate, somewhere people don't know me, and I don't know them. Somewhere I won't be reminded of Clayton and all the years I poured into my marriage for nothing. I'm ready to build something that's mine. But it's killing me knowing I'm leaving my brother behind when he needs me."

"Mack doesn't need anyone. He's tough. Isn't that his whole shtick?"

She searches my eyes. "Do you really not miss him?"

I shrug.

"Do you not even care that he's not doing okay right now?"

Her words flood my chest with anxiety and make my throat feel tight. "It's not my business to care anymore. You want a clean slate? Well, so do I."

She drums her fingers on the side of her glass. She's painted them a pale, sparkly, pearlescent pink. "I understand that. I guess I just… I don't know. Thought you'd worry about him the way I do. But that's not on you anymore. I'm sorry."

"Why are you worried about him?" I shouldn't ask. I should keep the door tightly closed on the feelings scrambling to sneak out underneath it. "Did something happen?"

Gia takes a big sip of wine.

*Uh oh.*

Time to backtrack.

"I shouldn't have asked," I say.

"He got jumped three nights ago."

"What?" I sit up straight, wine forgotten and sloshing over the edge of my glass and spilling on my pant leg. "Is he okay? What happened? Who jumped him?"

Gia drinks more before answering. "He's banged up and in the hospital."

Hospital?

*Shit.*

I'm on my feet.

"Wait," Gia says, hurrying to follow me to my front door, where I'm already reaching for my coat and car keys. "You can't go. He doesn't know I came here, and if you show up there? It's going to confuse him. He's all fucked up since you left, Charlie. He understands why. But if you go there to make sure he's okay, you're going to tear that wound open all over again, and he's already hurting enough."

My jaw is clenched so tightly I realize my teeth are starting to ache. I force myself to relax.

"Who jumped him?"

"Police are investigating."

"Where did it happen?"

"At work, when he brought one of the moving trucks back to the lot after hours. He was there alone, locking everything up, when six guys came onto the property."

My heart starts thundering in my chest. "Six?"

She nods, her complexion pale, her shoulders drawn forward like they're protecting her from the truth of it all. "Simon found him the next morning unconscious in one of the truck bays."

Suddenly, I need to sit down. I move into the kitchen and pull a stool out from my island and lower myself onto it.

Gia stands on the other side of the island from me. "He had a concussion, two broken ribs, a sprained wrist, and needed stitches in his eyebrow."

*Mack.*

"Simon provided the police with security footage from the property, and the whole thing is on film. Police are working on identifying the suspects, but they were all dressed in black and wearing masks, so it's going to be hard to tell unless Mack can remember personal details. But the memory is all pretty muddy for him still."

My brain is caught up in panic, still going over the list of his injuries and struggling to catch up with the rest of the information. But soon it all clicks, and I look Gia in the eyes.

"Does this have to do with Clayton?"

She licks her lips. "I think so."

"Is he still in jail?"

She nods. "For now."

"What does that mean?"

"His trial starts in a couple weeks. I'm not going to testify."

"What? Why?"

"Because I'm going to be in Jasper."

"Gia…"

"I can't sit in a courtroom with him, okay? Not after all this. Mack is still going to take the stand. I told him he doesn't have to, but he's dead set on it, and he's convinced those guys were sent to scare him off the idea. Now, he's even more hellbent on testifying against Clayton. I'm just terrified of what the consequences might be. I can't be here anymore. The fear is eating me alive."

"So you're going to let your brother fight your battle for you?" I ask sharply.

She nods. "I am."

That's not the response I expected, but it's honest.

And it pisses me off.

"Mack wants me to go," she adds. "When we talked about it before he was jumped, he offered to drive me out there and get me settled. Things are different now that court dates are set, but he still wants me to get as far away from this as I can."

"He's trying to protect you. He's not right. You should stay. You owe him that."

"That's what I told him. But he–"

"He loves you more than anything," I tell her, my irritation turning my words into daggers. He nearly killed for her. He served time for her. I understand that kind of love. It's the lies I can't accept. "Of course he's going to tell you to run. He'll keep you as far from this as he can. He'll pour gasoline on himself if he has to. It's who he is."

"I know."

"And you can do that in good conscience?"

"No, that's why I'm here."

"Well, I'm sorry to disappoint you, but Mack Carver isn't my problem anymore. And neither is this legal battle, the goons who jumped him, or the ripple effects you're going to cause by bailing and running away. You want to know a hard truth, Gia?"

She shies away from me.

"You go with you to Jasper," I say. "Running doesn't fix anything. It just wires your brain into thinking that you don't have to face your problems. It programs you to take the easy route. And I guarantee it will backfire."

"Maybe," she admits. "But didn't you run from Mack at the first sign of problems?"

"I ran because I couldn't trust him. Not because he had problems. It's *not* the same thing."

She moves to my door and lets herself out into the hallway. "If you say so."

# CHAPTER FORTY-TWO

OVER THE NEXT THREE DAYS, which are full of rain and gray skies, I struggle to stay away from the hospital. Mack is on my mind nearly every waking minute.

Are the nurses taking good care of him?

Is there security there to protect him if those guys try to go after him again?

Are the police taking this seriously, considering his record?

Is he scared?

Not likely. Mack doesn't frighten easily. But I'm sure he's lonely, and after talking to Gia, I'm sure he's got nothing else to do other than think about how things between him and me fell apart. On quiet nights, when I'm alone, my mind always circles back to the good times with him—to him making love to me and laughing with me while we cook dinner. To him throwing his head back when he laughs, or squaring up to me when I try to get competitive with him. To him sleeping in my bed with the sunlight turning his hair golden brown.

Does he still long for those things the way I do?

It's during one of these spiral sessions where I'm thinking about Mack that my phone rings, and the Caller ID is *Simon Says MOVE*.

I answer immediately. "Hello?"

"Miss Warren?"

I recognize Simon's voice immediately. "Yes, it's me. You can call me Charlie."

"Charlie," he says, his tone friendly but slightly strained. "I, uh, have some not-so-great news."

I assume this is about the attack on Mack, but before I have the chance to tell Simon that I already know what happened, he continues.

"We had some flooding in some of the storage units on site with all the rain we've had the last few days. Your unit was one of the ones that got hit. We can cover any cost, but can you come down when you're able and go through it? If anything is damaged, you can leave us a bill."

"Can I come now?"

"Of course."

~

THE RAIN IS COMING DOWN ALMOST HORIZONTALLY BY THE TIME I reach the lot. Three moving trucks are parked along the wire fence. All the lights are on inside the office, and I rush across the lot, the heels of my boots striking the concrete. I push inside, drenched and breathless, and immediately lock eyes with Simon, who is standing behind the counter.

He gives me a lopsided smile. "That was fast."

"Take me to the locker."

Simon leads me through a maze of hallways, and we arrive at the locker full of Daniel's things. I haven't been here in several months—not since Mack told me some items had been damaged in the move.

Simon hauls the storage locker door open.

I hold my breath, anticipating the worst. I expect the cardboard boxes to be soaked through and ruined. Daniel's clothes will need to be washed, which means I won't be able to smell his lingering cologne on them anymore. Before I packed all his things away, I used to pull his things out of his dresser drawers and smell them. What if I can never do that again?

What if everything is ruined?

The door hits the roof with a clang that makes me jump out of my skin. Simon apologizes with a sheepish smile and stands back so I can enter.

I stop in my tracks.

Everything looks different from how I left it.

There is a tarp over the wood furniture like the dresser, his desk from his study, and the dresser from our bedroom. One of his old bookshelves still houses all his books, but it's covered in a sheer plastic cover similar to what people use for a tiny greenhouse on their deck or something. There's moisture in the locker to be sure, but everything is protected.

I take the cover off the dresser and open one of the top drawers, finding Daniel's T-shirts inside have been vacuumed sealed. Same with his jeans and trousers. And his navy-blue waffle robe with his name stitched in white on the chest.

The same robe I wore the night he died.

"What on earth..." I breathe, turning to Simon. "Who did all this?"

"We assumed you did," Simon says, puzzled. "Although, we never had a record of you coming in. When I asked the staff about it, Mack said he did it."

I hold the vacuum-sealed bag of shirts to my chest and feel the emotions bubbling to the surface. It's all safe. Protected.

"Looks like it's all dry, doesn't it? Well, that's a relief. I wasn't sure what to expect." He looks at me like I'm a volcano that was on the brink of rupture. "Crisis averted, right?"

A sob of relief escapes me. I don't know what I would have done if I had walked into the unit to discover all of Daniel's things had been ruined. The drive here had been excruciating, and I'd made a thousand apologies to Daniel as I sat at red lights and the rain beat down on my roof. It was as wet and miserable as the night he died, and that felt like a bad omen, but as I hold the shirts tightly, tears pouring onto the vacuum-sealed plastic, the courage of Mack's actions shine brighter than all the other feelings surging inside me.

"When did he do this?" I manage through my sobs.

Simon retreats out of the unit and hovers at the threshold. "Uh, I don't know. The end of August, maybe? Before the rainy season started."

We were already broken up. And he still protected items he knew I cherished that represented a love that may very well have made him feel less than, as Mallory had pointed out. For me. For Daniel. For the future version of myself who might have needed to come here for comfort.

"Thank you," I whisper.

"Ah, it's nothing," Simon says, rubbing the back of his neck. "Take your time. I'll wait in the office for you."

I wasn't thanking him, but I don't correct him, and I take advantage of his offer to stay in the unit a bit longer. I sift through every drawer, every shelf, and every sealed bag, reminding myself of all the little treasures tucked away in here. Each and every item holds a memory, and as I pick up a paperweight, I recall Daniel coming home with it, complaining that someone at work had given it to him as a Secret Santa gift, and he hated it.

I find his ties, perfectly preserved, and think of all the New Year's Eve parties we had together. The time he got too drunk on the rum cocktails and puked his guts out in one of the indoor house plants—and blamed it on someone else for a good laugh. I find his cufflinks and think about the quiet moment we shared before his dad's funeral when I helped him put them on, kissed his closed eyes, and told him I would be there for him the whole day.

I uncover his baseball glove in the bottom drawer of the dresser. He swore he would wear it when he played catch with our future son in the yard someday.

*We missed out on so much,* I think, looking around the space, *but we also made the most of what we got.*

"I have to go," I say, even though I'm alone.

I hurry to put everything back exactly where it was, and then I close the unit behind me and take off running down the maze of hall-ways back to the main office, where I startle Simon when I burst through the door.

"Thank you," I holler as I run through the office to the second door that lets out to the parking lot. "Thank you!"

He responds, but his voice is cut off by the pounding rain striking the asphalt. I run to my car, raindrops stinging my cheeks, and jump in behind the wheel. Like a demon out of hell, I spin the car around, slam it into drive, and make an illegal left turn out of the lot onto Lougheed Highway.

The rain makes traffic insufferable. Brake lights glare against my windshield. I inch through traffic and take the first left I pass so I can drive the back roads. They're better, but not great.

It's only when I pull into Mack's driveway that I realize it's the first time I've driven in the rain without the impending sense of doom settling in my gut. Daniel died in the rain. Upside down. Bloodied. Alone.

I didn't get the chance to tell him everything on my heart that night. I wasn't going to make that mistake again.

# CHAPTER FORTY-THREE

THE OUTER EDGE of my hand aches fiercely after slamming it on Mack's door twenty times. He still hasn't come to answer it, but his truck is in the driveway, so I'm assuming he's home. Either that or he's still at the hospital. Shit. I should have called Gia and asked before I came all this way in that terrible rush hour traffic.

For good measure, I knock again, this time rapping my knuckles until they hurt, too.

Still nothing.

"Ugh!" I throw my hands up in the air and turn around to stomp back out into the rain, but I pause when I hear the soft click of the deadbolt unlocking. Spinning on my heel, I turn just in time to find Mack opening the door with heavy eyelids, slumped shoulders, and an arm gently wrapped around himself under his chest, presumably over his broken ribs.

He looks like shit.

Horrible, handsome, wonderful shit.

He straightens ever so slightly at the sight of me soaking wet on his front step. "Charlie. What the hell?" A grimace passes over his features, and he leans a little more heavily on the door. "Don't tell me you're here to yell at me some more. I've had a shit week and—"

"Can I come in?" I hold my breath.

His stare captures mine and holds for several beats. Every passing second feels like we're getting closer to him telling me to get lost and go home. But he doesn't do that. Instead, he stands back, opens the door all the way, and invites me in with a tip of his head.

Inside, I step out of my boots and shrug out of my wet coat. Little droplets of water collect on the floor beneath me. He offers to hang it for me but winces when he lifts it up to hang it on the hook by the door. Broken ribs will do that to a guy. So I take my coat and hang it up before following him into his living room, where we sit across from each other; him on the couch, me in the armchair by the window using my shirt sleeve like a towel to scrunch some of the water out of my hair so I don't get his furniture wet.

Even though it's a gloomy day, daylight still breaks in, casting shadows over his bruised face. The stitches Gia told me about are still in his brow. He has two black eyes, a bruised jaw, and more purple bruising near his collarbone that disappears under his shirt. He moves tenderly, minding his right side, and as he shifts on the couch, I can tell he probably hasn't been able to get comfortable for days.

"I heard what happened," I say. "I'm sorry."

"Is that why you're here?"

I lick my lips. "No, actually. It's not."

He lets out the quietest groan as he shifts again. "Great, Gia told you to come check on me, then? I don't need a fucking babysitter, Charlie. I'm fine."

"You don't look fine. And for the record, no, Gia didn't send me."

He arches a doubtful eyebrow.

"She came to see me the other day, yes," I concede. "But I told her you were a big boy who could take care of yourself." I soften my tone as much as I can. "She told me she's moving to Jasper."

He nods slowly.

This is the man I met on moving day. Guarded. Evasive. Careful. His eyes seem darker, his features sharper, the shadows around him pulled tight like a second layer of skin.

Did the six men who jumped him do this to him?

*Or is this my fault?*

"I'm sorry she's leaving," I say, even though that's not what I'm really sorry about. "And I'm sorry about what happened to you, too. And I'm sorry—"

"I don't need pity."

"I know that, I just—"

"If that's all you came for, you can go." He rises like he's brittle, like bones are grinding on bones, and muscle is deteriorating.

"Please let me stay." My words come out rushed, and I'm on my feet now, too. He stares at me, unmoving. I stare right back and lift my chin ever so slightly. "I came to thank you."

A bitter laugh comes out of him that he seems to regret because it's cut short, and he puts a hand on his ribs. "Fuck," he growls, shaking off the pain. "Thank me for what?"

He's barbed wire, and I'm scared of getting cut, but I answer him.

"For the storage locker."

He straightens just slightly but says nothing.

"Simon called me and said that some of the units were flooded with all the rain we've been having. He said mine was one of them and that I should come down and go through the damage to let him know what he owed me, or to make an insurance claim. But when I got there, I saw what you'd done."

He's still silent, rigid, and unreadable.

"Thank you," I say again, my voice trembling with gratitude. "If I had lost all of Daniel's things, I would have been heartbroken. And I know you did it after we broke up. I don't know why you did it, but I'm grateful to you, and I've never had someone do something so thoughtful for me before. Or for Daniel."

His jaw flexes, and he looks out the living room window. The neighbor who called the cops when he and Clayton were brawling in the front yard is outside unloading groceries from his Tesla while his wife waits in the open door, hiding from the onslaught of rain.

"Those units are old," he says finally. "I know how much his possessions mean to you. I would have called you to warn you so *you* could have gone and done it, but you blocked me on everything."

"Yeah, I did. And maybe I was wrong to do that. I don't know. All I do know is that I've missed you, and I've been doing a lot of soul searching."

"Don't," he says, his voice as barbed and sharp as his body language. "You're only here because my sister told you what happened and because I spent a couple of hours vacuum sealing a dead man's shit. This has nothing to do with you or me and what you missed. I'm not going to play along. If you came to thank me, consider it done. *You're welcome.*" He turns his back on me and starts to leave the living room. "Satisfied?"

"I'm not done yet."

He scoffs and draws short, looking over his shoulder at me. "Is that so?"

I sit back down.

He rolls his eyes, shakes his head, and massages his brow. "Fucking hell. I'm not in the mood for this shit, Charlie. You've made your position perfectly clear. I don't need gratitude, or pity, or someone coming around checking on me because I got my ass handed to me. Bones heal. Sisters move away. She deserves a fresh start."

"Yes, she does." I'm not sure how he's going to react to what I say next, so I hold my breath. "And brothers deserve to be mad about their sister refusing to stand up against her abuser and help put him behind bars where he belongs."

His eyes flash.

"She's leaving you to pick up the pieces for her," I say. "I'm pissed for you. I can't imagine how you're feeling. I wish she were brave enough to face him, but she's not ready, and the court never waits for someone to be ready. You're carrying a lot on your shoulders, Mack."

"You think I don't know that?"

"I think you need someone in your corner."

He laughs again, grimacing through the pain. "Oh yeah? And who would you suggest? *You?* Give me a fucking break."

"I get that you're angry, but I had every right to walk away from our relationship," I say firmly. "I got scared, Mack. *Really* scared. I'm trying to rebuild my life and the foundation we laid was built on half-truths. I understand why you went to jail. It was for Gia. And if you'd just told me, things might have been different." I pause, waiting for him to respond, but he doesn't. "You weren't a saint, and neither was I, and maybe the biggest thing I learned from my time with you was just that. I had to confront a lot of truths about myself and how I show up in my relationships. I made a lot of mistakes with us. Most of them, in hindsight. It's not all on you."

He cracks a smile that doesn't suit him. "Oh, it's not? How nice of you to say so."

"You're acting ugly right now."

"I'm just acting like the asshole ex-con you think I am," he says. "Now get out."

"No." I cross one leg over the other. "I want to fight."

"Why?"

"Because maybe I'm not done with you. Because I miss you. Because..." I trail off.

"What?" he snarls.

The truth bubbles up, demanding to be released, and I don't have the stomach to keep pushing it down anymore. Not after everything.

"Because I haven't stopped loving you," I say, my voice barely a whisper. "And now that I've seen what you did for Daniel's things, I can't help but believe that you still love me too. And all this anger you have? It just affirms that belief." I get up and move to him, stopping a foot away. I search his eyes. "Tell me I'm wrong. Tell me I'm wrong, and I'll walk out that door, and you'll never have to see me again. But please," I beg, "don't lie."

Mack glares at me like I just struck a match and threatened to throw it at him.

"Say something," I press.

*Anything.*

*Yell at me.*

*Call me names.*

*I can take it.*

Resignation settles in and chases away the tight angry lines in his expression. He looks suddenly defeated.

"I'm not him, Charlie. I'm never going to be like him. I'm never going to be enough. And I can make my peace with that."

That's not what I expected when I wanted him to say *anything*. Anything but that. What am I supposed to do with that?

"No," I say slowly, "you're not like Daniel. He was patient. A calculated decision maker. He didn't take risks. In fact, he avoided them like the plague. And he was a little predictable. He liked his things how he liked them. Type A, preppy, clean-cut, clean-minded. He had a clear picture of where he was going and what he wanted. He was driven and a workaholic. He–"

"I fucking get it," Mack snaps.

"Don't interrupt me," I snap back. "He was so many things that I needed, but he's gone, and I've changed since I lost him. I need other things now. Things that you have."

He waves me off. "I'm done listening to this."

"I need someone who will tell me when I'm being crazy." I follow his retreat into his kitchen, unwilling to let him turn away from me now. "And *need* isn't even the right word. If the last three years have taught me anything, it's that I don't *need* anyone. All I need is to be honest with myself, and that is what I've been practicing this month. I've looked in the mirror a hundred times over and confronted so many things about myself that I don't like. Like how judgmental I am. How black and white I am. How quick I am to run when I get scared."

At this, he looks at me. Really looks at me.

"I'm sorry it took me so long," I breathe, getting as close as I can before I feel like he might bite. I reach for him but don't touch. "I don't need you, Mack. But I want you. All of you." I manage a smile, praying like hell my words are landing somewhere he can hear them. "The bad attitude and all."

My body hums with nerves and uncertainty in the wake of my confessions. When I try to put my finger on the last time I was this vulnerable, I go back to the night that I fell apart in Mack's arms and screamed my grief into the world while he held me. I think about how he managed to make me laugh and breathe after the grief nearly ate me alive. About how he protected me from Clayton without hesitating. How he used to light up when I walked into Dixie's. How he saw right through me the very first day we met.

How could I walk away from this love without throwing my all into it one more time?

I search Mack's eyes, desperate to find a flicker of what he's thinking. Is he angry that I dumped all this on him? Has he been holding the same truths while we've been apart? Does he want me back? Does he miss us?

"Charlie," he says softly.

*God, I love how he says my name.*

The tension evaporates from his shoulders. He lets his hand fall away from his ribs so he can reach up and take my face in both hands. He draws me close, and right when I think he's about to kiss me, he bows his head, closes his eyes, and rests his forehead on mine.

We stay there for a moment in time that belongs to just us. The lightning and thunder cracking in my mind soften to a gentle hush of waves lapping up a white sandy shore. I can practically feel the sunshine on my face.

When I open my eyes, his dark brown stare pours into me.

"I love you too," he breathes.

And then he kisses me, sending licks of fire from my lips to the tips of my toes. As the kiss deepens, he backs me up against the wall, and my shoulder blade hits the light switch to turn on the hallway light. We both wince at the brightness and break apart. His bruises are even more visible now, and I run my hands up his shirt, lifting the fabric as I go, so I can look at the damage to his ribs. His torso is wrapped in white bandages, but I can see red bruising peeking out around the edges.

Gently, I run my fingers over the bandage.

Mack catches my wrist, guides my hand up to his mouth, turns it over, and kisses the inside of my wrist. He works his way up the inside of my arm before taking my elbow in one hand and pulling me firmly against him. If he's hurting, he's not kissing like it.

He's kissing like he wants more.

*Everything.*

So I pop open the fly of his jeans.

His lips quirk in a smirk as he breaks the kiss and looks down at my hand unzipping his fly. "Making up for lost time?"

"Something like that."

He chuckles, which hurts him, but I don't intend to cause him any pain. Any more pain, anyway. I hook my fingers in his unzipped jeans and gently guide him to the couch, where I coax him down onto it, and once he's sitting, I push his legs open and settle on my knees between them.

His eyebrows raise before that smirk turns into a panty dropper, and he drapes both arms over the back of the couch on either side of him. Spread open and ready, he's sexy even with the bruises. Perhaps even more so.

After everything he's been through, he deserves to feel good.

And I'm going to give him that.

Slowly, teasingly, I rub him over his boxers. He's already stiff and straining at the fabric, and when I pull his boxers down, he springs free. My mouth is already watering. I part my lips.

Mack groans as I take him in my mouth. With the pain he's been in, I can only imagine how good a little bit of pleasure feels. I hope he feels relief as I take him deeper, guiding him to the back of my throat with my tongue following the vein down his length.

His head falls against the back of the couch.

He's putty in my hands. Or mouth. He's mine, and it's a rush to have him at my mercy as I work up and down, taking him slowly, tenderly, and deeply. Intent on unravelling him, I swirl my tongue over his tip and tease him some more. His hips shift, and he grimaces in pain, and I can't deny that his anguished and lustful expression is absolutely fucking delicious.

If he weren't so battered, I'd take my pants off and fuck him right here and now.

But he is battered, physically and emotionally, and all I want is to ease some of that pain.

So I work him over until he's breathless and gripping the couch cushions, his tendons straining, muscles chiseled. He goes rigid seconds before he comes, and I take as much of him as I can, letting him release into my throat.

"Fuck," he grates, the tension snuffing out as his muscles relax more deeply into the couch.

I swallow everything, clean him up with my mouth, and press soft kisses to his lower stomach as he breathes heavily, his chest rising and falling.

He smiles and closes his eyes. "Good thing I didn't kick you out."

"Ass."

"Just remember," he says, cracking open one eye, "you wanted this. *Really* bad."

Giggling, I rise and curl up on the corner of the couch beside him. "Yes, I do."

For the first time after Daniel, I have a snapshot image of what my future might look like, and the view is pretty damn good.

# EPILOGUE

## FOUR WEEKS LATER

"We have to go," Mack hollers, banging on my bathroom door.

"Shit, shit, *shit*," I hiss, popping up from the toilet, pulling up my panties, and hurrying over to the counter, where I toss a towel over the evidence. "Shit."

"You good in there?" he calls. "Gia wants to be early for the bus."

"Coming!"

I wash my hands and stare at the towel on the counter, my insides churning, heart hammering, hands shaking. I have to keep it together. Gia leaves for Jasper today, and Mack and I are driving her to the bus stop to see her off in proper fashion. She's been crashing with him leading up to her departure, and Mack and I have been trying–and kind of failing–to ease back into our rhythm slowly.

After finally choosing each other and making it exclusive again, we both talked about how we didn't want to rush things this time. We wanted to move at a natural pace and savor all the little pin drops on the road map of our love story. He only spends the night at my place on Friday and Saturday nights. Outside of that, we stay in our separate places, and he made sure to spend good quality time with his sister before she leaves.

While I picked up more hours working reception for the real

estate firm, Mack landed a job as a mentor for inmates who are preparing for release to help set them up to better acclimate to normal life on the outside. He helps facilitate finding housing, building resumes, preparing for interviews, and hosts weekly meetings with ex-cons to offer support and community. So far, he's loving it, and he's only a few weeks in. I can see the purpose it filled him with. And quite simply?

He's never been sexier.

My job is okay. It gives me something to do, and I've connected with a couple of women who work there and made friends with them. Mack and I have gone on a double date with one of them and her husband and had a nice time, but I'm not sure I'll stay at the job much longer because Mack has inspired me.

I have a story to tell and a community I can help. Weeks ago, I started writing a blog, focusing my content on what it's like to live after losing my husband and then our child, and how I lost my entire sense of self as I drowned in my grief–but how I found redemption in time, new love, and friendships.

And forgiving myself for surviving–and Daniel for dying.

Several grief groups have reached out to me to join their meetings, and I agreed. Those are coming up in the next couple of weeks. I'm terrified, but Mack has an obnoxious amount of confidence in me and has already been telling me to put my notice in for the reception job.

He keeps saying he has a feeling this is my calling.

Time will tell.

In the past four weeks, the police successfully identified the men who jumped Mack in the moving company lot and arrested them all. They are each being charged with assault with a deadly weapon and attempted murder–and Clayton?

Charges have been added to his already existing case for orchestrating the entire thing with an inmate he met while he was being detained who had connections to gang members on the outside. Together, they arranged the attack on Mack.

And now, together, they are going to serve a minimum of fifteen years. Perhaps more.

The first court appearance isn't until January, but we will be ready.

Even if Gia isn't here.

Mack and I have had plenty of conversations with her about it all, trying to make sure she really is okay with walking away from it. Nothing we say sways her to stay and confront her ex in court. Mack is disappointed but accepts it and told her he will make sure Clayton is behind bars where he belongs.

The pride I feel in being his girl is unmatched.

His moral compass, grit, and reckless bravery in the face of a man who premeditated the attack on him are admirable. I will be there in court with him the whole while.

Simon has also agreed to testify as a witness considering it all happened on his property, and he has the video footage. There are other people from corners of Clayton's life who are going to be called to the witness stand as well, and our lawyer is wildly confident that things will go our way. In fact, he told us there is no other way the pieces can fall.

Clayton is staying in jail.

Gia is going to Jasper.

And Mack and me?

Well, we're *supposed* to be taking things slow.

"Charlie!"

I burst out of the bathroom, breathless. "Sorry, I'm ready. I'm ready! Let's go."

"Hold up, girl." Mack catches me with a strong arm around my waist and spins me into him like we're back on the dance floor at Dixie's. He dips me, his hand pressed to the small of my back, gives me a dangerous grin, and kisses me like I'm his morning coffee after a late night out.

I grab hold of the front of his shirt and kiss him right back. "Down boy."

Mack jerks me back up and gives my ass a smack that echoes in my bedroom. Giggling, I run out into the hall with him on my heels, winding back like he's going to slap me again. Luckily, I reach the kitchen before he has a chance.

Gia is washing her hands in the kitchen sink, and she shoots us a smile. "You two are *a lot* when you're together. You know that?"

"Better than not enough," Mack says. "You sure you don't want to stick around? You could have a front-row seat to the shitshow."

Gia pretends to gag. "No thanks." She turns and grabs her duffel bag from my kitchen counter. The rest of her bags are in Mack's truck, parked outside.

The pair of them spent last night at his house, just the two of them, connecting and enjoying each other's company before they put seven hundred and eighty kilometers between them. Mack invited me, but I said no. They needed that time.

Gia moves to my front door, opens it, and heads out into the hall. "Come on, love birds. I have a bus to catch and a new town to fatten up with cheesecakes."

Mack laughs. "Good luck with that. Jasper is wild country. If anything, you're gonna need to build some muscle."

Gia flexes her bicep and pokes at an invisible muscle, then frowns.

The three of us head downstairs and pile into Mack's truck. Gia sits between us on the bench seat, her tanned legs stretching out in front of her. In the past weeks, I've seen her really come into her own. Instead of wearing loose clothes that she could hide in, she now opts for more feminine pieces, and I gave her a bunch of my wardrobe that no longer fits me anymore and was from my old life with Daniel. She's wearing a pair of my white cut-off shorts right now along with a cute pink top. She looks pretty.

And ready for whatever comes next.

Even though I wish she was staying to see things through with Clayton, I'm happy for her.

I'm happy for all of us.

Mack cranks the music on the stereo, blasting Kate Bush, and Gia sings at the top of her lungs. On the horizon, as we head down the hill to the bus station, the sky is bright, sunlight peeking through some angry gray October clouds. I lift my voice to join Gia's, and she gives me a dazzling smile that's brighter than the sun trying to come out. I loop my arm through hers as we close in on the bus station.

After Mack parks, we help her with her bags, loading them into the undercarriage storage of her bus. All of her other belongings, of which she doesn't really have many, were sent in a moving truck provided by Simon at a discounted rate three days ago. Her stuff is already waiting for her in the condo she's rented out in Jasper, and I know she's chomping at the bit to settle into her new home and make it hers.

Once her bags are loaded, and all the other passengers are on board, Gia turns to us with tears in her eyes.

"I guess this is it, huh?"

"Guess so," I say.

Mack engulfs his sister in a hug that makes her disappear, she's so tiny. He holds the back of her head, cradling her to his shoulder. "You make smart choices out there, little sister. And call me anytime, night or day; I'll answer. And I'll come running if you need me, okay? No questions asked." He pulls back and holds her face in his hands. The way he looks at her is all love and kindness. "You're going to do great. Jasper has no idea what's coming for it. Take it by the balls. Make friends. And if you can't make friends?" he winks. "Give them your cheesecake. They'll be obsessed with you."

Gia grips her brother's wrists and holds back tears. "I'll come home to visit for Christmas."

"You'd better."

"Promise," she says.

They share one last hug before she breaks away and heads onto the bus, turning on the top step to look back at us and wave, tears streaming down her cheeks. I blow kisses. Mack wraps his arm around my shoulders and stands stoically in his feelings. I know saying goodbye to his only family member is ripping him up inside, but I take solace in knowing he's not alone.

He's got me.

He's got *us*.

The bus driver says something to Gia, and she finds her seat at the midway point of the bus as it starts to pull away. She waves through the window, and we wave back, Mack breaking away from me to walk a few steps alongside the bus and get a few extra moments to see his sister before the bus picks up speed and leaves us behind.

He stares after the bus, and I stare at his back.

Strong. Steady. Safe.

All the things I thought I would never find again.

Right here. Mine.

I wrap my arms around myself as gratitude swells up inside me. And then I drop my hand to my stomach.

Mack turns, a sad smile on his lips, and pauses when he sees me. His eyes fall to my hand, and then his smile drops to a frown. He walks over.

"Are you okay?"

I nod.

"You sure?"

I nod again, nervousness and excitement competing to overpower the other.

"We should head out," I tell him. "Devin and Brett will jump down our throats if we're late again."

He puts his hands on my hips. "You're keeping something from me."

"I am?"

"I see right through you, Charlie. What is it? Don't tell me I have to put more shit together at their place."

I laugh. It's a fair guess. Over the past month, Mack and I have voluntarily babysat Jameson twice so that Brett and Devin could get back to having some date nights and seeing their friends without their baby in tow. It was hard on Devin at first, who called or texted me every fifteen minutes, but I knew with a bit more repetition she'd become more comfortable with it.

And I can't wait because babysitting Jameson with Mack is hands down my favorite thing to do. He is a darling little baby with a joyful temperament and a smile that rivals Mack's. He has both of us wrapped around his chubby little fingers, and Mack and I are just grateful we can help give his parents a slice of their old life back.

Things haven't been going great between Devin and our mother lately. They have a lot to work through, especially with Mom feeling so entitled to Jameson, but they are taking baby steps, and Mom agreed to join Devin in some family counseling to learn how to set and respect healthy boundaries. Devin was a bit hesitant to confront all her issues with our mother in a way that left nowhere to hide, but as someone who has survived the worst part of my life because of therapy, I was able to give her some supportive words and encourage her.

Mom loves Devin and me. She loves Jameson. She just desperately wants her own place where she can stand on her own two feet and belong–and be needed. Now that I have opened my eyes to my flaws, and my mistakes, and all the things I did that hurt the people I love in the last three years, I have more grace when I look at my mother.

She and I are healing, too. Slowly, but that's just fine by me.

"You don't have to build any furniture," I tell Mack. Last time we babysat, Devin asked if he could hang shelves in Jameson's room while Brett was at work because he hurt his shoulder golfing. "But you do have to take this whole babysitting thing a lot more seriously now."

"Why?"

The sun fully emerges from behind the clouds and pours down on us as I take Mack's hand and guide it down to my stomach. His brow furrows as he looks from my face to my stomach. I wait for him to catch on, because I know the truth, which is hidden under the towel on my bathroom counter.

Two pink lines.

The air rushes out of his lungs suddenly, and he looks light-headed. "Wait. Are you saying…?"

Words are impossible, so I just nod over and over until Mack gathers me in his arms, lifts me off the ground, and spins me around. When he sets me back down, his eyes are as teary as mine. He grabs my face, kisses me hard, and lets out the kind of laughter that sounds like love. He wipes my tears with his thumbs, and his hands start to shake.

I'm shaking too.

And for a moment, I'm somewhere else.

I'm in the kitchen of the family home I shared with Daniel. Onions and peppers are frying in the pan, spitting oil. It smells like oregano. A candle burns on the kitchen table his mother gifted us all those years ago.

Daniel is sitting at that table, watching me with his all-seeing blue eyes. He's holding a coffee mug, which he holds up to me in a toast as he offers me the smile I've missed dearly. *"Here's to second chances, sweetheart."*

The kitchen grows hazy, the mirage vanishing as Mack's face comes back into focus. I hold on to him tightly, my fingers digging into his arms, and let the tears fall. Then, I find my voice, dragging it out of the pit of the past and bringing it into the light of the present.

"You're going to be a dad."

Thank you for reading! Book 2 will be out soon. You won't want to miss Gia's story!